PRAISE FOR NICOLE BYRD'S NOVELS . . .

## Beauty in Black

"The social whirl of Britain's Regency era springs to vivid life . . . [A] charming, character-driven novel."
—*Publishers Weekly*

"*Beauty in Black* is another delightful tale by the multitalented Nicole Byrd . . . Readers won't want to miss the latest adventures of the Hill/Sinclair families."
—*Romance Reviews Today*

## Widow in Scarlet

"Nicole Byrd scores again with her latest Regency historical . . . an exciting and engaging, almost Cinderella-type story with touches of suspense, sensuality, and the exotic . . . 4+."    —*Romance Readers Connection*

"A romantic tale filled with suspense and enough characters and plot to have you quickly turning the pages . . . a superb Regency tale you won't want to miss."
—*Romance Reviews Today*

## Lady in Waiting

## Dear Impostor

"One of the most entertaining romances I've read in a long while. The story line is inventive, the characters are dynamic, and the pacing is lively . . . *Dear Impostor* is the rare romance that . . . never hits a false note . . . Readers who . . . are looking for a well-paced story that sparkles with originality are advised to run, not walk, to their bookstore and seek out *Dear Impostor*. I highly recommend it."

—*The Romance Reader*

"A terrific story with heartwarming, realistic characters . . . Do not miss *Dear Impostor* . . . The tale is beautifully written and enticingly romantic and is a Perfect Ten for me."

—*Romance Reviews Today*

## Robert's Lady

"*Robert's Lady* is a most excellent debut."

—*The Romance Journal*

"Nicole Byrd has created a masterpiece . . . with the perfect blend of mystery, suspense, and romance. This is one romance story you hate to see end."

—*The Romance Communications Reviews*

"Highly recommended . . . more than a fabulous Regency romance. Rising star Nicole Byrd shows much talent and scope."

—*Under the Covers Book Review*

# Vision in Blue

Nicole Byrd

BERKLEY SENSATION, NEW YORK

**THE BERKLEY PUBLISHING GROUP**
**Published by the Penguin Group**
**Penguin Group (USA) Inc.**
**375 Hudson Street, New York, New York 10014, USA**
Penguin Group (Canada), 10 Alcorn Avenue, Toronto, Ontario M4V 3B2, Canada
(a division of Pearson Penguin Canada Inc.)
Penguin Books Ltd., 80 Strand, London WC2R 0RL, England
Penguin Group Ireland, 25 St. Stephen's Green, Dublin 2, Ireland (a division of Penguin Books Ltd.)
Penguin Group (Australia), 250 Camberwell Road, Camberwell, Victoria 3124, Australia
(a division of Pearson Australia Group Pty. Ltd.)
Penguin Books India Pvt. Ltd., 11 Community Centre, Panchsheel Park, New Delhi—110 017, India
Penguin Group (NZ), Cnr. Airborne and Rosedale Roads, Albany, Auckland 1310, New Zealand
(a division of Pearson New Zealand Ltd.)
Penguin Books (South Africa) (Pty.) Ltd., 24 Sturdee Avenue, Rosebank, Johannesburg 2196, South
Africa

Penguin Books Ltd., Registered Offices: 80 Strand, London WC2R 0RL, England

This is a work of fiction. Names, characters, places, and incidents either are the product of the author's imagination or are used fictitiously, and any resemblance to actual persons, living or dead, business establishments, events, or locales is entirely coincidental.

VISION IN BLUE

A Berkley Sensation Book / published by arrangement with the author

PRINTING HISTORY
Berkley Sensation edition / February 2005

Copyright © 2005 by Cheryl Zach.
Excerpt from *Truly a Wife* copyright © 2005 by Rebecca Hagan Lee.
Cover art by Leslie Peck.
Cover design by Lesley Worrell.

ISBN: 0-425-20110-4

BERKLEY® SENSATION
Berkley Sensation Books are published by The Berkley Publishing Group,
a division of Penguin Group (USA) Inc.,
375 Hudson Street, New York, New York 10014.
BERKLEY SENSATION and the "B" design are trademarks belonging to Penguin Group (USA) Inc.

PRINTED IN THE UNITED STATES OF AMERICA

10  9  8  7  6  5  4  3  2  1

*Dedicated,
with great love and pride,
to my daughter Michelle
as she embarks on exciting new journeys*

# Prologue

*The letter arrived on her birthday.*

Big-eyed at being entrusted with such an important errand, one of the first-year girls intercepted Gemma on her way to the music room.

"Thank you, Mary," Gemma said as she took the letter. It was larger and heavier than the usual quarterly note. Hope leaped, unbidden and unsought, from the place deep inside where she usually crammed it down.

"Yes, miss." The little girl dipped a curtsy as she would to one of the teachers before trotting back to her classroom.

Gemma hid a sigh. She was as old, in fact, as some of the instructors and to the younger students, she must look much the same. Although officially now a parlor-boarder, she sometimes helped out with the children, listening patiently as they played scales on the pianoforte or checking their spelling on ink-blotted essays, remembering when she had been this small. When she had been that age, the brick walls of the school had seemed a fortress, protecting and succoring her. Lately, they seemed more like a prison.

Today, she turned one and twenty. Many girls her age were already married, were mothers, even, and she occasionally received correspondence from friends she'd gone to school with, friends who had left three or four years ago to go on to the real business of life. Of course, they had somewhere to go.

She might have that chance, too, to fall in love and marry, create a family and defy the emptiness of her life, if she only knew if she had the right to wed a respectable man.

Gemma looked at the thick packet. The outer sheet, with her name and address: *Miss Gemma Smith, Miss Maysham's Academy for Select Young Ladies, Yorkshire*, was penned in the tiny precise writing of the solicitor who had, for years past, forwarded her quarterly allowance, along with a few impersonal lines noting that her school fees had been paid. But she had had her allowance only a few weeks ago; what was this about? She was not expecting birthday greetings: Certainly, the man had never written anything personal in all the years he had handled her affairs. Was it possible that—

She broke the wax seal and read the first sheet with increasing incredulity.

*Dear Miss Smith: Two decades ago, I was instructed to forward you this missive on the occasion of your one and twentieth birthday. I remain, your servant, Augustus Peevey, Solicitor.*

The inner packet, which was labeled only *Gemma*, had a wax seal, too, unbroken, though she could not make out its impression. The paper was of fine quality, and this script more delicate, with larger loops and swirls. Somehow, it suggested a woman's pen. Gemma's heart beat fast, now, and she felt her breath coming quickly. Trembling, she broke the seal and scanned the letter, then—not believing her eyes—read it again, and yet again.

Then she pressed the sheet to her chest and felt behind

her for the wooden bench at the edge of the hall. Her knees were weak, and Gemma collapsed onto it.

Her world had suddenly expanded outward, and nothing would ever be the same.

# *One*

*No doubt about it, money had its uses.*

Miss Louisa Crookshank straightened the seam of her new navy blue traveling costume and smiled, careful not to appear smug. She was known in some circles as "the Comely Miss Crookshank," and she knew that appearing satisfied with one's self did not generally serve to enhance one's natural beauty.

But the fact remained, being in possession of a comfortable fortune made all the difference. Since she had achieved her one and twentieth birthday during the final days of winter, she was at last in possession of the fortune she had inherited from her father. True, her uncle Charles still nominally controlled her funds, but her uncle was a dear, and it usually took little effort to coax him into agreement with her latest scheme. Which was how she came to be sitting in her own elegant, newly purchased chaise, on the way to her most cherished goal: London.

At long last!

She had tried last year to have a proper London Season,

a coming-out long delayed by the sad fact of her father's death and the resulting year of mourning, then by other family concerns. But when she had arrived in London, nothing had gone according to plan. Remembering the disasters that had brought her brief sojourn in the capital to such an abrupt and unhappy end, Louisa shuddered. But this year, it would be different, this year—

The carriage jolted to a stop. Louisa clutched the seat to avoid being thrown onto the floor. On the other side of the carriage, Miss Pomshack, her hired but very respectable companion, had been dozing. Now, the older lady jerked awake and gave a small shriek. "What is it, Miss Louisa? Are we attacked by brigands?"

"Of course not," Louisa retorted, trying to make out a familiar form through the rain-streaked window, but torrents of liquid obscured her view. She pushed open the door just a little, ignoring the wet gusts that dampened her skirt and the draft of cold air that swept through the carriage. Miss Pomshack screeched again and pulled her shawl closer about her thin shoulders, but Louisa persisted. In a moment, she had found him.

Her fiancé, Sir Lucas Englewood, curly brown hair plastered to his head—the wind must have knocked off his hat again—rode his steed closer to the carriage. He had insisted on riding, and although Louisa had invited him sweetly inside the chaise when the first drops began to fall, he had scoffed at her suggestion. "A little rain never hurt a fellow," he had said gaily.

He didn't look so happy now. "It's no use, Louisa," he told her. "The rain isn't letting up, and the road's turning to soup. The team can barely pull the carriage. There's a decent-looking inn just ahead. We're going to have to stop and wait for the weather to improve."

Louisa bit back a protest. She had so wanted to end the day with her long-awaited arrival in London. But, gazing at the sheets of rain that cloaked any view of the countryside, she nodded reluctantly and shut the door.

In a moment, the carriage moved again, lurching as the

team pulled hard against the grasping mud. Bracing herself, Louisa sighed.

Perhaps money couldn't accomplish everything.

*When they hurried into the inn, heads bowed against* waves of water that drenched them thoroughly, she found they were not the only travelers to take shelter from the storm.

Inside, the innkeeper bowed and smirked and was as obsequious as the most demanding member of the Ton could require, but the fact remained, there was no private parlor to be had. "But the travelers from the stage are a nice, quiet bunch, miss, and I'll make sure that no one bothers you. And me wife is cooking up a grand dinner, which will lift your spirits no end."

Sir Lucas frowned as he escorted Louisa to a seat in the corner of the room and helped her shed her sodden cloak. She would have preferred to be closer to the fire, which Miss Pomshack also eyed with longing, but Lucas was, as usual, more concerned with the proprieties.

The public coach, it seemed, had also had to make an unscheduled stop. Several men crowded around the leaping fire, lifting their coattails and drying rain-soaked coats and broad backsides all at once, talking in loud voices about market shares and the price of wool. The whole room smelt of damp wool, the scent mingling with smoke from the fire, as well as the fumes from one particularly noxious pipe, which an elderly man sitting by the hearth had clamped between thin lips.

Perhaps, all in all, Louisa favored her distant corner.

"At least I was able to obtain a bedchamber for you and Miss Pomshack," Lucas told her.

"We have to share a room?" Louisa protested, though she kept her voice low. Her companion was shaking out her pelisse and didn't seem to notice the quiet complaint.

"It's the last one," Lucas told her. "I'll have to camp out

in the parlor with the other men, so count your blessings."

Sighing, she nodded. "Thank you, Lucas, for looking out for me so well." She smiled up at him.

His chest seemed to swell visibly. "I promised your uncle I would see to your safety, didn't I?" he told her, his tone dignified. "You will not come to any harm this year!"

Not wanting to discuss last year's perilous adventures, Louisa frowned. Her near-escapes were now only painful memories, and she had no wish to relive them.

The innkeeper brought them all steaming cups of mulled wine. Glad she had not yet removed her gloves, Louisa held the hot pewter cup carefully and sipped.

A pleasant warmth spread through her, and some of her disappointment ebbed. She was on the way to London; this was only a momentary delay. Very well, not momentary, exactly, but still brief.

Lucas excused himself to check on the carriage and team, to be sure the horses, including his own handsome gelding, were properly rubbed down and fed. Left alone with Miss Pomshack, who seemed interested only in her cup of wine, Louisa glanced around the room. This time, she noticed one lone female sitting a bit apart from the group of men.

What was a woman, who was, Louisa noted, dressed most respectably—if not richly—doing alone on the coach? This woman, who looked not much older than Louisa herself, kept her gaze down and seemed to be doing everything she could to avoid contact with the other passengers. Did she have no one to travel with her?

Louisa's ready curiosity stirred. Besides, she was bored, and there was a long evening ahead with no one to talk to except Miss P, who was not much of a conversationalist, and dear Lucas, who would probably spend hours in the stables until he was sure that all the horses were seen to. Acting on impulse as she often did, Louisa stood, and before her companion could object, marched across the room.

She paused in front of the other woman, who looked up at her in surprise.

"Forgive me," Louisa said, her tone cheerful. "But you seem to be alone. Would you not like to share some wine with us?"

The young woman flushed. She had dark hair tucked beneath a somewhat soggy bonnet and unusual eyes, of a blue so dark and rich that they put one in mind of ocean depths on a sunny day. Her skin was fair, and when she spoke, her voice sounded educated and genteel.

"I would not wish to intrude," she said, looking unsure.

"Not at all. I know this is not precisely a proper introduction, but I am Miss Louisa Crookshank of Bath, but just now on my way to London for the Season."

The stranger still hesitated. "It's very good of you, but are you sure your mother will approve?"

"Oh, Miss Pomshack is my companion; my mother died years ago," Louisa explained matter-of-factly. "I had no female relatives available just now to chaperone. I have aunts, but one has a new baby and isn't interested in the Season"—she shook her head at such madness—"and the other is newly married and taking an extended honeymoon around the world. I get letters from the strangest places, I assure you. She was riding camels and exploring pyramids the last I heard. However, she does send the most delightful gifts. I have a Persian shawl—light as air but very warm, and such colors—that is utterly divine."

The other woman smiled. Louisa was glad to see it; the stranger had been looking rather downcast. Mind you, Louisa's bubbly good spirits usually had that effect on people. "Come along," she coaxed. "A more congenial group is just what you need on such a miserable day. And you can eat dinner with us, instead of with the men on the coach, which would be much more to your liking, I'm sure?"

The light outside the rain-streaked windows was fading, and the group at the fireplace growing noisier.

The young woman seemed to make up her mind. She stood and gave a small curtsy. "Thank you, you're very kind. I am Miss Gemma Smith, for several years a student

at Miss Maysham's Academy for Select Young Ladies, just
outside of York. I have only recently left."

Louisa led the way back to their corner, where she introduced Miss Pomshack and beckoned to the innkeeper to
bring more wine.

Soon they were comfortably settled. Miss Smith removed her damp bonnet and attempted to push her hair back
into order.

"Are you traveling to London for the Season or to visit
family?" Louisa asked politely, trying not to sound too inquisitive.

The other young lady hesitated. "It is for family reasons, yes," she agreed, taking a long drink from her cup.

This did little to enlighten Louisa. She decided to explain some of her own circumstances. Perhaps this would
put Miss Smith more at ease and more apt to share her situation.

"I am traveling with my companion and my fiancé, Sir
Lucas Englewood," she told the stranger. She glanced down
at the topaz betrothal ring on her finger.

"Oh, my felicitations," the other girl said.

"Thank you. Lucas wanted us to be married this spring,
but I have so wanted a real London Season first—I've
never even had a proper coming-out—that I saw no reason
to rush into matrimony, as dear to me as Lucas is. Not to
mention—" Louisa lowered her voice in respect. "After the
sad death last fall of Princess Charlotte in childbirth, well,
it somewhat lessened my eagerness to rush into the married state."

Miss Smith nodded. It had been a national calamity.
The princess had been very popular, unlike her volatile father, the Prince Regent, and her loss had been genuinely
mourned. The prince had been most cast about at losing his
only child, or so it was rumored. But the prince was a fun-
loving man, and Louisa was privately hoping that this
spring's Season would not be too much subdued by the
tragedy.

"Do you have a home in London?" the other lady asked, trying to rub away the water spots on her gray traveling costume as it slowly dried. "Or are you staying at a hotel?"

Louisa smiled. "I have rented a very nice house in town, fully furnished and with a small staff, at a quite reasonable rate," she explained. "Lucas has taken rooms for the time being. He's feeling very proper just now and doesn't think it would be suitable to stay with me, even with another lady to chaperone. But after Lucas and I are married, I hope to purchase the house or one like it. My uncle handled the lease, and I have not yet seen the residence myself, but he assures me I will be pleased."

"How lovely." The other girl sounded a bit wistful.

"And I suppose you are going to stay with family? You will have to call on me once you are settled," Louisa suggested. She liked the look of this girl, with her intelligent blue eyes and her reluctance to put herself forward; her manners were very nice. "Were you in London last year? I have the feeling I have seen you before."

For some reason, the girl flushed. "No, this is my first visit. I do have family in London, but, um, they are not yet aware that I am coming."

That was unusual, but it would have been bad form to remark upon it. Generally, a lady did not set out until she was sure she had a safe haven at the end of the journey; big cities—as Louisa's aunts were only too eager to remind her—could present many dangers for young ladies on their own.

"Perhaps your letters have passed in the mail," Louisa suggested, trying to sound as if this were not an odd-sounding situation.

"I'm afraid it's more complicated than that." The other girl took another sip of her wine and avoided Louisa's gaze. "But I do have a brother who lives in London. If you have been in company there, you may have met him?" There was the slightest question in the way her voice rose.

Curiosity inflamed once again, Louisa looked up.

"Perhaps, though I did not go about in Society last year as much as I would have liked. What is his name?"

The other young woman hesitated, then said slowly, "Lord Gabriel Sinclair."

Louisa gave a start of surprise. "But I do know him! In fact, my aunt is newly married to his older brother. He's a most charming and devilishly handsome man, and his—your—family is most well connected. No wonder you looked familiar—the shape of your eyes and that unusual dark shade of blue, and your fair skin and dark hair. Oh, how nice to meet another one of the Sinclairs!"

She hesitated, suddenly remembering that the stranger had given her surname as Smith. Fortunately, before the pause became too awkward, a serving girl approached with a large tray full of dishes. She pulled a table closer to them and set down the food. No one spoke as the table was laid.

But Louisa's ready interest was again at full alert. Was there some mystery or intriguing family scandal here? When the servant retreated, Louisa added, as delicately as possible, "I admit, I did not know Lord Gabriel had a sister."

"Actually—" Again, Miss Smith did not quite meet Louisa's eye. "Actually, he doesn't know it, either."

## Two

*L*ouisa almost clapped her hands. Only at the last moment did she realize that the other lady might take her gesture in the wrong spirit. But although she was able to hide her first intent by gesturing instead toward the serving dishes, saying, "I believe we are to help ourselves. We need not wait for Sir Lucas. He takes the welfare of his horse, and my team, very seriously," inside, she was aglow with delight.

A mystery indeed! And here she'd thought that the evening, stuck in a small inn with little congenial company, would be boring. The trick was in getting Miss Smith—it was obvious now that the name was a mere ploy—to unburden herself to Louisa. And since Louisa was almost family, it would only be fitting for her to know what twist of fate had given Lord Gabriel a sister of whose existence he was unaware.

But she knew the value of timing, so for now she simply filled her own plate, and the three women ate quietly of the roasted chicken and shepherd's pie, the potatoes and peas and hearty brown bread, that their landlord had provided. It was simple fare but tasty, and after a long day of travel, Louisa was empty enough not to complain about the unfashionable menu.

Conversation during their meal was dilatory. By the time they had worked their way to the apple crumble, cheese, and basket of nuts, Louisa felt as full as a hen fattened for tomorrow's dinner. But she felt better for the meal, and surely Miss Smith did, too; the other woman had gained a better color and no longer looked blue with cold. Miss Pomshack was yawning behind her hand. Perhaps Louisa could convince her companion to go up to bed and allow the two younger women the chance for a more intimate conversation.

But though she suggested it, Miss P was too true to her responsibility to consider leaving her charge unchaperoned in a common taproom. True, the men across the room seemed more absorbed in their shepherd's pie and their ales than in plotting any unseemly approaches to the young women, but, judging by Miss P's suspicious glance, a brazen seducer might yet lurk beneath one of those stout, wool-covered breasts. And anyhow, Lucas at last reappeared, damp and smelling a bit of horses.

The innkeeper was once again summoned and brought in a new platter of chicken and a tankard of ale to add to the other dishes on the table. Lucas bowed in response to the introduction to their new friend, which Louisa performed, and then set at once to his much-delayed meal.

"Don't believe the horses will come to any harm," he told Louisa. "They were wet and tired, of course, but we've rubbed them down well—don't trust the ostler here; the man looks ham-handed to me—and your coachman has them covered in blankets. I'll check on them again before I turn in. Hmm, not bad. I'm as hollow as a drum." He took another bite of his chicken, and Louisa, leaving him to his meal, gave up trying to make conversation.

When Lucas had finished, he suggested retiring.

Annoyed at his attitude, Louisa glanced at the clock on

the wall. "It's barely nine o'clock." She was no child to be sent up to her bed just because they had to share the one common room with other travelers.

"I know, but some of the men are getting a bit deep into their cups," Lucas told her, with all the authority of a young man who has enjoyed a few drunken sprees of his own. He scanned the other side of the room. The group in front of the fire had begun singing—off-key—a song whose lyrics even Louisa realized were most certainly not the thing. "It won't do for you to stay here, trust me, Louisa."

"Oh, very well," Louisa agreed, though she still felt cross. "I suppose you will wish to retire, too?" she added, turning back to her new acquaintance.

The young woman flushed. "Actually—"

Louisa blinked. "Oh, no. My darling Lucas was taking such good care of me that we have acquired the last bed-chamber! My dear, you cannot spend the night down here alone with a group of rowdy men."

Miss Smith bit her lip. "I didn't realize— I expected to be in London before night fell."

Now Lucas was looking concerned. "Surely, her maid—"

"Met with an unfortunate accident a few days ago, forcing her to be left behind," Louisa put in swiftly before Miss Smith could admit to traveling alone. "Miss Smith, you will simply have to share our bedchamber."

"I couldn't impose upon you," Miss Smith objected, although she, too, gazed across the room at the boisterous group with obvious misgivings.

"No, indeed, how could I sleep thinking of you suffering embarrassment, or worse, in such company. That is, I know Lucas would protect you from harm, but still, it would be neither proper nor comfortable."

"Certainly not," Lucas agreed. And Miss P looked scandalized at the very thought of a young woman left alone amid such male company.

So the lady was persuaded to accept the "very kind offer," and the three women went up to the bedchamber together.

The room was small, Louisa thought when she walked through the doorway. But she was committed to her good deed now, so there was no use in fretting. On two sides of the room the ceiling sloped halfway down, and outside in the darkness rain lashed at the panes of a dormer window. But the bed, inspected carefully by Miss P, was pronounced clean and free of vermin, and a cot had been brought in, which the older lady bravely volunteered to take.

"Will you be comfortable?" Louisa regarded the narrow pallet with doubt.

"Oh, I shall manage very well," her companion assured her, coming over to unbutton the tiny buttons on the back of Louisa's dress. "I can sleep anywhere, Miss Louisa. Don't concern yourself about me."

And sure enough, by the time the two younger women had washed their faces and hands at the china bowl on the dresser and donned nightgowns—Miss Smith's plain but clean and neat, Louisa's à cunning concoction of lace and fine linen—the older woman was undressed and stretched out on the cot, covered by a thick quilt and snoring discreetly like a plump cat.

Louisa climbed into bed. She snuffed out the candle on the table, bade her new friend good night, and turned over to stare at the rough plaster of the wall, but sleep did not come. As the only child of a wealthy father, she was not accustomed to having another person in the same bed, even though the other lady lay as far away as the mattress allowed. It was hard to repose herself.

Was Miss Smith awake, too? She lay still, but her body seemed stiff. And when a coal popped on the hearth, she started just a little.

Louisa blinked into the darkness and pulled the bedclothes closer to her chin. The air cooled quickly as the fire died. She wished they were in London, in her comfortable rented house, instead of this tiny inn. Still, it had led to an interesting interlude.

"Are you awake?" she whispered into the darkness.

The other woman shifted a little. "Yes," she answered, keeping her voice low, too. "It's hard to rest in a strange place."

"For me as well," Louisa agreed.

"And I know you would be more comfortable without having me thrust upon you. You've been very good, but you . . . you must think my situation very strange," the other girl suggested.

Louisa held her breath, then said carefully, "Not at all. I'm sure you have good reason—"

"I only just found out, you see," Gemma said. Somehow, talking into the darkness, which was lightened only by the faint glow of the fading coals on the hearth, it seemed easier for her to confess her secrets. "When I turned one and twenty last month, I received a letter from the solicitor in London, the one who has been paying my school fees and sending me my allowance. The missive inside was written by my mother—my real mother . . ."

Her voice shook, and Louisa could sense the strong emotion barely contained.

"She said that she regretted our separation, my absence from the family. She said I should contact Lord Gabriel, my—my brother—and he would make arrangements for us to be reunited. But although I wrote at once to the estate in Kent to which the letter directed me, he has not—he has not yet replied. And then I read in the London paper gossip about a great ball to be held at the end of April, and Lord and Lady Gabriel Sinclair were among the 'distinguished' guests to be expected. So I knew he was coming soon to London, and I felt I must try to see him. . . . See with my own eyes the first person of my family, my real family, that I have ever known. So I made up my mind to travel to town."

"You are very brave," Louisa said, a bit awed. She had jumped into some impulsive adventures, herself, but this—

setting out for London to meet a brother who had no notion that his sister was coming—

"Oh, no, I am quite terrified," the other young woman said, her voice trembling again. "But I wanted it so badly. I've always hoped to find out the secrets about my birth, you see, and I know so little." She hesitated, then added, "And surely Lord Gabriel will be pleased to see me, even if—the letter said—he has not yet been informed of my circumstance. I am coming at my—our—mother's invitation, after all. And I must know . . . I just wish to understand. She must have had good reason to send me away at such a young age."

Louisa was glad that it was dark; the other woman could not see how Louisa's eyes widened. My, what a tale! This was as fantastic a story as some of the novels she had read covertly when her aunt had thought her dutifully conjugating French verbs.

"Don't you think he will be pleased?" the other girl repeated.

"Oh, certainly, why should he not?" Louisa said quickly, and tried not to remember Lord Gabriel Sinclair angry. She had seen it occur only once, under unusual circumstances, but it was a memory impossible to forget. He had nearly killed a man that day.

"But you are courageous, indeed," Louisa insisted. "Setting out on such an odyssey and all alone, too. Did you not have a maid you could bring with you?"

She felt the other woman shake her head. "I didn't need one at school. And although I've been saving my allowance, knowing that hotels in London would be costly, I did not think I could manage two coach tickets, two people to feed. And while I hoped that my brother—that Lord Gabriel might invite me to stay, I had to consider that he might not yet be in town when I arrived, or, or that other problems might occur."

Not just brave but downright heroic, Louisa thought—even foolhardy—but she did not speak the opinion aloud.

"My own maid left me just recently to marry her childhood sweetheart," Louisa said. "I had planned to hire a

London dresser after I arrived, a woman who would know more about fashion and the ways of society. And I had Miss P to assist me and travel with me, of course, as well as Lucas."

She paused for a moment, aware of a strong curiosity about just how Lord Gabriel Sinclair would react to the appearance of an unknown sister. She heartily wished she could be there. And then it came to her.

"You must travel with us, Miss Smith!" she said, almost gasping at the simple logic of it.

"Oh, no, Miss Crookshank, you have done so much already," the other woman argued. But already, her voice sounded less tremulous, stronger, as if comforted by the idea of feminine companionship and increased safety.

"You must call me Louisa. Why, we are almost related. Trust me, it will be much more the thing, and I would be remiss indeed if I did not offer to help out Lord Gabriel's relation. He has been of service to me at a difficult time," Louisa explained. "I could hardly do less. In fact, you might stay a few days with me in London, if you do not go at once to your brother's house. He indeed has an estate in Kent, and while I expect he will soon be in town for the Season, it's possible he and his wife have not yet arrived."

"You are very generous," the other lady said, sighing— this time Louisa thought—with relief. "And please, you must call me Gemma. That at least," she added with the first spark of humor Louisa had glimpsed in her, "I know is truly my name."

Louisa giggled. "Oh, what fun we shall have together, and this Season will be a delight, the first for both of us!"

She was gratified to hear Gemma laugh softly. Louisa was careful not to show the rest of her thoughts. Because together, they could surely decipher the mystery behind Gemma's clouded past, and who only knew where it might lead?

# *Three*

*After Louisa's amazing offer, they chatted for a few minutes*—her new friend seemed full of ambitious plans for her first real Season—then Louisa drifted into sleep. The darkness of the chamber was lit only by glowing pinpricks from the dying embers on the hearth. Gemma could hear Louisa's light, even breathing beside her and Miss Pomshack's high-pitched whistle from the cot closer to the fire. The sounds did not disturb her; some of the girls at the boarding school had snored more loudly than this.

Gemma found that she was able to close her eyes at last and allow some of her tension to ebb. Only when she felt the stiffness fade from her body did she realize just how anxious she had been, setting off alone on this audacious journey.

True, her mother—her real, hitherto unknown mother—had invited her to come. It was this knowledge, this amazing burst of illumination lighting up a childhood shadowed by secrets, that had inspired and sustained her.

For years Gemma had puzzled over just who, in truth,

she was. It was a curious thing not to know your family, your origins, even your true class. Where did she belong, really? She could be an impostor, an intruder, as she sat in class with girls from respectable merchant families and daughters of minor gentry. Should she be outside scrubbing floors with the servants, or milking cows in a farmer's dairy, or walking the street selling rags, or worse?

Who was Gemma Smith? The older she grew, the more the enigma of her circumstances hung over her, and recently it had become vitally important that she know that, at the least, her birth was respectable. And then the letter had come, like a gift from the heavens. . . .

But there was also the fact that the letter was dated shortly after her birth, over a score of years ago. Why had her mother not contacted her since? What if, after writing the letter, she had changed her mind about meeting her daughter? Gemma considered how the missive had come, its wax seal unbroken, from the solicitor, with no explanation about its contents or the long delay. No, she refused to consider such an awful possibility.

Gemma thought of the wrinkled sheet of paper with its faded ink, which was wrapped carefully in her best linen handkerchief and placed inside her reticule for safekeeping, along with her small store of coins. It was the only thing she had from her mother, the only sign, aside from the quarterly allowance whose source had never been explained, to show that somewhere, someone cared for her, that she was not totally alone in an alien and uncaring world.

She could not begin to spell out what the letter's arrival had meant to her. Certainly she could not explain to Louisa Crookshank, as kind as this new friend was. Louisa might be an orphan, might have lost both her parents, but she obviously still had family about her. She had never been adrift on a sea of circumstance, prey to any random current ready to pull her under and drown her in poverty or danger with no one to know that she was imperiled. True, Gemma had the solicitor, but he had been a distant lifeline, appearing in her life only as a name at the bottom of short, formal notes. Gemma had been deeply grateful for the monetary support he had provided, even if the man had refused, when she'd asked, to identify its source.

Soon, perhaps, she would know the truth. Gemma would meet her mother, learn just why an infant had been sent away, too young to remember her true family and home. It did not have to mean that her parents did not care, she told herself, just as she had repeated the thought so many times since her childhood. There could be, would be, a logical reason for her apparent abandonment. How many times when she was lonely or frightened, or when the other girls had teased her, or during the horrible time at the foundling home, had Gemma repeated that refrain? There was a reason, there had to be a reason, why she had been cast away. Someone had loved her, even from a distance— surely, it must be so.

Now she would learn the answers, and the emptiness in her heart would be filled. She would meet her mother, receive the loving embrace Gemma had dreamed of so many times, and at last, she would know who Gemma Smith really was.

She shut her eyes and allowed herself to put away just for a little while the constant watchfulness that was the lot of an orphan of uncertain heritage, the continual sense of being on guard against unknown perils which might swoop down from any direction when one had no one else to count on except oneself. . . .

Tonight, she was not alone. Gemma slept.

*The next morning dawned cloudy but with the rain now* reduced to only a light patter of droplets. By the time they had broken their fast, a few feeble rays of sun peeked through the layers of cloud.

Coming in from outside, Sir Lucas announced that the road, though still muddy, appeared passable. Louisa had informed him of the new addition to their party, and if he had reservations—he treated Gemma politely but with a slight reserve—he kept them to himself.

Only once did Gemma overhear Louisa protesting, "But she is Lord Gabriel's sister, Lucas. Why should I need more introduction than that?"

And at his low-voiced answer, her new friend had pushed back a straying curl of fair hair and smiled. "We will find out shortly, will we not?"

Bending over to check the lace on her traveling boots, Gemma pretended not to hear. It would not be the first time she had been treated with suspicion or indifference. When one had no family name to give one credibility, slights were commonplace. She had developed a thick skin over the years, or so she told herself. If, deep inside, she still felt the pricks of hurt from raised brows or arch looks, or even outright rudeness and exclusion, she was careful not to show it.

Her family might be unknown, until now, but she would behave like a gentlewoman. Somehow, Gemma had always been certain that her mother *was* a lady, and that she owed it to her faceless parents to conduct herself accordingly. Others might doubt her, but Gemma would not offer anyone an excuse to further condemn her.

So her two modest valises were added to the luggage strapped on behind, and she took her place in the carriage beside Louisa, with the older lady on the other side, and Lucas once again riding.

The roads were slowly drying but still forced them to proceed at a leisurely pace. Lucas had to ride slightly ahead of them to keep from being pelted with mud from the carriage wheels. As the day went on, the sunshine grew stronger, and Louisa beamed just as brightly.

"We shall be there soon. I recognize that inn and that bridge. Oh, I am so happy! And having you as a guest will only add to the fun, Gemma."

Gemma's presence had rarely before been considered

an asset—she thought of some of the girls at school who had snubbed her and whispered behind her back—so she returned the smile with real gratitude.

This was so much better than riding jammed into the public coach with a fat merchant from Lincolnshire poking his elbows into her side or a sales clerk who smelled of garlic coughing into her face. Louisa's coach was better sprung, too, and did not toss one about as badly.

And best of all was having someone to chat with, laugh with . . . above all, the heady feeling of being accepted. Gemma felt her heart soar. If she had wondered in odd moments if this journey—embarking without an invitation from her unknown brother with no indication of what his reception might be—was rash and foolhardy, she felt much more confident now.

She was alone no longer. So it was a merry pair who hung out the windows and pointed out to each other signs of the approaching metropolis.

The sun was high in the sky by the time they rolled into the fashionable west side of the city. Gemma gazed at the wide streets and squares lined by handsome houses and felt quite awed. Louisa must be wealthy, indeed, if she could lease such a house without qualms.

And her brother—did Gemma's brother live somewhere about in a grand home? Residing in such a desirable location, he must be very self-assured. What if he didn't wish to claim a sister who had appeared out of nowhere, who was tongue-tied with nervousness and provincial naivete? If so, what would she do?

Gemma swallowed hard as her delight in her improved circumstances faded a bit. If Lord Gabriel rejected her, Louisa must surely do the same. She had accepted Gemma so easily only because of her claimed connection with the Sinclairs.

It always came back to that. Unless one had a family to give one credibility, a grounding and a place in Society that others could easily note and identify, it was like being a fragile sapling in a strong gale. Without deep taproots, such a tree would be blown away, tossed forever amidst a whirling maelstrom with no safety in sight.

Gemma shivered. But her mother had wished to see her—the letter said so. Surely, a mother would not reject her child?

Again.

They pulled up in front of a handsome town house, flanked on both sides by houses of similar proportions. The house that Louisa had rented had numerous levels rising to a slated roof. The door was painted a deep crimson, and the windowpanes were clean and bright.

When Sir Lucas dismounted and went up to rap on the door, a footman opened it at once. The groom put down the steps of the chaise, helping first Louisa, then Gemma, then Miss Pomshack, to climb out.

"Smelters, isn't it? This looks very nice," Louisa said to the servant, looking not in the least abashed as she took Lucas's arm and led the way into the front hall.

A lanky chambermaid and a stout lady, who was likely the cook, hastened to join the footman, to make their curtsys to their new mistress and then stand stiffly against the wall like a line of toy soldiers.

"I am Miss Crookshank," Louisa told them, with the calm matter-of-factness of someone who has dealt with servants all her life. "I am sure you will prove a most competent staff, and I shall enjoy my stay with you."

The footman introduced the other servants. "Brownley is our cook, miss; the housemaid is Lily. The scullery maid's below stairs—she's been scrubbing pots and she didn't wish to come up with a dirty apron. We have a right good dinner cooking for you and your guests, if I do say so, and would you like a light luncheon laid out in 'alf an 'our? When you didn't arrive last night, Cook made sure to keep the sliced beef and the apple pie in the cold safe. They'll make a nice bite after your trip."

"That would be excellent." Louisa smiled at the woman. "I was sorry to be delayed. The heavy rain made the roads impassable."

"Thank'ee, miss. The pie is still nice and moist, but we couldn't save the souffle," the cook said sadly, as if it were a relation who had passed on instead of a puffy egg dish.

"I shall take a tour of the house, and then you can serve luncheon. Oh, I shall be advertising immediately for a lady's maid. Until I find someone who suits, you might assist me, Lily."

"O' course, miss," the maid said, looking a bit awed to have acquired such a comely new mistress.

Lucas said, "I shall inspect the stables for you, Louisa, and see that the space is adequate, as we were promised, and that the horses are properly attended to."

"Thank you, Lucas," she told him.

The ladies proceeded through the house, and Gemma silently admired the handsome draperies and fashionable furnishings. Like many London houses, this one was tall with many levels, with kitchens and pantry and servants' hall below stairs, the dining room and tiny library on the ground floor, the drawing room a level up, then two floors of bedchambers, and at the top of the stairs, an attic with small rooms for the servants.

She was relieved to see that Louisa had a spacious bedchamber, and Miss Pomshack and Gemma would each have smaller bedrooms of their own. At least here Gemma did not have to worry about crowding.

After directing the footman to bring up the luggage, Louisa followed Gemma into the guest chamber and peered about at the rose-colored hangings on the bed and the windows. "It's small and a bit plain. I hope you will be comfortable," she said.

If her new friend thought this room small, Gemma was glad she could not see the tiny chamber at school, which several girls had shared. "It's lovely. I shall be most easy here, I know," she assured her.

"Good. I'll leave you to take off your bonnet. Come down to the dining room when you're ready," Louisa said.

She turned and left, and Gemma removed her bonnet and gloves and washed her face and hands. She had never had a room to herself before. Of course, she might not be here long. What was Lord Gabriel going to say when he met his new sister? How long would it be before Gemma could meet her mother? Did she reside in London, or somewhere in the country—on that estate in Kent, perhaps? Gemma hoped her mother's home was not far away. Sighing, Gemma put her worries aside and descended the staircase.

The others were already gathered at the table, and dishes were set out on the sideboard. Gemma accepted some cold beef and potatoes from the footman. Louisa was eating with a good appetite, but Gemma found it hard to swallow the food, palatable as it was.

"I'm going out to peruse some shops on Bond Street," Louisa announced. "My wardrobe is in urgent need of refurbishing with more stylish London fashions. Would you not like to come, Gemma?"

Flushing—her own clothes were less up-to-date than Louisa's—Gemma shook her head. "Thank you, but not today. I need to write a note to my brother and see if he is at home. Perhaps another time."

Louisa looked disappointed, but she nodded as the footman poured wine into her goblet. "Of course. We shall have much shopping to do before the Season starts, I have no doubt. I'll see you at dinner then."

*Although located near a village only a few miles outside* of London, the institution sat apart, looking isolated and unfriendly. The grounds were bare, with no flower beds or shade trees in evidence. The main building was tall and dark and somehow gloomy. Its windows were streaked with grime, and ivy clung in scraggly patches to the outside walls. Matthew could not imagine it full of laughing children, though he had tried to picture Clarissa in affectionate and protective surroundings, tried to pull his musings away from the images of dire circumstance and deadly dangers which had haunted his nightly dreams and waking thoughts.

Now he wondered if his worst fears had been true, after all. The guilt and the anguish conjured up by such a reflection turned his stomach and left his shoulders stiff with tension, just as they had been at Abourkir Bay when he had watched the French ships flood the horizon, their masts straight and their bright-colored flags tossing in the brine-scented wind as it pushed the two fleets closer and closer until the cannons boomed, emitting puffs of smoke and a rain of deadly shot. . . .

Now, as then, he took a deep breath and braced himself for battle.

He lifted the knocker and pounded, hard.

A child answered, a small girl wearing a faded gray-blue pinafore over an even more colorless dress, her brown hair pulled back into a severe knot. She had a smudge of dirt on her cheek. Her mouth formed an O as she looked up at him.

Matthew tried to smile, but he knew his expression must be more like a grimace. The sight of her had made his heart twist. Clarissa had been much this age, the last time he had seen her.

"I wish to speak to the matron in charge," he said.

The child looked doubtful. "Visitors ain't allowed," she said, her voice as small as her stature.

"She will see me," Matthew predicted, his tone firm.

As the girl bit her lip, as if unsure how to respond, a woman appeared from an inner doorway.

"Here, get along with you. Miz Craigmore don't see no visitors today," she said sharply.

Matthew gave her the look that had been known to make cocksure ensigns take a step backward. The woman hesitated, and her arrogant expression wavered.

"She will see me," he said. And neither female made any move to stop him as he crossed the dirty threshold and strode into the hall.

When she rose from the table, Louisa summoned the cook to confer briefly about the week's meals, then said good-bye to Gemma and to Sir Lucas, who was going—he announced with an air of great importance—to look in on his club.

Since she knew perfectly well that he only belonged to one men's club—and had just been accepted to that, his name put up by an old friend of his father's—Louisa hid her smile.

Miss P made ready to accompany her young mistress, and she and Louisa set out. Lucas had decreed that Louisa's team needed rest after its long journey, but it was not far to Bond Street, and Louisa was too eager for new fashions to consider delaying her first shopping excursion.

She could have sent her footman out to hail a hackney cab, but the day was mild and the rain seemed to have receded. Louisa was so happy to be in London that she thought everything gleamed, the handsome buildings and wide thoroughfares glistening not just from the recent storms, but reflecting her own happiness. She could have skipped along the paving stones, if such a gait were not undignified.

She had to content herself with a quiet smile as she pointed out the most interesting sights to her companion.

"Yes, miss," Miss P answered, her eyes down as she carefully skirted a puddle.

Sighing, Louisa wished that Gemma had come along. But of course, it was natural that she would want to send word to Lord Gabriel right away. Perhaps they could go shopping together tomorrow.

Soon they approached the first of the shops that Louisa had decided to honor with her patronage, and she pushed open the door and stepped inside. This was a popular hat shop, and several women were inspecting airy bonnets or lavishly trimmed hats, while one gentleman waited at the side, looking bored. Louisa stepped up to wait her turn, glancing about at the hats on display.

Oh, there was a particularly fetching model with osprey feathers dyed a deep crimson. Louisa moved closer to inspect it and almost collided with another customer, an older woman whose face was somehow familiar.

Heavens, it was Lady Jersey, the influential society matron and one of the patronesses of Almack's, whom Louisa had accidentally offended last year. Louisa felt as if she had been struck dumb. What should she say? Would Lady Jersey remember her?

If Lady Jersey maintained her animosity this year, Louisa would never obtain the vouchers to Almack's that she coveted so badly. The so-called Marriage Mart was reserved for the most exclusive circles of Society, just where Louisa craved to be. She tried to decide what to do. She could pretend not to recognize the noblewoman, or she could face the social dragon and see if she would be slain before her quest had even begun.

Never a coward, Louisa cleared her throat.

"Pardon me, Lady Jersey, but perhaps—"

"I'll see the maize-colored bonnet, too," the other woman said, hardly glancing at her. "And mind, I told you to bring back the one with the rose-tinted ribbons."

She thought Louisa was a shop girl! Louisa's quick temper flared. "I am not a clerk!"

Frowning, Lady Jersey raised her prominent eyes to focus on Louisa's face.

Her heart sinking, Louisa bit back any more rash words. She felt an ominous sense of deja vu. This could not be happening again! Oh, please, if she angered this woman afresh she would never get into Almack's!

Like a guardian angel, the gentleman who had been hiding a yawn behind his hand suddenly stepped closer. "This is not the girl who was helping you, Lady Jersey. The clerk will be back momentarily. I believe this lady was simply about to remark—" He paused and looked toward Louisa, his glance remarkably bold, his eyes holding a spark of cynical humor deep in their hazel depths.

"Yes, I was about to say that the hat you are holding

should look most becoming on you. The shade will complement your, ah, eyes," Louisa managed to say. "Forgive me for intruding."

"Oh, you think so?" The lady's gaze dropped back to the overlarge hat in her hands, and to Louisa's relief, the countess seemed to forget her existence. "Tell me, Lieutenant McGregor, do you think this one will complement my eyes?"

"No," the gentleman said, to Louisa's annoyance.

Why could he not agree and allow her to fade gracefully out of sight before she put her foot into her mouth again? She realized now that she should not even have spoken to Lady Jersey without a proper introduction. Why did she always barge into trouble without thinking first?

But he continued smoothly, "After all, how can any confection do justice to such lovely features, dear lady?"

Lady Jersey gave her somewhat shrill laugh and wagged her fan at him. "You are a shameless man!"

"Of course. Otherwise, I would wane into just another boring acquaintance," he pointed out, his tone unrepentant.

"Here you are, my lady." The real shop girl hurried from the back carrying an armload of hat boxes. Lady Jersey turned away to examine them.

Louisa sighed in relief and glanced toward the gentleman. Who was he, to be following like a footman after a lady so obviously older than he? He was dressed like a gentleman, and he had a roguishly handsome face, deep brown hair, those cynical hazel eyes, and, yes, although of middle height, a fine military bearing. And his smile made Louisa suddenly wish that she had taken more care with her appearance before she had come out. This was a man who knew women, and somehow, she wanted to be a face that he remembered.

Yet, he appeared to be neither rich nor titled. Lady Jersey had called him lieutenant. He could be one of the many officers who had fought in the long war against Napoleon and were now forced to sell out or exist on half pay during peace time.

As if he felt her stare, he looked back to meet her glance, and his eyes seemed to laugh. "Not that you wouldn't make a fine shop girl," he murmured, for her ears alone. His voice had just a tinge of Scottish burr, and its tone was rich and smooth.

Louisa opened her mouth to snap at him, then realized she couldn't risk anyone else hearing her rebuke.

"That is to say, anyone so lovely would convince me to buy anything," he added.

Louisa felt her cheeks flush with gratification and couldn't decide whether to laugh or frown. Before she could decide on a suitable answer to such bold manipulation while he waited, his eyes still twinkling, they were interrupted.

"Lieutenant McGregor, come here, do!" Lady Jersey called to her companion.

He moved away to solemnly view more hats and offer his opinion, making both his august companion and the salesclerk giggle with his flagrant compliments and wicked judgments. "That one, no. It looks like a barnyard run amok," he said as the clerk held up a wide-brimmed hat trimmed with what did look very much like small yellow chicks.

He'd called Louisa lovely. Although she had been complimented often enough before, his words seemed to carry the hint of a caress, and the graceful Scottish lilt lingered in her memory. A smooth-tongued devil, but perhaps he praised all the ladies. . . . Still, something about his easy urbanity and dashing good looks made Louisa regret his hasty departure. She could still feel the heat that had colored her face when he'd looked at her with that laughing gaze that seemed to see all the way inside her, past her fair hair and smooth cheeks, to her very essence. . . .

Of course, she was betrothed, so she had no business being attracted to some probably penniless ex-officer, just because he had merry eyes and a smoldering smile. Whatever would Lucas say?

Lucas didn't have to know everything, Louisa told herself.

Having a few acquaintances in town would make her time in Society much more pleasant. Besides, this gentleman obviously had Lady Jersey wrapped about his sunbronzed finger; he might aid Louisa in her quest for vouchers to Almack's. She was merely being practical, she thought, as she signaled to Miss P to depart.

Or perhaps she simply wanted to enjoy the gleam of those wicked eyes one more time.

*His gaze ostensibly fixed on a dreadful bonnet trimmed* in purple plumes, Colin McGregor murmured his responses to Lady Jersey while he watched—from the corner of his eye—as the fetching fair-haired lass slipped out of the shop. She was a treat to the eye, indeed, even if she did rush in like a mountain hare who does'na sight the fox lurking amid the heather.

He wondered who she was and if she was married or betrothed. He wondered if she had any money—her clothes were well-made and obviously expensive. This stupid hat he jested about just now carried a price that would have paid the rent on his miserable rooms for a sen'night. Most of all, he wondered how it would be to kiss those soft, delightfully pouty lips. . . . He felt his body respond to the vision and pushed such an idea hastily aside. He could not afford to offend Lady Jersey.

Hiding a sigh, he looked down at a new hat the salesgirl had brought forth, a straw bonnet trimmed with large berries dyed an unlikely shade of puce. He shook his head. "The crows would follow you down the street," he suggested, "hoping to devour the berries."

Both women giggled.

And Colin wondered, not for the first time, just how in the name of heaven he had ended up mired in such a miserable situation?

## Four

*Gemma dipped her quill into the inkwell and signed* her name with special care. Despite her uncertain background, or because of it, she must make every effort to appear educated and respectable. Her handwriting must look ladylike when her brother perused this note.

Writing it had taken her an enormously long time. She had discarded several drafts before she was satisfied. Feeling guilty over wasting expensive paper, she glanced at the wadded sheets of scratched-out first attempts. But she had done her best. Sighing, Gemma folded the letter carefully, then picked up the silver wax jack and dropped a dollop of melted wax onto the edges of the paper. She had no seal to affix, so the wax was left to stiffen into an irregular blob. When it was solid, she pushed herself back from the desk in the drawing room, put the crumpled paper into the fire, and went to find the footman.

Fortunately, she had discovered in conversation with Louisa that her friend had visited Lord Gabriel's London home last year, so she was able to give the footman directions.

Smelters nodded as he accepted the letter. "A connection of yours, is he, his lordship?"

Ladies did not write to unknown gentlemen, so she could hardly deny it, but neither did she want the servants gossiping about her.

"Something like that," she said shortly, and gave him a coin from her small store, hoping that it would be enough. If not, his curiosity seemed strong enough that he did not scorn the errand.

"I'll take it out right away, miss," he assured her.

Gemma climbed the stairs and found Lily, the housemaid, in the guest chamber unpacking Gemma's valises. "These gowns are sadly crushed, miss," the servant said. "It appears that your maid at home folded them very ill."

Gemma, who had packed the bags herself, grimaced. "No doubt."

"Mind you, traveling is always hard on a lady's wardrobe," Lily added, as if afraid she had been too forward. "Not to worry, I'll just press them for you. Which one would you like to wear for dinner?"

Gemma glanced at her small collection of dresses and hoped her brother would not expect her to venture much into Society. She did not have the wardrobe for extensive socializing, nor the funds to replenish her stock of gowns. And she could not ask him for money the moment they met! He would think she was a mercenary wretch who only sought him out for the advantages that might come to her.

Her cheeks flamed at the very notion. She did not mind scraping by on a small income; she had done that all her life. What she lacked was a family, a real family, and that was what she hoped to gain by this impulsive quest.

The pale green muslin was her newest and best-looking dress, but she would save that for the first meeting with her brother, and she could not know if that would happen at once or later in the week. "The jonquil-sprigged muslin, I think," she told the maid, nodding toward her second best.

"I'll see to it, miss," the girl said. With several frocks draped over her arm, she took her leave.

Thinking ruefully that she had now put most of her hostess's servants to work, Gemma hoped that Louisa would not mind. Or was that appropriate behavior for a guest? Gemma had no frame of reference. Once again, she wished for a proper childhood, a large and loving family, a mother who would have taught her daughter the finer points of social behavior. . . .

This was no time to sink into melancholy. She had received an amazing invitation, and soon her long-held questions would receive answers. Just remembering the letter from her mother lifted Gemma's spirits.

In the meantime, she wished she could make herself useful and find some way to repay Louisa's amazing kindness. Gemma thought of going down to the kitchen and offering her help with dinner, but she knew enough to know that would only make the servants stare and think her strange, indeed. Ladies of the Ton did not labor over a mixing bowl or a chopping board.

Gemma wandered downstairs again and found a few books in a glass case in the drawing room. She opened the door and looked over the sparse selection: a collection of sermons; a book of Latin verse, which reminded her too much of the schoolroom; and a two-volume set of Alexander Pope's poetry. She selected Pope and sat down to try to lose herself in witty couplets. But she raised her head every time she heard a carriage drive by or detected the sound of men's voices along the walkway.

When the footman reappeared, she shut the book at once and waited, knowing that her heart beat fast.

"Were you able to deliver the note?" she asked, trying to keep her tone even.

"Yes, miss; 'is lordship 'as a very nice 'ouse, if I do say so. But the servant who answered the door says that 'is lordship is not at 'ome, and 'e can't say for certain when 'e will be arriving in London."

Gemma's heart sank. "I see."

"But I left the note, and the footman says 'e will be sure to give it to 'is lordship as soon as 'e arrives."

"Thank you, Smelters." Gemma maintained her composure until the footman had left the room, but then she put her hands to her flushed cheeks. She felt like weeping.

This was folly. She had waited more than twenty years—what would a few more days matter?

But they did. She jumped to her feet and paced up and down on the slightly worn Oriental rug. What else could she do? Until her brother returned to London, until she could seek an audience and ask for his help in journeying to meet her mother, she had no other avenue to explore.

No, that wasn't true. Gemma thought suddenly of the London solicitor who handled her allowance and school fees. She had written to him once, when she was sixteen, and begged him for any scrap of information about her family. He had written back in his usual dry legal tone and advised her he was unable to answer her plea.

Did he not know, or had he been forbidden to say?

She would face him in person, this time, Gemma thought. And surely he must tell her something! Through their correspondence, limited though it might be, she knew the address of his office. She hurried upstairs and found a shawl to throw about her shoulders. Fortunately, she was still wearing the gray traveling dress.

Smelters caught her as she was about to go out the door. "Can I be of assistance, miss?" His eyes were bright with curiosity.

"I am going to see my man of business," she said, with as much composure as she could manage. "He is located at Lincoln's Inn."

"Ah, that's down by St. Paul's, the Inns of Court where the barristers and solicitors 'ave their offices," the footman told her, his tone knowing. He raised his brows. "It's not a place where ladies usually visit, miss, if you don't mind me saying."

"I must," Gemma told him, determined not to be put off. "It's business of a personal nature."

"You could send a note and ask him to come to you," the footman suggested.

And what if Mr. Peevey refused to come, she thought. It would be too easy for him to hide behind a note; she wanted to see him face-to-face. "No, I wish to see him at once."

Smelters looked resigned. "Then I will summon a hackney. And I'll tell Lily to prepare herself to accompany you."

"Oh, no, she's so busy—" Gemma started, then caught herself. Ladies did not walk alone in London; she knew enough to know that. "Very well. But I don't need a cab. I would quite like a walk."

"It's a fair distance, miss," the servant warned.

"I'm accustomed to walking," she persisted, aware of the small size of her cache of remaining coins.

"As you wish." After a trip upstairs to find the housemaid, he returned and explained how to find Lincoln's Inn. Gemma paid careful heed to his directions.

"I'm sorry to take you away from your chores, Lily," she told the housemaid as they started out.

"That's all right, miss," the girl said. "It's a lovely day, nice to be out a bit. I lived in the country before I went into service, so I'm not such a namby-pamby about walking a few miles as some of the servants here."

So Gemma felt able to set a smart pace. Indeed, the crowded streets and byways were a treat to see, crowded with men and women of all classes, from the hot pie seller and the ragman with his cart to fine ladies riding by in open carriages and men on sleek steeds. She tried not to stare like a country cousin, but she couldn't help but be impressed by the bustle and noise and energy of the city. No wonder Louisa had been eager to come to London.

Between the cry of the street vendors, the rattle of carriages and wagons passing on the busy street, and the *tlot-tlot* of horses that negotiated the wheeled traffic, she felt quite invigorated. The streets of York, a city which she had visited a few times with school parties, were nothing to this.

Soon they came upon a row of shops, with dresses and hats displayed in the window. Gemma couldn't help slowing for a moment to take a better look at a stunning dinner dress of indigo-hued silk set off with wide flounces of Brussels lace.

"Look out, miss," Lily murmured.

Gemma dodged a young page with his arms full of parcels. "Sorry, ma'am," the boy said as he hurried past.

"Thank you, Lily," Gemma said. Turning reluctantly from the enticing apparel out of reach beyond the glass panes—not to mention beyond the size of her purse—she resumed her trek.

Unhappily, by the time they neared the business district, not only were they getting curious stares from the increasingly male-dominated passers-by, but Gemma found she had gotten quite lost. And she did not fancy asking for directions from the men who already leered at her in a most unpleasant way.

So she resigned herself to paying a fare and sent Lily to the street corner to hail a cab. At least it would shield her from the stares of the men on the pavement.

The hackney delivered them the rest of the way, rattling north of Fleet Street and onto Chancery Lane. When Gemma climbed down from its high step and made her way through the archway and into the dark-beamed ancient set of buildings, she took a deep breath to fortify herself, asked a staring young man for directions to the right door, then marched into Mr. Peevey's outer office. Lily hurried after her.

A clerk wearing a collar that seemed almost as high as the stool upon which he perched looked up at her in amazement.

"I am Miss Smith and I wish to see Mr. Peevey, if you please," Gemma said, pleased that her voice sounded so firm. Her heart was beating fast at her own audacity, but having come this far, she would not stop now. If Mr. Peevey refused to see her, she would gain his inner office by force, if need be. The clerk was a slight fellow who looked unlikely to put up a spirited resistence.

But such drastic tactics proved unnecessary. In a moment, the clerk returned and showed her into the solicitor's private office.

"Wait for me here, Lily," she muttered to the maid and, squaring her shoulders, prepared to face the lion.

Or perhaps the tabby cat.

Mr. Peevey sat behind a broad desk. He rose and gave her the briefest of bows, then gestured toward a chair. She had always imagined him as big and powerful, Gemma thought as she took a seat. But, as slight as the clerk and not an inch taller, he was elderly and as withered as an autumn leaf. A good cough would blow him away. His cravat was tied just as precisely as his cramped careful script, and his dark jacket was untouched by any speck of lint. Gemma lifted her chin as he gave her a critical look, obviously examining her in his turn. She tried to sound as dignified as possible.

"We meet at last, Mr. Peevey."

"Indeed." He did not sound excessively pleased at the fact. "This is a surprise. I did not know you had left Yorkshire."

"I am newly come to London," Gemma agreed, then paused, trying to think how to begin. The silence seemed heavy, and he broke it first.

"How may I be of assistance, Miss Smith?" the solicitor asked, his tone guarded.

"The note you forwarded to me on my one and twentieth birthday—"

"I have no further information about its contents," he interrupted. "As I explained in my cover letter."

"I am not here about the note," Gemma told him. "It was self-explanatory. I was very pleased to learn the name of my mother, and as soon as my brother returns to town, I hope to arrange the meeting she invited me to pursue."

His eyes widened for just a moment, as if in surprise. Gemma felt her heart sink. Did he truly not know the details about her birth? But she had come this far, and she forged ahead.

"But as for the source of my allowance—"

This time, his eyes narrowed. "Miss Smith, we have addressed this subject before—"

"But not satisfactorily." She interrupted him this time, anger fueling her courage. She would not be dismissed like a child.

His skinny lips pressed into an even thinner line. "I am not permitted to tell you the source of that income, Miss Smith. I'm amazed that you should inquire. I should think you'd simply be grateful that parental responsibility has not been abrogated as happens too often in these cases—"

"So my allowance does come from a parent? Do the funds come from my mother?"

He looked alarmed. She had caught him off guard; he had not meant to tell her even that much, Gemma thought.

"I did not say that."

No, she didn't think that surmise was correct. He had seemed too surprised at the mention of her mother. Gemma bit her lip. "My father, then."

Peevey did not meet her gaze. "I did not say that," he repeated, shuffling the papers on his desk.

"No, you didn't." But it was the answer, Gemma thought, her heart beating fast, even if this dried-up little man was not going to reveal her father's name. "And what do you mean, in 'these cases'? You assume I was born out of wedlock?"

He looked pained. "If you please, Miss Smith, this is not a suitable topic for a female to discuss."

"My own family must always be a suitable topic for me to discuss, Mr. Peevey. Do you know for a fact that I was a child born . . . without benefit of marriage?" She leaned forward and tried to catch his eye, but he did not look up.

She thought he blushed slightly. "No, I do not ask questions about my clients' personal affairs. But—"

"But you assumed that would be the only reason for an child to be sent away by her parents," Gemma finished for him. She could hardly blame him for drawing such a conclusion. She could not think of another reason, herself, and she'd had years to dwell on the dilemma.

"The fact remains, as a solicitor, I am bound by certain rules. When I give my word, I do not go back upon it. I have pledged that this information will remain private, and I will never break that confidence. Not only would doing so ruin my professional reputation, such a breach would impugn my personal honor."

Even though she wanted to shake that scrawny neck until the hidden facts burst from his lips, Gemma had to admire, for one moment, the resolution that made him lift his head and at last meet her frustrated stare.

She made one last try. "You understand why this is so important to me?"

His expression might have softened just an iota, but she knew even before he spoke that the man would not budge.

"Your feelings are natural ones, but I fear that I am unable to oblige you."

Gemma felt tears flood her eyes, and she blinked hard to hold them back. She would not betray such weakness before this stiff little man.

He gave the faintest rustle of a sigh. "You must take your comfort from the fact that, ah, an unknown patron does continue to offer you financial support, and thus, you may assume, goodwill. When I sought out a boarding school after you left the foundling home—and it was not easy to find a good school willing to take a child so young, I assure you—it was impressed upon me that this time, we must be confident that you would be assured of comfortable and affectionate surroundings."

"You know about the foundling home?" She glanced at him in surprise, then shook her head at herself. Of course, he must. Someone had delivered her to the school, but she had only a vague memory of the shock of it, being swept up out of that hellhole with no notice at all and taken away by stage on what had seemed an almost endless jolting journey to Yorkshire, not knowing if her next home would be as brutal and uncaring as the one she had left. She had been beyond hope, at an age when no child should have such feelings. "Where is it? What is the name?"

He looked at her in surprise. "You were there—do you not remember?"

"I was barely six years old when I left, Mr. Peevey, and although some memories will remain with me for a lifetime— the worst memories, I fear—for the home itself I retain only an impression of a large, dingy building." She could not repress a shiver. The people in charge, those faces she would never forget, but she would not tell him that.

She could see him ponder the question, following her own thoughts as they ran in rapid circles. She might find more information at the home itself, but if she did, it would not, strictly speaking, be Mr. Peevey's fault.

"I shall locate it anyhow, in time," she added, hoping to encourage him. "But you might at least spare me some effort in searching it out."

He seemed to make up his mind. He drew a piece of paper toward him and dipped a pen into an inkwell.

She held her breath while he scratched out a few lines, then he blotted the ink and pushed the paper toward her. "There. I can tell you no more."

Rising, she took two steps toward him, snatching up the scrap of paper before he changed his mind. "Thank you."

She turned toward the door, but his dry voice made her hesitate. "Have you left the school, Miss Smith? Where shall I forward your next quarter's allowance?"

So the money was to continue? She had not even considered that question. In three months' time, she hoped devoutly to have found her mother, to have a home, but still, the thought of something to fall back upon was comforting.

"I'm not sure. I am staying with a friend—a respectable lady—just now. I shall let you know my direction before the next quarter arrives," she told him. She took another step, then, her hand on the doorknob, paused again to look back at him. "Thank you for your care in the choice of my school, Mr. Peevey. I was indeed happy there."

And then she turned to hide the fact that she had to swallow hard against the lump in her throat, and shut the door quietly behind her.

Lily was waiting, and the clerk, his expression inquisitive, stared at them from his perch on the high stool.

Gemma nodded to the maid and they left, making their way as rapidly as possible out of the cramped confines of the Inn's neighborhood and back to the wider streets of the west side. This time, Gemma did not lose her way, and she was just as happy to have the time that it took to go by foot so that she could think.

Several times she glanced at the paper before she tucked it carefully into her reticule. She must have something to do while she waited for her brother to arrive in London, or she would have screaming fits simply from frustration. So she would go to the home, which by the directions she'd been given was not far outside of London, even though the idea of revisiting it made her shiver. But she must see what facts she could uncover.

By the time they reached Louisa's rented house, Gemma found that her hostess and her companion had returned. Gemma washed the dust of the street off her hands and face and changed into the dress Lily had pressed for her. Louisa, too, had changed, and even Miss Pomshack had donned a dress of severe gray silk. Presently, the three women went into dinner together. As they sat around the table, Louisa extolled the beauties of several new gowns that she had ordered.

Gemma tried to appear interested in the litany of millinery delights that her new friend related, but her own thoughts kept returning to the journey she must make, and the trepidation she felt over the destination that lay at the end of it. She shared nothing of her own day, somehow not ready to talk about her double disappointments. Besides, she had been so accustomed to not speaking of her doubtful antecedents that it was hard, she found, to break the habit.

"And the last dress is a nice jonquil hue, as cheerful as

morning sunshine, and trimmed with white," Louisa finished. "Much like the sprigs on the one you are wearing, but a bit deeper in hue."

"I'm sure that, with your fair hair, the color will suit you admirably," Gemma answered as she nibbled at a piece of cake.

Louisa nodded. "I hope so. And, oh, I saw a length of deep blue that would bring out your eyes wonderfully, Gemma. If you decide to order a new gown, it's just the right shade—"

Gemma shook her head with unladylike vigor. "No!"

Louisa looked up at her in surprise. "But why? You have not even seen it."

"I just— I do not wear blue," Gemma said, bringing her voice under control with some effort. "It—it's a long story. I do not care for the color."

"It's your choice, of course," Louisa agreed, though she raised her brows for a moment at the vehemence of Gemma's tone. But then Louisa seemed at last to lose interest in the topic of dresses. Her expression dreamy, she dipped her spoon into a plate of blancmange. "And I met a man in one of the shops. . . ."

Relieved not to be pressed to explain herself further, Gemma said, "Really? Someone of import?"

Louisa blushed. "Oh, no, just a Lieutenant McGregor, but he did have a way about him." Her voice faded, and her thoughts seemed far away.

So they finished the meal in a companionable silence. Gemma thought of the high-pitched chatter of female voices at Miss Maysham's Academy, where mealtimes had never been silent, and how pleasant this was, in contrast. She felt a rush of gratitude for the new friend who had, with such trust, taken Gemma into her home.

Gemma only hoped that someday she could repay Louisa properly, and that, in the meantime, she would give her friend no reason to regret her hospitality.

When Louisa rose from the table, Gemma and Miss Pomshack followed suit, and they all returned to the drawing room where they chatted until they went up to bed. And although Gemma found her guest chamber pleasant and the bed comfortable, it seemed a long time before she could drop off to sleep.

*To Gemma's chagrin, she slept later than she'd intended.* When she opened her eyes to stare at the unfamiliar rose-colored hangings around her bed, she saw bright sunshine peeking round the corners of the draperies. She had to struggle for a moment to remember where she was.

As memory rushed back, along with a surge of both excitement and dread as she recalled her planned journey, Gemma sat up at once. Pushing aside the bedclothes, she rose, washed, and dressed, with some help from Lily, who entered the room in time to help her hook her gown.

"Is your mistress up and about?" Gemma asked.

"Oh, yes, Miss Louisa is downstairs, miss," the maid told her. "Breakfast is laid out in the dining room."

Gemma hurried down the staircase. When she entered the dining room, she found the other two women at the table. The post had come, and Louisa was examining a note.

"It's from my fiancé," she explained, adding to the footman who hovered in the background, "Smelters, tell Cook that Sir Lucas will be joining us for dinner tonight. And I have a question for you about the carriage. Lucas tells me that by the time we reached the city, he noticed a slight wobble in the right front wheel. He tells me it may need to be examined by a wheelwright before we use the chaise again. Do you know of a qualified craftsman?"

"Indeed, miss," the footman assured her. "Leave it to me. I shall go round and fetch Mr. Titmus at once."

While the two conferred, Miss Pomshack placidly chewed on a slice of lamb, and Gemma took a bite of toast. Louisa finished her coddled egg, then announced that she was ready to depart on another shopping excursion.

Again, Gemma begged off. When the other two women had left the house, and Smelters had departed to see about the carriage wheel, she was able to slip out the front door without being noticed. For this journey, she had no wish for witnesses. It was bad enough that the household knew her to be of limited resources and small wardrobe. She had no wish for Lily to witness the wretched institution in which Gemma had spent a part of her childhood.

So she hailed a cab herself and, wincing at the fee he demanded to take her to the village a few miles outside of London, set off on her journey, trying to quell the nervous tremors that made her stomach hollow and her head ache.

The trip was longer than the last, but because she dreaded the arrival, it still seemed too short. She clutched the side of the dirty seat as the hackney bounced over holes in the road and watched as the outskirts of the city fell away. They passed fields and greens where cows grazed, then the hackney slowed as it ascended a small hill, and suddenly she recalled this last mile before the home came into view. Gemma felt herself tense as memories flooded back.

When the cab rolled to a stop, the horse stamping its feet and making its harness jingle, she had to take a deep breath before she could force herself to climb down from the cab and face her memories. On the ground, she handed several coins up to the surly-looking driver, then looked about her.

The house was large and shabby. Its windows had panes streaked with dust, and some sickly looking ivy clung to the outer walls. Some of the leaves were brown, and the stringy vines seemed reluctant to take firm hold of the building. Gemma had every sympathy for such an aversion. Still, the structure was not as enormous as it had seemed to a five-year-old's terrified gaze when she'd first been delivered into the clutches of the woman who'd waited inside.

Was the matron she remembered still here? It had been more than a dozen years since Gemma had left. Perhaps there would be a new woman in charge of the foundling hospital, in which case Gemma could deal with a less formidable opponent.

Anyhow, she was a child no longer, she told herself. There was no reason to cower here before she had even knocked on the door.

"Wait for me. I shall not be long," she told the driver. He frowned as he clutched the driving reins and looked about him at the deserted road.

Gemma wanted nothing more than to climb into the shabby conveyance and hurry back to the relative sanctuary of Louisa's London home. But she might find some answers here, so she forced herself to take one step forward, then another, until she made her way up the short path to the wooden door with its peeling paint.

She clutched the knocker, and, to disguise her rapidly fading confidence, rapped smartly against the panel.

Waiting, she heard nothing. Was no one at home? That was impossible. And she would not be ignored. She had not suffered through the long drive and all her nervous qualms to be turned away unseen.

She knocked again.

At last, Gemma heard a faint rustle of sound, and presently, the door creaked open. For a moment, gazing toward the empty-looking hall, Gemma saw no one. Then she lowered her gaze and found a small girl peeping around the heavy door.

"No one is 'ome to visitors today," she chanted, as if this was a phrase she had learned by rote.

"I wish"—Gemma had to clear her throat before she could finish the sentence—"to see the matron. I have important business with her. Is Mrs. Craigmore still in charge here?"

Putting a thumb in her mouth, the girl nodded.

Looking down at the tangled dirty hair that needed washing and brushing, the faded dress of indeterminate color and the pinafore still faintly blue, both also in need of laundering, Gemma took a deep breath, then wished she had not. The hall still smelled strongly of cooked cabbage and half-rotten potatoes. That, and thin gruel for the morning meal, had made up the bulk of their sustenance during the year and more that Gemma had stayed at the foundling home. She recalled standing at the long table before each meal while all the girls chorused, "Thank'u, Miz Craigmore." And she remembered as well the ache of hunger in her belly and wished now she had thought to bring a sugar drop for the child standing before her.

"You'd better go," the little girl whispered. "Nothing 'ere for a pretty lady like yourself. Lest you want to hire a kitchen maid? I'd like to work for you, miss."

Gemma bent to touch the girl's cheek. "I was once just like you," she said, her voice very low. "And you can be much more than a scullery maid, you know."

Looking bewildered, the child shook her head.

Gemma heard a firmer tread, and she straightened quickly. The child, with fear again in her eyes, looked over her shoulder.

"Who is it, Polly?" The nasal voice made Gemma's mouth go dry. But no, it was not the matron, but another woman, thin instead of stout. "If it's the butcher, tell him—" The woman paused when she saw Gemma.

"Yes, madam? How may I be of assistance?" she demanded, her tone polite but her dark eyes suspicious. She made a motion of dismissal to the girl.

"Yes, Miz Bushnard." The youngster ran up the stairs and disappeared from view.

Had Miss Bushnard been here during Gemma's stay? She wasn't sure. Gemma braced herself, waiting for the woman to say, "Gemma Smith!" and order her, no doubt, back to scrubbing pots.

But Miss Bushnard did not seem to know her. The woman's expression was closed, and no gleam of recognition lit up her thin face.

"Are you looking for a servant girl, miss—?"

"No, not today. I come in search of information," Gemma said, trying to sound assured. "I wish to know some particulars about a young girl who was given into your care sixteen years ago."

The woman's eyes narrowed. "I regret that we have no records dating back to that time."

Gemma gazed at her in disbelief. "But the foundling home has been here for much longer than—"

Miss Bushnard shook her head. "We had a fire two years ago. It destroyed any records dating prior to that time. I'm sorry we cannot help you."

Gemma hesitated, trying to think of some way to refute the woman's statement. The words were too pat, she thought, and she did not believe them for a moment. Fire? Everything in this hallway was just as it had been those many years ago.

"If you will excuse me," the other woman added. "As you must understand, with all the children here to look out for, my duties leave me no time for idle chatter."

Gemma stopped herself just in time from blurting out that, as she remembered it, the staff's duties were mostly confined to caning children who fell asleep over their scrubbing brushes.

Before she could conjure up further argument, she found herself being ushered back over the threshold. The door shut behind her with a thud.

It was a lie—she knew it was a lie! Gemma studied the facade of the building and saw no sign of smoke damage, no recent repairs, and certainly, no repainting of the dingy outer walls. Nor had she smelled any lingering odor of smoke inside the hall. Fire, indeed. The matron here wanted no one to look at her records. Why? How could such scrutiny harm her?

Gemma climbed reluctantly back into the hackney, and the driver clucked to his horse and twitched the reins to circle back the way they had come. The cab rolled forward. Gemma felt the ache of unshed tears in her throat. The matron must know something about Gemma's background before she had been sent here. Someone had brought her—had it been the same solicitor who had taken her away again later? Gemma wished she could remember. Had her mother had any contact with her while Gemma was here? Had her unknown father visited, or at least paid for her support here, too? If so, there might be, must be, something in the home's ledgers that might give her a name, an address, some way she could seek out her parents.

"Stop!" Gemma called to the driver. They had passed out of sight of the foundling home as the road dipped behind a cluster of trees. "Let me out here."

"You gonna walk back to town?" the driver demanded.

"No, just wait here a few minutes," she told him, ignoring his frown. "I—I forgot something. I shall be back momentarily."

She hoped. As she hurried back up the narrow lane, Gemma knew she was being foolish. Most likely, Lord Gabriel would arrive in London within a few days. Most likely, he would be willing to help her set up a meeting with her mother. Her mother wished a reunion—the note said so.

Yet, her brother did not know that Gemma awaited his arrival. What if, despite the newspaper item, it was a week, a month before he came to town? What if, for some reason, he changed his mind and did not come at all this Season? And worst of all, what if he did not feel as her mother did, and he refused to help her?

Gemma would be left as ignorant, and as alone, as she had ever been. The day of reckoning had been delayed for so long that suddenly it seemed impossible to be patient for another hour. Inside that grim building, she felt with a sudden intuition, lay information that would be of value to her. Gemma would have bet her life upon it.

She would not be put off so easily. She was not a frightened child any longer, Gemma told herself. There was no reason for the matron to be so taciturn. Had she been sworn to secrecy, too, like Mr. Peevey?

Gemma was sick to death of questions with no answers. She had to make one more try. If those in charge here did not want to help her, she would help herself. God knew, she remembered the inside layout of the house all too vividly. On her hands and knees, she had scrubbed the bleached oak floorboards of every room on the first two floors. She knew the office in the back where Mrs. Craigmore kept a shelf full of ledgers and notebooks. It had not occurred to the young Gemma to wonder what was inside them, but the grownup Gemma did, and the hidden contents seemed to call to her. Her name might be written inside one of them, and could it also spell out the names of her antecedents?

The mere possibility spurred her on. Keeping herself screened by the trees, Gemma slipped around to the back of the building where a few sad-looking hens, as dispirited in appearance as the children inside the big edifice, pecked at the sparse greenery. The sun had dipped past its zenith, and the shadows were growing longer. Gemma looked about her, but she saw no one.

She heard a sudden muffled peal from inside the home, and she jumped. Then she remembered that it was the bell for the early dinner, which served as the children's main meal of the day. Gemma knew from her time here that all the staff and youngsters would be gathered in the drab dining hall in the basement.

Now was her chance! She ran lightly up to the back door and turned the doorknob, wondering if she were strong enough to break the lock.

To her surprise, the knob turned easily. Someone had been lax, Gemma thought. When she had been here, the doors were always kept latched, if for no other reason than to keep some angry, desperate inmate from running away.

This was no time for indulging in the memories that still haunted her. Fighting back her fear, Gemma eased open the door, stared down the dimly lit hallway, then took one step over the threshold.

A strong hand covered her mouth.

# Five

Gemma jerked in shock, but the hand muffled her shriek of surprise. Its touch felt slightly rough against her mouth and its grasp impossible to evade. Her arm had been seized in a steely grip. She tried to break the hold, but she couldn't move. Terror raced through her, and she thought for a moment she would faint.

"Do not scream," a man whispered. She realized she could smell starchy linen and a slight hint of male skin.

It seemed so unlikely for a murderer to smell of clean linen that some of her initial panic ebbed. What was this about? Who was it who held her so firmly?

Standing very close, he moved into her view. She saw a tall, well-made man with somewhat disordered fair hair and eyes the color of gunmetal. His face would have been handsome if his expression had not been so grim. Smudges of dust darkened his cheeks. He wore a black coat and had wrapped a dark scarf around his throat and chin, and he blended easily into the shadows of the hall.

"Are you a teacher at the foundling home?" he whispered,

glancing down at her drab but ladylike traveling costume. His voice seemed too genteel to belong to a thief and housebreaker, and yet, why else was he here?

She shook her head.

"I will release my hand, but if you make a noise, I will throttle you here and now. I have had sufficient practice in the art to do it quickly. Do you believe me?"

She nodded. His tone alone would have convinced her; his words made her once more cold with fear.

He removed his hand but held it a few inches from her mouth, as if not quite trusting her. His eyes were still dark with resolve.

Her mouth very dry, Gemma tried to swallow.

"Who are you?" he asked.

Her voice came out as a muffled croak. "I—I have come to slip into the matron's office and examine her records?"

He stared at her. Did he not believe her? It was a strange enough errand.

"Why?"

"It's too complicated to explain just now," she told him, keeping her tone low. "Listen, the children and staff are at dinner; there is little time before they come back upstairs. Just let me go into the matron's office down the hall. But you—why are you here? There is little here to steal, you know. Surely, you have not come to harm any of the children?"

She would have to scream for help, if so, even if it meant risking her own death. She would not sacrifice any of those pitiful youngsters below stairs.

He raised those slashing brows in apparent shock. "God forbid!"

If he were a twisted villain looking for some innocent sacrifice, he would not admit to it, one rational part of her mind told her. And yet, his voice held the deep note of sincerity, and she found that she believed him.

"Lead the way," he told her. "And raise no outcry."

She nodded, and he let go of her arm. She saw that he held a slim metal bar beneath one arm and realized he must have broken the lock on the outer door to get inside. Unease rippled through her again, but she refused to give up her quest. She tiptoed down the hallway, opened the door, and slipped into the office.

He followed, shutting the door very quietly behind them and sliding the latch into place. Biting her lip, Gemma thought for an instant how secluded they now were. This would be a better place to kill her than the hallway, where her struggles would more likely be heard from below. But she could not waste time on useless fears. She was here, and she would take her chances.

Gemma glanced about the room. Pewter candlesticks sat on the desk and table, and a small clock adorned the mantel, poor enough pickings for a thief. She saw him draw out a large sack of coarse cloth from beneath his coat, but she cared little if the matron lost her trinkets. Gemma went straight to the shelf of ledgers, which was just where it had always been. She picked up one of the books and opened it to scan a page, seeing a list of household expenses.

Eggs, 5 shillings
Potatoes, 10 shillings a bushel

The list went on, but none of it was what she sought. She leafed through the thin journal, then picked up another.

"Is there a list of students?" the man asked, peering over her shoulder.

She looked at him in surprise. "That is one of the things I am searching for," she admitted and continued her search.

Then she stiffened. She heard a muffled thud from below, and then the pounding of feet on the staircase. "The children have been released from the dining room," she told him. "Someone may come!"

He raised his brows again, but she forgot to be afraid. Time was slipping away, and she had to find out—

Then, to her shock, he took his bag, and, ignoring the clock and the pewterware, grabbed a handful of the shabby ledgers and dumped them, along with the metal bar, into the sack.

Staring at him for only an instant, she made up her mind. Gemma seized another armload and helped him. Together, they emptied the shelf.

Then the man turned his head. She heard it, too—heavy footsteps in the hall. She pictured the matron marching along with her usual ponderous tread, and the child inside her cringed in terror at the thought of being discovered. The sting of the matron's stick on her shoulders returned to her, as real as if the beating were just occurring. For an instant, fear veiled her vision so that she could hardly see. Oh, God help her . . .

"Come," he breathed into her ear. With long strides, he crossed to the window and pushed up the sash. Putting the bag on the floor, he held out his hands to her, and she allowed him to grasp her around the waist, lift her with an easy strength, and help her slide through the open window. She fell the few feet to the ground below, then scrambled out of his way as, bag in hand, he followed her through the opening.

"Make haste," he ordered. "We must get out of sight."

Nodding, she took the hand he offered, and they dashed for the trees. It seemed a long way. Gemma's heart pounded as she ran, and her shoulders tensed as she waited for an outraged Mrs. Craigmore to lean through the window and scream for them to bring back her lost ledgers, but she heard only the slight thud of their feet on the grass and her own pulse beating fast. At last the lush greenery and thick trunks offered them shelter. When the house was hidden from view, they paused in the deep shadow of a large oak. Out of breath, her pulse still racing from exertion and fear, Gemma leaned against the tree and stared up at him. He still held the sack over his shoulder.

"Now, who are you?" she demanded. "I cannot allow you to take away those ledgers. I need to study them. And they can have no value to you."

He gazed back at her without answering. Gemma lifted

her chin, trying to read his face in the dimness. She was, no doubt, in terrible danger, standing here with some unknown felon, yet she refused to relinquish her original goal. Somehow, she would find out her true origins. If Lord Gabriel never answered her, if he refused to see her, if—heaven forbid—her mother had changed her mind about a meeting, this could be Gemma's only lead. She had lived with uncertainty for too long to believe that it might really be lifted.

She put one hand on his cloth bag, now heavy with the books, but he did not loosen his grip. They both maintained their hold on the cloth, and Gemma tensed again. The man's eyes were heavy with purpose, but she met his gaze squarely.

"They are more valuable than gems. There is information here I must have, that I would die for," he told her. The melodramatic statement should have sounded ridiculous, but his tone was such that she believed him implicitly.

"The contents are just as vital to me, and I will not let you disappear with the books," she argued, even as she wondered how on earth she would stop him. He was more powerful, and she was alone.

She felt him stiffen as if preparing to pull the bag out of her grasp, and to delay a struggle, she added, "Why do you wish these ledgers?"

"Why do you?" he shot back. "Why would a lady wish to know the inner workings of a foundling home?"

"I was once an inhabitant," she told him.

To her surprise, his expression lightened. "You have lived here? So the home is not as bad as I have imagined?"

"It is worse," she said bluntly.

His face fell, and determination thinned his well-shaped mouth.

"But why—" He was questioning her, now. His dark eyes were intent. "Why do you wish to have them?"

"I need information," she said. "The reasons are complicated, as I said." And not ones she wished to confess to a stranger.

His lips relaxed enough to lift into a wry almost-smile as if he guessed the direction of her thoughts. "And you know nothing about me."

"No," she agreed. "I do not. If you let me take the ledgers, I promise to allow you to see them, as well. I will give you the address in London where I am staying."

And where she could meet him with people around her, a sturdy footman on call, she thought. Where a stranger would be less likely able to commit a quiet murder. She had not forgotten his first threat, while he had held her immobile with hands like forged steel.

He stood still for a moment, as if deep in thought. Then he looked back at her. "I think it is possible that we could help each other. If you once resided at the home, you may know other things that could be of use to me."

That depended on what his unknown purpose was, Gemma thought, but she would not argue now. "It is possible."

"How were you planning to return to London?" he asked, suddenly practical. "Surely not on foot?"

She shook her head. "I have a cab waiting," she said. "About half a mile from here."

He seemed to make up his mind. "Then you will come with me to collect my horse, and I will follow you back to London," he said.

Thereby being sure that she did not give him a false address, Gemma thought cynically. But if she distrusted him, he had the right to similar suspicions. She wondered suddenly if she was doing right to bring a housebreaker— although he had not stolen anything she would expect of a common thief—to Louisa's home. It was too late to change her mind, however, and she was desperate not to allow him to ride away with those ledgers.

"Very well," she agreed.

They had been so quiet that, reassured, the birds in the trees around them had once again begun to call. As the stranger lifted a branch for her, a thrush fluttered away in alarm. Stepping softly, he led her farther into the woods.

Gemma's fear flared again—until she made out a horse, a roan, tied to a young tree and waiting patiently for its rider to return. Here, under Gemma's worried gaze, the stranger transferred the ledgers to his saddlebags.

He saw her look of concern. "Do not worry. I will not disappear with them. As I said, I think we can help each other."

Knowing she was likely mad to trust a thief, she nodded. Gemma felt another qualm as he untied the horse, put his foot into the stirrup and swung himself into the saddle. She gazed at him in alarm, but he leaned over and held out his hand.

"Come, I will take you to your carriage."

She hesitated for a moment, then, suddenly aware that she did not wish to be found here alone when someone from the foundling home came searching after the loss of the journals was discovered, she gripped his hand and allowed him to swing her up behind him.

She perched awkwardly on the horse's back. Her skirt was not cut for riding, and although the sturdy fabric did not rip, she had to allow her hem to ride higher up her leg than was proper. Did he glance down at her stocking-clad calves? If so, he made no comment.

Her face flushing, Gemma put her arms around his waist. It was that or risk sliding off, she told herself, and gripped him more tightly than she would have wished. His back was broad, and his carriage very erect. Once again, she wondered just who and what he was.

He clucked to the horse and moved his foot against the beast's side, and the animal stepped forward.

Her face pressed against his back, Gemma clung to him. She was aware again of the vague smells of his clothing, his body. Even with the faint hint of the perspiration induced by their exertions, and now a slight horsey aroma, he still did not—as she had noted at their first contact—smell like a long unwashed street thug. But if he were not a ruffian, what sort of man was he, then, to be breaking into the foundling home?

She was all too aware of how near their bodies pressed together. His back was hard with muscle, and she already knew the strength in his hands and arms. She felt a faint and most unladylike response inside her to his closeness. To distract herself, she lifted her head and tried to stare around him. They had emerged from the trees, and the narrow road came into view. "Just over there, past the rise of the hill," she directed.

He turned his horse into the roadway, and they crested the hill. Gemma leaned to the side to see better, and she gasped.

The road was empty. The hackney was gone.

"It's not here," she said foolishly as if the stranger could not see the bare road for himself. "The driver must have given up on me."

She was stranded here, miles from London. Worse yet, she had been left alone with a stranger whose morals she had no reason to trust. All of Gemma's fears rushed back, and suddenly she could no longer endure their enforced and almost intimate contact. She let go of the man she had been holding so tightly and pushed herself off, sliding down the horse's flank.

She stumbled but managed to regain her footing and avoid tumbling into a heap. Now what? What would the stranger do, now that she had no other resources? With no witness here to see the crime, he could easily execute that quiet murder he had threatened her with on the instant of their first meeting.

He looked down at her, and she could not read his expression. "What are you doing? You can hardly walk back to London. It will be dark before you reach the city. It would be highly dangerous for you to trek through the night all alone."

"In case I should meet a man of uncertain reputation?" she asked, her tone dry. "A thief or housebreaker, perhaps, who might threaten me with harm?"

For a moment, she thought he struggled against a smile. "Point taken."

As she watched, he pulled the dark scarf from around his neck, revealing the neatly-tied white stock of a gentleman. He pushed his fair hair more or less back into place and used the scarf to wipe the dust off his face. Had he dirtied it deliberately to avoid being easily seen in the dimness of the hall? Suddenly he looked much less like a street thief and much more like a gentleman. Had he removed his disguise to reassure her?

It was hardly rational that his appearance should vouch for his honor, but Gemma found that she did feel a little better.

"But why—"

"As you said, my reasons are complicated. I think we should make our way back to London, and then we need to have a long talk."

She nodded slowly. "Yes. And examine the ledgers."

"Together," he reminded her.

"Agreed."

He leaned over and offered her his hand. She grasped it with both of hers, and without apparent effort, he pulled her up behind him once more. If he were indeed a gentleman, as it increasingly appeared, he was not an idle sort, Gemma decided.

She felt even more self-conscious about being pressed so closely against his body, but if she did not wish to fall, she could hardly avoid it. He would think nothing of it, she told herself. Or so she hoped.

And indeed, he made no comment except to say, "Hold tight. I need to put some distance between us and the home. There is only a crescent moon tonight, so it will be as well to get as far along as we can before darkness falls. The road will be hard to see."

She nodded and tightened her hold. It was not very comfortable, perching behind the saddle like this, but it was better than walking the miles back to the city, and she realized she did not at all want to be left on foot, vulnerable to assault by any passing vagrant.

So she gritted her teeth against the discomfort of the

horse's gait and allowed herself to lean into the comforting solidness of the rider's form. Did the man have a name? Soon, she must find out more about him.

Matthew was all too aware of her body as it pressed against his own. Her breasts were soft against the hard line of his back, her arms firm about his waist but still shapely and indisputably feminine. He ached a little, thinking how long since he had been this close to a woman—and not just any woman.

From their first encounter in the dark hall, he had liked the way she held herself, the soft curve of her throat, the dark silkiness of her hair. He remembered how it had felt to touch her face, her lips—her soft, so touchable lips—and again his groin ached.

A glimmer of regret stirred—he'd been rougher with her than perhaps he'd had to be. He hadn't wished to alarm her, but he couldn't allow his mission to be imperiled. He hadn't expected her to have such courage and such presence of mind. Most females, if assaulted by a stranger in the dark, would have screamed or swooned or engaged in hysterics. A surprising woman, this. No, she had spirit and enough courage to stand up to a man whose honor she had no way of judging. He tried to think about all the ways she had surprised him instead of the soft body that pressed against him, the feminine body so hard to ignore.

The sturdy little horse settled into a steady gait. After a time, the sun dipped behind the trees, and the blue sky faded into rose and lavender and then gray, then at last a soft darkness surrounded them. The air cooled. A sliver of moon rose, but its light was faint. When it slipped behind a cloud or trees shadowed the road and made the going more treacherous, Matthew tightened the reins, and the horse fell into a walk. If their steed stepped into a pothole and lamed itself, they would both be on foot. When the moon reappeared, he urged the horse back to a trot.

Even as he decided they would make their way back to town without problem, a hare darted across the road, passing just beneath the horse's nose. The roan shied.

Cursing, Matthew tightened the reins, but he felt the woman gasp and her hold on his waist slip. He could feel her sliding—she had been thrown off balance and was about to fall beneath the horse's nervously dancing hooves. He put one hand out to grab her arm and with the other tried to calm his steed. While he fought the frightened horse, he thought, in one corner of his mind, the only part not consumed with fear for her, that a flapping sail was easier to control any day.

But although she cried out, the woman did not fall. He clung to her, and he heard her moan with pain. When the horse quieted, at last, Matthew could release his grip on the reins and allow her to slide safely down. He jumped off the horse and tied the reins to a nearby tree, then hurried to her.

She was shivering.

"Are you all right?" he asked, taking her gently by the shoulders. She gasped.

"No, I am not bloody well all right!" she shot back. "I think you have broken my arm. It hurts abominably!"

"Let me see. Where does it hurt?"

He probed gently, in his concern forgetting both his desire and her sense of modesty. Her gasp of pain told him, and the feel of her body.

"It's not broken," he told her.

"Then why do I feel as if my whole shoulder is afire?" she retorted. He could see the glimmer of tears on her cheeks.

"You have dislocated it," he told her. "Hanging on to me with only one arm pulled the bone awry. But don't worry."

Even in the faint moonlight, he could see her look of skepticism. "No?"

"I have seen it before. I know what to do. Look, here is a nice broad tree trunk. Just lean against it for a moment."

"I don't think you should—I need a surgeon," she argued. But she did lean back, shutting her eyes for an instant. And he took his chance.

Eyes flying open, Gemma cried out. Such a flash of

pain—but now the agony was gone, leaving only a lingering deep ache in her shoulder.

"What did you do?" she demanded.

"Put it back into place," he told her matter-of-factly. He reached into his pocket and handed her a white handkerchief so she could wipe her eyes.

Gemma held it to her face a moment. "Why didn't you warn me? Oh, I wish I knew how to swear!"

To her fury, he laughed softly. "I will teach you sometime. If I had told you, if you had braced yourself, it would only have hurt more. Come, I will lift you up to the horse, and I will lead it."

"You have to ride, as well, or we will be hours getting back to town," she argued, still furious at him, and yet she knew she should be thankful, too. He had saved her several times tonight. Only, why did he have be so—so damned decisive about it, each time! "If I am gone all night, what on earth will I tell my friend?"

So he lifted her as gently as possible, settling her in front of the saddle, then untied the horse and somehow sprang up behind her.

And this time, her head spinning a little, Gemma had every excuse to lean against the comforting solidity of his shoulder—which didn't ache as hers did, damn him. She found his arm secure around her and once—she almost thought—his lips touched her hair. But she was a little giddy, still, and she might have imagined the last.

He nudged the horse into a walk. They made slow progress, and she thought they would travel forever before reaching town. Somehow, held tightly in his embrace, that did not seem such a terrible prospect. Eventually, buildings, scattered at first and then more densely clustered, rose up around them. For a time the way was even darker, but soon they approached the west side of the city, with its fine homes, gas streetlights, and better paved, wider avenues.

Money made all the difference, Gemma thought vaguely, that and a secure social class. It always came back to that.

She directed him to Louisa's rented dwelling. When he pulled up the horse in front of the tall edifice, he helped her down once more. Her back and thighs ached as well as her abused shoulder, and she knew that she would be sore tomorrow. Lights glowed from inside the house's draped windows, and she gazed at the stranger. If she brought him inside now, Louisa would see the man and would have to be told about Gemma's most inappropriate adventure. And yet, if Gemma let him ride away into the darkness, what if she never saw him again? After so much risk and fearful exertion, the ledgers would be lost to her.

Perhaps the man guessed at the nature of her quandary. "It would be remiss of me not to see you safely to the door," he told her. "Do you have family waiting?"

Sighing, Gemma shook her head. "A friend."

"Perhaps I should not come in tonight," he suggested. "I am not dressed for a social call, and it will seem odd."

"But the ledgers—"

She was interrupted as the door swung open. Gemma flinched, and he stiffened, as well.

"Gemma!" Louisa stood in the doorway. "I was growing most concerned about you. Oh, you have a friend with you."

What could she say? She did not even know his name. And worse, Gemma saw Sir Lucas come to stand beside his fiancé in the doorway. He was frowning. Seeing Gemma turn up with an unexplained male would only confirm his worst suspicions.

While Gemma hesitated, the man beside her made a smooth bow. "Captain Matthew Fallon, lately of His Majesty's Navy, at your service."

The slight tension in the air seemed to ease.

"My friend Miss Louisa Crookshank, and her fiancé, Sir Lucas Englewood, both of Bath," Gemma declared, as the two responded with curtsy and bow to the captain's greeting.

A naval captain? Was this true?

"Would you not join us for dinner, Captain Fallon?"

Louisa asked, her expression inquisitive. "We were just about to sit down."

"I would not impose upon you on such short notice," Captain Fallon told her. "Perhaps another time."

But the ledgers, Gemma thought. She turned to stare at him.

He nodded at her anxious expression. "I shall return tomorrow about our unfinished business," he told her, his tone low. "Ten o'clock, shall we say?"

"I look forward to it," she answered, unable to protest with Louisa and Sir Lucas watching. She prayed he would truly return. At least she had his name.

If it were genuine.

She could only dip a polite curtsy as he made his bow to her, then he remounted his horse and flicked the reins. Frustrated, she watched him ride away, then she slowly climbed the steps.

"You must tell us all about your friend, Gemma," Louisa told her. "Come into the dining room; dinner was just announced."

"If you will forgive me for not changing gowns, I will just wash the dust off my hands," Gemma agreed. "I shall not keep you waiting long."

And while she did that, Gemma thought, she must rally her wits to concoct a likely explanation for Captain Fallon's unexpected appearance!

When she rejoined them all shortly in the dining room, Sir Lucas stood while the footman held Gemma's chair for her. She took her seat across from Miss Pomshack, and Louisa's fiancé sat down again. For a few minutes they were all occupied with filling their plates. But Gemma knew that Louisa would not wait long to begin her questions.

"Tell us about your handsome captain," Louisa said. "I did not know you had another acquaintance in London."

"I don't know him well," Gemma demurred, dipping her fork into the beef and sauteed mushrooms on her plate. Dinner smelled delicious, even though her mouth had gone dry from nervousness. "We have a mutual acquaintance, that is all." The image of Mrs. Craigmore, the tyrannical matron at the foundling home, flashed into her mind, but she pushed the vision away and continued, "I did not expect to see him. He has only recently returned from sea." If he had truly been a naval officer, that seemed a safe enough conjecture.

Sir Lucas frowned at her. "And you went out alone with him, someone who, as you say, is not well known to you?"

Raising her chin, Gemma met his skeptical stare. "No, I went out with Lily," she said. That was true for her excursion yesterday, if not today. "But I sent her on a brief errand. I had taken a hackney, but the driver ignored my instructions to wait for my return and left me stranded. Captain Fallon, who had ventured out on business of his own, came to my rescue and escorted me home when another cab was not to be found. Forgive me for troubling you, Louisa. I had not meant to return so late."

Gemma took a deep breath. She only hoped they had not already questioned the maid and knew that part of her story was false.

Sir Lucas nodded, but Louisa shot her a sharp look. Louisa obviously recognized that some of her tale was concocted, but, to Gemma's relief, she did not speak, taking another bite of her boiled lobster instead. She looked thoughtful. At least Sir Lucas seemed satisfied by her explanation. He began to tell Louisa of the new coat he had been measured for.

"A man at my club assures me this tailor is all the crack in the best circles."

"Excellent," Louisa agreed. "I'm sure you will look most handsome in it. I have ordered more gowns, as well."

They discussed London fashions while Miss P applied her attention to her food.

Gemma was now free to eat her dinner as well. Her middle felt amazingly hollow and, despite all her aches, she savored the tender beef and crisp roasted chicken. Still, as the footman brought in more food, she could not help contrasting the linen-draped table before her, laden with its many skillfully prepared dishes, with the meager fare the children at the foundling home had shared. It made it hard to swallow the cunningly iced confections in the second course. Gemma put down her fork and waited for Louisa to signal the ladies' withdrawal. Even though Sir Lucas would be left to enjoy his port in solitary state, proper form must be kept.

And when she and Louisa and Miss Pomshack retired to the drawing room, Louisa took her arm and whispered, "All right, the truth now. I asked Lily, and she said she had been out with you yesterday to see a solicitor, but she did not know you had left the house today. You are not in any trouble, are you, Gemma?"

There was an undertone of unease in Louisa's query that, Gemma suspected, was not totally intended for her new friend. And she did not blame Louisa for her anxiety. Taking in a stranger had been very generous; it would be only human to be concerned about the possibility of scandalous secrets that might emerge, to Louisa's detriment as well as Gemma's.

"It's a long story," she murmured, glancing at Miss Pomshack as they took chairs close to the fire. The evening had turned cool. "I will tell you later."

Lucas soon rejoined them, but after a few minutes of conversation, stood once more to take his leave.

"Going so early? You're not venturing out to some horrid gaming den, are you?" Louisa demanded, eying him with some reserve.

"Ladies do not speak of such things," Lucas told her, his tone dignified. "I am meeting some gentlemen, if you must know, but I am past the first flush of green youth, Louisa. You have no need to worry about me."

Eyeing his round cheeks and unlined face, Gemma bit back a smile. He did not yet qualify as old and jaded, no matter how mature he thought he was, but she hoped, for Louisa's sake, that Sir Lucas was not inclined toward heavy gaming or deep drinking.

Louisa did not appear convinced, but his next statement diverted her.

"And I have engaged a box at the theater for tomorrow night, Louisa. I am sure you will enjoy the outing."

Louisa clapped her hands. "Oh, that sounds lovely, Lucas!" She followed him into the hall where they could take a private farewell and perhaps share a quick kiss. Miss Pomshack applied herself to some needlework, and Gemma picked up the book of poetry she had been reading yesterday. When Louisa returned, Gemma read aloud from it to amuse the other ladies—and also to keep Louisa's questions at bay a little longer—until the footman brought in the tea tray before bedtime.

When they went upstairs, Gemma shut her door and waited for Lily to come and unbutton the back of her gown. But it was Louisa who appeared, robed in a dressing gown, her fair hair hanging loosely down her back.

"I sent Lily to bed," she explained. "So we will not be interrupted. And Miss P is already snoring; I can hear her through her door. I want the whole story, now. I asked Lily first of all—fortunately, before Lucas had arrived—and she knew nothing of your whereabouts. What mystery are you up to, Gemma?"

She came across to undo the back of Gemma's dress. Gemma was glad for the chance to turn her face away for a moment, to hide her grimace as her sore shoulder protested, and to marshal her thoughts. When she had pulled off the frock and donned her nightdress, wrapping her shawl around her shoulders against the slight chill of the room, she climbed onto the bed. Louisa settled herself at its foot, from her expression ready to listen all night.

Gemma sighed. "I shall have to start with the errand yesterday," she told her friend. "First of all, I sent a note to Lord Gabriel's house. But when Smelters returned, he told me he had learned that Lord Gabriel has not yet arrived in town."

"Oh, no!" Louisa exclaimed.

Raising her brows, Gemma paused. Such distress seemed

exaggerated; it was not Louisa who was waiting for the answer to lifelong secrets.

Louisa blushed. "That is, I was hoping to renew my acquaintance with Lady Gabriel. I need a married lady who is familiar—and accepted—in London society to introduce me at some select gatherings so that I can begin my debut properly. And since my aunt is not yet back from her wedding trip, I had hoped that Lady Gabriel might oblige."

"I see," Gemma said.

"But most likely, they will arrive soon," Louisa added with her usual optimistic nature. "Go on. Lord Gabriel is not yet in London. You must have been most disappointed to hear it. I am aware, truly, that the urgency of your errand is greater than mine."

Gemma gave her a grateful look. "I was distressed, that is true. Then I thought of the solicitor who has handled my school accounts and who sends me my allowance. If I went to see him, I thought I might find out something about my parents."

She told Louisa of the trip to the Inn and the limited information she had obtained.

"A foundling home?" Louisa's fair brows shot up. "Oh, Gemma, my poor dear! I had no idea."

Gemma found that now she was the one flushing. "It was not a happy time," she agreed. "But fortunately, it was of short duration." And more than that, she would not say, she thought. She had no wish for Louisa, with her privileged background, to pity her even more than she might already.

"So I had the address of the foundling home, and I decided to pay it a visit. The matron there might know who had brought me as a child to the institution, and who might have provided funds for my stay."

Louisa's eyes widened. "You are brave, indeed, Gemma, but you should not have gone alone!"

"I know that," Gemma agreed. "But I hated to have the servants know—"

She didn't have to finish the sentence. Louisa nodded in

understanding. "So you went. Did you learn anything about your family? And where did you meet the captain? He really is scrumptious, you know."

Gemma thought about the man's handsome face. It was impossible to forget the strength of his hands and arms, or the firmness of his back as she pressed herself against it, or how secure she had felt cradled in front of him. Knowing that Louisa was observing her expression, she pushed those memories away.

"He was on a similar errand, though I have not yet heard the particulars of it. I'm sure he was not at the home himself; it has always held females only. And the hackney really did leave me stranded, and a pox on the driver, too!"

"Oh, how fortunate that Captain Fallon was there and could escort you back to the city," Louisa exclaimed.

"Indeed," Gemma agreed. She had no intention of telling her friend the rest, how the captain had threatened to throttle her, how they had stolen the matron's ledgers, or how she had almost fallen from the horse. Despite her impulsiveness, Louisa was well brought up and at heart as conventional as such a lady was supposed to be. Gemma did not want to distress her or alienate a friend of whom she was growing more and more fond. So she closed her lips on the balance of the story and tried to ignore Louisa's suggestive glance when she remarked that perhaps the captain would call again.

"Perhaps," Gemma agreed. "But I am not in need of a suitor, Louisa."

Louisa sat up straight. "You are engaged? And you did not tell me!"

"No, no." Gemma smoothed the bed linen with one hand to avoid meeting her friend's startled gaze. "I am not betrothed. But there is a young man in Yorkshire—"

"Go on," Louisa commanded when she paused. "Who is he? What is his estate—is it respectable? Where did you encounter him? What are his intentions?"

Gemma shook her head at the barrage of questions. Louisa sounded for a moment like a maiden aunt, eager to determine the young man's suitability. "He is the brother of a schoolmate, which is how I came to know him. A small miracle, since my opportunities to meet suitable males have been most limited. His name is Arnold Cuthbertson. He is the son of a local squire, and he has hinted that he wishes to offer marriage, but—"

"But?" Louisa prompted, her eyes gleaming with vicarious delight at this unexpected discovery.

"But he hesitates, not wishing to disgrace his own family by . . . by . . ." She found that she could not finish the sentence.

"By engaging himself to a woman whose birth might be—Oh, Gemma, I am so sorry," Louisa blurted.

Gemma blinked hard. She would not reveal how the stigma of her unknown parentage haunted her. "I must discover who I am," she declared, her voice strained. "I am determined to know, once and for all, if I have the right to even think of marrying a gentleman, or if I should simply hire myself out as a serving maid and be done with it!"

The force of her declaration startled them both. But the frustration, the anxiety, perhaps even the anger at Fate for leaving her fixed in such an uncertain state had been building inside her for years. Gemma sighed deeply as Louisa stared at her with wide eyes. "So, that is why I took such a dangerous and foolish risk today. I simply have to know."

"And you did not learn anything useful? Oh, Gemma, I am truly sorry. But you have the letter from your mother. You will learn all when Lord Gabriel comes to town, and surely, it will be soon. I pray so, for both our sakes," Louisa suggested.

Gemma tried to appear as hopeful as her friend. "If he agrees to see me and admits that I could be his relation," she murmured. "I hope so, Louisa."

"I am sure he will help you. No one could be so cruel as to deny you knowledge of your own family. And he will be pleased to see how ladylike and personable you are. I am sure of it," Louisa predicted.

She stood up, pausing to give Gemma an impulsive hug.

Gemma tried not to wince. "I will leave you. Try to get some sleep; it has surely been a most fatiguing day. Perhaps tomorrow you will hear from your brother."

Gemma wished she could be as sanguine. "Perhaps," she agreed, too tired to argue. And Louisa's good wishes, even if excessively optimistic, were comforting. Still, as Louisa left quietly, shutting the bedroom door behind her, Gemma was sure that with all her inner uncertainties, she would not sleep a wink.

But somehow, as she curled up beneath the bed covers, she remembered how it had felt to press herself against the hard-muscled torso of Captain Fallon and how much strength the man seemed to project. When she was inside his arm—

Gemma had never been embraced by a man, not like that. Arnold had been very punctilious in his courtship, afraid perhaps to go too far when he was not yet sure if he could—in fairness to his own family's honor as he had carefully explained—offer for her hand. So although they had gone for long walks accompanied by Arnold's sister Elizabeth, and he had bowed over Gemma's hand, they had not yet even kissed.

Would Matthew Fallon have held himself back so carefully if he had been the man who cared for her? Gemma remembered his easy strength and the intensity of those cool gray eyes. Captain Fallon was capable of passion, she had no doubt of it. Not that it would be for her, of course. Whatever had brought him to the foundling home, it had nothing to do with Gemma.

She should not be thinking of him at all. She was almost, if all went well, betrothed. But somehow, instead of conjuring up memories of Arnold Cuthbertson as she knew she should, her thoughts lingered on the stranger with whom she had shared the jolting ride home. Even the recollection of their brief and illusory closeness seemed to comfort her, and despite her aches, she drifted into sleep.

# Six

Gemma woke early, blinking at the pale sunlight slipping past the draperies and wondering why she felt a sense of anticipation. Of course, Captain Fallon was coming, or she prayed he would keep his agreement and come, and he would bring the ledgers. And if only she could find some information within them, her life could change, and she would be free to be courted like any normal girl. She would even be better prepared to meet Lord Gabriel, Gemma told herself, if she were not totally ignorant of her own background. She would not be merely a petitioner with nothing to offer, the beggar-girl soliciting the lord.

When Lily appeared with a cup of tea, Gemma sat up in her bed, thinking hard as she sipped the hot liquid. If the captain did not return, she would scour London for him, she told herself. Mind you, he had given her his word that he would come. She only hoped it—and he—could be trusted.

When Lily returned with a ewer of warm water, Gemma rose, washed, and dressed. Her rose-pink muslin was a tiny bit faded, but Lily had pressed it carefully, and it looked quite presentable, surely respectable enough in which to meet the mysterious gentleman who might help her solve some of the puzzle that had plagued her for years.

At the breakfast table, she and Louisa had a quiet, most civil argument.

"But if you think he will return, then I can put off my shopping till later in the day. I should stay and play chaperone, Gemma," Louisa protested. "It would not do to leave you alone with a gentleman caller."

"There will be servants all about; that is not alone, precisely," Gemma shot back. "And I fear he will not be forthcoming if someone else is present. I must have his candid explanation." And how would she explain the ledgers to Louisa? "No, you and Miss P should go on with your shopping, as you had planned."

Louisa took a delicate bite of toast and sighed. "I suppose if you feel the need, you can always call Lily down to sit with you." Lowering her voice, she added, "I would not wish you to disgrace yourself, in case you should be overcome by his manly charms."

"I should never—" Gemma hoped she was not blushing. Their intimate ride—then she glanced at her hostess and recognized the gleam of mischief in her eyes. "You imp," she whispered so that the footman standing at attention beside the buffet would not hear. "Take care. I shall suggest to Sir Lucas that you are too eager to appreciate the allurement of a good-looking man encountered in a hat shop—"

"You wouldn't!" Louisa raised her brows in alarm.

"Of course I wouldn't," Gemma agreed. She took a bite of her sausage and smiled sweetly.

Louisa shrugged. "Oh, very well. I shan't tease you. But if he comes, I do expect to hear all the particulars."

"Of course," Gemma agreed, though she kept her thoughts to herself.

So Louisa and Miss Pomshack set out for an extended shopping excursion, and Louisa retired to the drawing room, where she paced up and down, glancing between the mantel clock and the window that overlooked the street outside.

Would he come?

Fortunately for the state of her nerves, it was still four minutes before ten when she heard a decisive rap at the front door. Heart beating fast, she faced the doorway. In another minute she heard the murmur of voices and foot-steps on the staircase, then the footman appeared and an-nounced, "Captain Fallon to see you, Miss Smith."

And the captain was carrying a neatly wrapped parcel! She dipped a polite curtsy as he bowed, then she motioned to a chair.

"Thank you for coming," she said, and she meant the simple civility with all her heart.

He unwrapped the bulky package and she could see the stack of ledgers. But his expression was sober. "I sat up a good part of the night perusing them, but I did not find what I sought."

His disappointment was obviously heavy. Gemma felt a flicker of alarm. "There is no list of students?"

"There is, but only the name is noted, with the date the girl came to the school and the date she left. No mention of where she departed to," he said, his voice grim.

"Or from whence she came," Gemma mused aloud, feeling her heart sink.

He selected one of the books and opened its faded cover. Gemma stared at the listing, swallowing against her disappointment.

"Who are you searching for?" she asked as she skimmed the names.

"My sister," he said.

"How—" She looked up in time to see the pain cross his face. "No, pardon me. I should not be asking such a per-sonal question."

He turned away from her for a moment and put one hand on the mantelpiece as he gazed down at the fire. She suspected he was seeing something other than the crackling flames. While she continued to stare at his square shoulders and well-shaped form, he answered slowly.

"I was away at sea, you understand. My mother was a widow with limited funds, and we had no land of our own. Ironically, that was one of the reasons I went into the navy. I had no money with which to buy a commission in the army, and at sea there was the possibility of prize money from captured enemy vessels, which would help me make my fortune and thus keep my mother and sister safe. One of our neighbors helped me obtain a place at the Royal Naval Academy at Portsmouth, and I went to a ship when I was just a lad. In time, I was fortunate enough to rise in rank."

She suspected it was more than good fortune that had elevated him to a captaincy, but she did not wish to break his narrative. From the tenseness of his back, she knew it must be hard for him to tell this story.

"I sent money home regularly to a solicitor named Temming, whom I had charged with looking out for my family and conveying the funds safely to them. When I stopped getting letters from my sister—my mother had a disabling condition of her hands that made writing hard for her—I worried, but Temming wrote that all was well, and my sister was no doubt too busy at school to attend to her letters. I was hurt that Clarissa would forget me as she grew older, but I also knew that mail was often delayed and delivery uncertain when one is at sea, so I tried not to worry."

A coal popped in the fire, and he paused. Gemma held her breath, anticipating the bad tidings that deepened his voice when he continued.

"Not until I had a much-delayed letter from a neighbor sending me sympathies on my mother's death did I realize something was very wrong. And even then, I was hundreds of miles away, and it was months more before I could be released from my military duties and resign my commission. When I returned, I made all haste for my mother's home, only to find it sold, my mother in the local graveyard and"—he cleared his throat—"and no sign of my sister."

"Oh, how dreadful," Gemma whispered. "And you think she was sent to the foundling home?"

He drew a deep breath. "After questioning most of the village with little effect, I returned to London and sought out the man Temming. But someone must have warned him. The address I had written to for years is now untenanted, and I can find no one who will admit to knowledge of his whereabouts."

He turned, and the look on his face made Gemma shiver. She could almost have sympathy for the wretched man if Captain Fallon ever caught up with him.

"I searched his abandoned office, and in his files I found a letter from the matron of the foundling home that hinted at business between them. So I went at once to the home, but Mrs. Craigmore refused to tell me anything. She would not even admit that my sister had been sent to her, and Clarissa is certainly not there now. I forced them to allow me to see all the girls, small to large, currently in their charge."

"So you went back, unannounced." Gemma's thoughts had darted ahead, even as she winced for his pain and for his sister's possible danger. "And that was when I encountered you."

"I apologize for frightening you." He met her gaze directly, his gray eyes clear and as determined as ever. "But at first I assumed you were a teacher or assistant matron at the home, and I could not have the staff alerted to my presence."

Gemma nodded. "You did alarm me," she agreed. "But considering the urgency of your errand, I forgive you."

"And you were indeed in their charge?" He crossed back to sit down in the chair opposite her. "Having spoken to the matron, you have my sympathy. Do you know anything of how and under what conditions the older girls are discharged from the home?"

Gemma thought hard but was forced to shake her head. She saw his expression of disappointment. "I'm sorry. I was only five when I was taken there after the death of my guardian, and a little over a year later, I was sent away again, under conditions that are not clear to me."

"Where did you go?"

"To a girls' boarding school, where conditions were much more humane, and I was given a reasonable education."

"So why did you return to the foundling home?" Captain Fallon demanded. "I cannot imagine it was out of desire to see the place again."

Gemma shivered. "No, indeed. Like you, I wanted information, which the staff was not willing to share with me."

She paused for a moment. He had been candid with her, and she felt she owed him honesty in return. "You understand, I tell you in confidence."

"Of course."

"I do not know who my parents are, Captain Fallon. But after I left the foundling home, someone paid for my schooling." It was her turn to look away from his searching gaze. "I thought the matron might know something of my background. This is why I was seeking out her ledgers; I thought she might have included private information in them."

She risked a quick glance up and thought that his gaze softened. "Then you have my compassion, as well," he told her.

Gemma sighed. "I am disappointed, but at least I am not in imminent peril, as you must fear your sister could be. What shall you do now?"

"I will continue to search for her. If I have to choke the information out of the matron, even though she claims to have no memory of Clarissa, I will do it."

Gemma watched him in concern as he paced back and forth across the rug. "It will not help your sister if you are taken up before the magistrates and thrown into prison," she pointed out, though she kept her tone gentle. "Let me help you, Captain."

"How?" He turned back to examine her with his searching gaze.

Gemma thought. Her offer had been an impulse, but it felt right. "I still have unanswered questions, as well. If we work together, perhaps we can go further than if we both forge ahead alone. To start with, I will give you the address of the solicitor who took me away from the home. He might have some knowledge that would help you."

She turned to the desk and wrote down Mr. Peevey's name and location. "He knows more than he will tell me about my father because, he says, he is bound by oaths of secrecy. But at least he might have more information about Mrs. Craigmore, and if so, surely, he would be free to tell you about her history. He might also know something about Mr. Temming, since their calling is the same."

It was hard to read his expression, but something of the pain in the cool gray eyes might have eased. "It is good of you to offer your assistance."

"Whatever peril your sister may be in, and I pray it is not as fearsome as your brotherly concern leads you to believe, it might just as well have been I facing the same jeopardy," she told him. "I have every sympathy for her. We shall find her, Captain Fallon."

She held out the slip of paper, and as he reached for it, he surprised her by taking her hand for a moment. His grip was just as strong as she remembered, though this time, it did not appear deadly.

"Thank you, Miss Smith."

Gemma felt the leap of response inside her and hoped that she was not blushing. She looked up into those enigmatic gray eyes, as hard to read as the murky oceans he had once sailed, and thought what strength he had, and what compassion for the sister for whom he felt responsible. If only Lord Gabriel would reveal such brotherly concern!

Nevertheless, the feelings she felt just now for the captain were not at all sisterly. She felt the warmth of his ungloved hand as it clasped her own and saw the pulse jump in his temple. He was standing so close that again she had a faint impression of the scents of soap and clean linen and something else that might simply be male flesh, a faint and pleasing smell singularly his own. She felt a curious sense of turmoil in her belly, and she found she had somehow forgotten to breath. For an endless moment, he continued to hold her hand, and the silence stretched. Then a coal popped in the fire, and a wagon lumbered by on the street outside, its driver yelling and lashing a whip at the dray horses that labored to pull it.

He dropped her hand and bowed, effectively concealing his expression. Was he as confused, as confounded, as she? Feeling as if she had been suspended underwater and was just now emerging for air, Gemma drew a long breath as she made her answering curtsy.

"I shall seek out your solicitor," the captain said. Was it her imagination or was his tone more wooden, this time? He seemed to avoid her eyes.

"Let me know if you find out anything useful," she said quickly.

"I will. I shall leave the ledgers with you, in case you can discover some detail which I missed. Guard them well; they might yet prove useful to us."

"I will," she agreed.

"We will talk again soon." Then he turned smartly and was out the door.

Gemma put one hand to her cheek, knowing that it must be flushed. No man—not even Arnold—had ever made her feel so. She had no words for the sensations that had stirred inside her when he stood close, when he held her hand.

What was wrong with her that she should be so affected by a stranger? Gemma paced up and down the rug, then realized that Captain Fallon had paced just this way when his emotions had been the most agitated. Most likely it was only that she understood his dilemma, she tried to tell herself, that she had such empathy for his sister who seemed to have been cast adrift with no one to protect her, exactly like Gemma's deepest fear. Had she not dreaded just such a fate throughout her own childhood?

It was not the captain himself, despite his fair good looks or the force of his personality; it was not that, she assured herself. How base it would be if she cast aside Mr. Cuthbertson's long, careful courtship on such a short acquaintanceship with this gentleman, who probably had no interest in a penniless, nameless young lady. No, no, it was only pity for his sister she felt, that and a most sincere desire to help. And if they worked together, she might also find some answers to her own questions. She could not imagine even the dreaded Mrs. Craigmore defying the captain, not for long.

So Gemma pushed aside her guilt and picked up the first of the stack of ledgers, determined to examine carefully every listing of household purchase, every shilling and every penny, until she found some clue that would help them all.

*By the time Louisa had been measured by the mantilla-*maker and had selected two delightful hats, although not at the shop where she had encountered Lady Jersey a few days before—she had no wish to meet the formidable countess yet again—even she was ready for a short respite.

To Miss Pomshack's obvious relief, Louisa suggested that they go into a tea shop for a cup of tea and a biscuit. While they sipped their tea, Louisa remembered that they had passed a bookseller a few doors back.

"I think we shall retrace our steps and look into the book shop," she suggested to her companion.

"What a good notion," Miss Pomshack agreed at once. "I overheard a lady in the last shop mention that she was reading a most edifying collection of sermons by Dr. Fulsap, full of morals and precepts, just the kind of volume with which a lady might instruct herself."

For a moment, Louisa eyed her companion with positive dislike. She had not had sermons in mind, but a delicious and distracting Gothic novel full of unlikely adventure and thrilling romance, such as was penned by the slightly scandalous Mrs. Radcliffe.

"However, first I still have to find ribbon in the right shade to suit that new bonnet with the jonquil trim. There is a shop just down the street, which I remember from last season. I don't suppose you would take my sample and see if you could match it? Then you could meet me at the bookseller?" Louisa asked, her tone sweet.

"But of course, Miss Crookshank. I am only here to make your life easier, you know." Miss Pomshack looked genuinely pleased to be able to be of help.

Louisa felt a moment of guilt for her subterfuge, but she shook it away and dropped her gaze to her tea cup. "Thank you," she said. "You're too kind."

And Miss P's errand should allow enough time for Louisa to find a juicy novel before the older lady returned and peered over Louisa's shoulder, frowning in disapproval at her charge's selection.

They finished their tea in perfect harmony. Then, on the walkway outside the tea shop, they parted company briefly. Louisa made her way quickly to the bookseller and entered its door. She was pleased to see stacks of new books, some of them surely novels, arranged on tables near the entrance. She had just picked up the first volume of a handsomely bound set and opened the cover when she heard a distinctive voice just behind her.

"Oh, you rascal. You should not say such things!"

"Then who else will say them and make you laugh?"

The peal of laughter made Louisa wince. Oh, heavens, it was—it had to be—the countess of Jersey. No one else had such a shrill voice and peculiar laugh, and if the male voice belonged to the sardonic lieutenant, who must be hanging on her sleeve again . . .

Louisa risked a quick glance over her shoulder. Yes, just as she thought. The countess wore green today and long ostrich feathers rose from her turban as she lifted her face, her expression teasing, to her male companion. Louisa's first impulse was to turn, dip a curtsy, and speak. Her second was to press her lips firmly together—had she not vowed to avoid the countess till Louisa could obtain a proper and more seemly introduction?—and flee before she was seen.

And she did not even have Miss Pomshack here with her! What would the countess think of Louisa abroad in London all alone? No, no, this would not do.

Louisa closed the book and put it quietly back upon the stack. Without turning and exposing her face to the other woman or her escort, she pulled her shawl about her shoulders and, as an elderly gentleman held open the door, took advantage of his civility and hastened out onto the pavement.

Her only thought was to put distance between herself and the bookseller. She walked rapidly past several shop fronts, but, as if Fate were determined to taunt her, Louisa glanced over her shoulder and saw Lady Jersey, with her male companion at her side, emerging from the doorway. And of course, they turned in the same direction as Louisa.

She would cross the street, Louisa thought wildly, anything to get away unnoticed. She would not look behind her again and risk showing her face, just in case the countess's erratic memory should recognize her countenance. She was still some distance from a street crossing, but Louisa did not dare wait. She looked hastily up and down for a break in the traffic—being trampled beneath a coach or a team of horses would not aid her desire for anonymity— then she plunged off the walkway.

And felt her shoe sink deep into a soft, clinging mound.

Oh, dear Lord. She had not looked down at the street itself, where some passing steed had left its mark—a large, still steaming horse pie. She had stepped squarely into it. Had anyone noticed? She lifted her chin and tried to maintain a dignified expression.

But she thought a man driving a cart of grain smirked as his wagon rolled past. It was hard to appear dignified with one's foot in a pile of dung!

Louisa lifted her skirt and tried to pull her foot out of the odorous mess. She found to her dismay that her foot came away, but the clinging manure had effectively captured her shoe.

Wavering on her other foot, she almost lost her balance. Swaying, she struggled not to fall. She succeeded, but only at the cost of being forced to step down on her stockinged foot, which now was also stained from the muck of the street. And her shoe was still trapped. She considered reaching down for it, but she was aware of more stares from passersby. Going by in the other direction, a driver on a wagon full of onions guffawed and pointed. Louisa flushed in mortification.

Oh, she would never go out alone again! Where was Miss Pomshack when she needed her? In this moment of imminent need, the fact that Louisa had herself sent her companion away seemed immaterial.

The thud of horses' hooves alerted her to even deeper danger. Rolling along at a smart pace, a coach and its team approached her position. The coachman was waving his whip at her. "Hie, there! Make way!"

Gasping, Louisa scrambled back onto the walkway and out of the street, just in time. In her panic, she dropped her shawl into the mud. The wheels of the vehicle ran squarely over the pile of manure, as well as her hapless shoe, squashing it deeper and rendering it now forever lost to her. Her shawl had been ripped as well, in addition to being so fouled that she had no wish to reclaim it. And in one last passing insult, the coach splattered the dung, hitting her skirt and stockings with foul bits of the soft muck.

Louisa realized she was still holding her skirt several inches higher than it should be, and she hastily let her hem fall back into place, shaking her skirt to try to dislodge the filthy splatters. What else could happen? She was in one piece, but now she was abroad in London's most fashionable shopping area with a dirty gown, only one shoe and one nastily stained stocking. Oh, Lord, if the gossips got hold of this, she would be the laughingstock of the Ton! So much for her hopes for a successful Season.

Louisa blinked back tears. Had the countess noticed Louisa's ridiculous and humiliating plight? She glanced behind her, but Lady Jersey seemed to have disappeared from view. Thank heavens for one small boon, Louisa told herself. But now, what was she to do?

She seemed to have little choice. She would not—could not—go into a shop in such a condition. And people on the street were still staring. Louisa prayed Miss P would hurry back and could be sent to hail a hackney, which could take them quickly home. If only her carriage were not still awaiting the repair of one of its wheels.

The moments seemed to stretch into an eternity. Miss Pomshack did not appear; she seemed to be taking her ribbon search all too seriously.

"May I be of assistance?"

Louisa stiffened. She knew that deep masculine voice with its faintest suggestion of Scottish burr. If he still had Lady Jersey at his side, she would simply die, here and now, of pure embarrassment.

But when she dared to look around, she saw the lieutenant, his expression suitably grave, his bright hazel eyes sparkling with repressed laughter, standing on the pavement with no lady at his side.

She wavered between the urge to lash out at him and an intense need to know where her nemesis had vanished to.

"Lady Jersey is having a lengthy fitting for a new ball gown," the irritatingly perceptive man explained. "And you do seem to be in a quandary. I am reminded of the nursery rhyme, one shoe off, one shoe on—"

"Do not jest!" Louisa snapped. "I did not do it on purpose."

"I would never suggest such a thing. But you cannot loiter on the street like this; you are gathering a crowd of gawkers. So the question is, how are we to get you home?"

"Can you hail a cab for me?" Louisa suggested, hope stirring again. "It is true, people are staring."

Lieutenant McGregor looked up and down the street, but no vehicle for hire presented itself. "At this time of day, we may wait for some time before a hackney appears. I fear I have no carriage at hand to offer you. And I do think you need to get off the street and away from the peering crowd."

Louisa felt herself in complete agreement with his last statement, but—"How?" she blurted.

"As it happens, I have rooms on the next street. Perhaps we could make you more presentable—or at least less noticeable—and then you are much less likely to be remarked upon and remembered."

"Go to your rooms? Alone with a strange man?" Louisa stared at him in horror at such an improper suggestion.

He raised his slashing brows. "I make no claim to be a perfect gentleman, but even I have my limits. I would not take advantage of a lady in such dire straits."

Was he laughing at her again, or was he serious? The way his eyes twinkled so often, it was hard to tell.

Louisa swallowed. Only the thought of being an object of gossip and ill-natured laughter would make her consider such a thing.

While she hesitated, a passing child clutched at its mother's skirts and said loudly, "Ow, Mum, look at the lady all covered in poo!"

The woman glanced at Louisa and, frowning in disapproval, pulled her child closer as if to escape contagion.

Louisa made a decision. "Get me there quickly!"

He offered her his arm, and she took it, hoping to somehow thus divert attention from her shoeless foot. She hobbled a bit, with one shoe off and one shoe on—she thought of the nursery verse he had quoted with a new loathing—but he kept a firm grip on her elbow and steadied her as they strode quickly along the pavement.

He guided her past three shops, through a dark alley, which made her shiver, and back onto a more respectable but narrower street.

Sure enough, his rooms were quickly reached, and Louisa hurried up the cramped staircase to the second landing, then, looking about her with unease, waited while

he unlocked his door. By the look of the building, Lieutenant McGregor was not well endowed with funds. If only
no one witnessed her illicit visit!

The front room into which he led her was neat but
sparsely furnished. His flat seemed quite empty, and the air
was cool.

Louisa felt awkward again, but he merely gestured to a
straight wooden chair. "Sit down, please. And give me your
stocking."

She had just touched the chair, but now she jerked back
to her feet. "What?"

"I shall wash it out—the smell is rather strong, you
know—and we'll hang it in front of the fire. Your stocking
is light of weight; it should dry quickly."

Made by Miss Pomshack, it would have been a sensible
suggestion. Offered by a man whom she barely knew,
while she sat alone and unchaperoned in his rooms, it was
almost indecent.

He waited patiently while Louisa stared at him.

"Sometimes it is better to be practical than proper,
Miss—?"

"Miss Crookshank, of Bath," she told him, reluctantly.

"Miss Crookshank of Bath, you may trust me in this, I
promise you."

Slowly, she sat down again, but she eyed him with continued suspicion. "Turn your back, if you please."

"Ah, yes. I seem to be a bit rusty in the role of proper
gentleman." He wheeled and went to the hearth, moving
aside the fire guard and bending to stir the banked coals to
try and coax some small amount of heat from the tiny fire.

While he was safely occupied, his face turned away
from her, Louisa pulled up her gown and shift and unrolled
her stocking. By the time he turned, she had pushed her
skirts back down in a seemly fashion and she held the
stained, and, yes, smelly, piece of apparel.

He reached for it. She bit her lip. She hated to release
such a personal item to a man, and a gentleman—more or
less—to boot.

"Surely, your servant—"

"Is out, I fear."

Was more likely nonexistent, Louisa thought. "I could do it myself. It is an imposition to expect you to wash my clothing!"

"Ah, a modest maidenly sentiment. However, the only water in the flat is in the washbowl in my bedroom. That would be even more improper, I think."

Louisa blushed once more. Without further protest, she handed over the stocking and waited as he vanished into an inner room.

Shivering, she looked about her. The room was strangely impersonal. She saw a few books on a round table next to the only upholstered chair in the room, which was pulled up to the small fire. Otherwise, there was hardly any sign that someone lived here.

Oh, what was she doing in a man's rooms? She must be mad!

Presently, he returned with her damp stocking in hand. He took it to the fireplace and hung it carefully over the brass fireguard.

"You have no need to sit so far from the fire. The air is cool, and you are trembling, Miss Crookshank."

Unable to deny it, Louisa stood. No rug covered the plain wooden floorboards, and they were cold beneath her unclad foot. She crossed to the more comfortable chair and sat, holding herself very erect and striving to look as dignified as a lady with a bare foot could, alone with a strange man.

He looked at her, and then left the room again, returning soon with a basin holding a few inches of clean water, and a soapy sponge.

"We must finish the job," he said. Before she could realize his intent, he knelt and began to wash her foot.

Louisa shivered. The tepid water rolled over her bare skin, and he held her calf lightly as he sponged away the offending spots left by her stained stocking. A man touching her leg—good heavens, it was the most improper thing she had ever heard of!

And even more than the chilly air, barely warmed by the minute blaze on the hearth, his touch made her tremble. Yet it was not cold that washed over her, but a strange and unfamiliar warmth. He bent close to her, and he gripped her ankle lightly but firmly. Inside her, a flame jumped much more eagerly than any amid the pitiful fire. She felt stirrings she had not dreamed her body might possess.

"Th-that is not necessary. I mean, I should not ask you to perform such a personal task," Louisa stammered as she leaned forward to motion him away.

He looked up at her, his face only a few inches from hers, and this time, his eyes seemed to mirror the flames. Something leaped between them, something even warmer and more urgent than the dawning spark inside her. She wanted him to move his hand higher, to press his face closer, to touch her lips with—

Gasping, Louisa lifted her head.

The lieutenant stood abruptly. "I think that will do. I will bring you a dry cloth."

He took the basin away while Louisa struggled to make her expression bland and unrevealing. By the time he returned with a thin strip of towel, she thought she had hidden her unexpected response to his touch, his nearness. And for nothing on earth would she reveal that some part of her still hungered for more.

She almost snatched it from him, afraid he would dry her foot himself. But he made no move to touch her again, instead lifting the stocking and handing it to her. "I think it is dry enough. We must slip away before anyone sees you in a gentleman's rooms."

The stocking was, in fact, still damp, but she didn't care. "Yes, if you please," she commanded.

The lieutenant stepped to the window. Glancing to make sure he was watching the street and not her movements, Louisa ran the cloth over her wet foot and then pulled on the stocking so quickly that she pulled a thread. But as she had every intention of burning the thing when she got home, she didn't care.

Of course, she still had no shoe. Louisa looked down at her foot and felt an absurd desire to burst into tears.

"I fear I have no spare lady's slipper to offer you," he told her without turning from the window.

"Of course not." Louisa tried to calm herself. She could not reveal how disturbing she had found their enforced contact. He surely thought nothing of it.

"But perhaps we can better disguise its lack," he said suddenly. He came back and held out his hand.

She was still so unsettled that it was a moment before she realized that he wanted the strip of cloth back. She handed him the towel and was startled when he ripped it neatly into several lengths.

"What are you doing?"

"Something I learned all too well on the battlefields in Europe," he told her, kneeling again in front of her.

Before she could protest, he wrapped her foot and ankle into a neat-looking bandage. And was it her imagination, or did he touch her foot and ankle as lightly as possible? Did he sense her distress?

Despite his care, her body was betraying her yet again. She wanted his touch, wanted to feel the firm warmth of his hand, and she privately lamented the thin stocking that kept his fingers from touching her bare skin. Louisa knew her cheeks were afire; she tried to be calm. He would think her ridiculous. . . .

He glanced up, and this time, she saw that his eyes did not laugh. Whatever he was feeling, it was not amusement.

"Are you rich, Miss Crookshank?"

It was a most inappropriate question, but in the present circumstance, she had no sense of outrage left to spare. "Only a little," she admitted.

"Are you betrothed?"

"Yes." Louisa thought of Sir Lucas with sudden guilt. Good heavens, if her fiancé ever learned what had happened today, he would call out the lieutenant! But, looking back at the steady gaze and sure hand of the man half-kneeling before her, his position almost a parody of an anxious suitor's, Louisa knew that if that should happen, she would fear for Lucas, not for the battle-seasoned man with the wicked hazel eyes.

"Ah, I see. And I suppose you would not consider jilting him?"

"Of course not!" Louisa blushed even more deeply, glad that the lieutenant could not know that last year she had, most improperly, ended a too percipient engagement. She could hardly do it twice!

"Why are you asking such questions?" she demanded.

"Because I need a rich wife, Miss Crookshank. As you can easily see, I have no funds of my own, and now that the war with Napoleon has ended, no prospects. So I must marry for my money."

"Oh." She could not think what to reply to such bluntness.

But this highly improper man was not finished. "Just as well for you," he said, though his expression had darkened. "And if you are not available for courtship, then I advise you to stay well away from me."

"Why?" she could not keep from asking. Her pulse was still racing, and whether he realized it or not, his hand still rested lightly on her cotton-wrapped ankle. She was all too aware of his touch.

"Because I am your—or your parents'—worst nightmare, the half-pay officer looking to marry an heiress. I am a man with no social connections, no landed estate of my own, in short, the fortune hunter who is every mother's worst fear. So I give you fair warning, stay away."

"Why are you telling me this?" She stared at him.

"I may set my own rules, Miss Crookshank of Bath, but I always play fair," he told her.

"If you are so bad, how do you come to escort a countess?" Louisa said, before she realized her own words were almost as improper as his.

"Because I am charming and wicked, and the lady, being already married, has no need of a husband, only some amusing and worldly flirtation. And she opens the doors to the kind of Society I must join in order to find a suitable bride," he admitted readily.

He had no sense of shame whatsoever, Louisa thought. And his hand still lay against her ankle.

She should move her foot, but she felt frozen.

"I see," she said, her voice a mere whisper. "And if I don't stay away?"

"Then next time, I make no promises," he said. The light in his bright hazel eyes flared with a passion with which Louisa had no experience.

And for the first time, she thought that might be something to regret.

But she pulled herself together and stood up so hastily that she knocked a book off the table. Ignoring it, he stood more gracefully and offered her his arm again.

But she stepped away, her heart beating fast until he opened the door to the hallway. After she hurried through, he closed and locked it behind them. They descended the steps and, on the street, she accepted his arm, but only, she assured herself, so that her pose as the lady with the injured foot would be more believable. She bent her head and tried to keep her face down, hoping that no one would recognize her. For the first time she was glad to have few acquaintances in the city.

And at last, since she seemed to have suffered enough to satisfy even the most capricious of fates, her luck changed. At the end of the street, a hackney appeared. The lieutenant hailed the cab. When it slowed to a stop, he helped her inside.

"A gentleman should see you home, but, as I said, since my pretense at gentility is somewhat threadbare, it's better that I do not," he told her.

"Yes, I mean, thank you for your help," Louisa told him.

Colin watched the carriage drive away. Good God, what fires she lit in his blood! But she was out of his reach, in more ways than one. If circumstances had been otherwise, he might have tried to make her change her mind about this fiancé, and propriety be damned! He shook his head.

If only—if only he had not been born without a ha'penny to his name. If only he had not so rashly thrown away his chance for advancement during the war. If only he had not been a fool in so many ways, he would not now be in such an ignominious position that any decent woman would have every right to spur his advances and there were times he despised himself. . . .

Bitterness burnt both his throat and—perhaps—his soul. Colin braced himself and strode off to rescue Lady Jersey from the risk of an hour of tedium.

Louisa gave the driver the address of her leased house, then realized that she had forgotten about Miss Pomshack. The good lady would be frantic if Louisa simply disappeared. "No, go back to the bookseller's on Bond Street, first."

The cab pulled away, and Louisa leaned back against the cushions. Hopefully, no one had seen her come out of a man's lodgings. Hopefully, no one would remember who the lady was who had lost her shoe and soiled her stocking in such a ridiculous manner.

She would forget the whole incident, Louisa told herself. Except that she could still—almost—feel his hand against her bare skin, touching her leg, her foot. Just remembering made her belly tighten and her heart beat faster.

When the cab returned to the book shop, she found Miss Pomshack standing in front of it, holding a small paper-wrapped parcel and scanning the street with an anxious expression.

"Oh, Miss Crookshank, thank goodness. I was so worried."

"I'm sorry to have distressed you. Do get in," Louisa directed.

The older lady climbed up, saying, "I found the perfect color of ribbon, but when I returned and you were not inside the bookseller's, I feared the worst. I am so happy to see that you are safe." Then she looked down and saw the bandaged foot. Throwing up her hands and dropping her parcel, she shrieked. "Oh, dear girl, what have you done?"

"Only a slight mishap," Louisa tried to reassure her. "I turned my ankle, that is all. But we should get home."

"At once, and we will soak your poor foot in Epsom salts. And then I will make you a mustard plaster. My mother passed on to me an excellent receipt for healing plasters."

Miss Pomshack retrieved her shopping and took her seat, but she continued to fuss while they made the short drive back to the house. Louisa barely listened.

Her reflections echoed Miss Pomshack's words, but their meaning was quite different.

Oh, heavens, Louisa thought. Indeed, what had she done?

# Seven

.

$G$emma studied the ledgers for most of the afternoon. She soon found the list of girls who had resided in the foundling home. The most current were written carefully in dark letters. In the middle of the book, she saw the name of the captain's sister, *Clarissa Fallon*. Pages back in faded ink, she came across her own name: *Gemma Smith*.

Like the others, the dates of her arrival at the foundling home and her departure were scrawled beside it, but no clue, no indication of any family connection. Even the name was a disappointment; she had hoped for more than the anonymous *Smith*.

Sighing, Gemma read on.

The other books seemed to be the most innocuous accountings of household purchases, and if the matron sometimes seemed to pay very high prices for her produce and staples, especially considering the poor fare that Gemma remembered receiving in the dining hall, that was of little help to her.

She felt doubly disappointed. Aside from her own hopes,

she had wished to find something to show Captain Fallon. If the ledgers turned out to be no help at all, they had both risked a potentially disgraceful theft for nothing.

Her spirits low, Gemma was glad enough to be distracted by Louisa's return. She put the ledgers back into the wrapping paper and retied the string, then went into the hallway to greet Louisa and her companion. But as her friend came inside, with Miss Pomshack fussing beside her, Gemma was startled to see that her friend had a bandaged foot.

"Are you all right?" she asked.

Louisa looked more embarrassed than hurt. "Yes, indeed. It's only a small mischance. I shall just put my foot up for a while, and I shall be fine."

"And the theater planned for this evening." Miss P clucked her tongue. "We shall have to tell your inestimable Sir Lucas that you will be forced to cancel the outing."

"No, indeed," Louisa contradicted quickly. "He has taken a box! And I'm sure by dinnertime I shall be quite recovered."

"But—" The other lady wrinkled her nose.

"Why don't you go make up that mustard plaster?" Louisa suggested. "I'm sure I shall feel much better after its application."

Miss P looked pleased. "Indeed, I shall."

She hurried away toward the kitchen, and Gemma came forward to offer her friend an arm up the stairs. "Do you need assistance?"

But Louisa seemed to climb the steps without effort. "I'm really quite all right. I only twisted my ankle—it's not really even a sprain."

"And lost your shoe, I see, a pity. Who bandaged your foot?"

She saw that Louisa blushed intensely. "A, um, Good Samaritan," she said quickly.

"How fortunate," Gemma murmured. When they reached Louisa's bedchamber, Louisa rang for the maid. When Lily appeared, she helped her mistress take off her soiled walking dress. Louisa pulled on a dressing gown and sat down upon a chaise longue so that she could put up her foot.

It did not seem bruised or swollen, Gemma noted, but she kept her thoughts to herself as Louisa seemed strangely embarrassed by the small accident.

"Lily, I wish a hip bath prepared before I change for dinner, please," Louisa told the maid. "I feel very grimy, indeed."

"Yes, miss," the girl agreed. She took the dirty gown away, and Gemma stared at her friend.

"All right, what really happened?"

Louisa blushed again. "Just as I said. Well, no." Then the story of the misstep into the horse dung rushed out.

Gemma tried not to laugh. It was obvious that Louisa had been mortified. "Oh, I'm sure that was most distressing. And they were handsome walking shoes, too, and almost new. Though I suppose the cobbler can make a replacement to match the one that remains, so all is not lost."

"True," Louisa said. "I shall send the remaining shoe around with the footman tomorrow. And I shall insist that the repairs to my carriage be completed, so I am not again left on foot!"

"And who did help you? You said the countess did not witness your mishap, which is fortunate."

Louisa shivered. "Oh, yes. And as to the other, I think . . . I think I do not wish to say, just now."

Gemma stared at her. Such reticence from the impulsive Louisa was something new. "Of course, I did not mean to pry."

Louisa bit her lip. "No, no. It is only . . . well, you know I would do nothing unladylike, not on purpose, and if Sir Lucas ever heard of it . . ."

Gemma nodded.

Louisa sighed. "I know I can trust you not to repeat the tale, Gemma. I was forced to go to Lieutenant McGregor's rooms."

"Forced?" Gemma looked at her friend in alarm. "You don't mean—"

"That is, forced by the circumstance. I was on the street with only one shoe and a dirty gown, and people were laughing at me!"

"Of course, and the lieutenant was no doubt only trying to be chivalrous," Gemma said, making her tone as soothing as she could.

"Actually, I think he was." Louisa's distress seemed to subside. "And of course, nothing improper happened." But her cheeks reddened once more.

Gemma pretended not to notice, and now Miss Pomshack returned, carrying a truly noxious-smelling plaster.

"This will make your poor ankle feel much better, Miss Louisa."

She fussed about, arranging the plaster on Louisa's foot, offering to fetch tea or a healing tisane.

Eyeing the plaster, Louisa asked for tea, and the older lady bustled off again.

"The confounded thing burns! This is my punishment for lying," Louisa said glumly. "But we shall not give up our excursion to the theater. I have been looking forward to it since Lucas told us about it yesterday."

When Miss P returned bearing the tea, Louisa sipped it, then announced that her foot was miraculously healed. "You may take off the plaster, Miss Pomshack."

"Already?" the lady asked in concern. "Perhaps you should lie abed for a while."

"No, no, I wish a bath before dressing for dinner and the theater, and my ankle truly feels much better. Your plaster was just the thing."

Miss Pomshack seemed gratified, and Gemma hid her smile. "Do you need any assistance?" she asked again.

Louisa waved her away. "No, you go and change. We shall have a lovely evening. I shall enjoy showing you the theater."

Gemma departed, grinning a little now that Louisa could not see, and washed and changed into her only dinner dress, a demure silver-gray with rose-colored piping along the bodice. She was pleasantly excited about going to the theater, a first for her.

Sir Lucas arrived in time for dinner and pronounced Louisa stunning when she came down the stairs—with no sign of a limp, Gemma noted—wearing a white dress with pale blue silk roses around the flounce, and fine lace at the sleeves and bosom.

"You look first-rate, Louisa!" he told his fiancé, who blushed and smiled, then he offered his arm to take her into dinner.

Gemma followed with Miss Pomshack, who murmured, "My mustard poultice worked even better than I expected, did it not, Miss Smith? My mother's receipt is certainly an excellent one."

Gemma managed not to laugh. "A wonderful remedy," she agreed.

They all chatted gaily through dinner. Even Louisa's middle-aged companion seemed quite stimulated at the thought of the outing, and Louisa herself positively sparkled. When Louisa's restored carriage drew up to the door, the ladies donned their best shawls and were handed into the chaise.

The drive to Covent Gardens did not take long, although the street was crowded with vehicles as other play-goers descended and headed into the theater.

Gemma watched her footing, not wanting to duplicate Louisa's mishap with the horse dung, and not until they were inside and she could lift her head did she get a good look at the splendor of the building.

The gilding on the boxes and the handsomely adorned ceiling were quite amazing. But she could not linger to stare. The crowd was dense, and she hastened along, not wanting to get separated from her companions.

Sir Lucas led them to the second tier and to the box that he had procured for them. Louisa took the best seat, of course, and Sir Lucas sat beside her. Gemma was quite happy to sit behind them, with Miss Pomshack at her side.

She let her shawl drop to the back of her chair, and now she could look about her at the beautiful dresses of the ladies and the fine coats and dazzling white linen of the men. She felt again the usual tremor of uncertainty—did she have the right to be here, or was she merely an impostor? Lord Gabriel and his wife must come often to the theater when they were in town. Did Gemma deserve to sit among the Ton in a tiered box and enjoy this luxury? Determined to enjoy the evening, she pushed the thought away.

And when the curtain rose and the footlights shone on the elaborately painted scenery behind the actors, Gemma forgot everything else. Tonight the actors and actresses were performing *As You Like It.* As she watched Rosalind moving lightly about the stage, impudent in her man's clothing, her face very handsome and just as obviously painted as the panels behind her, Gemma leaned forward to hear every line above the occasionally noisy audience.

Many in the pit and even the boxes carried on loud conversations, oblivious to anyone else's pleasure, and some of the men below were flirting outrageously with women whose dresses seemed scandalously low-cut. But even this did not dint her delight. Time flew by as Gemma laughed at the jests and gasped at the near-disasters that Shakespeare's script inflicted upon his players, and she clapped heartily as the play ended.

"Wasn't it romantic, Lucas?" Louisa sighed, turning to her fiancé. She held out her hand, and he patted it.

"First rate," he agreed. "Very handsome, these actresses. Ah, I see some chaps I know from my club. Excuse me, please, Louisa. I shall be back presently." Sir Lucas bowed and disappeared into the corridor.

Louisa looked disappointed, but she turned to speak to her companions. "Did you like it?"

"Oh, it was divine," Gemma told her. "I have never seen such a delightful comedy. I read the play at school, but that was nothing to seeing it performed."

"A very handsome production, indeed," Miss Pomshack agreed. "Even my father, the vicar, always said that the Bard could not be condemned, though Papa did not approve of play-going in general." Despite this somewhat qualified praise, her cheeks were pink, perhaps from suppressed laughter, Gemma thought, grinning to herself.

Louisa glanced at the audience, the finely dressed ladies and gentlemen now chatting and moving about. She frowned for a moment, then gasped. "Gemma! Do you see—no, of course, you do not know his face. In the third box to the right."

Gemma scanned the boxes, but she had no idea what to search for. "What is it?"

"Lord Gabriel and his wife, Psyche!" Louisa hissed.

Gemma winced and turned quickly back, suddenly afraid they would be detected. Louisa might think she was being discreet, but her voice seemed loud. "Hush, pray do not let them hear you." She did not wish to make a bad impression before she had even been introduced to her brother.

"There's too much noise. I'm sure they did not. They are not gazing this way, look again," Louisa directed. "She is blond and he is dark, and they are the handsomest couple in the theater, I'd wager."

Such praise from Louisa was saying a great deal. Gemma looked cautiously to the side. Now, she saw them!

She felt a thrill go through her. Her brother—could it be so? He was regarding his wife, speaking to her ears alone, and Gemma could see his face only from the side, but there was no doubt he was an amazingly handsome man. And his wife, fair and well proportioned, her fashionable gown so elegant that Louisa was no doubt swooning over it, yes, they were indeed a fine-looking pair.

"I wonder when they came into town?" Gemma muttered. "He has not answered my note."

"Perhaps they only arrived today, and he has not yet had the time to read all his correspondence," Louisa assured her. "I'm sure he takes a box for the season, so it is really

no surprise to see them here. Oh, I shall write to Lady
Gabriel at once. I do hope she will agree to introduce me at
a few gatherings."

Louisa twisted her hands, but Gemma felt as if her
stomach was being wrung even more painfully. Her need
was more urgent than her friend's, though Gemma did not
begrudge Louisa her wish to succeed in Society.

"I think I shall take a stroll along the corridor," Louisa
decided.

"You're not going to their box?" Gemma felt a stab of
apprehension. If Louisa made them angry . . .

Louisa wavered. "Perhaps not, that might look too forward. But if they decide to take a stroll before the next per-
formance begins, I might meet them in the corridor and
exchange a few words. . . . Why don't you come with me?"

Gemma still felt unsettled "No, I wish him to read my
letter first—my situation is so complicated to explain."

"Very well," Louisa agreed.

"Shall I come with you, Miss Louisa?" Miss Pomshack
inquired.

Louisa glanced back at her companion and shook her
head. "No, thank you. I shan't be long."

Taking a deep breath, she stood and made her way out
of the box.

Gemma looked back toward the box where her brother
and his wife sat. They seemed totally absorbed in each
other and showed no inclination to leave their box; she did
not think that Louisa was going to be able to manage an
"accidental" meeting. And the thought of interrupting the
two made Gemma bite her lip with nervous qualms. She
hoped that Louisa would not be too precipitant.

Outside in the corridor, which was now filled with people coming and going, Louisa paused. Would it be this simple? Why not? It would be silly not to take advantage of
such an opportunity if one should offer itself. She strolled
past the box where she now knew that Lord Gabriel sat,
and at the end of the hallway came back again.

But after she had retraced her route at least three times,

and there was still no sign of the couple leaving their box, she was ready to give up. Perhaps after all, she would not be able to manage an easy greeting.

Louisa bit her lip and wondered if she were on good enough terms to pay a visit to their box to renew their acquaintance. Surely, it would be all right? But as she approached the box entrance again, she felt a quiver of unease. It had always been her habit to jump into action, but sometimes that had had unfortunate results. No, perhaps this time it was better to be circumspect. She would write a note to Lady Gabriel first thing tomorrow, or she could leave her calling card at their house and hope that the other lady would return the visit. There was no reason for Psyche not to wish to see her, Louisa assured herself. At least Louisa had not offended Lady Gabriel last year, as she had, totally by accident, angered Lady Jersey.

Sighing at the loss of this seemingly golden moment, Louisa turned back for their own box. Then she hesitated at the sight of familiar faces. She knew those two young women just ahead. Perhaps Lady Luck was, after all, going to smile upon her tonight, and she could renew an acquaintance.

She walked forward and paused to dip a bow. "Miss Hargrave, Miss Simpson, how nice to see you again."

She had timed her curtsy perfectly, and she knew it was graceful. Her voice had just the right mixture of surprise and polite pleasure. But instead of the prompt greeting she had expected, the two ladies glanced at her with blank faces.

Oh, dear lord, they were not going to just walk past her?

Louisa kept a smile on her face with enormous effort as the first young lady drew up the lorgnette that dangled from her wrist and stared at Louisa as if she were some toad who had crawled out from beneath a rock.

"We met last year when I was staying with my aunt, the former Mrs. Marianne Hughes," Louisa went on. "She has married since then, and . . ." But her words trailed off, and her throat felt dry. The two women looked completely uninterested. Had they really both—both!—forgotten her?

"Ah, no doubt," Miss Hargrave said, her tone somewhat vague. "I'm afraid my memory is shockingly remiss. Of course, the Season is always so crowded with events and new faces—with so many people coming to London from the provinces, it can be hard to recall. You came from, was it Liverpool, mayhap?"

"Bath," Louisa corrected, knowing that her cheeks felt aflame and hoping her face was not as deeply red as the curtains inside the theater. "My family has resided in Bath for many years now. But I have taken a house in London for this year's Season."

"How pleasant for you," the first lady answered, her tone still distant and her gaze now fixed beyond Louisa, as if searching for more congenial company. "If you are here for the Season, we shall no doubt meet you again at Almack's."

Louisa felt as if her tongue had thickened. Almack's, where the cream of Society gathered, those happy enough, deemed worthy enough, to be granted vouchers. What could she say to that? Admit she had not yet been, and might never be, granted admittance?

"Ah . . ." The two ladies glanced at each other. "Excuse me, I see a friend I must speak to," Miss Hargrave said.

And they swept past Louisa as if she were a crumb on the carpet.

Louisa gasped. They had never smiled. Miss Simpson had never even acknowledged her greeting, and they had made no effort to seem friendly or happy to see her.

And this was to be her glorious Season in London?

Louisa felt as if she had been slapped. She had never been so completely snubbed in her life. In Bath, where she had friends, where people had esteemed her, where no one had thought her ineligible of notice, she had never encountered such blinding indifference. Louisa felt a strong urge to burst into tears.

But a stout man in a gaudy waistcoat eyed her with obvious curiosity, and more of the spectators who thronged the passageway might be staring. She turned blindly and almost collided with another male figure.

"Miss Crookshank, good evening. Are you enjoying the theater?"

It was, once again, the improper Lieutenant McGregor.

This time, she was in no mood for flirtation, no matter how scintillating. And anyhow, Louisa had glimpsed him earlier, sitting beside some sallow-faced female in another box—a sight that had given her an unpleasant, if irrational, pang. So now she tried to control her expression.

"I—I—"

"Do not let them distress you," he told her in a low voice. "They are cats, and they like to scratch. You do not need their approval."

But she did. Still, his attempt at reassurance warmed her.

He offered his arm. "Let me escort you back to your box."

So, feeling less alone, she accepted his escort. She was secretly disappointed when they reached the entrance and he bowed in farewell and did not come inside with her. She took her seat quickly as the lights dimmed.

"I was afraid to look their way too often, but Lord Gabriel and his wife did not appear to have left their box," Gemma whispered. "Did you meet them in the corridor? Did they speak to you?"

Louisa shook her head. She did not feel capable of answering without revealing her still disturbed feelings, so she was glad to hear the musicians once again take up their instruments. She pretended to be deeply engrossed in the tune being played.

Next, Sir Lucas returned, too, and took his seat beside her. He pressed her hand and then looked down at the stage. She thought of telling him about her shattering rebuff, but changed her mind. It was too painful to admit, and dear Lucas had no idea, she was sure, that some ladies of the Ton might find Louisa not worthy of their company.

The thought brought tears to her eyes, but she blinked them back, determined not to succumb to her emotions, not here.

Gemma was surprised when the curtain rose again; it seemed that the evening's entertainment was not yet complete. It was not Shakespeare, this time, that was enacted upon the boards, but a comedy of broad humor and little finesse.

The farce that ensued would most certainly have been condemned by Miss Pomshack's father, the vicar, but although the older lady looked a bit scandalized, she held her tongue. The rest of the party laughed at the broad wit of the actors. However, Louisa's laughter seemed shrill and even forced.

But she ignored Gemma's concerned gaze, and Gemma turned back toward the stage and tried to make sense of the jests, some of which she did not comprehend at all. But she laughed with the rest of the audience over the humorous antics of the cast.

When the farce ended, people stood and began to leave. Gemma glanced quickly back at the box where Lord Gabriel and his wife had sat, but was disappointed to see it already empty. They had made their exit early.

"Come along," Sir Lucas told the ladies. "The traffic outside will be something fierce, and we have to find our carriage."

The passageway was jammed with people all headed for the stairway, and it took them some time to make their way out and then locate their vehicle amid the press. At long last, they were handed into Louisa's chaise and wended their way home. Louisa was very quiet in the carriage, and when the ladies stepped down in front of the rented house, Sir Lucas looked at her in concern.

"You all right, Louisa?"

"A bit of a headache, that's all," she told him. "Thank you for the lovely evening, Lucas. It was most thoughtful of you to take us to the theater."

He looked gratified. "I'm glad you enjoyed it. But I won't

come in since you're not quite the thing. Go straight to bed, that's the ticket."

Louisa agreed, and he bowed over her hand. But after he turned and walked away, Louisa stared after him, her expression desolate. And inside the house, Louisa murmured good night to the others, ignoring Miss Pomshack's offer to make her a tisane for her headache.

"Probably her ankle bothering her again," the older lady said, pursing her lips as she and Gemma watched Louisa hurry up the staircase. "I did warn her that she should stay in bed this evening."

Gemma murmured an answer and said good night. Although she would never tell the older lady, Gemma feared something more dire than a sore ankle troubled her friend. Louisa had been silent all the way home. Had something happened? Had she encountered Lord Gabriel, after all, and been rebuffed? Worried, Gemma went upstairs and allowed the maid to help her off with her dress.

But when the servant had departed, Gemma wrapped her shawl about her nightgown and made her way to Louisa's room. The door was shut, and she tapped lightly.

There was no answer, but she heard an ominous sound from inside, the muffled sound of weeping.

Oh, no. Gemma was emboldened to turn the knob; the door was not locked. Before she could lose her resolve, she stepped inside.

Still in her evening dress, Louisa lay facedown on top of her bed. Her gown was now sadly crushed, and she sobbed as if her heart were broken.

"Louisa! What is it?" Gemma hurried forward and sat down on the edge of the mattress where she could pat Louisa's heaving shoulders. "Did you see him after all? Did Lord Gabriel say something hurtful? It was not I, was it, who has ruined your chances?"

Gemma held her breath until she saw Louisa shake her head. But still the other girl sobbed.

"What happened, then?" Perplexed, Gemma stared at her friend. "Tell me, please do. It cannot be this bad."

"Y-yes, it is," Louisa stammered, hiccuping from the force of her tears. "I—they—Miss Har-hargrave . . ."

"Yes?" Gemma had never heard this lady's name before, so these words did little to enlighten her. "Please calm yourself, Louisa, you will make yourself ill. Shall I ring for some brandy or a cup of tea?"

That at least made Louisa push herself up from the bed-covers. "No, no. I sent the servants to bed; I didn't wish anyone to see me. And even Lucas—he could have noticed that it was something really serious! He paid so little attention to me at the theater. Oh, I feel so wretched!"

"I will go down myself and make you some tea," Gemma offered.

Louisa looked at her in surprise, but Gemma smiled. "Really, I know my way around a kitchen."

"No," Louisa said, hiccuping again. "Just give me a little water and sit with me a while, if you would. I feel—I feel very alone tonight."

Relieved that the torrent of tears seemed to have slowed, Gemma went to the table by the bed and poured some water from the jug. She took Louisa the glass and when her friend had sipped a little of the liquid, she took it from her and set it down again. Then she put her arm about Louisa's shoulders and said, her voice gentle, "Why do you not tell me about it, Louisa? It can't be this bad, really; it cannot."

"Oh, it is. I've never had such a direct—well, almost direct—cut," Louisa said, her voice barely above a whisper. She recounted the painful story, with many hesitations and an occasional gulp and sniff.

"And this Miss Hargrave is such an important person?" Gemma asked.

"I—that is, I don't really know. But she moves easily among Society, and she goes to Almack's, so she must be."

"And therefore the ocean will shift its banks if she does not smile upon you?" Gemma kept her tone light.

But Louisa was not to be so easily distracted from her despair. Instead of grinning at the mild jest, she swallowed another sob. "But it's not just her, it's everyone. I just—in Bath, people liked me, some of them even admired me, I think. They called me 'the Comely Miss Crookshank.'"

She tried to smile, but her expression was more like a grimace. "I know it's vain of me to consider it, but—but they liked me in Bath, Gemma. I've never . . . I've never . . . No one is ever going to accept me here. I have made a dreadful mistake. I have leased this house for the whole Season, but I don't care about the money. I think I shall have to give up and go home."

Gemma stiffened with anger. She stared at her friend's swollen eyes and reddened cheeks. Louisa was not the most comely sight just now, but who would be, after crying so hard and so long? Yes, Louisa could be a bit vain at times, but she also had a very kind heart, Gemma thought. Look at how she had taken in a stranger journeying alone to London, the kindness and consideration she had bestowed upon Gemma! How different it would be for Gemma right now if she were biding her time in some out-of-the way, run-down hotel, with no one in London to care about her safety and well-being.

"Louisa—" she began, but the other girl was already speaking.

"I know that my father made his wealth in the mills," Louisa said. "He owned shops, as well, I admit it. But even if he was not highly born, he was a most gentlemanly, kind-hearted man. He was the most wonderful, generous father any girl could ask for. I miss him so much, and to judge him—and me—as lacking in merit only because my family has not been wealthy forever, well, it is too bad."

"It is more than too bad, it is insufferable!" Gemma declared.

Louisa stared at her. "You don't think I've been too presumptuous, entertaining the idea of coming to London and hoping to join the Society of my betters?"

She sounded unusually meek, and Gemma found she could hardly bear this change. Perhaps Louisa's customarily untrammeled self-assurance might annoy others at times, though it had not bothered Gemma, but this pitiful humility was much worse.

"Better in what way? Certainly not in kindness or good manners," Gemma retorted. "Yes, I know how Society works, and I know, too, that I am not the one who can judge, since my own antecedents are still uncertain. But we cannot just give in to them, these arrogant and haughty damsels who think they can define who is allowed to enjoy London's pleasures and who is not!"

"We can't?" Louisa sniffed again and looked about her for a handkerchief.

Gemma jumped up and fished a clean square of lace-edged linen from Louisa's reticule. Her friend took it and blew her nose with vigor.

"No, indeed!" Gemma stood beside the bed and folded her arms in decision. "Louisa, I have been snubbed all my life. There have always been those girls who ignored me, who looked the other way when I walked by, who did not invite me to share special celebrations. Worse, sometimes they made sport of me, called me names that I would not repeat in good company." Gemma's lips tightened as she remembered. "Once when I was twelve, one schoolmate emptied a slop bucket in my bed."

"Oh, that is infamous!" Louisa exclaimed. She sat up straighter. "How could anyone behave so?"

"She was jealous because the dancing master had admired my form and had called her clumsy." Gemma smiled a little at that part of the memory. "He was quite handsome, the dancing master. All the girls had crushes on him."

Louisa still looked shocked.

Gemma added, "I maintain that those who are true ladies, who are real gentleman, who possess genuine class inside themselves as well as in their ancestors' pedigrees, would never behave so. There will always be those who try to make themselves feel superior by putting someone else down, Louisa. But that is the mark of a small mind and a petty spirit. And if we allow them to hurt us, then they have won."

Louisa sighed. "But how can you suffer such treatment and not permit it to hurt? I just wish for people to like me!"

Gemma hesitated, and Louisa said quickly, "Oh, how selfish I am. You have endured so much worse, and here I am making a fuss because two ladies did not wish to speak to me. I'm sorry, Gemma. I will do better, really, I will."

"That is the secret, Louisa," Gemma told her gently.

"What is?" Louisa blew her nose again, but she blinked hard, and her eyes were regaining their usual sparkle.

"If you don't care about their approval, their disparaging actions lose their sting. If you show them you are quite indifferent to their opinions, it unnerves them. In fact, sometimes, that can even make you quite sought after. People do not know what to make of it, you see."

Louisa managed a grin. "I doubt that Society will be seeking me out any time soon. But I shall remember what you have said, Gemma, and I will try. Thank you."

She held out her arms, and Gemma hugged her. For a moment, they both, perhaps, took comfort in their unexpected, but growing friendship.

And Louisa looked much better, though her cheeks were still mottled, and her eyelids swollen. She released Gemma and glanced into the looking glass over her dressing table. "I shall have to use a whole bushel of cucumbers," she suggested, her tone glum, "if I do not wish the household to see that I am upset."

Gemma laughed. "You will manage it," she predicted. "And we shall think of something to do tomorrow that will make us feel better."

Not until she had said good night and headed back for her own room did Gemma have a lowering thought of her own.

Lord Gabriel was in town, at last. He would read her note, and he would answer it—how?

Tomorrow, she might find out.

# *Eight*

*They both rose early. Gemma found Louisa already* at the table when she went down for breakfast, and if Louisa's eyelids were somewhat swollen, the condition was hardly noticeable. Louisa had been gazing dolefully into her tea cup, but she looked up and smiled when Gemma came into the dining room. "I hope you slept well," she said.

She was trying for her usual cheerful tone, Gemma thought, admiring her friend's effort. And she herself could hardly do less, even though she had had a restless night, wondering when her brother—when Lord Gabriel—would open her note and what he would reply to it.

"Tolerably," she lied. "A lovely morning."

"Oh, yes," Louisa agreed. "The sun is out, and the birds are a-wing. It's much too nice a day to stay abed."

Which was a lie, too, Gemma suspected, though a polite enough one. The truth was, they were both too anxious to sleep fashionably late. Miss Pomshack had not yet appeared from her bedchamber. And when Louisa reached for a slice of toast, Gemma saw ink stains on her friend's fingers.

Louisa saw the direction of her glance. "I sent a note to Lady Gabriel," she admitted. "Asking if she might be willing to sponsor me to a few events and introduce me to the Ton. We do have a connection, in a way, and she's by nature a gracious woman, so I am hopeful—" She paused and bit her lip for a moment.

Gemma hoped so, too. Louisa did not deserve another unkind rejection. And as for herself, she had her own hopes.

So they chatted a little over the meal, but Gemma saw Louisa start and glance up at every sound in the street. She knew that they were both listening for a tap on the door, a message returned in the post or by hand, carried by a servant, or even Lady Gabriel herself, if they were really fortunate, coming to call. And as for going out and missing a message or a visit, Gemma knew that neither of them considered such a thing.

When Louisa pushed back from the table—she had as little appetite as Gemma, judging by the food left on her plate—Gemma put down her napkin and followed her friend into the drawing room. Gemma picked up a handkerchief she was hemming, and Louisa flipped through a fashion periodical, but both still listened for a knock at the door.

The morning seemed to last forever, though the porcelain clock on the mantel inexorably ticked away the minutes. Gemma had stabbed her finger three times before there were—at last—sounds at the front door.

Sitting very still, Gemma heard the murmur of voices. She glanced over to see that Louisa had jumped to her feet and had gone very pale. Neither of them said a word, and in a moment it was easy to make out the thud of the door shutting. Gemma strained to hear more chatter, but apparently no one had come in. Then footsteps sounded on the stairs, and Smelters appeared. He held a note on a silver salver.

Gemma held her breath, but it was Louisa he approached. "A letter for you, miss."

"Thank you." Louisa flashed a look of apology toward Gemma. As soon as the footman had gone out, she ripped open the note and scanned its contents.

Gemma did not have to ask what Lady Gabriel's answer was. Seeing Louisa's expression cloud, she felt a wave of regret for her friend.

Louisa sat down heavily. "She says she would be happy to see me again, but at present she is going out very little, and she does not feel she would be very helpful as a sponsor."

"I am sorry," Gemma said.

Louisa was making a brave attempt not to cry. "If my aunt Marianne was not traveling abroad—" She shook her head as her voice failed. "It does no good to repine. I suppose I will think of something." But her lip trembled, and she said, "I believe I will lie down for a while, if you would excuse me, Gemma. I have a bit of a headache."

Suspecting that her friend wanted to be alone, Gemma nodded. "Of course. I will tell Miss Pomshack that you do not wish to be disturbed, even for one of her famous tisanes."

"Thank you," Louisa said fervently, then she hurried out of the room.

Oh, dear. Louisa had lost her best hope of a sponsor, and Gemma—Lord Gabriel had not even bothered to answer her letter. Had he read it, yet?

Presently Miss Pomshack appeared, coming from the dining room. She tsk-tsked over her employer's ill health, and wondered aloud if London had been such a desirable destination, after all.

"It does not appear to have been good for poor Miss Crookshank's constitution," she noted as she sat down with her embroidery.

Gemma made a noncommittal answer and went back to her own sewing, trying not to jump at every sound outside the window. Every time a carriage rolled past the house, or footfalls could be heard on the paving stones, she stiffened, hoping that another note—with a more favorable reply—might come to the house.

But by the time Smelters came to the door to offer them a light luncheon, there had still been no word.

Gemma went in with Miss Pomshack and sat at the table, but she eyed the sliced ham and mustard sauce with no appetite, despite her scanty breakfast. She wanted to scream. Why did she not hear something? How could he ignore her request for an audience over such an important matter?

Miss Pomshack was dipping her spoon into her bowl of soup. "Are you not hungry, Miss Smith?"

"No, not really," Gemma said. In fact, the smells made her feel a little nauseated. "I believe I have a headache coming on, too."

"Oh dear, I do hope it's not something contagious?" the older lady said, pausing with her spoon halfway to her lips.

"I'm sure you will maintain your usual good health," Gemma assured her, thinking, *and your usual good appetite!* But it was not the other lady's fault that Gemma's stomach was knotted with anxiety. "I believe I will lie down awhile, too. Please excuse me."

She slipped out of the room while Miss Pomshack was still offering homemade remedies. But in the hallway, Gemma hesitated.

What she really wanted— She turned toward the outer door. She had to go and see him face-to-face! She could not simply wait here, not knowing. Nor did she want anyone to know if she were rejected. She checked her first impulse to rush out the door alone. Walking down London streets without a companion would not reflect well on her sense of propriety, and she did not wish Lord Gabriel to think ill of her before she even had a chance to plead her case. She went upstairs to find Lily.

"I am going to pay a visit to a distant connection," she told the maid. "If you would not mind a walk—"

"Of course, miss," the girl said, her expression curious.

Gemma got her shawl and paused long enough to glance anxiously in the looking glass at her faded muslin gown. This was not the dress she had planned to wear for her first meeting with her brother, but she was too impatient to change. Besides, she could not pretend to be wealthy or fashionable when she was not. Perhaps it was just as well that he saw her as she really was. If he rejected her because of her less-than-stylish appearance, they would never have had a chance of a relationship, anyhow.

She asked Lily for directions to the square in which Lord Gabriel and his wife resided. Then they set off at a brisk pace, and after a short walk, reached their destination. The Sinclair home was located in a handsome square with a small park in the middle and expansive dwellings built on every side.

The house was of brick, very handsome, and bigger than the one Louisa had rented. It seemed to broadcast the prosperity and social prominence of its inhabitants. Gemma felt a wave of nervousness. And what if Lord and Lady Gabriel had just sat down for a meal themselves? It would be an awkward time to call. She should have considered that before she set out.

She almost turned back, but by this time they were standing at the doorstep, and she simply could not walk away. If she withdrew now, Gemma thought, she might never have the courage to return.

So she lifted her hand and took firm hold of the brass knocker.

*Lord Gabriel Sinclair had also risen early.* He woke as the first rays of sunlight peeked around the edges of the draperies that covered the windows in their bedchamber. Lying very still, he turned only his head to check on Psyche. She was asleep at last, her pale hair sweetly disordered and her breathing even. He knew she had had a difficult night. When she finally did slip into sleep, she had cried out, and shortly afterward had wakened with tears on her cheeks.

He had encircled her with his arms, kissed her wet face tenderly, and held her until she slept again. He didn't ask about her tears; he knew their source.

She had been resting very ill the last few months, he thought. Sometimes her beautiful blue eyes had dark circles beneath them, and her skin too wan, with a pallor unlike its usual healthy glow. It made his heart hurt to see her spirits so low.

He watched her for a while, then, afraid that even his gaze might disturb her, eased himself out of bed, lingering only to kiss the top of her head with a touch so light that his breath barely ruffled the fine hairs. Then he tiptoed into his dressing room and already had his nightshirt off and his trousers half buttoned when his valet appeared.

"My lord," Swindon said, his tone reproachful though he kept his voice low. "You should have rang for me."

"I managed to dress myself for years without help," Gabriel told him, smiling slightly to lighten his rebuke. "In those years, in fact, I was lucky to have a spare shirt to put on. I think I still remember how."

The servant didn't answer, but his dignified expression still managed to express his doubt. He helped his master finish robing for the day, then went away to make sure that tea was brewing and breakfast laid out.

Gabriel went downstairs. The house seemed very quiet. He almost regretted that he had allowed Psyche's younger sister, Circe, with her governess and a male servant, to travel to Bristol for two weeks in order to take special lessons with a renowned French painter. Perhaps having Circe with them when they first returned to London would have lifted her sister's spirits. There would have been art shows and exhibits to attend, museums to examine for offerings that had been added while they were in the country. But Circe had been eager for the opportunity since the artist was only in England for a short time, and Psyche had insisted that she go.

He sat down at the table in lonely splendor and helped himself to beefsteak and pickled herring. But he pushed his plate away after a few bites. In the name of all that was holy, if only he could do something! What kind of a man was he, to be unable to give Psyche what she wanted, what they both wanted?

He stood up, and when a footman hurried forward, shook his head. "Nothing else. I shall be in the library."

Gabriel went to the big room on the ground floor. His desk was piled with papers that needed attending to. But he found it hard to concentrate on accounts of investment earnings or stock reports or his man of business's description of a piece of property he had been considering making a bid on. Psyche was unhappy, and what else mattered besides that?

He paced up and down in front of the fireplace, then forced himself to come back and sit behind his desk. Whenever Psyche came down, he must look as usual and not add to her distress with his own.

So he was skimming a list of figures when one of the footmen came to the door. "Beg pardon, milord."

"Yes?" Gabriel didn't look up.

"There is a young lady . . ."

"Tell her Lady Gabriel is not at home to visitors today," Gabriel directed, wondering that it had not already been done. Their servants were better trained than this. "And on no account is my wife to be disturbed."

The footman cleared his throat. "No, indeed, milord. But she doesn't want to see Lady Gabriel, milord. She wishes—most fervently—to see you."

This time Gabriel put down the document and stared at him. The man's face was a bit flushed, but he held his ground.

The young lady must have been insistent, indeed, Gabriel thought, feeling a flicker of amusement for the first time.

"Very well, show her in," he said, then as the footman disappeared, realized he had not asked the visitor's name.

Not that it mattered. This was most likely a solicitation for alms for the charity ward or a new roof for the parish poorhouse. It could hardly be a social call.

He stood when the young woman appeared in the doorway. She had dark hair—he could see a strand peeking from beneath her plain straw bonnet—and was dressed in an unremarkable but respectable faded muslin gown, with a plain shawl thrown over her shoulders. Definitely, someone doing good works, Gabriel thought. Her face seemed familiar for a moment, but yet, when he gave her a harder look, he was sure he had not seen her before. He bowed when she made a brief curtsy, then motioned to a chair and waited for her to perch on its edge before he sat again himself.

If she was collecting money, she must be new to it, Gabriel thought. She looked very ill at ease.

"Lord Gabriel, I apologize for disturbing you, but the matter is so urgent—" She had a pleasant voice, not shrill or overly loud, and she spoke in an educated tone.

"How may I help you?" he asked courteously, pulling open a desk drawer as he spoke, ready to take out of his cash box a suitable sum and send the poor girl on her way.

"You have not read my note?"

He looked at her in polite inquiry. "It was regarding—"

She licked her lips. "Surely, you must recall. I have recently received a letter that indicates that I am—that we are—that I am your sister, my lord," she said in a desperate rush of words.

Gabriel stiffened. He knew he was frowning, but he couldn't help it. The room seemed suddenly cold. He tried to think what to say.

"I do not—" Then he checked his first response. Why deny it? Yes, he had opened that letter, glanced at the first paragraph and then consigned its remarkable bunch of tomfoolery to the wastebasket. He had judged it some ill-conceived form of blackmail—in which case they had picked the wrong man!—or else a woman of the streets with some fantastic scheme for ill-gotten gain.

He had lived among blackguards and scoundrels for enough years to have heard every type of poppycock, or so he would have said. Having an unknown relative turn up, eager for money, was not unheard of, and generally any claim to kinship turned out to be totally untrue. He was hardly so green as to be taken in by such outrageous lies.

But this did not look at all like the type of woman he would have expected to have penned that letter. He cleared his throat and spoke again, keeping his tone low. If he shouted at her, he thought the girl would swoon. She was pale enough as it was, and it obviously took all her courage just to sit there and face him. She clutched her reticule as if it were a lifeline and she a drowning sailor.

She was either a much-more practiced actress than he had seen lately on any stage, or perhaps someone else was using her as a tool to enact this ruse. Or her wits were addled. But in any case, he could not encourage this delusion. He tried to speak gently.

"I'm afraid you are mistaken, madam," he told her. "I have no sister."

"Oh, I was hoping—" She paused to take a deep breath. "I was hoping our—my—your mother might have already told you."

"My mother?" Gabriel felt it more and more likely the girl was deranged. "I could not have heard from my mother, madam." He knew his tone sounded flat.

The girl gazed at him anxiously. "I am unmarried," she explained.

He narrowed his eyes. "What does that have to do with the matter?"

"Only that you called me madam," she explained. "If no one has informed you of my situation, then I understand you must be shocked at the news, sir—that is, my lord. I regret to have to tell you in such a way. But it is so important to me—I must know. She has invited me to meet her, to be reunited with the family—my family!—and I have waited my whole life for this. You must understand!"

Her voice rose a little, and Gabriel winced. He hoped he could get her out of the house before she became hysterical. He did not wish for Psyche to be wakened in such a manner or alarmed without cause.

"I cannot—"

"But she told me you would help arrange a meeting!"

"My mother could not have done so."

"I have explained this badly," the girl said. She put one hand to her face. She was quite pretty, he thought absently. "Perhaps you should read the letter she sent me."

"Indeed, I think I should," Gabriel agreed, wondering if the paper the young woman withdrew from her reticule, unfolding it as tenderly as if it were her last hope of salvation, would be as unbalanced as her strange request.

But as he scanned the letter, Gabriel knew that his frown deepened. He read it once, then again more slowly. "This letter was written almost twenty years ago? Why did you wait so long?"

"As I told you in my letter, I have just received it." She watched him with anxious blue eyes.

"You realize this is an incredible story," Gabriel said, his tone gruff.

She blinked but faced him with her chin up. "Yes, I know that it must sound very strange. But if you could just speak to your mother, I am sure that she would tell you that this is indeed her letter and that she does wish to meet me."

"If there were any question of this being true—I mean, why should she have to meet you?" he began, then shook his head at himself. He seemed in danger of being drawn into this poor girl's fantasy world. "I cannot ask her," he said.

"Oh, but please! Just make an inquiry—it is essential. I beg of you!"

He thought for one alarmed moment she would kneel before him on the expensive rug. He said quickly, "You don't understand. I cannot ask her anything at all. My mother—my mother died some years ago."

And then he jumped to his feet, but not in time to get around the desk and catch her before she slipped to the floor.

*When Louisa came out of her room after indulging her-*self in a brief cry, she felt little better. Now her head was aching for real, and she frowned when she found that Gemma had gone out. Louisa had hoped for someone more congenial than Miss Pomshack to talk to. Her companion, the vicar's daughter, meant well, Louisa was sure, but the woman did have a tendency to slip into pat bromides, and Louisa was not in the mood to be told to count her blessings or expect that all would look brighter in the morning. . . .

Still pondering, Louisa wandered into the drawing room and sat down. At least Gemma had taken the maid with her, so Louisa had no fears about her friend's safety. And indeed, knowing where Gemma must have gone, she did not blame her for deciding to face Lord Gabriel Sinclair without a witness. If Gemma had asked her to accompany her, Louisa would have agreed, of course, but she shuddered at the thought of observing Lord Gabriel's surprise and possible anger.

Thinking of Gemma reminded Louisa once more of Miss Pomshack's list of platitudes. Perhaps, after all, she should be thankful.

Being mindful of Gemma's predicament—her friend not knowing who she was or even into what social class she belonged—did put her own problem into a different perspective. Louisa was privately sure that her friend had to be a lady by birth as well as disposition—Gemma simply had too many fine sensibilities—but it was still a very uncomfortable position for her.

Louisa herself enjoyed a much more fortunate situation, despite the distress caused by those malicious members of the London Ton. She had family who cared about her, the fortune left her by her father and thus no fears of want or deprivation in her future, and she even had a handsome and affable fiancé who was devoted to her. . . . Well, he was fond of her, she was sure, even if he had not been very attentive lately.

Louisa tried to reassure herself by thinking of Lucas. She wished she could see him. She had decided to share a somewhat edited version of her humiliation at the theater and seek his solace. She sat down at the desk to write him a short note, but before it was completed, the footman appeared, announcing her fiancé.

Pleased that he seemed to have read her thoughts, Louisa stood to welcome him. But when he entered the drawing room, she was much less pleased to find that he had brought a male companion with him.

"Mr. Harris-Smythe," Lucas said as introduction. "My fiancée, Miss Crookshank."

Lucas's friend was short and stout, and his sandy hair was already receding from his forehead. He gave her a deep bow. "Enchanted to meet Sir Lucas's future wife," he said grandly. His tone was almost as flowery as his purple waistcoat.

Louisa kept her expression pleasant and returned his salutation. "I'm delighted," she said, but she glanced back toward Lucas, wishing she could indicate that she wished a few words in private.

Lucas was blind to her significant look, however. "Just wanted to tell you that we—Smythy and me—are going out of town overnight with some other chums to attend a cockfight."

His friend looked shocked. "Lucas, you don't say such things to your fiancée! A subject not fit for a lady's ears, you know."

"Oh, she would have had it out of me, anyhow," Lucas explained, looking unperturbed. "Louisa doesn't mind me speaking frankly."

Louisa wondered if it was a disadvantage that she had known Lucas since they were both children. Sometimes of late he seemed to treat her more like a sister than his future wife. His expression remained guilt-free. "Anyhow, didn't want you to worry that you didn't hear from me. I'll be back by tomorrow, unless it's a really good event, and if so, we'll return by the weekend, I'm sure. I'll come and dine with you as soon as I return, if you like?"

"Of course," she agreed, but when the two men took their leave, she frowned at her betrothed's departing back. She had wanted a private chat, a comforting shoulder, a little sympathy and understanding. And Lucas had his mind on dueling chickens, blast it!

As the door shut behind him, it occurred to her that Lucas was having a fine time in London and seemed to have made friends already. He did not seem to have any problems being accepted! But then, masculine manners were so different, and men could get by with so much more than women. Feeling a little miffed, Louisa tossed her unfinished note into the fire and paced up and down the room. She had waited so long to come to London. It was ridiculous to stay caged in her own house, just because the more fastidious members of Society did not approve of her or her parents' background. She frowned again, thinking of the implied slight to her darling father.

When Miss Pomshack came downstairs from her usual afternoon nap, Louisa looked up in relief.

"I wish to go out, Miss Pomshack. Are you amenable to accompanying me?"

"Of course, Miss Crookshank. I'm sure that a turn in the fresh air would be just the thing for us both. I shall get my shawl."

Louisa donned her hat and gloves and ordered that her carriage be made ready. She had no intentions of again being stranded on foot. When it pulled up in front of the door, she gave directions to the coachman.

"We shall go to Gunter's," she told her companion when they were seated inside. "My aunt told me last year that the establishment is famous for their ices."

And, she told herself, one did not need vouchers to be admitted!

It was a short journey to their destination in Berkeley Square, where the groom helped Louisa and Miss Pomshack down, and they entered the confectionary shop.

Several patrons were seated at small tables around the room. Louisa led the way to a free table. After they had taken their seat, a young woman soon came to ask what they would wish. She offered a number of enticing choices, and Louisa chose a cherry-flavored ice embellished with chopped almonds and whipped cream, and Miss Pomshack, looking pleased at the prospect of this treat, selected peach.

Louisa was enjoying her dessert when she happened to look up and note Miss Hargrave seated, with two other ladies unknown to Louisa, at a table on the other side of the room. When had she come in? Suddenly, Louisa's ice tasted less sweet. She put down her spoon.

Her first impulse was to jump up from her chair and leave at once. But she took a deep breath and considered.

No, she told herself, remembering Gemma's advice. Louisa would not be driven away by that unpleasant young woman. Her jaw tight, she managed another bite, but the pleasure had gone out of her excursion. Was there nowhere in London where she could be safe from supercilious damsels?

Miss Pomshack devoted herself to her own dish, and Louisa had ample opportunity to glance about the room at the other clients, though she carefully avoided looking toward the table which held the superior Miss Hargrave. But then she received another shock. Louisa looked quickly down at the table and was sure that she had flushed.

"Is something wrong, Miss Crookshank?" Miss Pomshack inquired dutifully.

"No, not at all," Louisa lied. But inside, she was torn by conflicting emotions. She was sure that the handsome countenance across the room belonged to the outrageous Lieutenant McGregor. Did all of London assemble in the confectionary shop? And was she merely singularly unlucky today?

She glanced his way again, and she saw him look up and meet her eyes. Remembering his kindness at the theater, she could not help but flash a smile.

"Miss Pomshack," Louisa said suddenly. "If you are finished with your ice, perhaps you would go up to the counter and select a dessert for us to take home. They make some amazing confections here."

"That sounds delightful," the other lady agreed. "But tell me, do you not have a preference?"

"Oh, no, I am sure that whatever you choose will be delicious. Do take your time," Louisa added. "I am in no hurry."

The older lady stood and walked across the shop. Louisa darted one more glance across the room. Yes, he was rising.

Then she kept her gaze carefully upon the mushy remains still in her bowl as she dabbled her spoon in the sweet.

"Miss Crookshank, I believe?"

She looked up and widened her eyes. "Lieutenant McGregor, what a surprise!"

"Indeed? I read a clear invitation in the look you sent me." He arranged himself comfortably in the empty chair. He had the carriage of a military man, she thought, erect and with the hint of strength in his well-shaped torso.

"I should do nothing so unladylike," she told him, keeping her tone dignified. "As I recall, you told me not long ago that I should avoid your company at all costs."

"Ah, yes, I believe I did," he agreed, glancing, to her annoyance, down at her neat pink slippers. "I'm happy to see that you are in better condition today. And do you always pay attention to the good advice that others give you?"

"Perhaps," Louisa answered, her tone demure. "And perhaps not."

"My kind of woman," he said, and the glint in his eye said even more. Louisa felt a delicious tingle. The man might be a reprobate, just as he had said, but he was a most entertaining one, and capable of unexpected kindnesses, too.

"Why are you not with Lady Jersey today?" she asked, keeping her voice light.

He raised his brows. "I do not spend all my time with the countess."

"No? She must be a most amusing companion. I have heard whispers that she has been an—ah—intimate friend of the Prince Regent himself." Louisa allowed her voice to rise in the faintest suggestion of a question.

But the man across from her, for once, kept his expression quite bland. "I do not tell tales about ladies I have the honor to claim as friends."

Louisa should have been disappointed to lose the chance for some really scintillating gossip. Instead, she glanced at him with approval. "I am glad to hear it. What about the suggestion that she was the one who first introduced the quadrille, that most sophisticated Continental dance, into Almack's?"

"She is certainly a most accomplished dancer." The gentleman flashed his easy smile.

No doubt he had danced with the countess of Jersey often. Perhaps she should beg his help in ingratiating herself with Lady Jersey, Louisa thought. But as much as she wanted an invitation to Almack's, she felt distaste at the thought of seeking favor in such a way. And if the lieutenant felt no shame in flirtations with a social elite, well, he should, she told herself, wishing once more that men were not judged so differently. Then, too, the thought of the countess—or any woman—in the lieutenant's arms, even merely on a dance floor, provoked inside her a flicker of—what?—surely not jealousy.

"Is she your kind of woman, too? Or does that designation apply to any woman who smiles upon you, sir?" she suggested, more tartly than she had intended.

He grinned, looking totally unrepentant. "You begin to understand me, then."

"This does not bode well for the happiness of your future wife, when you find a suitably rich lady and manage to gain her affection," Louisa retorted.

"Oh, no," he told her. "I may allow my eye to roam just now; why should I not? But I always play fair. When I am married, I will be true to my bride."

"Of course you will, when you are married—" she began, then saw he was laughing at her again.

"There is no 'of course' about it, my dear naive Miss Crookshank. Many men do not give up their extra pleasures just because they have entered into the marital state. But as I said, when I do marry, I will not dishonor my vows or my wife." He leaned forward just a little, and she saw again just how broad were his shoulders and how wicked was the gleam in his eyes. It made her feel curious inside, shaky and exhilarated all at once.

"And your word is so dependable?" she flashed back.

"In fact, it is," he told her.

Louisa paused; he sounded serious just for an instant. And he had certainly been open enough about his present activities.

She had one hand lying on the edge of the table. He reached for it and lifted it to his lips. The kiss was only a faint brush of the lips, but she hoped he did not observe how she quivered with delight.

If so, he made no sign. Then, to her disappointment, he released her hand and pushed back his chair.

"You're leaving already?"

"I shall claim a dance the next time I see you," he promised. "Perhaps Wednesday night at Almack's. Lord knows, that assembly is boring enough that I shall need some pleasant diversion."

Louisa knew her expression had twisted. About to rise, he paused. "What is it?"

"I have no vouchers," she explained. "And it seems unlikely that I shall obtain any." She tried not to allow her voice to sound strained, but he seemed to read her disappointment and even to understand.

"You are not really missing a great deal. It's not the most exciting spot in London, you know," he told her.

Louisa did not reply, but her silence was answer enough.

"Think of all the many spots in the city you may enjoy, with or without the approval of the biddies who rule the Ton."

"Such as?" she demanded.

He smiled again, this time with less devilry and more real kindness. "You might stroll into Hookham's Circulating Library on Bond Street, and take out one of Mrs. Radcliffe's wicked Gothic novels. Or, at number 24, visit Sir Thomas Lawrence's studio, or nearby, Hoppner's, and gaze upon the portraits of the best of London Society. Why, one of them could likely be persuaded to paint you, too, you know, for a suitable commission. You're quite as lovely as any of his other subjects, more than most. You would require much less enhancing than our distinguished duke of Wellington."

Louisa laughed, but she felt a wave of pleasure. "Do you really think so?"

"Of course." And then there is Ackermann's print shop at 101 the Strand, another favorite spot for fashionable young ladies to enjoy. And of course, there are the theaters, the opera, the exhibits of wild beasts at the amphitheater—"

Louisa giggled again despite herself. "I am not a child."

"Oh no, I am quite sure of that." And as he glanced down at the discreet bosom of her gown, she felt again the prickle of those surely scandalous feelings that he always engendered.

But Miss Pomshack was returning, her expression disapproving despite the parcel she carried in her hands.

"It was a pleasure, Miss Crookshank." To her immense regret, the lieutenant stood and gave her a completely correct bow. "I'm sure we shall meet again."

"No doubt," Louisa agreed, her tone demure, determined not to show how enticing she found the prospect.

And if Miss Hargrave had noticed Louisa's tête-à-tête with
the dashing lieutenant, so be it!

*Gabriel supported the slim form, wondering about call-*
ing for the footman. He needed a maid, but again, if he
shouted out the door, he feared that his wife might hear and
be alarmed. To his relief, while he considered which
course to take, the girl stirred and sat up.

"What?"

"You swooned for a moment," he told her, helping her
back into the chair. "Let me pour you a glass of wine."

She was silent while he turned his back and poured a
glass from the decanter on the side table. When he looked
around again, he found that she was weeping silently.
When she felt his gaze, she wiped uselessly at her damp
cheeks. Her attempt to suppress her sobs somehow moved
him much more than noisy wailing would have.

"Here," he said, more gently than he had spoken earlier.
"Please, take a sip. It will help you calm yourself."

She drank a little of the port, almost choking on the potent drink. Not accustomed to strong wine, then, he deduced.

"I am sorry this has upset you, but—" he began.

"I feel as if I have lost her all over again," she said, staring past him. "I never knew a mother, not a real mother. I
thought I would see her face at last, hear her voice, and she
would explain it all."

"Explain what?"

"I apprised you of the facts about my life in my letter,"
she told him, her tone reproachful.

Gabriel wished he had read the bloody thing. But he
could hardly admit he had tossed it away. "I'm sorry. If you
would be kind enough to refresh my memory?"

She looked at him as if he were the one who had gone
mad—one part of his mind could not help appreciating the
irony of it—but she nodded. "I was raised for five years by

a kind lady who I was told was my caretaker, but who I knew was not my mother. When she died suddenly, I was sent to a foundling home, and it was, it was not the most . . ." For the first time she looked away and swallowed with obvious effort. "At any rate, after some time I was taken away and sent to a respectable girls' school in Yorkshire. My fees were paid by a solicitor, but he would tell me nothing about my background."

"And your name?" Gabriel asked.

She flushed. "I was known there as Gemma Smith," she said simply. "But when I turned one and twenty, the solicitor sent me this letter. He told me he had been bidden by my mother—two decades ago—to give it to me when I came of age. I came at once to London to seek you out, just as the letter said. I was—I was so happy." Her voice broke, and he looked away to give her time to compose herself.

"But you must see how fantastical this story is," he pointed out.

She nodded. "Of course I do. But I thought"—her voice wavered, but she regained her control—"I thought I could simply rely on my mother to confirm it, and finally, to answer all the questions about my past which have hung over my head for years."

"I regret that she is not here to do so," he said, then was afraid he had stirred her to fresh tears. "I'm afraid I know nothing—have been told nothing—about a sister. How could my mother have hidden a confinement? It all seems quite impossible."

She found a minute handkerchief in her reticule and wiped her eyes. "But perhaps your father—"

"Is also dead," Gabriel said, hearing his tone harden. "And my older brother is abroad, though if he had ever heard anything of this, he surely would have told me."

She blinked hard. "Does this writing resemble your mother's hand? You could tell me that, at least."

Gabriel glanced back at the faded ink of the letter, still lying on top of his desk. "I'm not sure."

"Can you not compare it to one of her letters in your

possession? Surely you must have saved some of them."
He was relieved to see that she was sitting up straighter, but
she also seemed to have regained her ability to argue.

"I don't—I fear I don't have any sample of her writing
at hand," he said.

She raised her brows, and Gabriel found it his turn to
feel ill at ease. "There are reasons why . . ."

"There must be something!" she protested.

Gabriel tried to think. "My wife has a housekeeping
book my mother used; the housekeeper saved it when she
died. It has some receipts and lists in her hand."

"That would do!" Miss Smith said eagerly.

"It is at our country estate, however," he told her.

She opened her lips, and he raised one hand to forestall
more debate. "I will send for it, and I shall compare it carefully with this." He turned back to lift the letter from the
desktop, but the girl was too quick. She darted around him
and snatched up the sheet, holding the letter to her chest.

"I'm sorry," she said, sounding breathless. "I cannot
part with this, even for a few days."

Was she afraid he would destroy it? Gabriel started to
tell her that he would not be so base, but she continued, her
gaze guileless.

"It is the only thing I have that was my mother's, whatever you think of my claim, and besides, she says in it that
she loves me. I will treasure this always." She bit her lip
and pressed the page to her heart.

Gabriel had no inclination to try to wrest it from her.
"Of course," he said. "I promise you I will inform you
when the book arrives. And I will write to my brother, although he is, the last I heard, in Constantinople, so I cannot
expect a quick reply."

She sighed. "Thank you for that and, indeed, for seeing
me at all. I had feared you would not even admit me."

He didn't tell her she owed her admission to the footman, and that Gabriel himself had been quite ignorant of
the quagmire she would open before him. He said only,
"May I ask where you are staying?"

She told him the address and then turned toward the door. Her expression was still doleful, but she had straightened her shoulders once again. The girl had courage, Gabriel thought reluctantly. If he could only be as sure of the soundness of her mind, it might be easier to decipher this strange tale.

She still looked a little shaky. "Allow me to call for my carriage to return you safely to your residence," he suggested.

She shook her head. "No, thank you, my maid is waiting." Her tone possessed as much dignity as a duchess's, and he bit back a smile, not wanting to wound her further. He stood and watched as she walked out into the hall.

But he motioned to the footman and told the man quietly to hail a hackney for the women and to pay the fare before they left the house. The servant looked startled, but he nodded and accepted the coins Gabriel held out, then hurried after the young woman and her serving maid.

Gabriel went back inside and stood by his desk, but he found he was listening to the faint footsteps as the mysterious Miss Smith took her leave. It was an insane suggestion, that his mother could have had a child in secret and have sent it away. . . . And never to tell anyone, no, it was impossible to even consider.

The stranger had not asked for money, he suddenly realized. When he had first scanned the note yesterday afternoon, he'd assumed it a ruse to obtain funds. He wished again he had read the letter more carefully. He looked at the basket beside his desk, but of course, it had already been emptied. The servants were punctual in their duties— Psyche saw to that.

As if his thought had summoned her, he looked up to see his wife standing in the doorway. Gabriel jumped to his feet and hurried to greet her.

"My love, how are you?"

"I'm well," she said, but she frowned as she accepted his kiss. "Who was that young lady who left looking so distressed? And, Gabriel, why does she have your eyes?"

# Nine

By the time Gemma returned to the house, she felt quite leaden with exhaustion and the weight of dashed hopes. It was very kind of her brother—of Lord Gabriel—to send them home in a hackney. She would have had more trouble with the walk than he could have guessed. Her knees felt shaky, her shoulders drooped, and her head ached. She felt as if she had received an enormous blow.

She had. As she had told Lord Gabriel, it had been like losing her mother all over again. If someone dashed up this moment out of the crowd on the street and informed her of the death of her parent, surely she would have felt just this sense of shock and grief and pain.

So her only thought was to go straight up to her room and abandon herself to her grief and despair. What on earth was she to do now?

But Louisa was waiting and must have been listening for their return because Gemma's hostess came out into the hall as Gemma untied her bonnet and pulled off her gloves.

"What—" she began, then paused when she saw Gemma's face. "Lily, take Miss Gemma's things upstairs and then please bring us some tea in the drawing room. Or would you rather go up to your bedroom, Gemma?" Her tone was solicitous, and the anxiety in her blue eyes sincere. And Louisa had had her own disappointment, important to her, even if not of the same magnitude as Gemma's loss, Gemma reminded herself.

She had to be strong.

"The drawing room is fine," she said, and if her voice wavered just a little, Louisa did not remark upon it. Her friend waited until they were inside the reception room and had shut the door against the servants' curious eyes, then she put her arms around Gemma in an impulsive hug.

"It did not go well?"

The sympathy was disarming. Gemma found herself dissolving again into tears.

Louisa held her for a few minutes while Gemma sobbed, this time without reserve, then at last sat up and reached into her reticule to find her already damp handkerchief.

"Here," Louisa said. "Mine is clean."

Gemma accepted the dry linen square and wiped her face and blew her nose. "I think I shall have to borrow some of your cucumber slices," she managed to say.

Louisa smiled obligingly at the feeble jest, though her expression still looked worried. "What did he say? Does he deny the claim? But how can he, with the letter from your mother to support it?"

Determined not to succumb to tears once more, Gemma drew a deep breath. "I suggested that he speak to her to confirm the statements in the letter, but, oh, Louisa, my mother is dead! So she cannot answer his—or my—questions." Her lips trembled, and with a great effort she maintained her self control.

Louisa gasped. "Oh, I—oh dear!"

She turned her head away as Lily entered with a tray. While the servant set down the tea and cups and some plates of small cakes, they were both silent.

"Thank you, Lily," Louisa said. Gemma felt the maid's curious glance before she curtsied and left them alone again, carefully shutting the door behind her.

Louisa poured out the tea and added sugar and cream, but her hand trembled. "Here, I'm sure you need this," she said, but her tone was hollow. "Gemma, you never said—I thought you knew. I feel terrible. I could have warned you."

"What?" Gemma demanded.

"I knew that his—and your—mother is deceased. I visited their country estate last year, and her death was mentioned. But I—there was a great deal going on at the time, and I—well, I behaved very badly. And I have tried my best to forget that whole time. Perhaps I succeeded too well." She frowned. "Oh, Gemma, I am such a wretch! I only thought you were anxious to be reunited with your brother. I should have made sure that you knew the situation."

Gemma swallowed against the lump in her throat. Yes, if she had known, she would have been better prepared for the interview with Lord Gabriel. On the other hand, knowing that her mother was not there to back up Gemma's claims, perhaps Gemma would not have had the courage to go to her brother at all!

"I have spent so much of my life not speaking of my situation, as you call it, that I am perhaps too secretive, even with my friends." She sighed. "It's not your fault, Louisa. And in a way, I'm glad I didn't know. It would only have crushed my hopes that much sooner. At least I had a few weeks to think that my mother still waited for my return, and that thought made me very happy."

Louisa's anxious expression eased a little. "Try to eat a cake; you took nothing at breakfast. It was wise of Lily to think of bringing it. Some food will make you feel better. At least, that is what my aunt would advise. And I must say, she always seems to be right."

Looking around, Gemma asked, "Where is Miss Pomshack?"

"Upstairs. She insisted on working on the ribbons we

bought yesterday. She is adding a trim to one of my hats," Louisa said. She held out a plate of small cakes, and Gemma accepted one.

"Thank you," she said, meaning her gratitude for more than the refreshment. Louisa nodded as if she understood.

For a moment, Gemma nibbled at a sweet morsel of cake and drank her tea, hoping it would steady her, fill a little of the great emptiness inside her. Yet she knew that the void in her heart was much too big for any amount of foodstuff to affect.

Still sounding worried, Louisa added, "You are not alone in that habit. The Sinclairs are very private about their family history—it's rarely discussed. The two brothers once had a great dispute—they fought a duel last Season, which I saw with my own eyes, and I truly thought someone would be killed. In fact, someone almost was! But I have heard almost nothing about the reasons for their estrangement. Even my aunt, who is usually most obliging, would not answer my questions. She loves the marquess, Lord Gabriel's older brother, very much, and does not want to distress him."

"I do not blame you," Gemma assured her again. "But I admit, the news is such a blow. I had so much hoped to at last meet my real mother. . . ."

Tears threatened again, and she blinked hard. "I think I shall go up to my room for a while," she said.

Louisa nodded. "If I can do anything, please call me."

Gemma smiled wanly at her friend, then pushed back her plate and went up the stairs to her room. Her emotions were so confused, and the sorrow of her loss—the shock of having all her hopes dashed—hung over her like a blanket of stone. She lay down upon her bed and shut her eyes, but sleep would not come. The tears did.

*Louisa paced up and down the drawing room, thinking* back on Gemma's earlier conversations. She could not

remember that Gemma had ever actually *said* she expected
to meet her mother, but then perhaps Louisa had simply
assumed—oh, she should have been more observant; it was
too bad!

The afternoon stretched ahead of her like an eternity,
and although she spoke briefly to Miss Pomshack when
that lady came downstairs for a cup of tea and a cake,
Louisa could not settle her thoughts.

After more than an hour had passed, she went up to the
floor where the guest rooms were located and paused outside Gemma's door. She was sure she could hear sobbing
from inside.

She knocked lightly. "Gemma?"

A pause, then she heard her friend say, her voice low,
"Come in."

She opened the door. One look at Gemma's face made
Louisa rush to sit on the edge of the bed and offer a hug.
"Oh, my dear, you will make yourself ill. What can I do?
Do you wish a dose of Miss Pomshack's laudanum? That
would make anyone sleep."

Gemma shook her head. "I don't care for the stuff; it
leaves one feeling even more wretched later. It's just that
my thoughts go round and round, and the pain is so
sharp. . . ."

Louisa felt her own eyes dampen. "I know how I felt
when my father died, and I had my uncle and aunt there to
comfort me. But I am here for you, Gemma."

"It's silly, since she died years ago, Lord Gabriel said,
but, but—" Gemma hiccuped, swallowing a sob.

"But it is new to you, and not silly at all," Louisa assured her. "It will take time for these feelings to ease,
Gemma. But you are not alone, I promise you."

"Thank you," Gemma told her. "I think I might as well
get up and wash my face. Perhaps we could go for a stroll
or a drive. Perhaps some diversion would take my thoughts
away from all that I don't want to think about, not now."

Louisa nodded. She felt a tremor of nervousness at the
thought of venturing out and encountering any more

high-sticklers who might snub her once again, but her own
fears were so paltry compared to Gemma's distress that she
pushed them aside.

"An excellent notion; you must not slip into a melancholy. I will order the carriage," she said. "Where is your
shawl?"

They both donned hats and gloves and shawls, then,
when her carriage was ready, they drove in a leisurely
fashion—the traffic on the London streets seldom allowed
one to do otherwise—to Hyde Park.

By the time they entered the park, Gemma seemed less
wrapped in her own fog of misery, and Louisa, keeping in
mind Gemma's earlier comments, had made up her mind
to be resolute and not cower out of sight of London's censorious elite. Since the afternoon was mild and quite lovely,
she instructed her coachman to pull up and allow them to
step down and stroll among the flower beds.

And indeed, they spent a pleasant half hour walking
along the pathways, enjoying the sight of the brightly colored spring flowers and the fresh new leaves just unfurling
to green the trees. Although on such a day the park was full
of people, she saw no one she knew, and Louisa was able to
put aside bad memories. With the breeze grazing her
cheek, and the scent of growing things in the air, Louisa's
spirits lifted, and even Gemma agreed that this had been a
good idea, after all.

Glancing covertly at her friend, Louisa thought what a
dreadful injustice it was to be forced to suffer the loss of a
parent all over again, and in such a lonely way, with no
family to share the sorrow, no funeral to attend, no way to
feel that one could express one's sorrow openly. She remembered her own dearest father's death and how painful
it had been. But at least she had had her aunt and uncle and
Lucas and many other family members and friends around
her, all ready to console her and offer her reassurance and
good wishes. And whom did Gemma have?

She had Louisa! Louisa told herself she would put aside
her own worries and think more about her friend, who must

not be left to suffer alone. She tucked her arm into Gemma's and smiled at her when Gemma looked up in inquiry.

"I was only—" But Louisa's voice failed as she glanced down the path. What she saw approaching drove away all recollection of her newly formed good intentions. Louisa stiffened in alarm.

"What is it?" Gemma raised her brows.

"I—I did not, that is, oh, it is Miss Hargrave and Miss Simpson, the two, um, acquaintances I spoke to at the theater, and they are coming right toward us! Oh, what shall I do?" Louisa glanced around a bit wildly, wondering if they had time to flee to her carriage. "I cannot bear to be snubbed again! They will give me a direct cut, I just know it."

"Certainly not!" Gemma said, her words crisp.

Louisa was still plotting the most direct path back to her carriage. They had been wandering along the paths as they observed the flowers, and now she wished they had stayed closer to the street.

"We shall not run away, Louisa," Gemma said, keeping her voice low. "That would give them too much of a victory over you—you cannot wish it."

"But I can't bear to be slighted so publicly once again," Louisa protested, feeling her heart pound at the thought.

"They will not," Gemma told her with quiet certitude. "We will not allow it."

"But we can't stop them!" Louisa swallowed hard against rising panic.

"Remember what I said," Gemma said, dropping her voice. "They can only hurt you if you allow them to do so."

Louisa wished she could be that steadfast or that brave. But she was not sure she could keep her face straight if she had to face the snobbish ladies again, so soon after the embarrassing encounter at the theater.

"I don't see how we can prevent them," she muttered, hoping she was not blushing from shame already.

"Easily enough," Gemma shot back. She put one hand

over Louisa's, which still lay on her arm. "Smile," she commanded as they strolled along the path. "Look as if you are at ease and enjoying a ramble in the park."

Louisa tried to do so, but the two other ladies were almost upon them. Just as she braced herself to either meet their indifferent gaze or to watch in mortification as the two looked away and pretended not to see her, Gemma swung them into another path so that their backs were turned to the approaching duo. While Louisa tried not to gasp, Gemma motioned toward a bed of tulips.

"A particularly fine shade, don't you think? Perhaps a new variety? We should inform your gardener to inquire about the variety of bulb. These do make a nice display."

Louisa bit back an attack of nervous giggles—she had no gardener to inform—but at last she understood Gemma's tactics: ignore them before they could ignore you! Oh, my, what could Miss Hargrave and Miss Simpson be thinking? She didn't dare to look to the side to see the answer.

She wanted to laugh, but she managed to keep her tone even as she and Gemma conversed at length about the no-doubt handsome tulips before them. Seldom had flowers been examined at such length!

When at last she was sure that the two women had passed safely by, she released a nervous hiccup. "Perhaps we should go home, now?" she suggested. "The wind is getting colder, I believe."

Gemma nodded, and they walked sedately and without hurry to Louisa's carriage. Only when they had been handed in and the door shut upon them, and the coachman had flicked the reins and the vehicle rolled forward, did Louisa give in to her pent-up feelings.

She collapsed against the seat and laughed until tears rolled down her cheeks.

Gemma laughed as well, and they hugged each other like small children who have pulled a prank upon their governess.

When Louisa finally wiped her eyes and sat up straighter, she said, "That was too bad of us, I suppose."

"They may not even have noticed. And if they did, I doubt their feelings were sorely tried," Gemma predicted. "But at least, neither were yours."

"You are very wise, Gemma," Louisa told her friend. "I am in your debt." She realized that much of her trepidation had disappeared, and already she was wondering why she had allowed the two women to upset her so much. Perhaps, she thought, because in her mind they represented all of the Ton, and she feared the same response from the rest of London's elite. She tried to explain as much to Gemma.

"But if they judge you only by how your father earned his money, are you losing so much?" Gemma argued. "Your friends will value you for who you are, for your character and your kindness, and if they slight you for other reasons, they are not really friends."

"I know," Louisa said, but she heard in her voice the trace of wistfulness that still lingered. "But Almack's—I did so want to be invited."

"But there are other events, other parties. And you are already engaged, so you do not even need to meet eligible gentlemen," Gemma pointed out.

"True. Thank goodness for Lucas," Louisa agreed. "He may not be very romantic, but he does not mind about my father's connection to trade. He knew my father and valued him for his integrity, his good sense, and his kindness." She sighed. "And I have you, Gemma. I am so thankful to have met you, even if it was due to a providential encounter. Your friendship means so much to me."

She made out a glint of moisture in her friend's eyes. "As yours does to me," Gemma told her, her voice husky. "Without your support, I do not know how I could have endured the intelligence about my mother."

They hugged impulsively, and then Louisa sat up and straightened her bonnet. "I think we should go and have an ice at Gunter's before we return home," she announced. The shop and its exclusive clientele would no longer frighten her. "In celebration of friendship!"

Despite her swollen eyelids and still pale face, Gemma smiled. "An excellent notion," she agreed.

Louisa tapped on the front of the carriage to alert her driver, and soon the carriage was making its way to Berkeley Square. After they had enjoyed dishes of flavored ices at Gunter's—this time with no distractions—they climbed back into Louisa's carriage and made their way home.

*Gemma was happy to see her friend looking more determined.* Louisa must not allow the high-sticklers of the Ton to cow her into meek submission, and Gemma would do all she could to help Louisa remain resolute. And in her resolve to aid her friend, some of Gemma's own pain and sorrow seemed to ease. When they entered the house, they paused in the hallway to take off their hats and wraps, and as Louisa spoke to the footman, a rap sounded at the door.

Now what? Had Sir Lucas come to call?

Gemma, aware of how much courage their outing had cost her friend, hoped for Louisa's sake that her fiancé had returned and would lift her spirits.

She thought about going upstairs to give them privacy, but Louisa gestured toward the drawing room. "See who it is, Smelters," she told the footman. Gemma followed her friend into the reception room where they sat down demurely and prepared to receive company.

They waited until the footman appeared in the doorway. His countenance totally impassive, Smelters stood very straight. Gemma had learned by now that this indicated that he was hiding intense emotion.

"A visitor to see you, Miss Crookshank," the footman announced in clear tones. "Lady Gabriel Sinclair."

Everyone froze, and the silence felt charged. Gemma felt as if she could not breathe. Then she saw that Louisa had gathered her wits and risen, and she struggled to her feet, too.

Lady Gabriel entered with a smooth, graceful gait and an elegant posture. Goodness, she was beautiful, Gemma thought. Lord Gabriel's wife had fair hair pulled up to the back of her head, icy blue eyes, and a face quite without flaws. Her outfit was stunning, and her expression suggested intelligence and a natural air of authority.

Feeling a bit awed, Gemma, like Louisa, sank into a deep curtsy. Lady Gabriel returned their greeting.

"Please sit down, Lady Gabriel," Louisa said. Her voice was a little breathless, but even so, Gemma admired her friend's self-possession. "It is so kind of you to call. I am most pleased to see you again. Smelters, please bring us a tea tray."

She nodded to the servant as Lady Gabriel sank gracefully into a chair. The newcomer glanced at Gemma for a moment.

Gemma hoped that her face was not as flushed as she feared it might be, and that the ride and the fresh air had obscured the lingering signs of her recent bouts of weeping.

When Louisa sat down, she seemed to realize she had not effected introductions. "Forgive me, Lady Gabriel, this is my friend, Miss Gemma . . . Smith." The pause after her given name was brief, and Gemma hoped, not too noticeable. "Gemma, this is Lady Gabriel Sinclair."

Her thoughts still awhirl, Gemma murmured a polite response.

Lady Gabriel smiled at Gemma, then turned back to Louisa. "I feared that my note might have sounded a bit curt, so I decided you would not mind if I came to see you so that I could explain my answer."

"Of course not," Louisa said. "That is, you have no reason to—I should not have expected—if I sounded presumptuous . . ." She paused, too tangled in her own words to find an end to her statement.

"Not in the least." Lady Gabriel, whose poise was impressive, smiled again, apparently to put Louisa more at ease. Gemma saw her friend take a deep breath.

Feeling a little wistful, Gemma drew her attention back to their visitor. Although only slightly older than she and Louisa, Lady Gabriel was still an example of the type of gentlewoman Gemma would have hoped to someday become, if she had any right to be deemed a lady at all. She suspected Louisa felt the same admiration. Was this what Gemma's mother had been like when she was young—gracious, kind, with intelligent eyes and a perfect bearing? But now Gemma would never know her mother at any age. The pain stabbed her again, and Gemma pushed it back.

"I confess I have been out of spirits," Lady Gabriel was saying. "Last year, I was very pleased to find myself expecting a child. It would have been my—our—first. However, it was not to be. This sad loss has been heavy on my heart, especially . . ." She paused, for the first time looking less than serene, her blue eyes troubled.

Had she not been able to become pregnant again? This was indeed a great blow, Gemma thought.

Louisa had flushed. "Oh, I knew that. I mean, I was there when you, well, you may not remember, as ill as you were. But I should have realized that such a disappointment could still haunt you. I am so sorry, Lady Gabriel, for bothering you with my frivolous request."

She sounded completely sincere, and her expression of concern was not contrived, Gemma decided. She was pleased to see that Louisa seemed to have put aside her own desires in her sympathy for the other woman. It showed her friend at her best, and Gemma privately applauded her for it.

They all paused for a moment as the footman came in with a tray with tea and dainty cakes and biscuits. As he made his exit, Louisa poured a cup of tea and handed it to their guest.

"Thank you, Miss Crookshank," Lady Gabriel said. "May I call you Louisa? No, indeed, I am glad you have applied to me for help. It made me pause and take stock, and I have decided I have been indulging myself too much. Aided by my dear husband, I must add, who cossets me in every way that he can think of. I am sure it would be better for me to resume a normal schedule and stop dwelling on sad reflections."

Louisa's expression changed, and Gemma saw dawning hope in her friend's eyes.

"Oh, please do call me Louisa—I should like that enormously. But, do you really wish, do you feel up to, that is . . ."

"Embarking upon one's first Season is also important, in its own way." Lady Gabriel smiled at Louisa, and Louisa colored with what Gemma was sure was pure happiness. But then Louisa hesitated.

"My lady, I think I should tell you, I would not wish to deceive you in any way." Her voice faltered, then Louisa took a deep breath and went on. "My family is completely respectable, I promise you. But it is a fact that my father— my father owned woolen mills in the north, and even several shops. If you find that distasteful, I would not wish to presume upon your kindness."

Their visitor gave her a thoughtful look. "I appreciate your candor, Louisa. But you need not fear. My own dear father, although from an old and much respected family, loved machines and was an inventor of some note. His wealth, and my inheritance and my sister's, was derived mainly from his patents and inventions; he may have made some refinements used by the new power looms in your late father's mills. I have no disdain for those who earn their money by honest toil and native ingenuity."

Louisa opened her eyes wide. "And you are not—and no one has slighted you because—oh, I beg your pardon."

"If they did, I should take no notice of such foolishness," Lady Gabriel declared. "I know well enough how particular some of the Ton can be, but one should not give any heed to such small-minded fancies. Though, mind you, I admit I cannot imagine anyone daring to slight a Hill or a Sinclair."

Waving the notion away, she continued, "One of my close friends, Mrs. Andrew Forsythe, is giving a ball next week. It's not a prodigious affair, but Sally is a wonderful hostess, and a good selection of the Ton will attend. She has begged me to come, but I was not sure. I have decided that I will go, and I will see that she invites you and your fiancé—and your friend as well."

Gemma drew a deep breath. She was to be invited, too?

As Louisa stammered her thanks, Lady Gabriel turned to Gemma, who sat motionless with surprise. "And now, my dear, I hope you will forgive me for asking, but I promise you it is not merely idle curiosity. I believe you called on my husband this morning with a rather incredible narrative? The footman heard you give the hackney driver your address when you departed, and I could not help but notice that it was the same as the one Miss Crookshank had inscribed on her letter to me."

Gemma lifted her chin and met the other woman's gaze squarely. "I know it is a fantastic tale—" she began.

"Which does not automatically mean it is not true," Lady Gabriel said gently.

Prepared for skepticism, not a receptive listener, Gemma paused in confusion.

"Gabriel says that you have in your possession a letter that you believe was written by the woman who was your mother, and perhaps also my husband's mother? Would you allow me to see it?"

Gemma swallowed. "Of course," she said, knowing that Louisa watched her anxiously. Neither of them wished to offend Lady Gabriel, and if she were disposed to be more open to Gemma's quest . . . Telling herself not to allow new hopes, which might once again be quickly crushed, Gemma withdrew the note from her reticule and unfolded it with anxious care.

As if she understood how precious this creased sheet of paper was to Gemma, Lady Gabriel put down her tea cup and moved across to sit on the settee next to her so that she could consider the few lines on the paper.

Everyone was silent. Then Lady Gabriel looked up. "I cannot say for sure, you understand—my husband has sent a message to our country estate to have sent to us the housekeeping book, which has some of his mother's handwriting in it—but it seems similar. We will need to compare the two more closely."

Gemma found that she had been holding her breath. She let out a long sigh. "Thank you," she said. "I do not blame your husband for doubting my story. But I wish so much to find out more about my mother, and—"

"And why she would send away a daughter?" Lady Gabriel sounded sad, just considering such a thing. "And without telling her sons?"

Gemma looked up and saw that the other lady had paused. "I know the most obvious answer," she said slowly. "It would be that I was, was—"

"That you were, perhaps, not her husband's child?" Lady Gabriel's tone was mild and her glance at Gemma without judgment. "It does happen, you know, but seldom are such infants sent away from the family. Sometimes it is common knowledge. The gossip among the Ton—well, that is beside the point. What is to the point is, I must tell you, having endured one brief visit with my husband's father before his death, that I cannot judge the theory impossible. He was a most intolerant man. If he was so unfeeling as to drive my husband away for a suspected transgression, the late marquess could conceivably have had the same vicious reaction to an infant he felt might not be his."

Hungry for any scrap of information, Gemma nodded eagerly.

"Whatever proves to be true, it is no reflection upon you, you know," Lady Gabriel added. She leaned over to pat Gemma's hand. Only then did Gemma discover she had twisted her hands together in her lap so tightly that her fingers ached. She drew another deep breath and tried to loosen them.

"It will affect my social standing, however," Gemma argued, trying not to sound bitter. "And make a respectable man hesitate to choose me as his wife."

"Do not think of it!" the other woman retorted, her eyes

suddenly bright. "If he truly loves you, this will be a small thing."

Gemma wished she could be so sure. Arnold did not think it a small thing. But she would not contradict their visitor. "You are very generous. Thank you for allowing me to hope that I may yet find some answers."

Lady Gabriel lifted her brows. "I would not wish to be unkind to someone who may be related to my beloved husband! And there is, you know, the matter of your eyes."

Perplexed, Gemma repeated, "My eyes?"

The other woman nodded. "Many English have blue eyes; it is not an unusual attribute among our countrymen. In fact, all three of us here are blue-eyed." She gestured to Louisa, and then back to Gemma. "But even so, there are many shades of blue."

Gemma glanced from one to the other. It was true. Lady Gabriel had eyes of an icy clear blue. Louisa's shade was softer. And as for herself—she could not keep from glancing into the looking glass above the corner table—the familiar deep-hued eyes that she had known all her life gazed back at her.

"Yours are just the color, and even the shape, of my husband's," Lady Gabriel explained, adding, "My younger sister is a most talented artist. Perhaps her keener observations of the human form have rubbed off a bit on me."

Gemma was only surprised she had not remarked upon the similarities when she had been sitting in front of Lord Gabriel. But she had been most perturbed at the time, and besides, she had gone there expecting him to be her brother. She did not need proof.

"Would you feel it impertinent if I invited you to tell me about your life?" Lady Gabriel asked.

Her tone was warm. Gemma found that she could talk much more freely than she had done when confronted with Lord Gabriel's obvious skepticism. She told the story all over again, explaining about the woman who had fostered her, the foundling home, then the school in Yorkshire.

Gemma also told how she had visited the foundling home in search of information and met Matthew Fallon there on a similar errand, though she did not tell her possible sister-in-law about stealing the ledgers. Anyhow, the audacious theft had gained them nothing.

"There is no reason that the matron should be so unhelpful," Lady Gabriel declared, looking over their heads for a moment. She stirred her cooling tea but seemed to have forgotten to drink it. "I think we should pay another visit to this place, Miss Smith. Or may I call you Gemma?"

Her hope stirring again for the first time since it had been dashed so low this morning, Gemma sat up straight. "Please do! Do you mean you yourself wish to see the home?"

"I do, indeed. And perhaps I can persuade this formidable matron to be more forthcoming," Lady Gabriel declared.

Anyone who withstood this lady's cool gaze and air of authority would be doughty, in truth, Gemma thought. Perhaps even the formidable Miss Craigmore would unbend before Lady Gabriel. Gemma found herself almost speechless with anticipation.

Louisa was less restrained. "Lady Gabriel, you are an angel!"

The beautiful matron laughed. "Call me Psyche, please. I am sure we are going to be wonderful friends."

*Matthew set out for the inns of Court immediately after* breakfast. He was staying in a modest hotel on the other side of the city, so he hailed a cab and rode to his destination. After he stepped down, he first tried the office of the solicitor whose job it had been to look out for his mother and sister, the duplicitous Mr. Temming. Once again, the door was locked, and again, no one came in answer to his pounding.

He had pried open the door upon his first visit to the

office and searched the place, but someone had repaired the lock. Interesting. Perhaps Temming had not gone too far, then. Although it could also be someone hired to look after the place in its proprietor's absence.

Matthew considered knocking the damned door down; he doubted there was any new information inside, but it would relieve some of his pent-up frustration—but someone might come and report him to the magistrates. He had already disclosed news of the man's disappearance and likely malfeasance to local authorities, but to little avail. Even sending out a Bow Street runner would do little good if the runner did not know where to start.

Where was the wretched man? Temming had so much to answer for, and Matthew was increasingly maddened at the absence of anyone available to respond to his questions. He had to find Clarissa, if—he prayed—she was still alive. If not—if not, he would be sure that someone paid, and even then, he knew he would blame himself for the rest of his life.

Feeling the weight of his guilt heavy on his shoulders, Matthew frowned and, glancing at the address that Gemma had given him, made his way to a different office located in a much more reputable-looking court. This door had a brass plaque with *Augustus Peevey, Solicitor*, engraved upon it, and the plaque was polished to a high shine. The knob turned obligingly to his hand, and inside a clerk sat on a high stool.

The young man looked up. His collar was so fashionably high that he had to turn his head to gaze upon the visitor. "Yes?"

"I wish to speak to Mr. Peevey."

"Do you have an appointment?"

"No, but I will be brief. I have an important matter to discuss with him."

"I shall see if he is available, sir," the man said. "Your card?"

Matthew took a card from his pocket and passed it over. The clerk disappeared into an inner office, and reappeared quickly. "Mr. Peevey can spare a few minutes, Captain Fallon."

"Good of him," Matthew said, his voice dry. But he entered the office and found the solicitor standing to greet him.

"Good day, Captain Fallon," the older man said. He motioned to a chair. "How can I be of assistance? Is there a legal matter with which I can offer you aid?"

"You could assist me greatly if you could tell me where to find a solicitor named Temming, Ewart Temming," Matthew told him.

Mr. Peevey raised his narrow brows. "Ah." He sat down slowly behind his desk. "You have had dealings with Mr. Temming?"

"To my regret, yes," Matthew admitted.

"That is most unfortunate," the solicitor said. "I fear he does not have a blameless character."

"That, I have realized, but too late," Matthew retorted. Trying to keep his voice even, he told the other man briefly about his mother's death and his sister's disappearance.

"If not for a letter from a neighbor, I might not have heard about my mother's death for even longer. Temming sent me no word and, I now think, continued to pocket the money I sent that was to be used for my family's welfare," Matthew told him. "I'm not even sure if he had been forwarding them all of the funds I had sent earlier."

Mr. Peevey looked affronted. "That is a serious breach of ethics," he declared. "You have more than adequate grounds to take him to court."

"No doubt, but I have to find the wretch first. And I have a graver concern. My sister's whereabouts are unknown. Finding her is much more important to me than the chance of recovering any of the money. She was sent, I believe, to a foundling home you have had some dealings with."

He told the older man about his attempts to trace Clarissa through the home, and the intransigence of the matron there.

"That does not surprise me, either," the solicitor said.

"These places are often ill-run, and I was not impressed when I made my one visit to the foundling home, years ago. But I was not responsible for its choice, originally. The young woman I represented had been sent there before I was informed of her guardian's death, and I fear I have had little contact with the institution or the matron."

Matthew felt a wave of frustration. "And Temming? If there is anything you can do to point me to him?"

Mr. Peevey sat up straighter. "I assure you, I have not now, and have never had, any association with that man. He has had a most uncertain reputation for some time."

Matthew frowned. "So you can tell me nothing that might assist me in tracking him down?"

The solicitor shook his head. "I regret not. If you will leave me your address, however, I will certainly inform you if I should hear any account of his movements."

Matthew grimaced, but he said, "Thank you." He gave the other man the name of his hotel, then rose reluctantly.

When he went out, he found he felt even more discouraged, and more angry, than ever. Why did every possible lead end up a blind alley?

He couldn't keep himself from retracing his steps and heading back one more time toward the dingy side street where Mr. Temming conducted, or had once conducted, business. Matthew knew there was little chance he should catch anyone at the deserted office, but he felt he must keep trying. As he walked, his footsteps quiet on the grassy walkway, he recalled the last time he had seen his sister. Clarissa had hugged him and wept and told him she would pray every day for his safety at sea. The irony was bitter. He had come home more or less unscathed, and she was the one who had been endangered. At the thought, his heart seemed to twist inside him.

So he was paying little attention to his surroundings when he turned a corner into one of the less populated alleys.

A man leaped out at him.

Matthew stepped instinctively back a pace. "What do you—"

He had no time to finish. The roughly dressed man raised a club and swung it at Matthew's head.

London streets did indeed seem more dangerous than the high seas! Wishing vainly that he had come out with a sidearm, Matthew ducked and put up his fists.

But forced to keep out of reach of the crude weapon, he could not get close enough to land a blow of his own. The attacker swung again.

Matthew twisted and once more evaded the impact. But now he saw that his attacker was not alone. A second ruffian circled them both, trying to put Matthew between himself and his mate. If they managed to sandwich him between them, Matthew would give no odds as to the outcome. Both the men were burly, and their expressions determined. And if the second man managed to pin Matthew's arms . . .

Putting his back to the wall to keep them from stepping behind him, Matthew swore briefly and tried to think.

The first man swung once more. Matthew dodged the attack. The years he had spent on a ship's shifting deck had made him light on his feet, but in doing so, he was forced to step away from the building. Now he could not prevent the second man from sidling behind him. They were going to encircle him. Very well, then. All his senses on the alert, he waited for the man with the club to make his next attack.

This time, when the first ruffian advanced and swung his cudgel, Matthew feinted. He sidestepped the swing of the weapon. But instead of moving completely away, he grabbed the man's shoulders as the impetus of the attacker's rush carried him past Matthew. Then he thrust the villain toward his mate.

Swearing loudly, they collided. Matthew made his escape.

They still blocked the alley, and he could not go back the way he had come. He ran, scanning the alley for a quick way out of their sight. When he saw an arched doorway, he dove into it. Coming through the arch, he found himself in one of the many small courts that pocketed the area, but there was no other exit that he could see. The doors around the courtyard were all closed, and no one else was in sight. Where were all the hardworking clerks and lawyers? Or had he ventured into a different section of the neighborhood altogether? He had had little time to acquaint himself with the city's geography.

And now he heard footsteps pounding behind him. He caught a glimpse of the first man's ugly face as he peered through the archway.

"Hallo there?" Matthew called into the court.

A door opened at the end of the building and a head poked out. But as the two men ran into the courtyard, one of them brandishing the club, the head disappeared even more promptly.

Coward!

No one else seemed to hear, or if so, no one responded. Matthew turned and put up his fists, resolved to give the villains the best pummeling he could before they overcame him by sheer number.

Panting, the two ran into the court, then paused. The first one smirked. "'Ere 'e is," he sputtered. "Just like I tol' you. Let's make quick work of it now."

"You will be disappointed," Matthew declared, his voice controlled. "I have little blunt in my purse."

The first man sneered. "Don't matter, do it?" he said, his expression disdainful. "We already been paid, gov'nor. So whatever we take off your lifeless body is gravy, ain't it?"

Matthew braced himself and watched the man advance. He kept his gaze especially on the cudgel, now raised once again. But just then, from the corner of his eye, he saw a form emerge from one of the doors that opened onto the small court. To Matthew's relief, instead of fleeing from the altercation, this man came forward.

"What's this, then?" The newcomer's voice held a faint Scottish burr, but it was an educated inflection.

"These gentlemen, and I use the term loosely indeed, have an interest in my purse," Matthew said, keeping his attention focused on the two ruffians.

They glanced at the new addition, but neither seemed overly concerned at the change in odds.

"Best get out of here, gov'nor," the more talkative scoundrel advised. "You don't want to feel my club, too."

"Oh, I doubt that's a real concern," the stranger said.

Gentlemen did not generally carry concealed blades about their person. So Matthew was startled when, again from the edge of his vision, he saw the stranger reach down and pull a slim dagger from inside one of his boots.

"I think my blade might just trump your cudgel," the man suggested. "I think I'd run along now, if I were you, before we summon the watch."

Matthew felt a surge of relief and triumph, and the second ruffian grunted in alarm.

But the leader of the duo shook his head. "Sorry, gov. 'Fraid I got a higher card than that."

Tossing the club he had been wielding to his associate, he reached inside his rough-cut coat and drew out a large pistol.

# Ten

"*Bloody hell*," *Matthew muttered.*

Matthew's Good Samaritan hesitated. "Well put," he agreed. But as the man with the gun raised it and swung it back and forth between the two of them, as if not sure now which was the most pressing target, the stranger drew back his arm.

The flash of metal was almost too quick to see.

The first ruffian shouted, and the air seemed to explode. Blinking instinctively against the flash, his eyes stinging from the haze of powder that surrounded them all in a suffocating cloud, Matthew swung before the man could attempt to reload his pistol. It was hardly necessary. Although his fist connected with a satisfying thud with the man's weak-natured chin, Matthew saw, when his vision cleared, that the ruffian already sported the dagger impaled in his shoulder.

Their assailant looked down at the blade and swore profusely even as he stumbled backward from the impact of Matthew's blow, stepping on the foot of his mate.

The second man yelped. Although surely little hurt himself, he seemed disheartened by this unexpected turn of events. Turning, he lumbered away, leaving his wounded crony to fend for himself.

Matthew grabbed the man by the lapels of his dirty coat and jerked him forward. "Who sent you to attack me?"

The man blinked at him. "'Ere, now, I'm 'urt. Give a fellow some air, then."

"You were eager enough to hurt me! I don't care whether you suffocate or bleed to death. You said someone had paid you to harm me. I want to know the name!"

"Don't know 'is name," the man said.

Matthew stared into the man's face. "You would accept a commission of murder from a man whose name you don't know?"

"If 'e paid enough." The man started to shrug, then winced at the pain in his wounded shoulder.

"Then where did you encounter him?"

"Come on, gov, I'm bleeding to death!" the man whimpered.

"We should be so fortunate! Where did you receive this commission?"

"I dunno. Me mind is fogged. Just let me go, gov, and I won't bother you again, I swear it."

"We'll see to that," Matthew promised him grimly. "And you've strength enough to talk my head off! Tell me!"

"I meet 'im at the Rosy Rooster," the man said, his tone sullen.

"And where is that?"

"A tavern in Whitechapel," the man muttered. His voice did seem to be faltering, or else he was playing a good role. His unshaven face had paled, what Matthew could see of it. "Near the river, it is."

"And what did this man look like?"

But the man was slumping against Matthew's hold. Sighing, Matthew pushed him toward the door where the timid spectator had earlier looked out.

"Retrieve my blade," the stranger suggested from behind him.

Matthew took hold of the hasp and pulled hard. Ignoring their assailant's groan, he wiped the bloody blade on the wounded man's coat and tucked it into his waistband. Pounding on the door, he waited for someone to open it.

In a moment, the door opened just a crack. Matthew made out a narrow face and wide eyes.

"Go away, or we'll summon the watch!"

"That's exactly what I want you to do," Matthew snapped. "Here, make sure this rubbish is collected."

He dumped the wounded man onto the doorstep, while the clerk inside protested, his startled voice rising into a squeak.

Matthew ignored him and turned back to the man who had come to his aid. He was of middle height and dressed, if not richly, at least like a gentleman.

Matthew held out the blade. "Thank you," he said. "You may have saved my neck. A good thing that he was such a poor shot."

"Ah, as to that—" The stranger seemed to waver for a moment.

Matthew put out one hand to steady him. As he grabbed the man's arm, the stranger winced. Matthew felt dampness in the man's dark coat.

"You are hit?" Matthew exclaimed. "How bad is it?"

"A mere bagatelle," the other man answered.

But his color did not look good, and he put up little resistance when Matthew pushed back the dark coat, which had so far concealed the extent of his wound. The white shirt beneath revealed a spreading scarlet stain.

"We need to stop the bleeding," Matthew said, frowning. "Are any of these offices inhabited by men of more sense than that last fellow?"

"Not that I have noted," was the unhelpful answer. "I have rooms not far away—"

"I will take you there and we will summon a surgeon," Matthew began, but the man shook his head.

"Ah, no. Regrettably, there is a slight misunderstanding with my landlady. She seems to have locked me out of my flat."

"Behind on the rent, are you?" Matthew deduced. "We must do something, and my hotel is much too distant. Wait, I have an acquaintance who lives not too far away. . . ."

Draping the man's good arm around his neck, Matthew supported him back out to the street.

Several people stared curiously at them, but no one offered help. To his relief, Matthew soon saw a hackney coming along the pavement and was able to call to the driver. When he got his Good Samaritan inside the cab, Matthew gave the driver Miss Smith's address. Turning up on a lady's doorstep with a wounded man was not precisely your average social call, but he could think of nothing better. Perhaps he could convince the footman to allow him to bandage the wound and call for a doctor without disturbing the ladies of the house.

While they rode, he pulled off his linen neckcloth and made a pad to press against the wound. It seemed to slow the bleeding.

For once, traffic allowed them to proceed at a brisk trot. Still, Matthew was relieved when the cab pulled up in front of the residence where he had visited Miss Smith. He jumped out and tossed the driver a coin.

"You may have to help me," he said.

The driver frowned, but he tied up the reins and got down to help pull the wounded man out of the carriage.

"It'th nothing," the man they were supporting protested. But his Scottish burr seemed thicker and his words slurred, and the dark spot on his coat had spread.

They got him up to the door, and Matthew grabbed the brass knocker. It seemed as if all he had done today was bang on doors, he thought. That, and fight off an assault or two along the way.

The door opened, and the footman stared at him in suspicion. The hackney driver had driven away, and the wounded man leaned against the doorframe.

"Do you remember me?" Matthew demanded. "You should recall that I was here the other day to see Miss Smith."

"Yes, sir, but—"

"I require urgent assistance for my friend."

The servant frowned at the sight of the slumping man. "You don't wish to call upon the ladies with your friend in a besotted state, surely, sir?"

"He is not drunk. He needs a physician's aid right away. We were set upon by robbers. Is there a doctor in the neighborhood you can summon?"

Without waiting for an invitation, Matthew supported the stranger and moved them both inside the door. "Show us into a room the ladies do not use," he suggested.

The footman was staring at the bloodstains on Matthew's hand as he shifted the man's weight. His eyes wide, the servant blurted, "I—yes, sir, at once! Perhaps in the study." He hurried to open the inner door, and Matthew propelled the man inside.

"And tell the maid to bring hot water and clean cloths."

The footman set off at once, and Matthew was able to partially recline the wounded man upon a leather-covered settee.

At last he could pull off the coat.

"Damn shame," the other man muttered, his words marked by a Scottish cadence. "Haven't even paid the tailor afore some fool puts a bullet hole in't. What did you do tae that rascal, anyhow, me lad?"

"I have no idea," Matthew said. "I'm a bit busy just now. I'll explain the matter to you presently."

With the swiftness and efficiency born of long practice—he had assisted the ship's doctor more than once back when he was still an ensign—he stripped off the ruined shirt and examined the wound more closely.

At least the bullet seemed to have gone quite through the flesh, ripping the skin and perhaps bruising a rib, but it had not lodged inside, so the man would not have to bear the pain of its removal. Despite all the blood, no vital area appeared to have been hit. Matthew did not think it would be a dangerous wound, so long as it did not suppurate.

When the maid brought warm water and clean linen strips, he washed the torn flesh. At last Matthew made a neat bandage over the wound, while the stranger lay back and gritted his teeth.

"Surely they ha' some wine in this place?" he inquired.

"I'm sure they do." Matthew nodded to the maid, who looked somewhat pale. She took away the bloody water and rags and went into the hall, hopefully to fetch some strong drink.

Gunshot wounds always ached damnably, Matthew knew from his own experience. "It was good of you to come to my aid," he said.

The other man shifted as if seeking a more comfortable position, though the movement only made him wince again. "I would ha' thought twice if I'd known I would stop a bullet for my trouble," was the astringent answer.

Matthew laughed.

Then he looked over his shoulder, and his grin faded. Both the young ladies of the house stood in the doorway. He had hoped to avoid alarming them.

"My servants seem to be trying to shield me, Captain Fallon," Miss Crookshank said. "But I will not be kept ignorant in my own house. Are you in some difficulty? Is there something we can do to help?"

Behind her, Miss Smith looked apprehensive. Matthew threw her an apologetic glance. "I'm sorry that we have had to trouble you, but my friend was injured by street ruffians, and I had to find help quickly."

He stood and made a proper bow.

Miss Crookshank gasped.

Matthew looked around quickly. Had he not put away all the bloodstained rags? But nothing objectionable was in sight, and when he turned back, he saw their hostess was gazing at the man's face.

"You?" she exclaimed.

"You know him?" Matthew realized that he, on the other hand, did not even know the stranger's name.

"Lieutenant McGregor and I have met, yes," Miss Crookshank said. Her cheeks had flushed.

"Colin McGregor?" Matthew asked, knowing his voice had sharpened. "Major Colin McGregor?"

"Don't you know your friend's name?" Miss Crookshank demanded. "But he's not a major—"

"Not any longer," the man on the settee muttered. He had closed his eyes. "How did you know?"

"I had a friend in the light infantry. It was a much-repeated story, you know, bound to be," Matthew responded.

McGregor frowned and didn't answer.

"Then surely you can share it!" Miss Crookshank demanded.

"Louisa, it may not be something that can be repeated outside military ranks," Miss Smith put in. She sounded worried as she glanced from the wounded man to Miss Crookshank.

McGregor opened one eye. "It's na' anything improper, ma'am—miss—at least in the sense I think you mean. Only a near court-martial and a demotion in rank."

"But why?" Miss Crookshank sounded genuinely disturbed. "Did you do something dreadful? I don't believe it!"

Matthew took pity on her. The truth was less disgraceful than they would likely imagine, anyhow.

"McGregor disobeyed a direct order," he explained. "Given by an idiot of a colonel, to lead his men into direct range of French cannon for no good reason whatsoever. They would have been cut down like wheat before a scythe."

Both ladies made sounds of distress at the image.

"So the major led them round the flank, instead, and captured half a company of French and a score of cannon."

Miss Crookshank's expression warmed as she turned to

the lieutenant. "But, you should have been a hero!" she exclaimed. "You should have been advanced in rank, not demoted!"

He did not meet her eye.

"Nonetheless, I still disobeyed an order," McGregor explained, his voice low. "I was lucky not to be shot, but they needed officers, just then. It was a dicey time, and Boney—General Bonaparte—was still at the height of his power."

"But it makes no sense," she argued.

"It was the army, it does na' ha' to make sense," McGregor retorted.

The housemaid returned with a decanter of wine and glasses, and Matthew motioned toward it. "If I may?"

"Of course," his hostess said.

"And the surgeon is here, miss," the servant added. "Shall I show him in?"

"Yes, indeed. Tell him to hurry."

Matthew poured the wounded man a glass of wine. "You may need this," he muttered.

A stout man carrying a surgeon's bag appeared in the doorway. "Madam, sir. Ah, this is my patient, is it? Had a run-in with some street thugs, I understand? Dreadful, the way these scoundrels roam the city without a 'please' or 'thank-you' from anyone. Where is the watch when you need them, I ask you!" He shook his head, then suggested that they might wish to withdraw while he examined the injured man.

Sure that the women did not wish to watch poor McGregor be tormented further as the doctor probed at his wound, nor observe a half-naked man, and even surer that McGregor would not wish witnesses to his discomfort, Matthew ushered the ladies out, even though Miss Crookshank showed signs of wanting to stay and hold the fellow's hand.

But when the doctor, his expression adamant, shut the door, their hostess sighed and led them back to the drawing room. They sat down, and she poured a cup of cooling tea for Matthew.

Matthew accepted it and took a polite sip, though he would have preferred wine, himself. Their little adventure at the inns of court had made for a trying day.

"Why did those men set upon you?" Miss Smith asked. "Do you think it was a mere coincidence?"

He shook his head and put down the tea cup. "No, I do not. One of the men admitted they had been paid to put me out of action."

"Who would do such a thing?" Miss Crookshank looked shocked.

Matthew hesitated, then glanced toward Gemma Smith. "I am attempting to find a solicitor who has behaved dishonestly and who has information I very much need. It may be that I have annoyed him enough so that he is trying to retaliate."

"You must take care," Miss Smith told him, her tone anxious. "What are you going to do now?"

"I shall hire a Bow Street runner and send him to watch the tavern my attacker mentioned. I do not know if I have a good enough description of the solicitor Temming to make the watch pay fruit, but I cannot ignore any possible lead."

Gemma nodded. "And Lady Gabriel Sinclair has been to see us. She and I are going back to the foundling home tomorrow! I have hopes that the matron of the home will be more cooperative when dealing with a lady of influence than she was with me."

At the mention of the home, Matthew looked up and knew his gaze had sharpened. "Then I think you should have a male escort," he suggested.

She smiled at him, and her tone was warm. "I'm sure Lady Gabriel will appreciate your protection."

"I will be here," he promised.

When the surgeon reappeared and proclaimed that Lieutenant McGregor was fit to travel—"You didn't leave me much to do, sir," he told Matthew jovially—he accepted his fee and took his leave.

Matthew thanked the ladies again, settled the time to

meet for their journey tomorrow, then he and McGregor departed in another hackney.

Since the lieutenant had said he could not return to his lodgings, Matthew had no better idea than to take him back to his own rooms at the hotel. When they arrived, he helped him out of the cab, and with one arm supporting McGregor, Matthew led the way up to his door. He had taken a suite—a bedroom and sitting-room, with another small room off the bedroom for his valet's use.

His man was waiting. Short and stout and graying, he nonetheless reflected the air of quiet competence that had made him so indispensable aboard ship.

"This is Pattock, my purser during my last years at sea," Matthew explained to the wounded man leaning on his arm. "He was good enough to follow me into retirement when I left the navy."

To the servant, Matthew said, "My friend has had an accident. He came to my aid when I encountered a gang of thugs. His wound has been looked after, so let's get him into one of my nightshirts and put him to bed."

"Yes, sir," Pattock murmured. "And what, Captain, if I may ask, about you?"

"Tell the chambermaid to bring up a cot for me, for tonight, then we'll see."

McGregor protested, but his voice was still weak. Ignoring his objections, they stripped him, pulled a nightshirt over his head, and careful not to dislodge the bandage, tucked him into the bed. The doctor had given them a dark bottle of noxious liquid guaranteed to help the wounded man rest, and now Matthew poured out a spoonful. McGregor swallowed it, though he choked a little and swore briefly at the taste.

Then the lieutenant lay back against the sheets and sighed. "Have na' had a bed this comfortable in years. Not bad, this place. Beats my little rooms all hollow. Came home with prize money, did you?"

Matthew nodded.

"I should ha' gone into the navy instead of the army," the man on the bed muttered.

"Why didn't you?"

"Nae enough good sense. Besides, I'm afraid of water," came the drowsy answer.

Matthew looked at his valet. "Go and get us some wine, and tell the kitchen to make up some broth for the lieutenant. When he wakes from his nap, he will likely be hungry."

After Pattock departed, Matthew drew a chair up to the bed. "When you're on your feet again, I can advance you some blunt to pay your rent."

The other man shook his head. "'Fraid I don't know you well enough to borrow money," he muttered. "Nae offense."

Matthew swallowed a laugh. "None taken. Then how do you plan to get back into your lodgings, at least until you draw your next—"

"Pitiful half-pay packet? When my mind is sharp again, we'll have a hand of cards. Nae doubt I can win a few pounds off you." The lieutenant flashed a sudden grin.

"Don't be too sure," Matthew told him, still amused. "I'm a fair hand with a deck, myself. What were you doing at the Inns, this morning, if I may ask? Not that I'm not pleased you were there, as it turned out."

"So I could take the bullet meant for you?" The lieutenant scowled for a moment. "I'd been called there by a damned solicitor. Seems a lady I've been seeing has a father who wanted to warn me off—threatened action against me if I pursued any further the fair lady's hand."

Matthew nodded in comprehension. Many men married for money when they had no other prospects, but the lady, and her family, had to consent, of course. "Sorry to hear that. Bad luck for you."

"Oh, as to that, the lady in question has the disposition of a warthog, so I'm not totally devastated, I must admit. I may lack capital, but I'm still only human." McGregor grinned, displaying no sign of a bruised heart. "Inconvenient, however, as I'd spent the last of my funds—hence the small problem of the missing rent money—dining her and taking her to the theater in order to advance my suit."

"Then I suppose I must wish you a more amiable, and still wealthy, lady," Matthew suggested, watching as the other man yawned. The medicine seemed to be taking effect. "I'll leave you to rest, now."

The wounded man did not reply; his eyes had shut. Matthew went back into the sitting room, determined to think more about the duplicitous solicitor he sought, and how he might run him to earth. And if the image of a certain blue-eyed, dark-haired lady came often into his thoughts, instead—well, as the lieutenant had said, Matthew, too was only human. . . .

*After everyone had left, and the excitement had faded,* Gemma and Louisa were left to talk over their amazing day. Because Lady Gabriel had decided that she must go equipped with, as she said, every ammunition, she had told them she had some letters to write before their journey. For that reason, she had postponed their trip to the foundling home until the following morning. Gemma had been ready to set off at once, but she had to believe that Lady Gabriel had good reason for the delay.

So Gemma and Louisa, along with Miss Pomshack, shared an intimate dinner at home and discussed both the wounding of the brave lieutenant and Lady Gabriel's visit again in every detail.

"I would wager his war record is most distinguished," Louisa declared. "I just knew he must be a gallant soldier."

"Why, because he dallied with you in a shop?" Gemma murmured.

Her friend threw her an indignant look. Gemma grinned but kept silent as Louisa continued.

"And he was so modest, never mentioning his heroic

incident before this. I do hope the wound is not severe, and there is no infection."

"Of course, we wish for a full recovery," Miss Pomshack agreed. "I will add his health to my nightly prayers. We all will, I am sure. Although—" A new thought made her pause with a spoon halfway to her lips. "I trust, when the captain attended to his wound, you were not allowed to see him unclothed, Miss Louisa?"

"Of course not." Louisa kept her face impassive, and Gemma tried not to giggle.

"That would have been most improper," the older lady went on. "For two unmarried ladies to witness a man not in full dress—"

Gemma thought it best to change the subject, so she remarked, for the dozenth time, "Lady Gabriel is being so generous." And indeed, the thought of Lady Gabriel's assistance made Gemma feel almost giddy.

Her ploy succeeded admirably.

"Indeed, I am so distressed that I missed her call," Miss Pomshack muttered as she sipped her soup. "A very distinguished patron, Louisa. You are most fortunate. Why, the Hill family goes back three centuries, at least."

Louisa nodded, but didn't encourage her companion to indulge in flights of genealogy. "She is a truly gracious lady, and I am so gratified that she has decided to sponsor me. And her friend Mrs. Forsythe must be a charming lady, as well."

Gemma's thoughts were on the coming return visit to the foundling home. "I cannot imagine what Lady Gabriel—Psyche—meant by 'ammunition'? Do you have any idea, Louisa?"

Her friend did not appear to hear. "I shall not sleep a wink for the next week; wait until I tell Lucas!"

"Lady Gabriel has such a commanding presence. I can't think what else she would need. I find it most hard to call her by her first name. I am more apt to feel I should prostrate myself before her like some Eastern serving girl before the Pasha," Gemma mused.

Louisa looked up from a bite of boiled lobster. "Fie, Gemma. She may very well turn out to be your sister-in-law. You must try to be more at ease with her."

"I will try," Gemma agreed. "But it would be much easier—or I hope it will—if I knew for sure about my birth and my family. When the housekeeping book arrives, with my mother's handwriting in it—"

Louisa's thoughts had already strayed. "Oh, I must order a new ball gown! There is just enough time, I should think, to get a new one made up—"

"The Hill family supported the king during the Civil War," Miss Pomshack was saying as she sliced her beef into thinner pieces. "They were not among the Roundheads, I am glad to say. Even my father, the vicar, did not think much of the dictator Cromwell, I must tell you, despite the general's incessant Bible reading—"

"If the handwriting is the same, perhaps Lord Gabriel will give more credence to my story," Gemma said. "I wish he would receive a reply from his older brother, the present marquess. How long do you suppose it takes to get a letter back from Constantinople?"

"Perhaps a very pale pink—pink becomes me, don't you think, Gemma?" Louisa asked, taking a sip of her wine.

"And then, under the dear departed Queen Anne, there was a Hill, who was ambassador to Russia, no, I think it was Sweden?" Miss Pomshack continued her account.

Gemma looked from one of her companions to the other and tried again not to giggle. No one was paying heed to anyone else.

As if to disprove her, Louisa looked up suddenly. But it turned out, her mind was still focused on the weighty subject of attire. "It just occurred to me. Do you have a ball gown, Gemma?"

Aware of her wardrobe's deficiencies, Gemma flushed. "We had very few balls at the school for girls."

Louisa nodded. "Of course not, but don't worry. I have a ball gown from last year that we could alter very easily to fit you, and no one here has seen it."

"You're very kind," Gemma told her and meant it. But she was much more concerned with the imminent return visit to the foundling home than with the upcoming ball.

*Gemma spent a restless night.* At last morning dawned, and she could rise and dress and wait for Lady Gabriel—Psyche—to appear with her carriage. At least this time, she would not have to worry about a hackney deserting her miles from London, Gemma told herself as she sipped a cup of tea in the dining room. There was food on the side table, but she was too nervous to be able to swallow more than a bite of toast.

On the other hand, if the cab driver had not left her there, she could not have shared that ride home with Captain Fallon, snuggled so close against him as the horse trotted back to the city. Just remembering that close contact made a thrill run through her, her body reacting to the memory of his nearness. She had never before felt that response with any man.

When Louisa came downstairs, she greeted Gemma cheerfully. "You are up early! Are you sure that you do not wish me to accompany you? I would be happy to do so."

Gemma shook her head. "I shall have both chaperone and protector," she pointed out. "You might as well spend your day on more cheerful pursuits."

Louisa filled her plate and sat down. "An amazing story, is it not?"

Gemma looked at her. "What?"

"About Lieutenant McGregor. You must agree he was dreadfully wronged. Do you think his wartime experiences might account for his somewhat cynical approach to life?" Louisa looked dreamy.

Gemma frowned. "You told me yesterday he plans to marry an heiress, Louisa, and you would be a prime target if you were not already betrothed, which you are. Do not allow yourself to become too fond of him. I do not wish to see you hurt. Besides, what would Sir Lucas say?"

Louisa flushed, and her tone was defensive. "Of course not. I am simply sorry that he has suffered so much, that is all. And he has his own way to make in the world. That is not such a crime."

"He makes his way, as you put it, using his charm and impudence. Those attributes, along with his handsome face, should suffice to gain him the rich wife he seeks," Gemma pointed out.

Louisa frowned. "You needn't say it like that. At least he is honest about his intentions, you know. And I believe you prefer Captain Fallon's sterner good looks, so you have little room to talk. What would your Arnold say about that?"

For a moment, they glared at each other. Then a knock at the door could be heard, and Gemma drew a deep breath.

"Let us not quarrel," she said. "I am only thinking of your welfare, Louisa."

"I know," the other girl murmured. "But please, do not quote me uplifting advice. I get enough of that from Miss Pomshack."

Gemma grinned, and the tension eased just as the footman appeared in the doorway to announce, "Captain Fallon, miss."

He was a little early, also impatient to be off, Gemma deduced.

His glance toward her was warm, and she was irked to find herself blushing again, knowing that Louisa was watching.

But her friend said only, "Would you like a cup of tea, Captain?"

"Thank you." Matthew Fallon sat down and accepted the tea.

"How is Lieutenant McGregor?" Louisa went on, though she was careful, Gemma noted, to keep her tone merely polite. "I hope he is recovering?"

"He spent a somewhat restless night," Fallon told them.

"But he seems improved this morning. I left him still abed and hope he will remain there."

They both looked at him in surprise. The captain added, "He has had a difficulty, that is, I thought it best that he come back with me to my lodgings instead of staying all alone. He has no live-in servants."

"That was most thoughtful of you," Louisa told him, her tone approving.

Gemma was about to add her own praise when she turned her head. "Is that a carriage out front?"

Louisa pushed herself back from the table and hastened to the window. "Yes, a very smart chaise. It must be Lady Gabriel."

"We will not keep her waiting," Gemma said. She had already brought a shawl and bonnet and gloves downstairs. She donned them quickly, and then Captain Fallon escorted her outside to the carriage and helped her up. She introduced him to Lady Gabriel.

"Good morning," Psyche said.

Lady Gabriel looked very smart in an elegant pearl-gray costume trimmed with a sable collar. Large pearl eardrops and a long pearl necklace completed her outfit. If this lady, with her fashionable apparel and air of command, could not intimidate the matron of the foundling home into releasing information, no one could, Gemma thought. Her hopes rising again, she took a seat on the other side of the carriage.

Captain Fallon had brought his horse, which was tied up in front of the house, so he mounted and rode beside the carriage as they headed out of the city.

Aside from a few polite comments, they said little. Gemma was too eager to reach their destination, and Psyche also seemed to have her own thoughts. She did say, as they left the outskirts of London, "My husband is most concerned that we all find an answer to this puzzle, Gemma. I hope you will not judge him too harshly for his doubts."

Gemma shook her head. "Oh, no. I am aware that it is a very unusual situation."

Psyche sighed. "The most difficult possibility for him to

accept is the thought that his mother might have had a lover. We tend to see our parents as above reproach, not as ordinary mortals who sometimes make mistakes. I think men, especially, are inclined to view their mothers as blameless creatures."

Gemma nodded.

"For myself, having met the late marquis and judged him cruel and controlling, I am only happy that his poor wife might have had someone in her life who loved her and perhaps gave her a few interludes of happiness," Psyche said.

Gemma had not considered the matter in that light. Poor woman indeed, she told herself, tied for life to a tyrannical and unkind husband. Her mother had suffered deep tribulations. They both fell silent, and as the carriage rolled along, Gemma's reflections returned to the foundling home and the reception they might expect there.

When the home came into view, Gemma tensed. She waited impatiently for the carriage to roll to a stop. Captain Fallon dismounted while Psyche's groom helped them both down. "Wait for us here," Psyche told her coachman, and she led the way to the door.

The captain rapped smartly upon it, and again, they had to wait several minutes for any response.

At last, the door opened, and another small girl peeked around it.

"No callers today," she said, her tone uncertain.

Was that the invariable response, Gemma wondered? It had not worked before, and it was certainly not going to deter Lady Gabriel.

Psyche pushed the door wider and smiled down upon the child. "It's all right. Mrs. Craigmore will wish you to admit us. You may tell her that Lady Gabriel Sinclair, and friends, are here to see her."

The child gazed at this fashionable vision with widened eyes. She remembered belatedly to dip a curtsy, then ran back down the hall to summon the matron.

"Where is this woman's office, Gemma?" Psyche murmured.

"This way." Gemma led them down the hall to the door at the far end.

Psyche tapped on the door lightly, and without waiting for a response, opened it. The room was empty of inhabitants and not very tidy.

Gemma glanced about, unable to prevent a quick look toward the shelves where the missing ledgers, which were still sitting in her bedroom at Louisa's house, had once sat. If only they had revealed more!

Psyche examined a wooden chair and apparently decided to stand. Now footsteps sounded in the hall outside, and in a moment, the matron appeared. Mrs. Craigmore was breathing a little fast, whether from climbing the steps from the lower level or from apprehension, Gemma was not sure.

Gemma braced herself as the older woman threw them all a sharp glance.

"What's this about? You have no business here, and why are you in my office! You, you were here before! I'll have you know—"

"You will not send us away today," Captain Fallon declared, his tone stern.

The woman bristled. "You don't tell me what to do. This is my establishment, and I shall have you put out!"

"I very much doubt it," he told her.

Gemma did, as well. When Captain Fallon spoke in that tone, she could easily imagine a whole shipload of sailors jumping to do his bidding. Even the matron looked taken aback, but in a moment, she rallied.

"I got nothing to say to you," she managed, "none of you. You might as well be on your way."

The captain lifted a brow, and Psyche took a paper from her reticule. "I am Lady Gabriel Sinclair. I have a note from your local magistrate, Mrs. Craigmore, appointing me to head your board of directors."

"We—we ain't got a board of directors," the other woman sputtered.

"Yes, I discovered that, and the magistrate was shocked

to hear it. This institution should not be operating without supervision. I shall collect some like-minded, charitable matrons to aid me, and we will put this place into order. The magistrate, you see, was also alarmed to learn that there have been reports that the children here are not being properly cared for. I have come to see for myself and, if necessary, to remedy the situation."

"Lies!" the matron exclaimed. "Who would cheapen me good name in such a way? Think you're so important with your high and mighty airs, do you? You can just take yourselves off, title or no, and leave off slandering me reputation! If you wish to arrange a visit, say in a week or two—"

"Oh, no," Psyche continued, her voice calm. "I intend to see all the children today, their lodgings, their clothing, the food they eat, the lessons they are given. We will also examine all your records—"

"You can't! Anyhow, me books were stolen by some scurrilous thief just a few days ago." The matron narrowed her eyes.

"Very convenient," Psyche noted, her expression skeptical.

Gemma swallowed, glad that Psyche did not know everything that had happened here. She threw a quick look toward Captain Fallon. A gleam lighting the depths of his dark gray eyes, he met her glance. But like her, he remained silent.

"I shall see the children first," Psyche declared. "If you would come with me, please, Mrs. Craigmore?"

A vein throbbed in the matron's temple. Gemma braced herself for the roar she knew would come, but—to her amazement—the woman swallowed hard, instead. "I left me shawl in me room. The halls are drafty."

Without further ado, she turned and hurried up the hall.

Psyche raised her brows as they watched the woman's back. "It *is* cold inside the building. Do the children have any wraps?" she wondered aloud.

"If you will allow me, Lady Gabriel." Captain Fallon

nodded toward the desk. "I will take a quick look to see if any records are here."

"Of course," Psyche agreed. Her expression grim, she paced up and down as she waited for the matron to return.

Gemma went to look over the captain's shoulder. But although he worked his way steadily through the desk, its drawers and shelves revealed only a scattering of papers, and none of them appeared significant.

"Perhaps you should look—" Gemma began, when an exclamation made her pause.

"Look!" Psyche pointed to the window.

They hurried closer. Through the dirty pane, Gemma made out the remarkable sight of Mrs. Craigmore, the matron's plump figure moving at an unexpectedly rapid pace. The woman was making for the trees. She carried a small carpetbag under one arm and clutched a shawl about her shoulders.

"Stop!" Matthew Fallon shouted, but the rapidly departing figure paid little heed.

He pushed up the sash of the window and climbed through. Landing with a thump on the hard ground, he sprinted after her.

"Oh, my," Psyche said. "This is unexpected. I'm sure she was annoyed to have me come and question her methods and poor management, but why would the woman run away? Are conditions here so bad she thinks I will have her up before the magistrate?"

Gemma wrinkled her nose. "She is afraid of something, obviously." She wondered if she should chase after the woman, too, but she was sure the captain was more fleet of foot, and it was doubtful that even he could catch the fugitive. Despite the woman's years and girth, she had a considerable head start, and she must know the paths behind the foundling home better than they would.

By the time they had gone downstairs and inspected the kitchen—its dirty tables and filthy floors made Psyche blanche, and the empty larder caused her to look grave—Captain Fallon returned to report that he had lost the woman in the woods.

He was frowning. "I fear she has taken any knowledge of my sister's fate with her," he told them, his tone short.

Gemma had similar fears about the information she searched for, but even so, her heart went out to him. The pain and worry that darkened his gray eyes made her put out one hand, but she drew it back, blushing, before he noticed.

The other two seemed absorbed in their own thoughts. Psyche had just discovered the cook asleep in a back room and was informing her, in no uncertain terms, of the change of direction that the foundling home was about to take.

"If you wish to keep your position, you will scrub every inch of this kitchen," Psyche instructed, her tone crisp. "At once!"

Rubbing her eyes with her dirty apron, the woman came into the kitchen and gaped at them. "But who be you to say? Miz Craigmore don't fret herself about a little dust—"

"Mrs. Craigmore is no longer in charge," Psyche interrupted. "What were you planning to give the children for their dinner?"

"The usual—soup." The cook nodded toward a large kettle at the side of the hearth.

Lifting its lid, Psyche shook her head at the thin, oily-looking liquid inside. Gemma felt her stomach roil as the once-familiar odor, from soup composed mostly of boiled cabbage and onion with a few chunks of rancid meat, wafted toward her.

"I shall send my coachman to the nearest village to buy foodstuffs. I expect you to have the kitchen clean enough to cook them by the time he returns!" Psyche told her.

"But, Miz Craigmore 'as all the money," the other woman argued.

"Just get to work."

The comment made Gemma glance toward Captain Fallon. "We should go through her bedchamber," she suggested. "She might have hidden something there."

They made their way to a room at the back of the
ground floor, while Psyche continued to the next level
where the drone of children's voices could be heard. When
they opened the door, the matron's room revealed evidence
of her rapid flight. A wardrobe door stood ajar, and items
of clothing littered the floor. Gemma stepped over a dirty
shift and looked about her.

"There." Gemma pointed.

Captain Fallon crossed to the small chest at the foot of
the bed. Its lid stood open. Except for several bottles of
gin, there was little left inside. They found a small metal
box, with one farthing overlooked at its bottom.

"Her cash box," he said. "I suspect she took the rest of
the money with her."

They searched the room quickly. Gemma wrinkled her
nose at the stale scent of the bed linen but forced herself to
check beneath the pillows and mattress, without luck.

"What about the school rooms or the children's bedrooms?"

"There are only long dormitories in the attic," Gemma
told him. "And she would surely leave nothing of importance within the children's reach. Let's look in the office
one more time."

They made their way down the hall and back into the
by-now familiar room. The shelf where the ledgers had sat
looked bare, and they had already checked the desk, but
Captain Fallon went again through its drawers.

Watching him, Gemma felt an old memory stir. "We
were not allowed to dust her desk," she said suddenly. "We
were not supposed to even touch it. I forgot the admoni-
tion, once, and had my ears boxed for my trouble."

Captain Fallon paused and looked at her. "Really? Do
you recall exactly where you were dusting?"

"The molding along the top," Gemma said, "just there."
She held her breath as he touched the wide wooden edge of
the desk, pushing and prodding.

Then she heard a small click. It sounded loud in the
quiet of the room.

"What was that?" Gemma whispered.

"Something opened—here it is!" Captain Fallon pushed the small door wider and motioned to a compartment that had been hidden behind the thick trim.

Gemma leaned closer and saw several rolls of paper. "What is it?" Her heart was beating so fast that she held tightly to the desktop for support.

He unrolled the papers quickly. She saw a list of names. Oh, had they found it at last, Mrs. Craigmore's cache of secrets?

# Eleven

*H*e *turned to her and grasped her shoulders. Before* Gemma could guess his intent, he pulled her close and gave her an impulsive kiss.

At the firm touch of his lips against hers and the closeness of their bodies, Gemma felt heat rush through her like a bolt of lightning exploding out of a hitherto calm summer sky.

She felt weak and strong at the same time. Exhilarated, her ears roared and her vision blurred. The kiss seemed to last forever, and it was much too brief. When he stepped back just as abruptly, she knew she should be shocked, but it was disappointment she struggled to contain.

"I beg your pardon," he said, his voice stiff. "That was inexcusable."

But despite his words, his face betrayed him, his eyes still bright with, surely, the same intoxicating emotions that had overwhelmed Gemma all too briefly. She wanted to grab him and pull him back, but of course, a lady could not behave in such a way.

For the first time, she regretted that she was, very likely, a lady.

"I was simply—I was overcome with—with . . ." he stammered.

"I understand," she said, managing a smile that she hoped was not too wide. "If this tells us where your sister may be—and where my antecedents can be traced—it is certainly a cause for celebration!"

He nodded, and, to her regret, released her shoulders. But he appeared to be in control of himself again, although she noted that he still breathed quickly, as if he had been running. Her own breath sounded ragged, and her pulse raced. She looked away from him and tried to pull her mind back to their mission.

He turned back to the desk and unrolled the largest sheet. They both scanned the contents. They found his sister's name, first: *Clarissa Fallon.* After it was scribbled another word and a figure.

Gemma narrowed her eyes to make out the crabbed script. "*Clapgate, 20 shillings?* What does that mean? And why would there be a sum of money noted?"

This time the look in his dark eyes made her shiver, and not at all in the delightful way she had felt a moment ago. But he did not share with her the concern that caused him to look so grim. After a moment, he answered.

"Clapgate—I have not heard of it, but it may denote a town or a village. Are there any maps in the schoolroom?"

Gemma nodded, but she was still searching the list for her own name. She found it toward the very top of the paper. Of course, it had been more than fifteen years since she had lived in this horrid place. But to her disappointment, she was listed only as *Gemma Smith*, though there was a small question mark after the surname, as if Mrs. Craigmore had doubted its authenticity, too. And beside it was written only: *taken away, no fee.*

She sighed in regret. Was this all there was of the matron's records? If only Gemma could have shaken the rest of her secrets out of the woman before she had decamped so abruptly!

Looking up at the man beside her, his face still dark with emotion, Gemma knew he felt an even deeper frustration. She had thought him lost in his own worries, but now he caught her eye. "I regret there is so little here to help you," he said.

Surprised that he should remember to think of her when his own concerns were so intense, Gemma felt warmed inside, and some of her disappointment eased. "Yes. And I am sorry, too, that we have no better clue to your sister's location. Come upstairs, and I will show you where any maps might be found."

They climbed the steps together. Since the kiss, she had a new, even stronger, awareness of him as a man, the masculine scent of him, his strong step on the stairs. She felt her lips tingle again, just remembering the contact they had shared.

On the first landing, a pail of dirty water and two scrub brushes lay abandoned, and down the hall they saw more brushes and cleaning rags left untended. Gemma smelled the usual mixture of stale linen and unaired rooms. But they saw no children until they reached the big empty hall that had served sporadically as a schoolroom. Here Psyche had apparently gathered all the foundling home's inhabitants. More than two dozen children, eyes big at this unprecedented turn of events, sat huddled together on benches. The assistant matron, Miss Bushnard, stood at the side, shifting from one foot to another as she eyed Lady Gabriel with nervous apprehension.

If she had questioned the newcomer's authority, that battle had already been concluded, and Gemma had no doubt as to who the victor had been.

Her tone pleasant but firm, Psyche was speaking. "You have no reason to be afraid. Mrs. Craigmore has departed, but after even the most cursory inspection, I should have seen to her dismissal regardless, so it's of no matter. We

shall be making inquiries for a new matron, and Miss
Bushnard, if she can follow my directions, will oversee the
home until a new head is chosen. We are going to see to a
thorough turning out of the building, and all the children
must have baths, immediately. The bed linen will have to
be boiled, and some of it may have to be burned." She
turned to the cowering assistant and added. "You are very
lucky not to have had an outbreak of disease, already. I
have seldom seen such conditions!"

Miss Bushnard sounded meek and completely demoral-
ized. "I were only following orders, ma'am—milady."

Psyche went on. "The girls all need new clothes, regular
baths, and, first of all, a decent meal. Then we shall draw
up a daily schedule of studies for the children."

"But their chores—"

"A reasonable program of household duties will be included, but I wish to see them do more than scrub floors!
They must learn some skills in order to prepare themselves
for the time they leave the home," Psyche told the other
woman.

Miss Bushnard snorted. "These lot? They're only fit for
scullery maids and worse, 'ardly a brain in their 'eads!"

Psyche bristled. "I am sure you are mistaken. My own
mother, who was admittedly advanced in her views, advo-
cated education for all females, whatever their class. Not
all of the children may turn out to be scholars, but they can
all learn to read and write and do their sums. They can
learn to sew; seamstresses are always in demand. And
some might surprise you by progressing much further. As
long as I am on the board of directors, they will at least be
given the opportunity."

Gemma looked over the children with their dirty faces
and matted hair; she had seldom seen a more unprepos-
sessing group. They were all in need of clean clothes and
baths, several had runny noses and, obviously, no hand-
kerchiefs, and most either stared down at the floor or
showed eyes blank with alarm. Had she looked much like
this during the time she had stayed here? She remem-

bered the days of drudgery and the nights of wrenching loneliness. . . . Poor mites . . . She found that she had a lump in her throat.

Psyche glanced down at one of the smaller children. The little girl was weeping quietly. "Here, now," Psyche said, her tone gentle. She knelt and put her arms around the child. "There is no reason to cry. What is wrong? If you are missing Mrs. Craigmore—"

The girl shook her mop of tangled hair. "No, miss. She only just walloped us a lot. But—be you going to send us away, too?"

Psyche tightened her grip. "No, no. You will have better food and a safer home, that is all. I promise you."

Her own eyes brimming, Gemma had to turn away. She blinked hard to hold back the tears, then felt a strong hand on her shoulder. She lifted her face to see that Captain Fallon stood beside her. His gaze was rich with compassion and understanding.

For a moment, their eyes met, and without a word being said, something passed between them that she could not have defined. But she felt comforted. Presently, he reached inside his coat and drew out his handkerchief to offer her, and she wiped her cheeks.

"Thank you," she said softly. "And I have a thought. You might want to ask the older girls if anyone remembers your sister's stay and how she left."

"An excellent idea," he said, and she thought that his voice sounded husky. They turned back to the group, and Gemma selected a knot of taller girls at the back.

Psyche was still comforting the younger ones. Gemma explained briefly that this gentleman was searching for his sister.

"Do any of you remember Clarissa Fallon? She resided here several years ago."

"She had blond hair with a hint of red in it, and hazel eyes," the captain added. "Her face is narrower than mine, but she has the same brows."

Several of the older girls, who might have been eleven

or twelve, shook their heads, but one pursed her lips, as if thinking. "I remember 'er. She often nattered 'bout a brother who was at sea. That you?"

His expression eager, Matthew Fallon nodded. "Yes. Do you remember when she left?"

The girl shrugged. "Dunno. A long time ago, five summers, maybe six."

"Where did she go?"

"Never was told," the girl answered. "Miz Craigmore called 'er to the office and then she just never came back."

The captain's mouth tightened.

Gemma felt disappointment flow through her again. "Thank you," she told the girl. "If you think of anything else that might help us, please let us know."

Gemma touched Captain Fallon's arm. "Over here are the books." She led him to the corner and the small collection of books, all that the foundling home boasted. Among the lot was an atlas of England, its corners frayed and its pages faded. The captain opened it and scanned the maps of the counties.

"I will go and help Psyche with the children," Gemma told him.

She joined Lady Gabriel and sat down on a bench to talk to the children, offering hugs and reassurance to the big-eyed urchins in their grimy pinafores, uniforms whose blue hue—now barely discernable—had long ago faded toward varying shades of gray. Even the sight of that apparel made her shiver with memories, just as the smell of the home still turned her stomach. She had never worn blue since the day she had left the foundling home. Fortunately, the school in York had allowed her to select her own gowns. They might have been of simple muslin and plain in style, but they had been a color of her own choosing.

After a time, Captain Fallon closed the atlas and came back to her side. "I have found two villages with the name of Clapgate," he told her in a quiet voice. "One is in Hertfordshire, and another at the far end of Cornwall. I will hire a runner to go into the West Country, and I myself will travel to the hamlet in Hertfordshire and make inquiries. It is closer and seems somewhat more likely."

She nodded, although she felt a moment of loss thinking of his departure. But of course he must continue the search for his sister. If only her own brother had been so diligent about her well being . . . if only her brother had known she was in need of him! And most of all, if only he would believe her now. . . .

"Do let me know what you find out," she told him. "God speed, Captain Fallon."

She put out her hand, and he pressed it. She relished the warmth of his touch and wished wildly that she could prolong the contact. For a moment longer he held her hand tightly inside his own, and she could not read his gaze. Then he turned away and bade farewell to Lady Gabriel.

Matthew Fallon was a curious paradox, she told herself. He was obviously still ruled by his long years of self-discipline, a habit necessary if he were to command a ship at sea, yet she felt certain that passion surged inside him, hungry to be released. He possessed such strength and such gentleness at the same time, and the combination moved something inside her. She watched him as he walked through the doorway and out of sight, observed his wide shoulders and well-shaped back, his fair hair— everything about him pleased her, even when she saw him only from this vantage point. She tried to imprint it all in her mind's eye.

"God speed," she whispered again. "I hope you find what you are seeking."

Then Psyche called to her, and Gemma turned.

"Can you find paper and pen?" the other woman asked. "Before we leave, we should make an inventory of the linen that needs to be replaced and get some idea of how many dress lengths should be ordered."

Gemma went back to the corner where the meager supplies were kept and found paper and a jar of ink and a quill, though she had to search again for a penknife to sharpen its point. But while she wrote down, at Psyche's direction, *four dozen sheets, three dozen pillows*, her thoughts were heading north with the captain.

⌒

*Louisa found the day long without her friend's company.* With Miss Pomshack to accompany her, she went out in the morning and spent several hours selecting fabric and trimmings and a design for her ball gown, which the couturier promised to have completed in time for Mrs. Forsythe's ball.

They returned in time for a late luncheon, and shortly after, Miss Pomshack retired for her afternoon nap.

"Should you not have a lie-down, too, Miss Crookshank?" the older lady suggested. "You seem a bit melancholy today."

"Thank you, Miss Pomshack," Louisa answered, her tone polite. "I shall likely go upstairs soon. I have a letter to complete, first."

And she did sit down at the desk in the drawing room and finish a missive to her aunt and uncle in Bath. She wrote only cheerful tidbits of information. She had never shared her humiliation at the theater or her growing doubts about the success of her mission to gain admittance to the Ton. And now, at last, she had good news to report: Lady Gabriel's amazing kindness and the invitation to the ball, which Louisa eagerly awaited.

When she had blotted her last line and folded the letter, Louisa looked up to see the footman come to the door of the drawing room.

"Sir Lucas Englewood, miss," he announced, then stepped out of sight.

She jumped up and ran to meet her fiancé as he entered the room. "Lucas, how lovely to see you. Did you have a nice time?"

"Oh, yes. Jolly good match," he told her, gripping the hand she held out for a brief moment. "Not that you would have cared for it, with all the blood and feathers flying."

Louisa shuddered. "No, I should think not. But I am glad to see you back. The most wonderful thing, Lucas—"

"Find the perfect new bonnet?" He grinned at her. "That shade of pink looks very well on you, Louisa. London seems to be agreeing with you. Oh, I have to beg off for dinner tonight, came to make my apologies."

His tone was quite cheerful, and he didn't seem to be paying attention to her announcement. Louisa nodded in acknowledgment of the compliment, but her smile faded quickly at the statement that followed. "But why? I have hardly seen you this week."

"I know, but there's a dinner at my club tonight that I don't want to miss. There's a bet on about how many oysters ol' Pikestaff can consume without casting up his accounts."

"Obviously, not something one would wish to miss," Louisa agreed, knowing that her tone sounded dry. "I am glad you are having such a good time in London, Lucas. Especially since I was the one who urged our coming up for the Season."

"You were quite right, too," he told her. "I give you full credit for it. London has much more to amuse a fellow than Bath."

"But you might remember to include me occasionally in those amusements, you know," she snapped. "We are to be married, Lucas. That does mean you are supposed to enjoy sharing my company now and then."

His expression wary, he stared at her. "Now, don't take a pet, Louisa. Of course I enjoy your company. We shall get up another party for Vauxhall, soon. I know several new fellows to invite, too, this time. We shall be very merry."

Louisa tried to hold on to her temper. "I am glad to hear it. And I do enjoy the pleasure garden. On Monday night, perhaps?"

"We'll see. I think I have another commitment that evening," Lucas said vaguely. "But soon, I promise."

"What about dinner tomorrow?"

"Ummm, I'll let you know," he said.

"Lucas!" She wanted to stamp her feet, but restrained herself.

"I don't have to show up at your table every day, Louisa," he pointed out with maddening calmness. "You have your shopping and your tea parties, all the usual stuff ladies do. And after all, it's not as if we are already married."

Louisa bit her lip. "And when we are? Lucas, do you mean to spend this much time out with your male friends, then?"

He didn't meet her eyes. "No one spends all his time sitting at home with his spouse, Louisa. Thought you were up on all the Ton's fashionable habits."

"I never said I put fashion above affection," she said simply. "I don't want to hold you prisoner, Lucas, nor do I wish to pick a quarrel, but I do like to know that you are still sincerely attached to me. Our marriage would hardly prosper, else."

"Of course I am." He leaned over and gave her a quick kiss on the forehead. "And yes, that's the ticket. No need for a spat."

Louisa bit back a quick retort. Why could he not grasp her meaning? Or perhaps he did not wish to, she thought.

After a few more pleasantries, he made a quick departure. Louisa listened to his footsteps fade as he clattered rapidly down the stairs. She had never even told him about Lady Gabriel and the upcoming ball.

He didn't seem to have any great interest in whether or not Louisa was making progress with the Ton, the whole purpose of her visit to London. That thought, and more, brought her more hurt than anger. She stared into the empty grate, and although the day was mild, she felt strangely cold inside.

*Lord Gabriel Sinclair was growing concerned by the* time his wife returned. He had already responded to an inquiry from their butler, telling him to convey a message to the cook to hold dinner back, when at last he heard the front door close and her voice in the hallway.

He went to the doorway of the library and looked out. "How did it go, my dear?"

She looked tired as she removed her hat and gloves, but she raised her head and smiled at him. "There is a great deal to be done. The foundling home is in a dreadful condition, and the children shockingly neglected. But I intend to remedy all that in very short order."

"I have no doubt that you will," he told her, pleased to see the familiar spark in her blue eyes, the fighting spirit that had been sadly missing for many months. He held out his arms, but she shook her head.

"You don't wish to hold me close, my love, at least not until I have bathed and changed my clothes. I held several of the children on my lap and hugged them, as well; it was impossible not to. I may even have to send my dresser out to purchase a fine-toothed comb! As I said, they have been most poorly looked after."

Regardless of her warning, he pulled her into his arms. "Then we shall share the comb," he declared, kissing her soundly. "A small price to pay to see you looking ready, once again, to take on the world."

She returned his kiss, and some of the ache inside him eased. Somehow, tending to the orphaned children seemed to have released the sorrow inside her more effectively than any of his pampering had been able to do. Whatever was the outcome of the strange story of the girl who claimed to be his sister, if she helped Psyche heal, the mysterious Miss Smith would have earned his gratitude. . . .

*Louisa was waiting downstairs when Gemma at last* arrived home, conveyed safely by Lady Gabriel's carriage.

"Gemma, how was it? Was Lady Gabriel shocked at the

children's state? What did she say? And did the matron tell
you anything helpful?"

Gemma sighed "I am sorry to be so late. There is much
to be done at the home, and Psyche wished to make a start,
so we did not leave until we saw the children fed and a beginning made on the cleaning, though it will take weeks to
turn the place out completely. I hope you did not wait dinner for me? I would not wish to spoil your plans, and I
know Sir Lucas was expected."

"He could not come," Louisa said shortly. "Miss Pomshack and I have eaten, but Cook is keeping your dinner
warm. Would you like it in the dining room or in your room?"

"I should like to wash, first." Gemma shuddered. "I feel
as if the stench of that place is on my skin, and I do not
think I can eat a bite until I am free of it!"

"It was brave of you to go back at all. I know your memories are not good." Louisa looked at the footman. "Tell
Lily we wish a hip bath prepared for Miss Gemma, please,
right away. Then afterwards, she will have a tray in her
room."

"And you can tell me everything," she added to Gemma.

Gemma nodded. Aching with fatigue, her still-healing
shoulder throbbing, she slowly climbed the steps. She
scrubbed herself thoroughly, as if to rid herself of all
trace of that wretched home, then soaked herself in the
tub and, with Lily's help, washed and rinsed her hair.
Then she dried herself and sat by the fire to brush out her
dark locks. Afterward, she wrapped a thick shawl around
her nightdress and was ready when Lily brought up a
tray.

At least, knowing that the children at the foundling
home—to their obvious astonishment—had enjoyed unaccustomed largess today in the form of fresh-baked brown
bread and a thick chicken and vegetable stew, Gemma
could eat her own dinner with a clear conscience.

Louisa came and sat in the other chair and waited with
commendable patience until Gemma had cleaned most of

the food on her plate, then she said, "Now, tell me every-thing."

So Gemma told her about Mrs. Craigmore's flight, which made Louisa gasp, then the discovery of the hidden lists, and the scraps of information it had contained.

"Just fancy!" Louisa said. "A shame it was not more ex-plicit. Why would she hide them, Gemma, when there seems to be so little there?"

"The money may be the key," Gemma said slowly. "Most of the names had a sum of money after them. I think that is what worried the captain the most."

"But . . ." Louisa paused. "You don't think—"

Neither of them could bear to spell out the worst fate that might befall a helpless young girl with no family or friends to look out for her, but dark thoughts had been tor-menting Gemma almost since she'd seen the list.

"We shall hope for the best until we know for sure," Gemma answered, suppressing a shiver. "But I know that Captain Fallon feels even more pressed to find his sister as soon as possible."

If the girl were still alive, Gemma reflected. To change the direction of her thoughts, she added, "Tell me about Sir Lucas. Was his return to London delayed? I'm sorry you were not able to see him for dinner. You must be missing his company."

"More so than he seems to be missing mine!" Louisa re-torted, more tartly than Gemma had expected. "I hardly seem to know him anymore."

Keeping her tone soothing, Gemma said, "He is most likely simply caught up in the pleasure of new confidants and a wide variety of amusements. Surely, you do not think his affections toward you have altered?"

Looking down at the edge of her wrapper, Louisa hesi-tated. She stroked the smooth lace trim absentmindedly. "I'm not sure, Gemma. He seems to show little concern about my happiness, or lack of it. He doesn't pay heed when I am low in spirits or when I am thrilled. I never finished telling him my wonderful news about Lady Gabriel and the ball, and he didn't even notice."

Louisa sounded truly troubled. Gemma felt a pang of sympathy. She put aside her dinner tray and reached out to pat her friend's shoulder. "He is likely just being somewhat heedless. I don't have a great deal of experience, but I believe young men sometimes are."

"But I have an even greater concern," Louisa added, her voice now very low. "I am afraid my own feelings may have changed."

"Louisa! Are you in earnest?" Gemma sat up straighter. "But I thought you adored Sir Lucas?"

"So did I—think that I adored him, I mean." Louisa sighed, still not meeting her friend's gaze. "Last year, when we had our disagreement and were parted for a time, I missed him enormously. I cried myself to sleep many a night. But now . . . I wonder, Gemma, if what I missed was the certainty of having someone there for me. . . . After my father died, it was a comfort knowing that Lucas would be at my side whenever we went out, and I did not have to worry about feeling alone. Perhaps I was more enamored of being in love than of loving Lucas himself. I mean, we grew up together, just about. I have known him since we were children. And sometimes, indeed, he seems to treat me more like a sister than a sweetheart."

Gemma started to point out that she had no idea how a brother might behave to his sister, but decided that might sound bitter. And she did not wish to check the flow of confidences. "Really?"

Louisa nodded. "He rarely steals kisses from me anymore." She blushed a little. "He kissed me on the forehead today, as if I were a child. I just wonder—"

"You cannot marry him if you are not sure!" Gemma asserted. "It's not as if you will go hungry if you do not wed, Louisa. You are fortunate to have money of your own, thanks to your father's diligence."

"Yes, I know I am blessed to have my own income. But

as to the marriage—I ended an engagement last year, Gemma. I cannot do it again!"

Gemma stared at her. She had heard nothing of that. Obviously, the usually open Louisa was still sensitive about her actions if she had not shared the tale. And no wonder, Society could be harsh on those who did not honor their betrothal vows. "I'm sure you had a good reason."

"I did." Louisa sighed again. "I rushed into a commitment too quickly, partly to assuage my hurt after Lucas broke off our relationship. It was precipitous and unwise. As time passed, I saw that we were not a good match. And the—my former suitor—did not end up brokenhearted. But the fact remains, I cannot jilt another gentleman!"

Feeling real concern, Gemma stared at her friend. "But, Louisa, it's your whole life we are talking about—"

"I can't!" the other girl repeated, her expression stubborn. "So I shall just have to hope for the best. Whatever I feel, I will be a loyal and attentive wife. And perhaps I am mistaken about Lucas's indifference to me. I do pray that I am."

She wiped her eyes, and with an effort, Gemma held her tongue. No need to point out all the pitfalls that lay ahead if the marriage turned out to be truly loveless. Louisa would have thought of it all without help from anyone else.

Gemma stretched out her hand, and Louisa clasped it. They were both silent. Presently, Louisa relaxed her almost desperate grip and stood.

"I know you are tired. I will leave you to sleep," she said. She went out and shut the bedroom door behind her.

Gemma sighed as she watched her friend go. As she reached to extinguish the candle by her bed, she wondered if either of them would sleep tonight. She knew her thoughts would be with Captain Fallon, and Louisa had her own worries. Gemma's mind flashed back to the day they had arrived in London, both of them giddy with optimism and splendid plans.

So far, the city had not served them well. She pulled the covers up to her chin and shut her eyes against the darkness.

~≈~

*Matthew rode most of the day, changing horses when* needed, and after stopping several times to ask directions, arrived at the village of Clapgate just before sunset. He found it to be little more than one unpaved street of dwellings and a couple of small shops. A tavern sat in the middle of the buildings. Beyond the huddled double row of structures, the spire of a church reached toward the sky, which was just now streaked with pink and purple as the sun dropped behind the horizon.

He rode up to the tavern and dismounted, feeling the strain in his thighs and back from the hours of hard riding. He was shockingly out of shape, he thought in one corner of his mind, too much leisure time since he had given up his command.

He gave his horse over to the lad who came from behind the building and told him to give the beast extra oats, as it was obvious there would be no horses to hire here.

Matthew had to duck his head to step inside the doorway. The air was redolent with the strong smells of unwashed bodies and traces of smoke from the fire, as well as aromas of food, which made his stomach rumble. For a man who had been long accustomed to the cramped, crowded space belowdecks, it was only a minor annoyance. And the food, at least, smelled savory enough.

He went up to the small counter. "Can you provide dinner and a pint of ale for a hungry traveler? And do you have a room for the night?"

The man behind the rough wood bar nodded. "Right you are, gov'nor. I'll have you a bowl of the best mutton stew in the shire. And our best room, too."

"Since it's your only room, I guess that's true enough." A bent elderly lady had entered the room behind Matthew. She cackled at her own wit, adding, "But I'd give a careful look at the sheets, if I was you."

"Ah, now, Grandma Poole, you will have your little jest," the landlord said, his tone easy enough even though he threw her a baleful glance. "Best mind your tongue. Your own cottage ain't seen a good turning out for many a season!"

He handed Matthew a brimming tankard of ale. "Our best home brew," he told him.

Matthew sipped cautiously. Not bad. He nodded his approval and said to the woman, "Can I buy you a pint of ale, Grandmother?"

She smiled, revealing pink gums almost devoid of teeth. "Aye, thank'ee, sir."

The landlord brought another tankard and put it down before her. Then he turned, saying, "I'll just see about that stew," and disappeared through a back doorway toward the kitchen.

Through blue eyes faded with age and framed by deep wrinkles, the woman regarded him with approval. "You're a good boy, you are. What's such a fine gent doing in our little hamlet?"

"I'm looking for someone, and I would wager you know all the inhabitants hereabouts." Matthew watched as she took a deep drink from her tankard, then she smirked.

"I should say so. Who be you searching for?"

"A young lady who might have come to this village about five or six years ago," he told her. "She would have been around twelve at the time." His pulse quickened and he thought he held his breath, waiting for her to respond.

She had pursed her mouth into a small O as she thought about his question. "Don't remember such a one coming here. The vicar's niece came for a visit one summer three years past, but she's not a newcomer, exactly."

"What does she look like, the vicar's niece?" Matthew asked, even though it was a faint hope.

"She's a sturdy girl with narrow eyes, brown locks and broad hips," the elderly lady told him. "But she's past two and twenty, even if she does claim to nineteen!"

Aware of his deep disappointment, Matthew exhaled slowly. "No one else?"

She shook her head. "Did your sweetheart run away

from you? Silly girl. If I was thirty years younger, I'd make it up to you, dearie." She gave him a rakish grin, which again revealed pinkish gums and a few blackened teeth.

He managed not to shudder. "You're too kind. Tell me about the village and those who live here."

She listed the families, shopkeepers, and farmers, who lived in and around the village, but it all sounded depressingly normal. Matthew could detect no hint of any possible connection with his sister.

"There's no one by the name of Temming who lives in the area, is there?" he asked when she paused.

She shook her head and refreshed herself with another draw of her ale. "N'er heard of such a family hereabouts."

"Is there a squire, a gentleman farmer, any bigger houses that I have not seen?" Matthew suggested.

"Just Mr. Nebbleston," she answered. "And he spends most of his time in London. He's not much of a farmer and as for a gentleman—" She cackled again, and the landlord, reappearing with a bowl of stew and a loaf of hard brown bread to go with it, threw her a hard look.

"This Mr. Nebbleston, did he have any guests that year? Any young ladies who came to visit?" Matthew persisted. "Does he have a daughter?"

She shook her head. "Naw. Just a son, and the poor lad's not right. A sore trial he is to his dad. And Nebbleston's wife is dead, poor lady, these ten years. Not that Nebbleston is lonely, mind you. . . ."

"Leave off the gossip, Grandma," the landlord told the old woman. "Wouldn't pay no mind to her," he added to Matthew.

Matthew wished he had heard something to pay mind to. He dipped a spoon into the stew. If he avoided the large bits of fat, it was palatable. Appetite was the best spice, he had heard. He broke a piece of hard brown bread off the round loaf and soaked it in the stew. Still, compared to the weevily hardtack and salted beef served aboard ship, this wasn't so bad.

After he finished the simple meal, he drank the last of

his ale and handed over several coins to the landlord. After a brief look at the tiny attic bedroom that was to be his, he went back down the narrow stairs and checked on his horse, then walked toward the church, wondering if he could get a glimpse of this Mr. Nebbleston. If Nebbleston were the only man of substance in the area, he might have more news of any newcomers, or even any young girls who might have passed through the village years earlier.

Before the old lady had left to return to her own hearth-side, she had explained where the Nebbleston house was located and that the local vicar served two small churches, including the one in Clapgate, but his vicarage was in the next village. Matthew would question him tomorrow, after his horse had had time to rest.

Tonight the moon was half full, and Matthew was able to make his way up the lane to the larger house located a half mile past the church. But when he approached the square stone building, he was disappointed to find the windows dark and to see that the door had had its knocker removed, a sure sign that no one was currently in residence.

Sighing, Matthew retraced his steps. When the moon slipped behind a cloud, he slowed, stumbling a little over uneven clods of dirt. He paused until the clouds moved on and the pale moonlight reappeared, allowing him to again make out the path.

Would he ever find his sister? Had she disappeared into oblivion for all time, never to know that her brother had cared, had striven desperately to locate her and redeem her from whatever plight she might have suffered after their mother's death?

How had he come to fail her so completely, when all he had wanted was to make his fortune and ensure his family's well-being? Matthew bit back a groan.

Glancing toward the church, its pallid stones silhouetted against the deeper black of the night, Matthew felt a sudden wave of cold wash through him as he noticed something else.

Pale in the darkness, oblong forms rose up from the

straggling grass, tombstones that marked the church's graveyard. Matthew drew a deep wrenching breath.

In the middle of the older graves, he made out a freshly dug mound, its dirt not yet blended into the surrounding earth.

Was this where his sister had come—to die?

# Twelve

*M*atthew *felt his heart beat faster. A low stone wall* surrounded the graveyard. He was over it before he even thought and then he stumbled across the uneven ground until he reached the newest mound. Then, just as he made out *Mistress* on the headstone, the moon slipped once more behind a cloud.

He cursed once, then, aware that this was hardly the place for profanity, swallowed the rest of his oath and ran his fingertips across the stone. Tracing the letters by touch, he made out that the grave held Mistress Prudence Barry-more, age three score and twelve.

By this time, sanity had returned, and he straightened, taking a deep breath. The air was musty with the scent of decaying leaves, and an owl hooted in a tree behind him.

He was going mad with guilt, Matthew thought. Why had the grave sent such a chill through him? People died every day; he could not picture his sister in every grave site. He had to stop rushing about and think logically. The village had been a dead-end, that was all. He would return to London in the morning and decide what to do next.

There had to be more that he could do than stumble about in the darkness!

When he reached the tavern, he warmed his cold hands before the smoky fire in the taproom, then lit a candle and made his way up to the tiny bedroom.

He inspected the sheets, and even by the light of his solitary candle, the dirty linen made him shake his head. Deciding against sharing a bed already so well occupied, he wrapped himself in his greatcoat and settled himself on the large oaken settee placed next to the tiny fireplace. It made a hard couch, but he had known worse.

He slept in fits and starts, and by the first light, was on his way back to London. He paused his journey only to interrupt the local vicar at his breakfast, question him briefly, and then set out again, arriving in the middle of the afternoon. He was weary, sore, and more than ready for a decent meal. So when he returned to his rooms at the hotel, he ordered bathwater to be sent up and dinner to follow.

"Pushing yourself too hard, Cap'n," his man muttered, shaking his head at the sight of his employer. "As you always did."

"Just see to the bathwater and a meal, please, Pattock," Matthew told his valet, having no energy left to argue.

After helping him out of his dusty greatcoat, the valet nodded. With the coat over one arm, he disappeared down the hallway to pass on the orders to hotel staff and then brush the coat into respectability.

"Back from Hertfordshire, eh. No luck?" McGregor asked, coming out of the bedroom.

Matthew turned to look at his guest. The lieutenant was back on his feet. A sling held up his left arm, but his color was better, and his voice sounded normal again.

"Is it so obvious?"

"I have seen more cheerful men come off a two-day battlefield," the other man answered. "Here, take a chair. I can pour wine with one hand—I think you need a glass."

Sighing, Matthew accepted the drink and sat down.

McGregor took the other chair. "I'm giving you your bed back tonight, as well."

"What about you?"

"Oh, I'll take the cot, as long as you are still minded to be generous. I'm locked out of my rooms until I can pay my back rent." The lieutenant shrugged as if this were a normal turn of events. "And I've helped myself to one of your clean shirts, by the by. Your man regards me with veiled disapproval. But tell me, what will you do now?"

Matthew frowned into his wine glass. "I have a Runner on his way to Cornwall, but that may lead to nothing, as well. I wish I knew what that damned woman's list really meant!"

"And the solicitor you were seeking? Any word of him?"

Matthew shook his head. "I have a Runner watching the tavern in Whitechapel that our would-be assassin mentioned."

McGregor snorted. "If he's as subtle as the muscle-bound ex-trooper you sent into the West Country, he will only scare off your prey. Let me take a turn at it."

Raising his brows, Matthew looked across at the other man. "You?"

"I have a debt to settle with this fellow, too." The lieutenant glanced down at his wounded arm. "And I would wager I can blend into the background more effectively than your Runner."

Matthew gazed at him thoughtfully. "You might be right, at that."

"Sadly, I know I'm right," McGregor retorted. "I'll need a really old coat and a few coins to start a game with."

Despite all his anxieties, Matthew couldn't help grinning. "Of course."

"I said I had to blend in, didn't I?" the Scot protested, his own smile raffish.

They shared a grin. But all jests aside, there would be the devil to pay, Matthew thought, when they caught up with Temming.

∽

*The next morning, Gemma rose early and waited for* Lady Gabriel's carriage to arrive, departing to spend another day helping Psyche supervise the refurbishment of the foundling home and the improvement of its inhabitants.

Louisa realized this was a worthy endeavor, but she found she sorely missed Gemma's company. She went out for a walk with Lily and then returned home to interview several women for the position of her lady's maid, eventually deciding on a redoubtable older woman with a French accent, which might actually have been real, who had until recently worked for a baronet's lady and had excellent references.

"Lady Stirling was a joy to dress," Madam Degas explained. "She had an unfailing air of style."

But just as Louisa wondered uneasily if she would be forever compared to the late Lady Stirling, the other woman added, "Although, sadly, she lacked your lovely erect carriage, Miss Crookshank."

Smiling, Louisa made up her mind. When generous terms of employment had been offered and agreed to, she rang for Lily to show the newcomer her room and acquaint her with the servants' hall below stairs.

"I'm sure I will enjoy working here," the older lady said, bestowing a small smile upon Lily. The younger servant smiled back and seemed impressed by the woman's poise and air of decision.

With that settled, Louisa and Miss Pomshack shared a light luncheon. Then, with her companion beside her, Louisa went out for a fitting of her ball gown and looked in at the bookstore, this time without any alarming encounters with Society matrons. She also did not see any gentlemen of her acquaintance, and she thought a bit wistfully of Lieutenant McGregor. What was he up to, today, escorting Lady Jersey again?

Louisa and Miss P returned home with an armload of

parcels, and Louisa sent her purchases upstairs with the footman. She followed, stopping in her room long enough to shed her pelisse and her hat and gloves and to glance into the looking glass.

A cup of tea would be just the thing, she told herself. She had sent Miss Pomshack off to enjoy her usual afternoon rest, and sitting alone in the drawing-room would allow Louisa to dip into the new novel she had purchased.

But just as Louisa had settled herself at the end of the settee, she was surprised to hear a knock at the front door. Was Gemma back so early? Or perhaps it was Lucas, feeling guilty for ignoring her!

Louisa closed her book and waited for the footman to appear, but to her surprise, a strange man stood behind him in the doorway.

"Mr. Arnold Cuthbertson, miss," Smelters announced.

Mystified, Louisa stood and dipped a curtsy as the gentleman bowed. He was of medium stature and had brown hair of a medium hue. His face was ruddy from outdoor living, and his clothes were those of a gentleman, although they lacked the stylish appearance of those crafted by a London tailor. She tried to remember where she had heard the name before.

"It is kind of you to receive me," the visitor was saying. "I am really in search of Miss Gemma Smith, whom I understood was staying with you? My sister had a letter from her not long ago."

"Of course." Louisa flashed him a smile. This was the young man from Yorkshire who had been courting Gemma, that was it! "I'm afraid she is not in, just now, but she may be returning before too long. Will you not have a cup of tea?"

"Thank you, that is very kind," the gentleman said, his tone complacent. He waited for her to nod to the footman and then take her seat, then he sat down across from her.

"Have you just arrived in London, Mr. Cuthbertson?" Louisa asked politely. Was he missing Gemma? Was this a true romance? If it made her heart ache a little, especially with Lucas's easy disregard of her company, Louisa would still be happy for Gemma if her suitor proved so constant.

"I came into town yesterday," he told her. "But I was too travel-stained to seek Miss Smith's company last evening, and anyhow, it was too late to pay a call."

He had good manners, Louisa told herself, another good sign. When Smelters returned with a tea tray and cakes and sliced bread and butter, she poured out the tea and encouraged the visitor to chat.

As it turned out, he was quite willing to talk, mostly about himself. Louisa had been hoping to hear something of his courtship of Gemma, perhaps a declaration of his feelings for her friend. Instead, she learned how lush were his father's pastures and how well bred were his sheep.

"Our wool is the best in the district," Mr. Cuthbertson was explaining. "We are quite proud of our breeding record. Our ewes have dropped more sound lambs than any farm for half a league around."

"How lovely," Louisa said, trying to maintain her air of interest. But she was sincerely glad when she heard the sound of a carriage outside the house, and soon Gemma herself appeared in the doorway. She paused, looked at their visitor in astonishment.

Gemma had stepped out of the carriage thinking only of her aching back—she had found it impossible to stand by and watch the children wrestle with the soiled, heavy mattresses they were removing from the dormitories without coming to their aid—and the usual longing for a warm bath, which a visit to the foundling home always engendered. When she entered the house and looked up to see the man who, at her entrance, stood and made his bow, she felt a jolt of surprise.

Somehow, he seemed as out of place in Louisa's drawing room as if York's great cathedral had uprooted itself and marched south.

"Arnold!" she exclaimed. "That is, Mr. Cuthbertson. This is a surprise. Your sister did not tell me you were coming to London."

He had bowed to her, but to Louisa's obvious disappointment, did nothing more, his manner more crisp than loverly. "Since we are not formally betrothed, it would have been improper to correspond with you and tell you of my impending journey. Still, I decided to come and see how you were faring."

"That's very good of you," Gemma told him slowly. She had forgotten how he pomaded his wavy hair in the old-fashioned style still favored by his father, the squire. And his coat did not sit well across the shoulders, not like Captain Fallon's, but then, she could hardly fault her Yorkshire admirer for not having access to a London tailor.

"And my mother has been telling me I should visit the capital. Everyone needs a little town bronze, you know," he told them both.

She had also forgotten how pompous he could sound. Surprised at her own response, Gemma nodded. Had Arnold altered so much during her short tenure in London, or was it possible that it was she who had changed? What could explain her response to him, her initial feeling of dismay, when she should have been delighted that he cared enough to come?

"My mother and sister send their regards," he added.

"That is kind," Gemma said. "I hope Elizabeth is well, and your parents."

"My father is troubled by a tinge of gout," he answered. "But otherwise, they are doing quite well, thank you."

While they talked of his family in Yorkshire, Louisa sipped her tea and tried to hide her own thoughts. This squire's son seemed rather tame, compared to—to—well, she could not compare every man to the dashing and somewhat wicked Lieutenant McGregor. And if Gemma loved him, that was all that mattered.

But when she heard a note of censure appear in the man's voice, Louisa looked up again. Gemma had been explaining where she had spent her day, and Mr. Cuthbertson had frowned.

"Why on earth would you devote time to such a place,

Miss Smith? You will appear little more than a nursery maid!"

He sounded as prosy as Louisa's last governess.

Gemma sounded defensive when she answered. "The children are greatly in need of help, Arnold—Mr. Cuthbertson, and—"

"I know that you came to town hoping to nose out intelligence that would tell you more about your parents' identity, a worthy goal. You must think about appearances, my dear. This will not advance your quest to establish your true class. My mother is eager to welcome you to our family, as, I hardly need to add, am I, but first we must know if your background disqualifies you as a suitable candidate."

"It was for that reason I approached the foundling home to begin with," Gemma argued, her cheeks a bit flushed. "And when Lady Gabriel—"

"Lady?" he interrupted.

"Yes, Lord Gabriel has been kind enough to agree to look further into the matter of my parentage. And when his wife saw the condition of the home, she was moved to help improve the situation for the orphans there. I wanted to give her any help that I could."

"Ah, then it is a very different matter," the gentleman declared. "I understand you now. Gaining the approval of Lady Gabriel is worthy of your time."

"Helping the children is also worthy of my time!" Gemma retorted, and for a moment her blue eyes flashed.

He gave her a patronizing smile. "Of course it is. We understand each other perfectly."

Feeling uneasy, Louisa glanced from one to the other. She was not so sure that he did. But Mr. Cuthbertson seemed a man who was very sure of his opinions and the rightness of them.

"Will you not stay and have dinner with us, Mr. Cuthbertson?" she asked, with more politeness than enthusiasm. It was for Gemma's sake, she told herself, even if they did have to listen to more lectures about sheep.

But to her private relief, Mr. Cuthbertson stood and

gave her another correct, if not very graceful, bow. "I would not presume upon your hospitality without proper warning, Miss Crookshank. Perhaps another day. I shall allow you ladies to enjoy a quiet evening. I'm sure my dear Miss Smith—not that we do not hope to eventually replace that name with her true family designation!—requires rest after her exertions. But I shall call on you again soon."

"We shall look forward to it," Louisa lied.

And when he had shaken Gemma's hand and made his exit, Louisa turned to peer at her friend.

"I suppose you are pleased to see him," she suggested somewhat tentatively.

Gemma didn't answer for a moment. She stared after their visitor, and her expression was twisted. "You must understand, I met very few gentlemen during my time at the girls' school in Yorkshire. When Mr. Cuthbertson seemed interested in me, I was gratified. . . ."

And perhaps now that she had had the opportunity to widen her acquaintances, Mr. Arnold Cuthbertson did not look quite so appealing, Louisa thought.

"You are not yet engaged to him, Gemma. Don't commit yourself if you are not sure! You know what you told me—"

Gemma bit her lip. "It would be base of me to cast him aside just because—because—he might not quite measure up to more sophisticated gentlemen. It is not his fault he has spent his whole life in Yorkshire."

No, it was not a crime to be boring, Louisa thought, but it could hardly add to one's happiness if one were forced to spend a lifetime with such a man. Boring and pompous and judgmental . . . None of these traits sounded appealing in a future husband!

Gemma was still speaking. "It's ironic, actually. He has the same concern about me, that my antecedents might not measure up, that marrying me would dishonor his family name if my own is not certain."

"If he cares enough about you, he should not mind that—" Louisa began, but Gemma shook her head.

"No, I cannot fault him for thinking of his own family's reputation. Surely he has the right to know whom he is marrying!"

Louisa sighed. Perhaps Mr. Cuthbertson would improve upon further acquaintance. At the moment, no one's suitor seemed to be acting very loverly. She thought of Lucas, spending his evening with his new friends, and even of Lieutenant McGregor, likely dancing attendance on the unyielding Lady Jersey. A pox on them all!

*But in fact, Colin McGregor's thoughts were far afield* from the subject of titled ladies. In the end, he had decided on his own coat, the one that had been ruined by the bullet. With an obvious patch covering the hole and the scorched edges that surrounded it, the coat looked disreputable enough, to his sorrow, just the kind of garment that might have been bought off a used-clothing cart.

Captain Fallon and his valet had offered several other choices, but the two men were not quite of a size, and Colin found he was more comfortable with his own much-abused garment, even if its appearance did make him sigh, knowing what it had cost and how quickly it had met a bad end.

After they shared a quiet dinner in the captain's rooms, Colin left the hotel and waved down a hackney, giving the address of the tavern in Whitechapel.

"You sure you want to go there?" the driver inquired, looking uneasy. "I can take you to a dozen better spots for drinking, with warm bodies for fondling if that's your hunger, all closer and safer, too."

Colin raised his brows. "Sadly, it's this establishment I need," he said. "I'll add a shilling to your fee."

The driver shrugged. "Your grave," he said. "But you'll have to walk 'ome. I'm not coming back there in the middle of the night to pick you up."

Colin nodded, hoping he lived through this experiment

in philanthropy. However, it was not only benevolence that motivated his offer to help. He had meant what he'd said to Fallon. He now had his own grudge against the cowardly weasel who hired other men to kill for him. Colin's side seemed to be healing, and he had put aside the sling that had kept pressure off the sore muscles, but though it was a small wound, it was still painful, and there was always the price of his coat. . . . For a half-pay officer, barely eking out an existence, determined to maintain his status as a gentleman, a well-made and almost-new coat was no small loss.

As the carriage wound its way out of the more re- spectable areas of London and bounced down narrow, less well-lit streets, Colin remembered his childhood in the southwest corner of Scotland. His father had held a small farm in Ayrshire; his mother had been a vicar's daughter from the north of England. Neither had had any great wealth, although the family had never gone hungry. He had worn patched clothing often enough then, hand-me-downs carefully mended by his thrifty mother. As a young man, he'd been tempted by the dashing red coats of the King's army, even though his father had scoffed at the notion.

That was, perhaps, what had sealed his fate, Colin re- flected now, grinning ruefully into the darkness. He'd had no wish to be a farmer, and anyhow, he had an older brother who would take over the farm when his father passed on. A small inheritance from a great-uncle had been enough to buy his commission, and since the war with Napoleon was still at its height, he had gone off dizzy with ambition and long-repressed energy, sure that he would defeat the French single-handedly, and advancement and fortune would soon follow.

But, although he had not made such a bad officer, he thought, the tides of a fickle fate had thrown him up against unexpected shoals. And here he was, having survived the dangerous currents of combat only to find himself adrift in peace time, surviving on half-pay, no more battles to fight and no resources within his grasp.

But he was a survivor, and bitterness buttered no bread, as his old granny had always said. He had enough Scot in him to be both quick-tempered and fatalistic. He'd never thought to fall so low as to strive to marry for money, even though better men, more prominent men than he, did it every day, but this was where he'd ended. If he could choose any woman to wed—his thoughts flew unbidden to the impulsive and appealing Miss Crookshank. She had money, true, but even without a farthing to her name, he would have been drawn to her. But she was already spoken for, and as he had warned her, she deserved better. He shook his head. And now the crowning irony—he'd survived more battles than he could easily remember only to be wounded by some street thug hired by a dishonest solicitor. The idea offended him. He did have some pride left!

So when the cab pulled up at a narrow crossroads in what looked to be the worst part of a bad neighborhood, Colin was ready. He handed over the fare and climbed out. The driver lashed his horse and made a quick turn, then the hackney hied its way back to safer streets.

Colin entered the tavern.

Inside, the murky air reeked of stale beer, of smoke drifting from an ill-swept chimney, and strongest of all, the stench of unwashed clothes and even grimier bodies. Most of the tables were crowded with men whose coats were much less pristine than Colin's and whose expressions, when they looked his way at all, were far from welcoming.

He knew all about being unwelcome. Colin had survived his first years in the army enduring the not-always-innocent baiting of his fellow officers—his fellow *English* officers—until he'd learned to moderate his strong Ayrshire accent and had also met two of his fellow subalterns with bare blades, easily drawing first blood. After that, they had treated him with respect, and in time, he'd even made friends among his fellows. Now, he hesitated not a moment. He made his way to an empty table, pulled up a three-legged stool and waited for a slatternly woman in a soiled apron to approach him.

"Ale, please," he said, passing over a coin. This was the type of establishment where one paid first. With his own pockets empty, it was a good thing he had Fallon to back him. His gaze deliberately idle, Colin looked around. Yes, the stalwart Bow Street Runner Fallon had hired to watch the place would have stood out here like a ripe ear of grain amid a field of nettles.

As for Colin, he had no doubt he could appear as disreputable as anyone here. Most of them, anyhow, he thought as he glanced at the next table where sat a man with a peg leg and a missing ear. By the time the woman returned with his mug, Colin had located a game of bones in the corner. Taking his drink with him, he rose and made his way across the room.

"Mind if I take a turn?" he asked.

The men huddled on their knees on the stone floor glanced up. A couple scowled, but the one who seemed to control the game shrugged. "Let's see your coin," he said.

Colin withdrew a few pennies from his pocket and let the man glimpse them. No need to flash too much blunt— he'd have his throat slit before he could leave the place. Then he knelt on the cold flagstones with the other men and accepted the greasy squares of ivory and bone.

He rolled them between his palms, judging just how unbalanced they were—no question as to whether or not this was an honest game—and then tossed them toward the floor. The rough-hewn cubes bounced across the hard surface, and when they stopped, the crowd around him guffawed at the mishmash that showed on the upturned faces of the dice.

"My loss," Colin agreed without heat. He passed over a penny and surrendered the dice, settling down to bet sparingly and observe closely. By the time the throw came his way again, he had a better idea of who was winning, who was losing—with many curses—and how the dice were being manipulated.

Most of the men appeared to be common laborers, if they were honestly employed at all, but one wore the leather apron of a blacksmith or a farrier. A big burly man with arms knotted with muscle, he had lost every time his calloused fingers touched the dice. By the time Colin picked up the bones again, the smith had already forfeited most of his small cache of coins, and he watched eagerly, hoping for another bad throw from the newcomer.

Colin rolled the dice in his hands, feeling their weight and their balance, and selected the one that was most obviously weighed. He put it down "This one is bad," he said.

The leader of the game, a thick-set man with scowling dark eyes, snorted. "Poor loser, are you? I'll take it ill if you cast aspersions on me honor, mate!"

"Then I cast them more easily than I will this weighted die." Colin met the man's baleful stare with steady eyes. "I think I'd rather use the other one."

The men around them muttered.

The thickset man frowned. "What other one?"

"The die in your left pocket," Colin answered calmly. "The one you've been replacing this one with, when it's your turn to roll."

"You'll pay for that—" the scoundrel began, but he didn't have time to finish.

The other men in the circle growled, and the smith reached for the speaker and gripped him with strong, smoke-blackened hands. "You been cheating us, Grimby? I'll crack your 'ead like a walnut, I will!"

"No, no, he's lying—" the man tried to argue, but Colin interrupted with another suggestion.

"Check his left pocket."

With one wide hand, the smith kept the smaller man firmly in his grasp; with the other, he reached into the pocket indicated and pulled out a small cube of ivory.

"Try rolling with that one," Colin suggested, his tone pleasant. "I'm sure you will have better luck. You can even take my turn."

The smith roared and shook the owner of the weighted dice in one hand till the man's teeth rattled. "You lyin' cheatin' whoreson!"

The other men were shouting, too, but it was the smith—his angry glare daring anyone else to dispute his right—who reached to scoop up the cheater's pile of blunt.

No one else protested, but Colin said, his tone mild, "I'll not argue over the winnings if you allow me to decide his fate."

The smith took a moment to think about this, then nodded reluctantly. "Since you cottoned to 'is cheating, I guess that's fair."

Face now damp with sweat, the man still gripped in the smith's big hand stuttered, "I d-didn't—I wasn't—"

"Oh, put it by," Colin advised him. "I'll deliver you from the beating you so amply deserve for the right price."

"'ow much? 'E just took all me blunt," the swindler argued.

"I don't want money, just a nugget or two of information," Colin told him.

Looking relieved, the man tried to nod without much success—his throat was still caught up in the folds of his coat, which was locked in the blacksmith's implacable grip. Colin motioned to the blacksmith, who reluctantly lowered the man back to the stone floor and released him.

Pocketing the coins, he cast a baleful eye upon the owner of the dice. "You'd best not show your face in 'ere again," he told the bonesman, then headed toward the front of the tavern to buy himself a drink. The rest of the circle followed, perhaps hoping for a moment of generosity from their mate.

Left alone, the man rubbed his throat and shivered. "You did me a bad turn, you did," he said to Colin, his tone resentful.

"I also saved your wretched hide," Colin reminded him. "You'd have been caught with your loaded dice sooner or later. Now, this is what I want to know."

❦

*A few hours later, Colin was ensconced in the corner of* the tavern, nursing only his second mug of ale—he might need a clear head before the night was done—and watching the doorway without seeming to. Eventually, his patience was rewarded. When the small, scrawny man with the dark coat and thinning hair combed across a rapidly balding crown entered, going straight to the counter to order a tankard of brew, Colin felt his pulse quicken.

This was the man, he was sure of it. Temming looked slightly more prosperous than most of the tavern's habitues, but just as furtive. Glancing around him, he took the mug of ale and gulped it down quickly as if he waited for something.

To Colin's increased interest, the man behind the counter handed over a slip of paper, and Temming pushed it quickly into an inner pocket of his coat, and only then did he pass over a coin—he must be well-known to the landlord if he did not have to pay before he obtained his brew—and then turned to leave.

He looked around again before he moved toward the door, but Colin's gaze was on his own mug, his body relaxed despite the pounding of his heart. Colin noted from the corner of his eye as the solicitor's gaze passed over him without pausing.

Colin waited until Temming had turned his back and pulled open the heavy door, then he stood and strode over the threshold after him.

Colin knew—from the information he had wrung out of the dice player—in which direction to look, and a good thing, too. In the darkness, he could detect only the barest hint of motion as the man's dark coat blended easily into the blackness. Determined not to lose him after all this, Colin walked even faster.

Temming must have heard the sound of his pursuer's footfalls. He broke into a scudding run, like a beetle disturbed when one turned over a stone.

Colin ran, too, and his legs were longer and younger. Just as the smaller man ducked into a side alley where he would have disappeared into the blackness, Colin narrowed the distance between them. He reached out and grabbed the back of the man's coat, jerking him up without regard for his dignity or his thin neck.

"We'll have just a word, if you please!"

"I didn't do it!" the little man squealed.

Colin marched him back down the block until they stood in the faint circle of light that slipped past the grimy windows of another tavern, so he could see the man better. Temming's thin face quivered. He looked so much like a rat caught by the tail that Colin could almost forget how dangerous he truly was.

"And what did you not do?" Colin inquired, his tone icy. "Other than pay a couple of street thugs to put a bullet through my side?"

"T'wasn't me," the man insisted. "You got the wrong man."

"And your name is?"

"Smith," the man said quickly.

"Really? I believe I have met one of your relatives," Colin told him. "And you have a card on you with that name engraved upon it, I have no doubt?"

The solicitor hesitated and licked his lips.

"Ah, yes. Perhaps you also answer to the name Temming?"

"Don't matter, I didn't do it," the solicitor repeated sullenly. "You got no proof."

"I suspect that we will find proof enough," Colin told him. "And if not, at least I can give you a sound thrashing. Let me see that paper you got from the landlord of that vile establishment we were just in."

Temming's narrow eyes widened in alarm. "I got no paper!"

It was something significant, then. Colin reached inside the man's coat with his other hand.

Temming lashed out and delivered a blow that struck the just-healing wound. Colin cursed as pain surged up his side and shoulder, but he kept his grip, and, unable to do much with his weakened arm, ended the man's brief but frenzied struggle with a swift kick to the back of his shin.

Temming swore. "You've broke me bloody leg!"

"Not yet, but that could be arranged. Let's have it," Colin said again.

The man quieted. For a moment he looked fearful, then his expression eased into a sly smirk.

Colin had heard it, too, the sound of footsteps behind them, stealthy footsteps coming closer. He frowned, but he maintained his grip.

"Best to let me go," Temming muttered. "If you want to live another hour."

Without answering, Colin moved to put his back to the wall of the dwelling behind them, holding the solicitor's body in front of his. He strained to see past the faint glow of light, and in a moment, made out Temming's confederate. And, oh, a true pleasure, it was the second man from the encounter in the alley near the Inns.

"Old friends, ain't we, gov?" the newcomer sneered. He held a cumbersome pistol in one hand, the muzzle pointed straight at Colin's heart. Despite the smaller man blocking him, the assassin still had a fair shot, and he was too close for his aim to waver. "Me mate was a poor shot, but me bullet won't go astray. I'll see you bleedin' and lifeless in the muck of the street."

# *Thirteen*

"Oh, I think not," Colin said, his tone polite. "But you have no idea how happy I am to see you again."

Startled, the hired killer hesitated an instant, and that was enough.

From the darkness that surrounded them, another voice spoke, deep with purpose and a cool controlled ferocity.

"Put down the pistol—if *you* wish to live another minute."

Matthew Fallon stepped into view, and behind him was the Runner who had taken Colin's message back to the hotel after he'd forced the information out of the dice thrower. The Runner uncovered a lantern. Both were armed, and both guns were held at the ready.

Temming's face sagged, and the other ruffian looked panic-stricken. He lifted his gun, but Matthew was too quick.

A shot rang out, and it was the thug who slumped this time, against the near wall.

"See to him," Matthew snapped to the Runner. He

stepped forward to reach into the solicitor's pockets, patting each until he could pull out the paper that Colin had been seeking.

He read it aloud, his tone heavy with disgust. "Fair hair, age ten to fourteen." He put one hand to the solicitor's throat. "Procuring, are you? Is that what you did to my sister?"

"No, no," the other man protested in a muffled voice.

"Tell me the truth, or I will kill you here and now!"

Even Colin, who had witnessed more battlefield violence than he cared to remember, was impressed by the savagery of the captain's voice.

No wonder that Temming's voice was little more than a whine. "I swear, I don't know what you mean."

"My name is Matthew Fallon—surely you remember me? You were entrusted with my family's care, empowered to pass on the money I sent home during the war. When my mother died, my sister vanished, and you kept the rest of the funds—you were likely taking a good part of them all along. And shortly after, my sister disappeared from the foundling home to which you sent her. I want to know where she is!" His grip tightened.

"I'm an honest man," Temming croaked out. "I never—"

"Tell me the truth, damn you!" Matthew thrust him against the building until the man's head cracked against the wall and his eyes rolled briefly back in his head. "Or I'll pluck your heart out of your chest here and now!"

"Won't do you any good," the small man whispered. "You'll never know then, will you?"

"Is she dead?" Matthew demanded, his tone still savage.

Temming shook his head. "No, but if you kill me, you'll never find her! In less than a week, she'll be out of England, and you'll never see her again—unless you let me go now!" His head was forced back by the captain's grip, but he managed a grin that was more grimace than smile and seemed to radiate evil.

"Oh, I will find her," Matthew said, though even in the

faint light, Colin could see that he had paled. "And I'll see you hang at Newgate afterward!"

He shook him again, but the little man pursed his thin lips and refused to answer more questions.

And later, when they took him and his hired thug before a magistrate, Temming denied any knowledge of Clarissa Fallon, denied he had been involved with the matron at the foundling home, and denied he had made any statement to Matthew Fallon about his sister's fate.

Colin observed the grim set of the captain's jaw with real sympathy. After Temming and the other man had been taken away to jail cells, Fallon wiped his face. His expression was still set, but he looked gray with desperation and despair.

"Perhaps after all, I should have tried to buy him off," he told Colin.

Colin shook his head. "That kind never deals fairly," he told the ex-mariner. "He may have made the whole thing up, you know."

Fallon grimaced. "I am afraid he was, for once, being truthful. If I have only days to locate my sister—" His voice faltered, and he seemed unable to finish. "England is a large country, and there are so many places for one girl to be hidden!"

"We will not give up," Colin told him. "We will find her."

Fallon put one hand on Colin's shoulder, but he had to clear his throat before he spoke. "Thank you."

Squaring his shoulders, he drew a deep breath. "I shall go at once into the West Country. I have not yet heard from the Runner I sent to Cornwall. It's possible it could be a village there where my sister is secreted away. There are seaports enough, if someone is planning to take her abroad. And I will send out inquiries to all the major ports. You could help me write out the letters."

"Of course," Colin agreed. And if he thought the captain was grasping at straws, it seemed they had nothing more substantial to build their hopes upon.

~~~

*Louisa had planned a simple dinner party for the next* evening, but her hopes for a quiet, congenial evening faded quickly. First, there were notes from Captain Fallon and Lieutenant McGregor, explaining that the captain was about to leave for the West Country and McGregor was supervising the dispatch of Runners to several seaports as they continued the search for Fallon's missing sister.

Then shortly before sunset, she got a note from her fiancé. Unwrapping the single sheet of paper, Louisa saw that he, too, was making his apologies, for the second time this week.

Frowning, Louisa pulled the bellrope to pass on the news to the kitchen that they would be short several guests for dinner.

While she waited for the footman to appear in the doorway, Louisa turned the paper over in her hands and suddenly noticed that, hidden by the folds, a line of scrip was written on the other side. She glanced at it, then gasped.

"What is it?" Gemma asked from the other side of the sitting room. She had been rereading Captain Fallon's note for the third time. She folded it and put it down. "Is something wrong with Sir Lucas?"

"No, except that he has begged off for dinner, again. But look at this, Gemma! It says, "On my way to Clapgate for the evening.""

"Clapgate? That is the name that was written next to Captain Fallon's sister's name on the matron's secret list," Gemma exclaimed. "We thought it was a village. But how—has Sir Lucas gone out of town?"

"He doesn't say so, only that he is unable to come tonight. And he usually informs me when he is leaving London," Louisa said. "Besides, I don't think this is Lucas's writing. The script does not look at all like his usual hand."

Gemma jumped to her feet, and Miss Pomshack, who had been nodding off over a collection of sermons, looked up. Gemma hurried across to look at the few words written on the paper, turning it once to compare with Lucas's own message. "I think you're right. Look at the *e*'s and the *l*'s; the loops are quite different. But then who wrote this, and why is it on the back of Sir Lucas's correspondence?"

Louisa frowned at the paper. "It might be from his friend, that fellow, Mr. Harris-Smythe. Lucas has been spending a lot of time lately in his company. If he sent Lucas a note, perhaps Lucas, without noticing, picked up one of the sheets to write to me."

"That would make sense," Gemma agreed. Her gaze was far away. "But is it possible that we have overlooked another place named Clapgate? Could it be much closer at hand than we knew? If so, I must let the captain know, at once, before his departure. His note says that he was about to leave for the West Country!"

Louisa looked up. The footman had appeared in the doorway.

"You rang, Miss Crookshank?"

"Yes," Louisa said, though all thoughts of tonight's dinner had flown from her mind. "Smelters, do you know of a place in or near London called Clapgate?"

To her astonishment, the usually impassive footman paused, and a deep blush crept slowly up his face all the way to the edge of the powdered wig. Even his neck—what she could see of it beneath his neckcloth—had reddened.

"Smelters?"

He blinked. "Ah, that is not a place that ladies would visit, miss."

"What kind of place, precisely?" Gemma demanded, her tone sharp.

He looked downright alarmed. "A place that ladies would not visit," he repeated stubbornly.

"Are you quite sure?" Louisa asked.

He nodded vigorously.

"But if I took a hackney and was quite circumspect—" Gemma argued.

"Whitechapel is not a location fit for respectable women, miss. It's a most dangerous part of London."

"Certainly not a place you should even consider, Miss Smith," Miss Pomshack added, sounding agitated at the idea. "My father, the vicar, always said—"

"Thank you, Miss Pomshack," Louisa interrupted. She nodded to the servant. "Very well, you may go."

"No, wait. I shall write a line to Captain Fallon, and you must take it to his hotel at once. It's possible we might catch him before he leaves," Gemma said. She hurried across to the desk, found a clean sheet of paper and dipped the quill into the inkwell. Very soon she blotted her words, folded the sheet, and handed it to the waiting footman. "Be sure that it goes straight up to the captain's rooms."

"Yes, miss," the servant said. He seemed relieved to leave the drawing room.

But as soon as he was out of sight, Gemma turned to her friend. "I am going," she said. "I will call a hackney—"

"No, indeed—" Miss P began, but Louisa interrupted.

"Gemma, you cannot! You heard what Smelters said, and he is right. I'm sure that section of London is not safe, and certainly, not at night!" Louisa felt a stab of alarm.

"But you know what Captain Fallon told us in his note, what that scoundrel Temming has threatened—time is running out for the captain's sister. And if she is near at hand, if I can help her—"

"Wait, wait, we must be sensible." Louisa grabbed her friend's hand. "Come up to my room with me."

Gemma seemed ready to resist. Louisa had to almost pull the other woman to the door. In the doorway, Louisa paused. "Miss Pomshack, this turmoil is bringing on one of my headaches. Would you mind very much going down to the kitchen and making up one of your inestimable tisanes?"

"I should be delighted," the older woman said, her tone dignified. "And I shall make one for Miss Smith, as well, to calm her agitated nerves."

"Agitated nerves, my eye!" Gemma muttered, but Louisa hissed at her.

"Shush! Come up with me." They hurried up the stair-case, and when they encountered the housemaid on the landing, Louisa told the maid, "Go out to the stable, qui-etly, and tell my coachman to prepare my carriage, Lily."

Gemma gaped at her.

"It's safer than a hackney. You've been left by one of those already in most dangerous circumstances," Louisa reminded her. "And you will not go alone."

"I cannot allow you to go with me," Gemma argued. "This is obviously not a respectable place, Louisa."

"It's a place Sir Lucas appears to be familiar with!" Louisa shot back. "I know that he and his new friends have spent a lot of time at their clubs and at gaming houses, and some of them may be quite low. Gentlemen do not seem to mind that."

"But you know that gentlemen can frequent many estab-lishments that ladies cannot! It cannot be a gentleman's club, if the name horrified your footman so. It must be some odious gaming den, or tavern, or some such."

"And you will risk your good name visiting such a place, but I should not?" Louisa countered.

"I would not except for Matthew—Captain Fallon—and his sister. Her life may be at stake!" Gemma lifted her chin. "You know what they told us about that villain Temming's threat! Anyhow, I do not have—and may never have—any family name to risk, but there is no need for you to suffer. If someone should see us—"

"Ah, but that is part of my plan." Louisa opened her trunk and bent to dig through layers of clothing and linen. "My maid back home packed these by mistake. I noticed them the other day."

In a moment she had emerged with two swatches of dark netting in her hands.

Gemma looked mystified. "What are they?"

"The mourning veils I wore after my father's death," Louisa explained. "I said we must be sensible."

Gemma grabbed her, and for a moment the veils were

crushed between them as they exchanged an impulsive hug. Then Louisa reached for a hat to drape one of the veils upon, and Gemma ran up to her own room to find her own hat and wrap.

By the time the carriage was ready, they had crept downstairs, happily avoiding any sign of Miss Pomshack, and slipped out the door.

To the coachman, Louisa explained their errand. "You may have to stop and ask for directions," she added.

The groom and the coachman exchanged worried glances. "I've, uh, heard of the place, miss," the coachman said. "But I think there's some mistake. This is not—"

"I know, I know. Not a place a lady would visit. That is why I depend on both of you, after tonight, to forget this journey ever took place."

The men still looked worried, but Louisa stepped inside to join Gemma, and after a short pause, the carriage rolled forward.

Gemma sighed. "Oh, no matter how vile it is, if we can only find Clarissa! What if she has been kept a prisoner there, forced to wait on tables and be subjected to vile language and dreadful company?"

Louisa reached over and gripped her friend's hand. Gemma seemed tense with worry and anticipation, and Louisa found that her own stomach had knotted.

The ride seemed very long, though later Louisa thought that must have simply been due to the perilous state of her nerves. And when they at last pulled up, in a narrow littered street where most of the surrounding houses showed fronts that appeared dark and empty, she leaned forward to stare out the carriage window.

It was a large house, with flambeau flaring on each side of the door, creating a small arc of light in the darkness. Sounds of laughter and an occasional shout could be detected past the draped windows.

The groom came to open the door, but he looked apprehensive. "Are you sure about this, miss?"

"Yes," Louisa said, knowing that nothing would stop

Gemma now. "But you are both to be on the alert. When we return, be ready to spur the horses and head immediately for home."

"Yes, miss," the groom assented, apparently finding one thing on which he agreed with his mistress.

Louisa pulled her veil down to cover her face and stepped out, stumbling a little on the uneven ground. Despite the flickering light of the torches, she could barely see with the dark veil covering her face, but she would have to do the best she could. It was essential that no one suspect they had visited such a place.

Louisa felt her stomach quiver with nervousness, but she could not stop, now. With Gemma at her elbow, she marched up to the door and gave a solid rap with the knocker.

In a moment, a burly footman opened the door. He wore neat enough olive green livery, but he was broader across the shoulders than the average house servant, and his prominent jaw appeared in need of a shave. He stared at them in surprise.

"What you doing 'ere?" he demanded. "We don't need no extra girls tonight."

Then women were indeed allowed here? Louisa tried to think.

"We're, um, meeting a gentleman," she improvised, adding, "He will offer you a coin or two, I'm sure, if you are helpful."

"Someone up to some fancy tricks, eh?" The man smirked. "Very well, don't suppose you can do any 'arm."

He pulled the door open and as they entered, asked, "You know where to go?"

Louisa hesitated, but from beneath her veil Gemma muttered, "Yes."

They came a few feet into the hall and paused. A man, by his dress a gentleman although his neckcloth had been loosened and one button opened on his coat, came out of the nearest doorway. From beyond it, loud chatter, music, and raucous laughter could be heard. Flushed with wine, he stared at them and tried to focus his eyes.

"Hey, sweetlings. Is this a new game? Let me see your face!"

He reached toward them, but Gemma slipped around him, and Louisa hastened to follow.

"Not tonight," Gemma told the man, her tone firm. She grabbed Louisa's arm and they made their way, not toward the wide doorway from which he had come, but on to the foot of a broad staircase.

Louisa had no clue where they were headed, but she suspected the important thing was to keep moving and not reveal their ignorance. She climbed rapidly, and halfway up the stairs, whispered to Gemma, "Now what?"

"If we can find a servant, we can bribe him or her to tell us if any lady here is named Clarissa," Gemma answered, her voice equally low.

"Oh, an excellent thought," Louisa agreed. Beneath her veil, her face felt damp with nervousness. She had no desire to enter that noisy drawing room downstairs and be subjected to inquisitive stares, which might penetrate their disguises.

At the top of the first flight of stairs, they found a hallway full of doors, most of them shut. Where could they locate a servant?

"Come away from the landing so the man downstairs cannot see us," Gemma urged. Louisa followed her halfway down the hall.

Then, to her relief, she caught sight of a maid—at least, Louisa assumed it was a maid. The woman wore a dark low-cut dress with a frilly apron over it, not exactly the normal uniform for house servants, but perhaps they were somewhat lax in this area of town. Louisa put out a hand to stop the stranger from walking past.

"Can you tell me if a young lady by the name of Clarissa Fallon is employed here?" she asked, keeping her voice quiet.

"Huh?" The woman stared at them. Her eyes were slightly bloodshot, and her voice just a little slurred. "Why are *you* looking for a woman?"

"It is an acquaintance of ours," Gemma added, holding out her hand and revealing a coin in her palm, just short of the maid's reach.

"Oh, you're in the trade, are you?" the woman said. She shook her head. "I don't know no Clarissa here. We got a Carrie, though."

"That could be her," Gemma said quickly. "Can you tell me where we could find her?"

"She's busy," the woman demurred.

"We will not detain her long," Gemma promised. She held the coin closer, and the woman stared at it.

"What the hell, she's in the second room on the right."

She pointed, and Gemma passed over the coin.

"Thank you!"

They waited until the woman went into another room and closed the door, and then Gemma hurried forward.

"Wait for me," Louisa whispered, running after her friend.

Gemma tapped lightly on the door the first woman had indicated

"Go way," a feminine voice called from within.

But Gemma turned the knob anyhow. The door was not locked, and it opened easily. Louisa crowded closer to look over her friend's shoulder.

She made out a bed with tumbled bedclothes. The woman in it had lifted the sheet to hide her face. Was she ill? Even if it were not Captain Fallon's sister, if this woman was in trouble, they would help her, Louisa told herself. She had a bad sense about this place, and to be forced to work here must be—

A woman's head emerged from behind the sheets. She had reddish hair and a pert, pretty face, and her eyes were narrowed. "What the 'ell you want?"

Louisa felt a surge of hope. The captain had said his sister had reddish hair!

"Carrie? Is that your name? Your real name?" Gemma demanded.

"What's h'it matter to you? Go way!"

"We are looking for a girl named Clarissa Fallon. She may have been brought here against her will," Gemma explained. "It's urgent we find her. Are you sure you remember just what your family name is? Clarissa was taken away when she was only a child, and—"

"'Course I know my own name. I grew up two streets from 'ere, now get out!" the woman exclaimed, her expression peeved. "I'm busy, can't you see."

"You don't know where we might find Clarissa?" Louisa added. "Has she ever been employed in the neighborhood?"

Then a muffled grunt sounded. To her horror, another head appeared from beneath the sheets. It was a man, a brown-haired man whom she knew at once, even seeing only the back of his curly head

"Lucas!" she shrieked and—without thinking—pushed up her veil to see more clearly, hardly believing her own eyes.

He twisted and pulled the sheet up to cover his torso. He appeared to have—Louisa drew a breath deep in shock— no clothing on at all.

He was—he was—he was on top of a naked woman!

"Louisa, we must leave!" Gemma whispered. "At once! This is not a gaming house—it is a brothel!"

Louisa was not listening. "Lucas, what are you doing here?"

The girl in the bed chortled. "Sweetie, ain't you got eyes? You need a few things explained to you, don't you?"

Louisa felt as if she were frozen—she could not get a breath. "Lucas?"

He stood up, pulling the sheet off the bed to wrap around him like a toga. The woman in the bed squealed in protest and tugged a·blanket up to cover herself. "Louisa, why in the name of all that's holy are you here? This is not a fit place for you!"

"And it's a fit place for *you*?" She put one hand to her chest, feeling a queer constricted pain inside her. "A place you prefer to my drawing room?"

"It's different for a man," he said, hitching up the sheet to take a step toward her. "You must leave at once. Let me get on my clothes—"

"Lucas, we are engaged! How could you be—be—be doing that with another woman, when we are to be married soon?"

"We're not married yet," he argued, but he did not meet her eyes.

"Lucas, how could you? I would never have credited it," Louisa exclaimed, still aching from the pain of her discovery. "You are being unfaithful to me!"

"No, I'm not."

"Louisa, we must go!" Gemma begged, tugging at her arm. Louisa shook her off.

"Lucas, I'm not blind!" Louisa raised her voice, ignoring Gemma's whispered pleas. "I find you in bed with a woman, and you tell me you have not betrayed me?"

"It's not like I was courting another *lady* behind your back," Lucas protested, looking about the room and snatching up a pair of discarded trousers. His sheet slipped a little and he jerked it hastily back up. "This is different. It doesn't really count."

"Thank 'ee very much," Carrie said from the bed. Her expression sour, she had sat up, the blanket tucked beneath her arms as she watched them. "Gonna cost you double, this is!"

"Louisa!" Gemma hissed.

"Very well, go back to my chaise and tell the coachman we are leaving and to make speed. I shall be right behind you," Louisa promised.

Gemma hesitated, and Louisa gave her a push. "Go!"

Her friend slipped out, but Louisa paused long enough to pull off the topaz ring upon her finger. She tossed it toward the man whom she thought she had known. He was hampered by trying to pull on his trousers without dropping the cloaking sheet, and the ring bounced off his arm.

Her voice shaking, she said, "It counts to me, Lucas. You may have your ring back. I shall inform my uncle that our betrothal is at an end and to take the necessary steps."

The girl on the bed, ignoring her naked state, dropped her blanket and dove to snatch up the ring. "Ooo, 'ow pretty!"

"Here, Carrie, give that back, it cost me five guineas!" Lucas snapped. "Louisa, you cannot do this. Be sensible! Tomorrow, when you are past your state of hysterics, we will talk."

"I have nothing to talk to you about," Louisa retorted. "If you call, you will not be admitted!"

He ignored the interruption. "When we are married, I will have no need to visit places like this."

"Not what you tol' me," Carrie muttered. She had shoved the ring onto her finger and was admiring its sparkle.

Revolted, Louisa drew a deep breath. "I have no need for a husband I cannot trust. You have spent little enough time in my company of late. Now I know where you prefer to be."

"Louisa! Every one does it, every man, I mean. I tell you, it's nothing of import."

"Nothing, am I?" Carrie muttered, but no one paid her heed. "Men are no good, dearie. If you got money already, you're better off without 'im!"

"If you had stayed home where you belong"—Lucas at last had his trousers up to his waist and he kicked away the sheet—"this would never have happened."

"I beg to differ," Louisa told him. "It is important." She turned for the door, which Gemma had left ajar, and paused in confusion when she saw another man standing there. Worse, it was a man she recognized—Mr. Harris-Smythe.

"Englewood, what the hell you playing at?" the new arrival demanded. "You don't bring your fiancé to a house of pleasure, man. Don't know what you do in the country, but it ain't done, sir, not in the city!"

"Of course I did not bring her," Lucas answered. "And you—you must not tell anyone you saw her here."

The man chortled. He was obviously deep into his cups. "You're a lu—lucky man, old thing. Found a wife who don't mind playing with you and your mistress? Damned lucky."

"I intended no such thing!" Louisa snapped. Too late, she remembered to pull her veil down to cover her face.

"Smythe, go away," Lucas begged.

But the newcomer had sagged against the door, holding it open. She heard more voices in the hall, attracted by the commotion. What if someone else saw her? Louisa felt her heart beat faster. She had to get out of here.

"But it won't do," the man said, his tone suddenly mournful. "She'll be ruined, you know. People bound to hear of it."

"Not if you keep your bloody mouth shut!" Lucas flung back, pulling on the rest of his clothes.

"Oh, you know me, could never do that," Harris-Smythe answered simply. "You'll have to divorce her. It'll take an Act of Parley—Parley—Parliament, of course, but must maintain your honor. Poor girl will never be received by any respect—respect—proper lady again. Too bad, such a pretty girl, too."

"We are not yet married," Louisa said, but her voice was faint. This impertinent toad was quite right. If news of this got out, she was ruined. Forever.

She took a deep breath, then tried to slip around him.

He put out one hand to grab her arm. "But you're not married yet," he parroted, still deep in his drunken musing. "Have to get married at once, then get divorced!"

"Brilliant idea," Louisa told him, then managed to break loose of his hold. Several partly clad men stood in the hall or peered out of doorways. Averting her eyes from their state of undress, as well as their staring faces, she ran down the steps, ignoring Lucas's call.

"Louisa!"

"Oh, tell everyone my name, why don't you?" she muttered.

In her haste, she almost fell down the staircase, catching

herself by grabbing the bannister before she lost her footing completely. In the entrance hall, the footman still stood by the door, and he gaped at her but did not try to stop her as she rushed past him. The door was heavy, but she pulled it open and hurried across the threshold.

She must get away! Louisa paused on the step and looked wildly around her.

Outside the brothel, the street was empty.

# *Fourteen*

*H*er heart beating so loudly she was surprised that it
did not alert all the house's inhabitants to her flight,
Gemma ran down the stairs. At the bottom she glanced
over her shoulder, but although she strained to see through
the thick veiling, she did not make out her friend following, as she'd hoped. Where was Louisa? Turning, Gemma
took one step back up the staircase, then hesitated. Haste
was imperative. What if Lucas was taking Louisa down a
back stairway to avoid more exposure? They might waste
precious time searching for Gemma if she ran back up the
stairs instead of continuing to the carriage.

So Gemma ducked her head and, without a word to the
doorman who eyed her with curiosity, hurried outside.

She pulled open the chaise door herself before the
groom could get to it. "As soon as Miss Crookshank comes,
make haste!" she told him as she climbed inside. "We are in
danger of being found out!"

But before she was even properly seated, the carriage
lurched forward.

"No, no!" Gemma yelled. "Wait for your mistress!"

But either the coachman had misinterpreted her warning, hearing only the word *danger*, or in his nervousness, he had given the wrong cue to the team because the chaise rolled ahead. Gemma knocked on the front panel to stop him, but the man apparently misunderstood, lashing the horses to a faster pace.

"You idiot!" Gemma shouted. Bouncing around inside the chaise as it jolted over the rough streets, she tried to get to the carriage door. At last, she was able to let down the window and push her head partly out the narrow opening. "Stop, you have left your mistress behind!"

Amid the rumble of carriage wheels over an uneven surface and the staccato beat of the teams' hooves, no one seemed to mark her words. The carriage continued to roll forward as she shouted once more, but again without result.

Then, just as she'd decided that the only chance of catching the panicked coachman's attention was to open the door and throw herself from the carriage, at imminent risk of life and limb, the vehicle slowed. She heard shouts and horses neighing. Now what?

She looked out the window again and craned her neck to see, but when she did, she felt a chill run through her. A man on horseback partially blocked their way in the narrow street. Worse, he held a gun pointed toward the coachman's head!

Gemma gasped. Then the man urged his steed closer, and in the faint light of the carriage lanterns, she made out a glimpse of his face.

"Lieutenant McGregor! Oh, please, you must help us!"

"Are you hurt?" He lowered his pistol. "What has occurred? This witling is speechless."

Gemma swallowed. "It's Miss Crookshank! In the coachman's haste, she was left behind at that horrid place. She may be in the greatest danger. Oh, please, convince these blockheads to turn about—I must go back for her!"

He shook his head. "You must go home," he told her, tucking his pistol back inside his coat. "You are in peril, too, in this neighborhood. I will go on to Clapgate and re-trieve your friend."

Gemma stared at him. "How did you know where we had gone?"

"When the note came to Fallon's rooms at the hotel, he had already departed. I took the liberty of reading the letter before I sent it on after him. Your man said the message was urgent, and I had a feeling—it's just as well that I did."

"Thank heavens," Gemma agreed. "You will make sure she gets safely home?"

"Indeed," he said, his tone grim.

Gemma stared at the set of his jaw and found that she believed him. Taking a deep breath of relief, she settled back into the seat. This time, when the carriage moved forward at a more sedate pace, she sat quietly, but her thoughts were still agitated.

Oh, poor Louisa, what a shock to discover Sir Lucas in the bawdy house, and in such a way! Gemma blushed to recall the scene, and it was not *her* betrothed who had been sharing a bed with a prostitute. Even at the boarding school, she had heard whispers of what some men did, and how much more latitude gentlemen were given than ladies, but it was still a shock to see such behavior with her own eyes.

Would Louisa ever forgive Sir Lucas? And what if word got out about Louisa and Gemma's visit to the brothel? And, oh, worse than anything, this was all Gemma's fault. After all Louisa had done for her, what a way to repay her friend—to involve her in such a scandal! Gemma found her eyes brimming, and she wiped her damp cheeks use-lessly.

She would willingly sacrifice all her own hopes to make this up to her friend, but she could think of nothing that would erase the damage that might have been done. Going to Clapgate had seemed a necessary step in the search for Clarissa Fallon, but, oh, Gemma should not have been so foolish as to go to such an unknown destination, or at least, she should not have allowed Louisa to accompany her. If

Gemma herself had had her reputation compromised, she would have lost little. No one knew her, and she would likely never be admitted into the Ton's august inner circle, anyhow. But, poor Louisa, who had so badly wanted to be accepted . . .

Gemma took a deep breath. Falling apart would help no one. She must compose herself and swallow her tears so that she could present a calm appearance when she faced Miss Pomshack. She would pray that somehow they would find a way out of this. In the meantime, Gemma, at least, must not give away their awful secret.

*Colin urged his horse on. Within a few blocks, he pulled* up before the torch-lit entrance to the whorehouse. He jumped off and rapped at the door.

When the doorman opened it, Colin tossed him a coin. "Keep an eye on my steed, if you please."

"I can send 'im round to the stables in the back, gov," the servant offered, though he palmed the coin quickly.

"No need, I shall be making only a brief visit," Colin told him. He didn't stop to hear the answer but pushed past the big man and into the entry hall.

He frowned at the scene before him. A group of men, and a few of the house's women, the latter highly rouged and clad in low-cut and nearly transparent dresses, milled about the hallway. All watched the stairs or gazed up to the next landing.

"What's all the commotion?" he demanded of the nearest spectator.

His voice a little too loud and his face flushed with wine, the man answered, "A great scandal! Some gentleman has been followed here by his fiancé, or maybe his wife, but a lady, if you would believe it, and she's caught him naked as a jaybird with his whore. She's upstairs in the room with him and his fancy woman, pulling out the whore's hair. Or some are saying maybe she came along for some revelry of her own, I dunno. But it's the best on-dit I've heard these half-dozen Seasons. I can't wait to tell—"

He stopped abruptly, perhaps because of the pistol that was now leveled directly at his loose-lipped mouth.

"You are mistaken," Colin corrected, his tone steely. "There is no lady upstairs. If there were, it would be that she came as the result of a malicious prank, summoned by an ill-wisher to a place she had no way of knowing was a house of ill repute. And the man upstairs is not her fiancé. I am."

"Who the hell are you?" the man sputtered. "I—"

"It doesn't matter. Just remember that I would take great personal offense with anyone who would repeat this story or sully the—hypothetical—lady's name."

The crowd around them had quieted at the sight of the weapon. Tension hung in the air, and though they gaped at him, no one broke the silence. The rest of the group stared as Colin glanced about at each blank face.

"And that goes for anyone else here. If you wish to be called out, and I will warn you I am a crack shot, you have only to repeat any version of this incident. I will find out who passed on the gossip, do not worry! I hope I make myself clear?"

One nearby gentleman shrugged. "None of my business," he muttered, pulling the woman next to him closer. "Come along, Nan. Let's find our own room and make merry without wasting more time here."

The others drifted away, too, and the man at the end of Colin's pistol, who had paled considerably, licked his lips. "Here, no offense meant, sir. I mean—"

"Just remember what I have said," Colin told him. He lowered the gun and waited for the man to scurry back into the parlor. Then Colin took a deep breath and mounted the stairs with long strides.

Upstairs, it was easy enough to find the right room. Several girls stood outside in the hall, and a number of curious male faces could be glimpsed peering out past half-open doors. Colin motioned to one buxom lady, her hair hennaed and her face painted, who was frowning at the shut door.

"Not good for business, this ain't!" she announced, then she frowned toward Colin. "Put the gun away, sir! I'll 'ave no bloodletting in me 'ouse."

The madam, then. Colin nodded but did not put the gun away just yet. "I'm told there is a lady here."

The woman rolled her eyes. "Such a commotion I never saw. What kind of lady comes to a 'ouse like this?"

"A lady who was misled," Colin said shortly. "Just release her—"

"You don't think I'm 'olding 'er 'ere, do you? I don't need this kind of trouble," the madam exclaimed, her tone indignant. "She's barricaded 'erself inside the room, and it's one of me best rooms. I want it back! I'm losing money with all this caterwauling, takes the men's minds off their pleasure, it does!"

He nodded. "I shall see about taking her away, then, shall I?"

"Not too bloody soon for me." The madam snorted.

His gun still held at the ready, Colin glanced about the hallway. The men who had been watching covertly all seemed to have thought better of their voyeurism and had disappeared from view. He motioned to the other prostitutes, who drifted back inside their own rooms. When only the madam stood in the hallway, her arms folded and her expression still incensed, he tucked his pistol inside his jacket and tapped on the door.

"It's me," he said, his voice low, not wanting to use the lady's name before so many listening ears.

"Lieutenant?" He would recognize that light trilling voice anywhere, even though it was just now tremulous with fear. "Is that really you?"

"Yes, open up," he said. "I'm here to take you home."

"Oh, thank God!" was the fervent response. He heard sounds of furniture being pulled away, and then the door opened, just a crack.

He saw a heavily veiled lady peek past the door, but although her face was effectively obscured, he knew the way her throat, its pale skin so enticing, dipped in that pleasing curve toward her shoulder blades. And he had seen her wear that dress before.

"Come," he whispered. "We must see you out of here."

She opened the door farther and threw herself into his arms. "Oh, it was awful, awful," she wailed.

He wrapped one arm around her and suspected that the thick veil, already damp against his neck, must be receiving a new sprinkling of tears.

"I did not mean—I didn't know—" she murmured.

"I believe you," he said, trying not to be aware of how his body responded to the warm fragrant armful he now held. Hellfire, he wanted her! He'd wanted her since that day he'd bathed her foot. . . . But even if she were not spoken for, this was hardly the time. "We must get you away— we will talk later."

"Oh, yes, please," she agreed.

With one arm still around her, he looked back to the madam. "Can you point us to the servants' staircase so we can slip away a little more quietly?"

She still frowned. "This lackwit has cost me money," she repeated. "And I think she's broken one of me best tables."

The hint was obvious. Frowning, Colin pulled out a couple of coins and passed them over. The woman took them, and her expression eased. "This way," she said. "Just make sure she don't never come back! We don't need 'er kind 'round 'ere."

"I believe I can promise that," he agreed drily.

They slipped down a back staircase and into an alley, then Colin, taking out his pistol again just in case, led her back to the front of the building where his mount waited. She would have to ride behind him; there was little hope of finding a hackney in this neighborhood, especially at this hour.

The doorman stared at them. "What's afoot, gov?"

"Nothing to be repeated," Colin told him, and passed over one of his last coins. An expensive rescue, this. "Help the lady up behind me."

The man lifted Louisa easily up to sit behind Colin and clutch his waist.

"Hang on," he told her, and slapped the reins. His horse moved forward into an easy canter, and Louisa clung tightly to him.

She leaned against him and he could not help but be aware of how warm she was, and how her breasts pushed against the taut muscles of his back. Conversation was impossible. He heard her sob once or twice, but when they left the darker, more noisome neighborhood behind and approached the west side of the city, she seemed to become more calm.

When their mount drew up in front of her house, Colin reached back to grasp her hand and allow her to slip smoothly down from her awkward perch.

"You're coming in?" she asked, her words a plea. Although she sounded more composed, he thought that deep distress still lay just below the surface. "I must have the chance to thank you properly and explain—"

"Of course, if you wish it." He dismounted and tied up his horse at the post provided at the side of her doorway. Offering her his arm, which she seemed more than ready to lean upon, he rapped at the door.

It flew open almost before he had drawn his hand away. He saw in the doorway, not a servant, as usual, but Miss Smith.

"Oh, thank heaven," she breathed. "Come in, come in."

Looking very pale except for reddened eyelids, she reached to hug her friend. The two women clung together for a moment.

Colin hoped he would not have two hysterical women on his hands. The immediate physical danger was over, but their trepidation was not unfounded. Much damage could yet ensue from this foolish escapade.

"Come in to the sitting room," Miss Smith urged them. "I'm sure you could both use some brandy."

"An excellent notion," he agreed, following them down the hall.

"Where is Miss Pomshack?" Louisa asked, her tone shaky.

Gemma winced. "When I returned home without you, she had a fit of hysterics. I finally got her to retire to her room with a dose of laudanum. I shall tell Lily to explain, as soon as Miss P wakes, that you are home safe. But I must tell you—"

When they entered the drawing room, Louisa stopped in surprise as a man rose to his feet and gave her and Colin a stiff bow.

"Oh, heavens—I had forgotten—I mean, good evening, Mr. Cuthbertson," Louisa said. "I'm so sorry about our dinner plans. . . ."

"I have explained that you were called away by a sick friend. Arnold was just going," Gemma said, her voice sharp.

"Ah, but since we are now adequately chaperoned," the squire's son and heir said, with his usual pompous tone, "I can stay and render assistance or advice. You appear most distressed. I gather that some further calamity has befallen your sick friend? Has she succumbed to her malady?"

"No, indeed," Gemma contradicted, glancing from one to the other. "Miss Crookshank has only had a bit of a shock, a—a minor carriage accident. But happily, her friend Lieutenant McGregor came to her rescue and was able to bring her safely home. I'm sure that now all will be well. She is only somewhat unsettled."

"Ah, but with females, especially well-bred females, that is hard to predict. A woman's constitution is not as hardy as that of a man's, of course."

Gemma stared at him, and her expression was disgusted. "This is hardly the time to reflect on a woman's frailties!"

He didn't seem to listen. "Perhaps you should send for a surgeon? It's likely that she may need bloodletting to rid her of her hysteria."

Judging by Louisa's expression, the only thing she wished to be rid of was Mr. Cuthbertson, Colin thought. But to his admiration, she drew a deep breath and pulled herself together sufficiently to say, "Thank you, an excellent notion."

"We will invite you again soon, when my friend is recovered. I'm sure you do not wish to stay and watch the surgeon perform his task," Gemma said.

"But until he arrives—"

Gemma took him firmly by the arm. "I must take my friend upstairs, but I will see you again soon, Mr. Cuthbertson."

The man cast a resentful glance toward Colin, who kept his own expression impassive. He also maintained his stance beside the fireplace—on the battlefield, the side that commanded the most advantageous site had a marked advantage—and at last, their unwanted visitor surrendered to the inevitable. He bowed and took his leave, and Gemma escorted him out.

In a few minutes, Gemma hurried back into the drawing room. "Oh, Louisa, what happened? I did not mean to leave without you, I give you my solemn oath. The coachman misunderstood or lost his head—I don't know—and we were suddenly galloping down the street. I could not make him stop. I was about to jump from the carriage just to draw his attention when the lieutenant appeared and forced the carriage to draw up."

Louisa gazed at him, and Colin shook his head. He did not deserve such a look of gratitude. "Anyone would have done the same," he muttered.

He explained again how he had come to know of their peril, reading the note that Gemma had sent to Captain Fallon.

"I suppose you have visited the house and so knew where to come," Louisa said, looking away.

"No, not at all," he told her. "In fact, I had to send Fallon's valet to the stables to question the grooms. How on earth did you learn of the place?"

Both women spoke at once.

"It was on the note that Louisa received from her—from Sir Lucas—" Gemma started.

"It was scrawled on the back of the sheet, and we thought—" Louisa said at the same time, then paused.

"It is all my fault," Gemma confessed. Despite her obvious attempt at self-control, a sob escaped her. She wiped her cheeks with a damp handkerchief. "I should not have gone, and I should never have allowed Louisa to go with me. But we knew that time was short, and I felt constrained to look for Clarissa there."

Colin felt a surge of anger toward Sir Lucas. How could the calfling have been so careless with his correspondence? Colin moved across to the sideboard, where a silver tray held several decanters of wine and liquor. He poured three glasses of brandy, bringing the first to Louisa, then handing the next to Gemma, who appeared just as agitated as her friend. He motioned them toward a settee. When they—looking equally doleful—had settled themselves side by side, he took a chair opposite them and drank from his own glass.

"I gather you had no luck finding the captain's sister?"

"No, sadly. Or at least, not sadly. If she had been held captive in such a place!" Gemma shivered. "But by mistake, we happened upon—upon—"

"My former fiancé!" Louisa snapped.

"Former?" Colin murmured. For the first time, he observed that the betrothal ring was absent from her finger.

"We have ended the engagement," she said. "I discovered Sir Lucas in the midst of—in that establishment. I told him I no longer wished to marry him, and then I ran downstairs, but my carriage had gone. And when I went back up, Sir Lucas had also departed."

"Without waiting to be sure that you had safely gone?" Colin interrupted.

Both women stared at him—he had spoken more loudly than he'd intended. He took a deep breath, resolving to take up this matter privately with the young man later. He would wring that silly pup's neck! For now he said only, "Careless of him!"

Louisa bit her lip. "Yes. I did not know what to do. Despite my veil, men were staring at me in such a way, and some of the girls were making comments. I shut myself in one of the rooms, and since there was no lock on the door, I pushed a bureau against it. I'd thought of tying the sheets together and trying to lower myself from the window, but then you arrived. . . ."

Again, she cast him a grateful glance. "I shall always remember how you saved me, Lieutenant."

Gemma smiled at him, too. "You are a true hero."

Colin shook his head. "The greatest danger is still to come," he warned them. "If this gets out, and it's bound to, although I did what I could to avert talk, Miss Crookshank will be greatly compromised."

"Oh, heavens, it's true what that awful Harris-Smythe said!" Louisa moaned.

Colin cocked an eyebrow at the unfamiliar name.

"A friend of Sir Lucas,'" she explained. "He saw me there without my veil. Oh, I shall be ruined!" Louisa put one hand to her face. "No lady will recognize me or allow me into her drawing room, and the men—I shall be the joke of the streets!"

"But it's my fault; you must not suffer for it!" Gemma declared. "I shall say it was me that they saw."

"So that we are both ruined?" Louisa asked. "It will not help, Gemma. That wretched man knows my name."

Colin found he was drumming his fingertips on the polished cherry side table. This was little different than an unexpected calvary attack or a sudden foray by the infantry. Sometimes, one had to move quickly, and the best defense was an offense. "I want you both to prepare an overnight bag, at once. We shall leave here within half an hour. Miss Smith, you must play chaperone for your friend. Miss

Pomshack is incapacitated, and we cannot wait for her to wake. Anyhow, you can be trusted to hold your tongue, at least until we desire it loosened! But I wish to be out of London before daybreak. We will have to stop at an inn when the moon goes down, but—"

"Running away will not help!" Louisa interrupted. "The scandal will simply follow me wherever I go." She bit back a sob.

Looking almost as anguished, Gemma put an arm around her friend's shoulders.

"Perhaps not," Colin told them, wondering if even he could pull this off. "But we shall not run away from the scandal. In fact, we are going to create a greater one to replace it!"

Both of the women gazed at him as if he had suddenly gone mad. Perhaps he had. But with little time to consider, it was the best subterfuge he could think of.

"Go," he said.

Gemma took her friend's hand. "We have to try," she said. "And I do not believe the lieutenant will fail us."

Louisa nodded. "No, you are right." She glanced at Colin, and his heart contracted at the trust in her blue eyes. If he disappointed her, how could he live with himself?

Without further argument—and to his private relief—they both hurried up the stairs.

He summoned the footman. "Tell Miss Crookshank's coachman to prepare the carriage at once—and yes, I know the horses have been out already tonight but only for a short journey. If he wishes to retain his post, which at the moment is in great jeopardy, he will have the equipage in front of the door before the half hour."

"Yes, sir," the footman said, eyes wide.

Colin took a sip of the brandy. He felt both calm and exhilarated, just as he used to before going into battle.

The carriage was ready on time, and the women hurried down only a few minutes late. They descended the stairs carrying a couple of small bags and a hatbox, which he put into the carriage after he handed them up.

"You are not coming into the carriage with us?" Louisa asked.

He shook his head. "I will need my horse later. I will ride," he told her. "Let us go, before we lose the moon completely."

He mounted his horse and nodded to the coachman. Colin had already given orders, and the man, still somewhat ashen of face, slapped the driving reins. The carriage moved forward.

They trotted through the streets, which were almost empty at this time of the evening, passing only the occasional carriage or horseman as other late revelers made their way home.

By the time the moon dipped behind the horizon and its pale light faded, leaving the evening sky dark and the road hard to see, they had reached the small inn that Colin had suggested to the coachman earlier. The carriage rolled to a stop, and he motioned to the coachman to wait.

Dismounting, he went in to get a room for the ladies, then returned to explain the halt.

"It's too dark now for the carriage to safely continue," he told them. "I've obtained a room for you. Stay inside and have your meals sent up. I have told the landlord you are hurrying south to visit a sick relative. But it's better if you are not seen, not yet."

"But why—how is this going to help?" Louisa demanded.

He looked at her face, still drawn with fatigue and apprehension. "I will explain it all in the morning. Try to put your fears aside and sleep. We shall pull out of this yet—if not unscathed, at least not mortally wounded."

She bit her lip, but she nodded. For a moment, a hint of her usual fire showed in her eyes. "Good soldiers are supposed to be as brave as their commander, I take it? We shall not disappoint you." She led the way, and he saw them inside the small inn, but he paused at the foot of the staircase. "I shall see you in the morning."

"You are not staying here?" Louisa asked.

He shook his head. "I must return to London."

"But it is too dangerous!" Louisa protested. "You said yourself, the darkness—"

"I have ridden through much more murky nights during the war," he told her. "And I have a bishop to see."

She blinked in surprise.

"I will explain later," he promised. And then, although she called after him to wait, to tell her more, he strode rapidly back to his steed.

*The room was small, but it smelled pleasantly of herbs.* The bedclothes appeared clean, the sheets had been aired, and a small fire burned in the fireplace. Louisa had never felt so weary. Now that she had nothing else to distract her, the weight of all the night's agitation and alarm seemed to settle upon her shoulders. She sank into a chair and found she had barely enough strength to shed her clothes and don her nightgown. But she roused herself to undo the back of Gemma's gown, and her friend returned the favor. Soon they both climbed into bed.

As she pulled the linen sheet up to her chin, Louisa recalled the last time they had shared a bed, on the way to London, when her future had still seemed so bright and promising. And now she was ruined forever—she could not see how this strange flight was going to help, and she did wish that the lieutenant had been more forthcoming. . . . But Lieutenant McGregor had some notion in his mind, which was more than Louisa herself could manage.

Coherent thought was impossible. Her head could have been stuffed with wool like the rag dolls she had once played with. She felt sodden with the burden of all her failed hopes. And Lucas—she rubbed her cheek, wiping away what promised to be a new onslaught of tears No, she would not spend her life with a man who so easily betrayed her. She did not care how many other men also made a practice of such things! To see with her own eyes . . .

Gulping back another tear, she tried to banish the horrible scene of Lucas beneath the blankets with the naked woman. She felt Gemma's light touch on her shoulder.

"Try to sleep," her friend whispered. "I am here if you need me."

Thank heavens for that. Louisa sighed. "Thank you," she said. She shut her eyes against the darkness. Although she would have sworn she was too perturbed for slumber, her body sought its own relief. Presently, the awful memories faded into blackness.

*They slept later than they had meant to, but it hardly* mattered since they had to await the lieutenant's return. Although when she woke, Louisa glanced with some concern at the sun's position in the sky—it must be close to noon— she had no fear that Lieutenant McGregor would fail to return. Despite her former fiancé's perfidy and despite the lieutenant's reputation—if it was as bad as he asserted— she had looked into his eyes, and she felt certain he would keep his word.

And indeed, by the time they had washed and dressed and supped, a maid came in with news that the lieutenant awaited them below.

They put down their tea cups at once, Louisa told the servant to have their bags sent down, and then they donned hats and gloves and followed. The lieutenant had told them not to wear the black veils—he wanted nothing to connect them with the mysterious ladies in the bawdy house—but Louisa kept her head down as she descended the narrow steps.

When she looked up to see Lieutenant McGregor smiling at her, her heart lifted, and life did not seem so bleak. He looked tired but satisfied.

"Come," he said. "I shall ride awhile in the carriage with you. I'm leaving my mount here for the time. The beast is exhausted, and anyhow, we need to speak privately."

He had been very scrupulous about not coming upstairs, Louisa realized. He was guarding her reputation, although since she had none left, or would not when gossip of the trip to Clapgate got out, it seemed a pointless effort. But his care still warmed her heart.

He assisted them both into the carriage, and Louisa had an irrational urge to cling to his hand and not release it. When they were seated and the carriage moved forward, at last he told them his plan.

"We shall create a bigger scandal, but one that is less irrevocable, I hope," he told her. "I trust that people will not credit that you could be the lady who visited the bawdy house—"

"Why not?" she demanded.

"Because on the same night that the veiled lady visited Clapgate, you were on your way out of town for a secret elopement."

They both stared at him. It was so audacious that for a few moments even Louisa could think of nothing to say.

Louisa drew a deep breath. She—eloping? Scandal, indeed!

"We are going to Gretna Green?" Gemma asked, her voice faint. "I thought we were headed south."

"We are. I have obtained a special license, with the help of more borrowed funds from the captain's purse," the lieutenant told them calmly. "The things are not cheap! We shall be married in Brighton as soon as we arrive."

"And a marriage—why did you bring me, then?" Gemma persisted. She looked bewildered, a frame of mind Louisa could well understand.

Louisa still could not find her voice.

"Because you must chaperone your friend and be able to swear that we were never alone."

"But—"

"Miss Crookshank must be able to apply for an annulment," he explained. "Aside from the fact it would require an act of Parliament, divorce would be *too* scandalous, no better than the visit to the brothel, and we would gain nothing in our effort to salvage Miss Crookshank's reputation. But a marriage that is not consummated is much more easily ended, and your uncle, who is a barrister, will be able to assist you. I believe that if her friends stand by her, Miss Crookshank will survive the ignominy of an annulment and still be able to be received by Society."

At last Louisa cleared her throat. "But why would I do such a thing, elope, I mean?" she asked, hearing how husky her voice sounded.

"Because you were persuaded by a greedy half-pay officer who many of the Ton already know has been on the lookout for a rich bride. Then you came to your senses and refused to continue with such an irrational decision. With any luck, you will have all the sympathy of the Ton, and I shall come across as the villain of the piece."

"I cannot allow you to take such blame, only to help me!" Louisa exclaimed.

He shook his head. "It's too late to change our course, now," he told her. "Trust me."

She did, against all reason, although something inside her chest ached a little at the price he himself was willing to pay . . . for her!

"But—" Gemma looked distressed.

Louisa pressed her friend's hand, and Gemma fell silent. There was only the sound of the *tlot-tlot* of the team that pulled the carriage and the light hum of its wheels rolling along the road. But despite the relative quiet, Louisa was sure that all three of them had minds filled with tumultuous thoughts. She leaned back against the squabs and surrendered to the vibration of the moving vehicle.

Her heart felt light, suddenly, and it was all due to the man who sat opposite them, the man who now refused to meet her gaze.

Louisa shut her eyes, but her thoughts still whirled. But long before they reached the outskirts of Brighton, and the lieutenant had directed the coachman to a reputable-looking posting house, she knew what she had to do.

"Why did you pick this town?" Gemma had asked,

staring out the window as they rolled into the fashionable watering place.

"Because Miss Pomshack has a cousin who is a vicar here and can marry us," Lieutenant McGregor answered.

Louisa looked up, and they both stared at him.

"She was kind enough to share the information with me not long ago," he explained. "As we were chatting."

The audacity of it made Louisa swallow, although this time, it was to hold back her laughter. "Do you think he will do it?"

"There is no reason for him not to. You are of age, and we have a license," he said.

And knowing the lieutenant's charm and powers of persuasion, Louisa could really have no doubts, either.

They left their bags at the inn and, after a quick luncheon, asked for directions, then made their way to the church and nearby vicarage where an elderly maid showed them in. When the reverend appeared, he greeted them politely, if with some bewilderment when he heard their request. He was a stout man with the same hooked nose that Miss Pomshack shared, and the same complacent air of staid and perpetual virtue.

"I am happy that my cousin recommended me," he told them. "She is not with you?"

"No, she had a slight attack of gout," the lieutenant told him easily. "She was forced to remain in London."

"Ah, her father was much troubled by that ailment, rest his soul." The vicar shook his head. "I am sorry to hear that my cousin is having the same concerns. But why were you not married in London?" As he spoke, Mr. Pomshack glanced at Gemma's respectable attire, and Louisa was very glad that Lieutenant McGregor had made sure to have another lady with them.

This time it was Gemma who supplied the answer. "Miss Crookshank lost her father only just over a year ago," she explained. "My friend prefers a quiet ceremony."

Louisa nodded.

"Ah, I see," the man said, though his expression still

seemed somewhat befuddled. But after he looked over the license, he agreed that no impediment existed to prevent their union.

He sent the maid for his prayer book and asked the "happy couple" to stand before him in front of the hearth.

He read the solemn words, and Louisa felt them penetrate her heart. She had dreamed of her wedding for years—she had expected to have a new dress and a church full of family and friends. And yet somehow, just now such things did not seem to matter. Standing in this tiny parlor, dressed in her plain traveling costume, she was aware only of the man standing beside her.

"For better or for worse, for richer or for poorer . . ."

The words droned on, and she and Colin made the required responses. The lieutenant's tone was resolute, and Louisa was surprised how calm her own voice sounded.

Gemma's eyes glistened with a suspicious glint—whether from happiness or concern Louisa was not sure—and the maid, summoned as their other witness, watched them with open curiosity.

When the ceremony was complete and Lieutenant McGregor had slipped a plain gold band upon her finger, they shared a brief kiss.

It was only a slight brush of the lips, yet Louisa felt her pulse jump.

But the lieutenant—her husband!—pulled back at once. Thanking the clergyman and shaking hands, they soon made their farewells.

They returned to the inn where evening shadows were falling in the courtyard. Despite their new titular state of intimacy, her new husband seemed strangely distant. He did not touch her again, walking several paces away and not offering his arm, quite unlike his usual courteous escort. He ordered dinner for the three of them sent up to a private parlor and arranged for two bedchambers, at different ends of the hallway.

"Miss Smith will spend the night with you," he told Louisa while the three were eating. "I will take the other room. In the morning, at first light, we will be on our way back to London. By the time we arrange for the gossip to begin, the annulment should be underway. You may wish to return to Bath long enough to confer with your uncle or to receive your family's support, but we can decide that after our return to the city."

Louisa nodded but made no comment, taking another bite of the sliced beef instead. It was quite delicious, or perhaps this was the first time she'd had an appetite since the sky had fallen in shreds about her shoulders. She suddenly felt like humming, but her mouth was too full.

Gemma, who appeared worried, glanced her way once or twice. Louisa flashed her friend a smile, and Gemma returned it with obvious effort.

"All will be well," Louisa muttered.

Gemma looked skeptical, but she nodded.

After dinner, they said good night to the lieutenant, leaving him staring somberly into his wine, and went up to their room. When the door was shut, Gemma turned to her.

"Shall I unhook your gown?" Gemma asked. "The maid is bringing us warm water to wash with."

"Good." Louisa twisted the gold ring on her third finger. It felt smooth with age and wear. Who had worn this ring? A woman, obviously; it was barely big enough for Louisa's slim fingers. Had that woman loved the man who had slipped it on, loved him completely with her body and soul?

"I would like a bath. Besides, we must see if she would enjoy a trip to London," Louisa said.

"What?" Gemma demanded.

Sitting down on the side of the bed, Louisa explained.

# Fifteen

*H*is elbows on the bare table, Colin sat for what seemed like hours, trying to think of something, anything, except the woman in the room upstairs. She must be shedding her dress by now, allowing her traveling gown to drop lightly to the floor, the fabric sliding past her slim hips and shapely legs—legs whose form he could sometimes glimpse beneath the thin fabric of her muslin skirts—and puddling at last around her trim ankles. The maid would lift a nightgown above Louisa's head, and the light garment would slip over that petite figure with its soft curves, caressing it just as his palms ached to caress every inch of her. . . .

His body responded to the images he was too weak to push away, and he almost groaned. No, he must not torment himself like this—it was insane. He took a long swallow of wine, but still, although he turned his gaze toward the coals dying on the hearth, he saw only the inner vision of her long pale hair and her expressive soft blue eyes, eyes big with chagrin or gleaming with merry mischief.

When Louisa Crookshank took a husband for real, she would lead him a merry dance, Colin thought. A man would have to be firm with her, this lighthearted woman with her impulsive and generous and sometimes foolhardy whims, so that she did not get herself into more scrapes, and yet at the same time her husband must be sweet and gentle. No man with an ounce of honor in his soul could bear to make such a woman unhappy. Or if one existed capable of causing her grief, and if Colin ever heard of her woe, he would ram his fist down that stranger's throat. . . .

Young Sir Lucas, that green and inconsiderate boy, would never have made her a good husband. Colin could not consider the abrupt ending of that engagement with any regret.

Did Louisa regret it? Sweet heaven, he hoped not, just as he wished fervently that she would not have cause to rue this strange conjugal fraud. His plan could come undone in so many ways—he had gambled with her good name, risking it to try to save it. Perhaps he had been just as impetuous as Louisa. . . . No, in life as on the battlefield, sometimes one had to move fast. He would see her through this, somehow, and if the ruse of the elopement did not shield her from the other, greater scandal, he would call out every man in London if need be!

On this highly impractical thought, Colin pushed himself back from the table. More wine would not help; his groin ached with unslaked desire already. But she didn't know how much he wanted to touch her lips, wanted to caress her neck and her smooth white breasts. . . . His body responded again, and he stood, shaking his head as if to cast aside such treacherous thoughts.

It didn't matter what he wanted. The only thing that mattered was Louisa's happiness, that she be allowed to maintain her good name. He wanted to see her flash that bright smile again without any shadow to darken her eyes.

He went slowly up the stairs, his footsteps heavy on the wooden treads, and the inn was quiet around him. He had sent the servants off long ago. When he swung open the door, he stepped into near darkness. Although a fire burned on the hearth, a brass fireguard had been placed in front of it, and in the dimness he could make out only indistinct forms. He closed the door and bolted it behind him. Pausing to put down his glass, he lit the candle waiting on the side table, then loosened his neckcloth. Perhaps he would not bother to undress. He had little hope of enjoying any sleep this night.

A small sound alerted him, and perhaps a trace of lilac scent. Turning quickly, he was startled to see in the small circle of light now stretching across the room, someone sitting in a chair by the window. The slender form was pale against the dimness.

His hand went automatically to the weapon inside his coat.

"Don't shoot, please," she said.

He knew that voice, that same light, trilling, sweet tone he had heard in the brothel. But this time she did not sound frantic with fear, only a little breathless.

"Louisa—Miss Crookshank—" he began, his voice sharp with urgency.

"Mrs. McGregor, you mean," she suggested.

"Only for a few days," he told her. Good lord, was she so innocent that she did not comprehend—did not realize—he drew a deep breath and tried to explain.

"Miss Crookshank, you must leave. You must be chaperoned at all times. We cannot spend any time alone together."

"But we are husband and wife," she pointed out, without making any effort to depart. "It is quite proper." She sat too far from the candle's faint glow, and it was difficult to make out her expression.

He felt the blood surge through him, the deepening ache in his groin. She was wearing only her white nightgown with a light wrapper over it. That smooth curve of her neck that led to the breasts he had yet to glimpse—the breasts that were now almost completely unfettered, with only a light layer of fabric to keep them from his hands—

He gave himself a mental shake.

"You don't understand. We will not be able to obtain an annulment easily, or at all, if there is any suspicion that we have been—that we—that we have come together as husband and wife." He heard the stiffness in his tone. Good lord, he sounded like someone's maiden aunt. But how did one explain to a lady as sheltered and as young as this just what she was risking? She couldn't know how the blood roared in his ears so that he could hardly make out her soft words, or how his passion swirled around him until he felt like a drowning man being drawn deeper and deeper into the whirling maelstrom of his need.

"I trust you," she said simply. At last she stood, but instead of walking toward the door, she took a step closer to him.

Colin drew a deep breath. "You shouldn't," he said, hardly knowing his own voice, it sounded so strange and so harsh. "You can't. You will walk out that door right now. You will go straight to your room and not leave your friend's side again. I am human, Louisa, and as frail as any man, more so than many. I cannot allow you in my room, nor sleep by your side—even if we could risk such closeness, which we cannot—without doing—without showing you what marriage truly means. And then we will never obtain the annulment—"

"I don't want an annulment," she said.

He didn't believe what he'd heard.

"Louisa, be sensible. If this is some momentary expression of gratitude . . . You can do much better, lass, than a paltry half-pay officer with an uncertain reputation!"

She lifted her head and met his gaze. "I don't care about your reputation. I don't care how much money you have. You have never failed to put my welfare before your own. You took pity on me when I fouled my shoe, and you never made sport of my ridiculous dilemma. You washed my foot! When I was downcast, you made me smile. You came to the bawdy house to take me safely home. You are sacrificing your own welfare now. Even if this preposterous plan works—and I think you *must* care for me to see any logic in it or any hope of its success, my dearest—how will you ever find a wife when news of this so-called seduction gets out? You're ready to give up your reputation to save mine, just as you sacrificed your hopes of military advancement to save your men."

He shook his head. "Louisa, you are being a fool!"

She took another step closer.

There seemed to be a humming in his ears. He could smell her lilac scent again, stronger and sweeter, and he saw her breasts rising and falling beneath their thin covering.

"You are either the most honorable man I have ever known or thought of knowing, or perhaps . . . you do love me?" Her voice lifted a little to make it half statement, half query.

"Louisa—" He tried to concentrate on her words, but he felt befogged by her nearness.

"Would it be so bad, being my husband?" She was untying the ribbon that held the light wrap together.

He watched the ribbon untangle itself beneath her fingers, saw her push the garment back and allow it to fall unheeded to the floor.

Now there was only the nightgown, its lace dipping low against the curve of her breasts.

"Oh, sweet heaven," he said, not knowing he had lifted his hand until the curve of her breast rested inside it, like a bird coming home to its nest. It fit naturally, easily, perfectly, as if she had been made only for his touch, created round and soft and smooth only for him to fondle.

Louisa sighed in relief. She saw the flame of the fire reflected in his eyes, and she felt the shudder that went through him. Surely, he could not be indifferent to her.

"I do not wish an annulment," she repeated. "Colin, I love you."

"Then God help us both," he muttered. He stroked her breast, and Louisa felt his touch send strange tingles through her, as if her skin had melted away and he touched something primal deep inside.

"If you change your mind——" he muttered. "Oh, Louisa, my bonny lass——"

"I won't," Louisa assured him, although her voice quivered a little because his hand had moved to pull the nightgown down, exposing her breasts to his view. He brushed the nipples lightly, and her stomach clenched. Who would think such a faint touch could provoke such sensation?

"I hope not, because it's too late," he told her. This time his lips lifted, his smile at once sweet and wicked, and his eyes held that gleam she had come to love. And at last, his voice had lost its harshness, although its tone sounded deeper than usual. "I will not—cannot—let you leave now, sweet Louisa, guileless, cunning Louisa. I warned you long ago to stay far from my path. You are here now, and you are mine, and I will not give you up, not now, not ever. Tonight, you will become my bride in truth as well as in name."

Knowing that her smile must be as wide as his, Louisa flung her arms around his neck. "My husband," she said. "Show me, please, what marriage is."

He lowered his head and kissed her, a deep, warm lingering kiss that was like nothing Louisa had enjoyed before. It made recollections of Louisa's chaste embraces with her former fiancé float away, memories banished by the sudden rush of new feelings, responses such as she had never felt. Colin's lips were firm, and he seemed to know just how to meet her own, just how much pressure made her pulse jump, and just how long to linger. She found, instinctively, that she could kiss him back, meet him—with less skill but no less fervor—halfway.

And then, just as she relaxed into his kiss, his tongue slipped past her half-opened lips. Louisa jumped, startled for a moment by the new sensation. Then she realized she liked this touch, warm again and sure, and again, it tantalized and teased her. . . . And his hands were slipping the nightgown down, and cupping her breasts, both at once, even though he still held her mouth beneath his.

It was almost too much sensation and it rushed through her whole body. His lips, his hands, the way they stroked her skin and left traces of fire behind, as if she were the tinder and he the spark . . .

For a few minutes Louisa forgot to think. When he stepped away for a moment, she opened her eyes and her lips to protest, but she saw that he had shrugged out of his coat and was pulling off his shirt.

Yes, she approved of that! She looked over her new husband with interest. Back in Bath she had young cousins still in the nursery and had occasionally helped with their care, but she had never seen a grown man naked. His chest and arms were just as nicely muscled as she had thought they might be. An old scar on his shoulder and another on his torso made her wince for him, but then she forgot her concern when she saw he was pulling off his boots. Or trying to pull off his boots.

He looked up at her. "Don't giggle, wench! I shall have to call a manservant. There is no bootjack here, and it would ruin the finish of my best boots if I used such a thing!"

"Can I do it?" Louisa asked.

"Do you wish to?" He sounded surprised.

She nodded. "Why not? You have done as much for me and when I was in much greater disorder. At least your boots are clean."

"Sit on the side of the bed," he suggested.

She did, and he lifted one foot, putting the well-polished boot between her legs, resting his foot against the bed frame. The leather felt cool against the inside of her thigh, and she felt again a quiver of unfamiliar sensation.

"You will have to grip it tightly," he suggested, with a hint of mischief in his voice.

She put both her hands around the heel, braced herself and pulled. For a moment, she thought she did not have the strength, but then the tight-fitting boot released its grip, and she fell back against the feather mattress.

But his foot was free. Colin took the boot from her and dropped it on the floor. "One more time," he said. Again, he lifted his foot and braced it against the frame, again she tugged.

This time, it came more easily.

"If you need a reference as a gentleman's valet—" he murmured.

She giggled again. Louisa watched as, free of the tall boots, he rapidly shed his trousers, then his stockings and underclothes.

He came out of his remaining garments with a smooth grace, and before Louisa could do more than blink, she was staring at her husband in the flickering light of the candle, marveling at the masculine potency so obvious to her startled gaze.

This was the shape of a man, then.

"What if—what if I don't like this?" she asked, hearing the wobble in her voice.

Colin grinned at her. "Trust me, lass," he suggested. "You are going to like this very much indeed."

She bit her lip. "Are you sure?"

"Oh, yes, sweet Louisa. My word as a gentleman and officer." He leaned over to kiss her lips again.

This part, she understood. Louisa shut her eyes—it was easier to enjoy the sensations when she did not have the intimidating sight of him in front of her—and enjoyed the touch of his mouth against her own.

Then he touched her breasts again, and she shivered with the thrill that coursed through her. He caressed one nipple, then another, then both at once. Louisa felt an unfamiliar ache deep in her belly, and tried to think why one part of her body would feel so when it was her breasts that he stroked . . . then he lowered his lips to take one of her nipples inside his warm supple mouth, and she forgot to think.

She gasped, and then as his tongue lingered over the firm pressing center, put her hands behind his head and pulled him harder against her. Oh, yes, yes. He kissed and suckled and fondled until her body moved without her volition, and when he released one breast, she had no time to protest because he bent toward the other, kissing it, running his tongue lightly, teasingly over that nipple, too, stirring even more of the strange yearnings deep inside her.

He paused long enough to kiss the side of her neck, and Louisa was surprised that this part of her, too, was sensitive to his touch. And the underside of her jaw, and her ear—every part of her held unexpected sensations, new responses that she'd never suspected might exist.

He ran his hands over her arms and then back to her shoulders, her neck, feathering down to her breasts again, and while she waited, breathing quickly, for the wonderful touch once again, his hands slid lower.

Her stomach, too, could quiver with delight as he stroked and kissed and stroked again. And his hands dipped even lower, and suddenly Louisa felt sensations so intense they were almost—oh!—almost painful. He slipped his hand between her legs, and the skin seemed aflame, and there was something she needed, a distinct ache she had not felt before. . . .

And his hand was there—just where she yearned for it.

She moved away, for an instant, almost alarmed by how deep the need was, how sharp her response to his light touch.

"Don't run away, my own true love," he said, his voice low as he kissed her neck, her lips, her cheek.

The words as much as his touch warmed her. She relaxed against him, allowing his long fingers to ease against her and then—she held her breath for an instant—to slip inside her, touching what must be her very core. Nothing else could feel so exquisite, so intense, so deeply pleasurable.

Louisa found she was making soft noises deep in her throat, and she blushed, not sure if this was proper. But Colin—her husband—smiled down at her, and she saw the love shining in his eyes. And she forgot to worry that she might not do this right.

He stroked her, gentled her, and provoked her until Louisa found herself moving against his hand, wanting something more but not sure what it would be.

And then he lifted himself over her, and before she even

could think about his change in position, she felt his body against her, slipping inside her.

And he was large, indeed. For a moment she tensed. He put his arms around her, holding her lightly, kissing her breasts again, bringing back the waves of pleasure that rolled over her until her stiffness faded. Then she felt him push, just for an instant, then again, and suddenly he sank deeper inside her. She gasped at a sharp, quick pain, and then he was kissing her, stroking her, cupping her breasts in his hands, and she forgot the momentary discomfort.

He moved again, and she braced herself for the pain to return, but instead, this time a ripple of pleasure seemed to turn her inside out. She gasped again, but this time in delighted recognition. There was a bigger ache inside her, a pleasant urgent insistent need, and now she was at last able to see what it was that would ease her.

He moved in and out. Her body arched against his, inviting him further inside, and he thrust against her, slowly at first, then faster and harder, falling into a rhythm older than time.

Louisa forgot everything except the circles of pleasure that coiled around her, wrapping her in sensation, lifting her in delight.

There was no one else in the world except she and Colin, no sounds except the rhythm of their bodies moving together and the faint rustle of the bed linen, no feelings beyond the deepest joy that his body created inside hers. They were the world, they were the music, they were the joy.

And still the feelings grew, and she learned how to meet him, move with him, till she found herself rising, soaring like a flute's highest notes lifting to a crescendo, and someone cried out—she did not know who—when she reached the topmost note of all.

Then she was falling, falling, and he was there to catch her, hold her, kiss her lips while she tried to form words in a language she didn't know, inarticulate sounds of surprised and languorous satiation.

When at last he lay his head back against the bedsheet, she rested inside his arms. They seemed to be fused into a tangle of damp limbs, sprawled across the bed in a living love knot more pleasing and more potent than any her sewing lessons had ever produced.

One part of her mind wondered why on earth she had not wed years earlier, even as the other part told her wisely that this marvel could not have occurred in such a way until she had met this particular man. It had to be Colin McGregor, with his strange prickly pride and the love he had fought so hard not to confess. No one else but this proud and impoverished Scot, who avowed a greed he did not feel and tried to deny the honor and decency that was part of his soul, could have moved her so.

And while he held her close, while he kissed the tangled fair locks that clung to her moist forehead, he sighed.

"Lass, you could have done better," he whispered against her hair. "They will say I married you for your money, you know that."

"I don't care what they say," she told him, looking up to meet his troubled gaze once more before the candle guttered in its pool of wax, and the darkness closed upon them. "I know the truth—that I am the one enriched."

*Louisa had supplied the money for Gemma and the maid* from the inn, with another male servant engaged as escort, to hire a carriage from the posting house and return to London. Gemma had departed with many mixed feelings, worrying whether Louisa had made the right choice. Yet, when the two women hugged before Gemma made her way out of the inn, Louisa had seemed very confident, and the light in her friend's eyes was as bright as Gemma had ever seen it.

Louisa loved Lieutenant McGregor—Gemma did not doubt that. And she was nearly positive that the lieutenant returned her friend's regard. Yet there was always the chance that he had arranged the whole elopement to gain the wealthy bride he had, by his own admission, been seeking. . . .

So traveling once again by moonlight as Gemma made the first segment of her trip, she struggled against her anxiety. Still, Louisa had made the decision, and under the circumstances, what were her alternatives? Go back and reconcile with Sir Lucas? Try to endure the scandal if gossip of the brothel visit leaked into the Ton? Go through with the annulment? And in the end, it was Louisa's choice to make, no one else's.

The hired coachman knew this route well, and when the darkness became too deep, they stopped in the next village and took rooms. Although she tossed and turned most of the night, Gemma rose early, eager to complete the trip. When she arrived at Louisa's rented London house in the afternoon, she climbed out of the carriage feeling both relief and a strong sense of fatigue.

Smelters appeared to take in her baggage. Gemma ignored the inquisitive gleam in the footman's eyes, but as she spoke to the hired servants, giving them their fee and arranging for their journey back to Brighton, she saw the curtains move in the sitting room.

Oh, dear, Gemma would have the task of breaking the news to Miss Pomshack—not a task she looked forward to. At least she could spare Louisa that ordeal. And, if she could pour oil on roiled water, Gemma told herself, it would be one thing she could do for her friend. Mentally bracing herself, she entered the house.

Sure enough, the older lady was waiting in the sitting room. At least today she was on her feet and seemed to have overcome her hysterics.

But she seemed poised for a scene of high drama. When Gemma entered the room, Louisa's companion lifted her chin. "Miss Smith, thank heavens! But where is Miss Crookshank? I have been prostrate with anxiety! If I have failed in my duty to keep her from harm, to guarantee her propriety and her good name—"

Gemma smiled and made her tone reassuring. "She is

safe and well, Miss Pomshack, and most grieved to have caused you concern."

"She did not go to that terrible place?" Miss Pomshack looked down her hooked nose, and for an instant, Gemma remembered the cleric cousin who so resembled her.

"No, indeed," Gemma lied. "We summoned Lieutenant McGregor, who talked Miss Crookshank out of such a precipitous action. However, he had something else to discuss with her, and—this may seem somewhat sudden, but I must explain that Miss Crookshank and Sir Lucas have ended their engagement."

"What?" The other woman raised her brows in horror. "But Sir Lucas was such an eligible gentleman."

"And the lieutenant then found himself free to profess his own love and deep feelings for Miss Crookshank. And they have married."

"What!" This time it was a shriek. Miss Pomshack, who had been standing as erect as a vengeful saint, collapsed into the nearest chair.

"Yes, we came back to pack our bags, and of course, Miss Crookshank would have invited you to accompany her, but you were sleeping deeply after your earlier distress, and we didn't wish to risk your health. So I went with Miss Crookshank to play chaperone until the wedding was conducted."

Gemma took a breath, but the other woman seemed still too shocked to speak, so Gemma hurried on. "They were married in Brighton by your cousin, because the lieutenant remembered how highly you had spoken of him. Then I returned home, and Miss Crookshank—Mrs. McGregor, I should say, and her husband will rejoin us shortly."

For a moment, the other woman struggled between affront and relief, the emotions chasing each other across her face. At last she seemed to decide upon gracious acceptance. "I am happy to hear that the lieutenant paid such heed to my words. I'm sure my cousin was pleased to be of assistance."

"Oh, he was, and sorry that you were not able to be

there. But Louisa felt a quiet marriage was appropriate."

Miss Pomshack frowned for a moment. "Since she has just ended one engagement to marry another man, I should think so. But I do hope she has made the right choice. Lieutenant McGregor is quite charming, but he has no great estate. And what Society will say about this—I know that Miss—Mrs. McGregor still had hopes of entering the Ton."

"True, but I believe they will be happy together, and we must hope for the best," Gemma was saying when the footman appeared in the doorway. Had he been listening outside? It didn't matter. The servants would learn the story, or the modified version of it, soon enough.

"You have a caller, Miss. Lady Gabriel Sinclair and a friend."

Gemma had been so consumed with Louisa's predicament that for some time she had had little time or energy to worry about her own fate. She stared at the footman for a moment, then jumped up.

"Show her in, of course!"

Was this simply more to do with the foundling home, where Gemma was happy to add her small efforts, or could it be about Gemma's letter?

"Lady Gabriel Sinclair and Miss Circe Hill," the footman announced.

When Lady Gabriel—Gemma still found it hard to think of her as Psyche—appeared in the doorway, she was accompanied by a young girl of about thirteen, with straight brown hair and a plain angular face, who nonetheless showed signs of beauty yet to come.

"This is my sister, Circe," Psyche explained as the ladies exchanged curtsies. "We have been at the park so that Circe could sketch, but I also have something to show you." Psyche held a small parcel in her gloved hands.

"How nice of you to come," Gemma said, trying to keep her voice even. "I'm pleased to meet you, Miss Hill. My friend Louisa is not at home just now, but I am anxious to see what you have found. Bring us some tea, please." She motioned to the footman, who bowed and left the room.

Lady Gabriel took a seat and unwrapped the parcel she had carried. Inside the brown paper was a small book.

Gemma felt her pulse jump.

"We have been so busy with the foundling home, I fear you must have thought that we—my husband and I—had forgotten his promise to you. But yesterday I received the housekeeping book, which has his mother's handwriting in it, and I thought we would compare it with your letter."

"Oh, yes!" Gemma exclaimed. She hurried across to the desk where she had locked her prized letter for safekeeping, opened a drawer and drew out the paper.

The two women sat down side by side—Miss Pomshack sat across from them, but Gemma could tell the older lady peered hard to see the script, too—and compared the two missives.

They looked at a receipt for pear preserves and a list of household linen, which Psyche was sure that Gabriel's mother had written herself, and then compared the faded handwriting in the book to that in the note.

After a few moments of silence, Psyche said, "The shape of the letters look very alike to me."

Letting out the breath she had been holding, Gemma nodded. She thought the same, but it was better to let Psyche make the first assertion. "Yes, I agree. Of course, I realize that this may not completely convince your husband, but—"

"But he is a fair-minded man, Gemma, and I'm sure he will weigh this piece of evidence, for we must consider it that. And there is something else." For some reason, Psyche exchanged a glance with her younger sister. The child had quietly opened her sketchbook and seemed to be doodling.

"Although we have not yet heard from Gabriel's older brother, who is traveling abroad and difficult to reach, Gabriel remembered some items that John sent to us some time ago."

She opened her reticule. This bundle was even smaller

than the book. Gemma watched as Psyche unwrapped a piece of cloth and revealed a small velvet box, of the kind that often contained jewelry. Inside was a broach, edged in gold, with something painted in the center. It looked like an eye.

What on earth? Gemma blinked at it, and Miss Pomshack leaned closer to see.

"My husband thinks that this must have belonged to their mother. His brother told him last year that after her death, he found a cache of hidden letters—"

"Letters?" Gemma looked up, hope leaping inside her.

"Yes, but John burned them, thinking them too personal to read," Psyche said. "As it turns out, that may have been an unfortunate—if honorable—decision. But this was one of her other hidden treasures. However, we do not know what it signifies."

"It seems to show an eye, a human eye." Gemma noted the obvious. "But I have never seen such an ornament."

This time, it was the child who answered. Except for a murmured greeting, she had been silent until now, occupied with her pencil and her sketchbook. "The eye painted on the broach is very similar to both your eyes and Gabriel's. You can observe the shape and the unusual shade of dark blue."

Gemma gazed at her in surprise. This young girl, who had seemed so quiet and demure, spoke with all the authority of an adult. Miss Pomshack, always a stickler for decorous behavior, looked disapproving.

Psyche said quickly, "My sister is an artist. She has studied anatomy, as well as artistic technique, and is just now returned from several weeks of instruction with a noted portrait painter who was visiting England to fulfill some commissions."

"And I hope to travel to the Continent myself, soon, to pursue further studies," the girl added.

Psyche sighed. "Circe, I said we will discuss that later. You are too young."

Circe frowned in obvious disagreement, but she turned back to Gemma. "Psyche was quite right about you, however.

You and Gabriel have many features in common. I do believe you must be related."

Gemma blinked at this candid assessment. Taking a deep breath, she said, "Thank you. Do you think this broach was painted to show Gabriel's eye, or even mine? Though I cannot think what the purpose would be."

The child shook her head. "This is obviously an older person, probably a man if you look at the shape of his brow, though I cannot be sure. Observe the small wrinkles about the eye. It cannot be of a child, and I think from the style of the painting that it is not of recent creation. It could have been painted twenty years ago or more."

Now that Circe pointed them out, Gemma saw plainly the tiny laugh lines about the eye. What an unusual child, she thought briefly, but she was more concerned with the puzzle of the broach itself.

"Miss Pomshack, have you ever seen such a thing?" she asked the older lady.

Miss Pomshack shook her head. "I'm afraid not," she said, with obvious regret.

"If it is an out-moded fashion, I know someone who might be able to tell us more!" Psyche said suddenly. "I think we should pay a call on a friend of mine."

# Sixteen

*"Like a wildflower,
love sometimes blooms in unexpected places—
but its scent is still as sweet."*

—MARGERY, COUNTESS OF SEALEY

*They all crowded into Psyche's carriage.* It was obvious that Miss Pomshack would have been devastated to have been left behind, and Gemma felt she owed the woman something. Louisa's companion had missed the wild elopement journey, and even though she would have disapproved of the whole idea, she was human enough to regret being left out. So this time Gemma invited her politely to come along, and Miss Pomshack eagerly accepted.

Psyche gave directions to her footman. When her groom shut the door and the carriage moved forward, she explained.

"The countess of Sealey is a confidant who was also my late mother's close friend. She has been part of the Ton's elite since she made her own debut and her first marriage several decades ago. She is twice widowed and a dowager countess now but still active in Society. She knows all the gossip, current and passé."

Gemma must have looked anxious because Psyche added, "And I promise you, Gemma, she is completely trustworthy, with a shrewd mind and a kind heart. She will not betray our secret."

Gemma nodded, although she found that she had gripped her hands tightly together. She was silent through the short ride as Psyche chatted a little, telling them more about the countess, then even she fell silent.

The atmosphere inside the fashionable chaise seemed tense. Would Lord Gabriel ever accept Gemma as his sister or maybe half-sister? Why had her mother not confided in someone, anyone? Some secrets were too important to be taken to the grave! For a moment Gemma felt a flare of anger at the mother she had never known, then she sighed and pushed the emotion aside. Who knew what her mother had endured? The marchioness had written the letter to be given to Gemma and that was still the lifeline that Gemma held to her heart. In some way, at least, her mother had cared. Lady Gillingham had wanted to reclaim the daughter she had perhaps been forced to put away from her.

But Gemma's stomach was knotted with anxiety when they arrived at a large and elegant house and were shown inside. Upstairs in an exquisite peach-colored drawing room, they found the lady of the house. Psyche performed the introductions, and the countess was welcoming.

"What a pleasure to see you," she told them, her tone gracious. Despite her age, Lady Sealey was a lovely woman, with natural silver hair and gently wrinkled skin stretching across a fine bone structure, the wrinkles softened by a light coating of face powder. Her lavender and gray silk dress was as fine and as costly as her surroundings. Her eyes bright with intelligence and curiosity, she waited with well-bred ease as Psyche unfolded the broach with its painted eye and held it out for the countess to examine.

"Have you ever seen anything like this, Lady Sealey?"

The older lady took the ornament and held it up to inspect through a lorgnette she drew from her reticule. "Of course, but not for many years."

The silence seemed heavy with suspense. But their

hostess considered for a moment before she went on. "You may have heard that when our esteemed Prince Regent was a young man, he took a lady to be his wife, even though the law of the land forbade a prince and heir to do such a thing, considering certain facts about her situation."

Tactful, indeed, Gemma thought. She had heard of the young prince's love of an older woman, who was considered unsuitable to be a future queen of England.

"The connection had to be kept secret, except from his close friends, and so—despite a lot of whispering among the rest of Society—did his adoration of the lady. But in defiance of his critics and the prohibitions that prevented him from making the lady his queen, the prince had a broach painted with her eye in its center. He could wear it as an unobtrusive declaration of his love, but one that would still shield her identity. For a few years it was quite the rage for others in the Ton to do the same. Later, he had to put the lady aside and marry a suitable—by class and lineage, at least!—queen, and the fashion died. I doubt you would find any of these worn nowadays." She paused and looked up at them, too well-bred to ask the obvious question.

Psyche sighed. "No, you're right. It is a mystery as to what it signifies, but you may have helped us unravel it."

Lady Sealey touched the surface of the broach with the tip of her finger. "Whoever wore this was most likely declaring a private and perhaps forbidden love, just as the prince once did." She glanced at Psyche, then toward Gemma. "And since the eye painted here is the same unusual shade as that of your husband's eyes, and, I must note, of this lovely young lady—"

Shrewd, indeed! Gemma blinked, not sure what to say.

Psyche answered for her. "Yes, we think there is a connection here that we had not known about earlier. We are trying to make out what is true and which has also been hidden from us."

"What does Lord Gabriel think?" Lady Sealey asked, raising her silvery brows.

"He is . . . torn," Psyche admitted. "He was deeply devoted to his mother."

"You must remind him that his mother had a most unhappy life with her husband, and despite the late marquess's violent and unkind nature, it would have been well nigh impossible for her to leave him. I know it is difficult for Gabriel to consider that Lady Gillingham might have had another man in her life. Men, especially, often wish to envision their mothers as saintly. But in the end, she was not a saint, you know, only a person who desired love just as most of us do." The countess's tone was gentle but firm.

Psyche nodded. "I shall tell him. What he will decide, I do not know. I do wish that his mother had left us a more definite explanation."

"If she had outlived her husband, perhaps she would have," Lady Sealey pointed out. "She died first, did she not? Perhaps she felt it was not safe to leave a clear detailing while her husband still lived and might yet have discovered her secrets."

"That's true," Psyche said slowly.

Feeling the heat in her cheeks, Gemma stared down at the hands she clenched tightly together in her lap. They were discussing her fate, her origins, and it was hard not to be self-conscious. Was she, after all, born of a union not sanctified by marriage? And would Gabriel ever consider acknowledging that she might be his relative? Her mother was dead, her father unknown and seemingly likely to stay that way. Lord Gabriel was perhaps the only chance she had left to have a family to claim her, certainly the only connection she knew about for certain. The old loneliness swept back over her, the sense of separation she had lived with for years, and she blinked hard against betraying tears.

Then she realized that Lady Sealey was speaking to her.

"Do not be distressed, Miss Smith. I am sure this must be very trying for you. If your mother was Lady Gillingham, she was a gentle and loving woman and a parent who would have cherished you if she could. Remember, in the end, you are what you make yourself, no matter what your origins."

Many in the Ton would never agree with that! Including Arnold, Gemma suspected. She remembered that Psyche had described the countess as forward thinking. Yes, indeed. But the lady was still speaking.

"The people who know you best will accept you, and you must accept yourself. With such secrets in your family history, you may have a more difficult time than those more fortunately situated, but the extra trials will make you strong, and you must not allow yourself to become bitter. Cultivate the same loving nature that your mother possessed, and be proud of the added strength that your ordeals have given you, a firmness which she may not have been able to find inside herself. In the end, we all do the best we can." Her tone was kind, and the blue eyes, faded with age, seemed very wise.

Swallowing incipient tears, Gemma said, "Thank you."

"I shall be happy to receive you at anytime in my salon, my dear," Lady Sealey told her. "And I get about quite a bit. If you decide to go into Society, you will find friends there."

"Thank you," Gemma repeated, her voice husky.

The ladies chatted for a few more minutes on less serious topics. Then Psyche rose, and the rest of their party followed suit as they made their farewells. When they were back in the carriage, Psyche reached to press Gemma's hand.

"I will speak to Gabriel and tell him what we have learned."

She said no more, but she could hardly promise what her husband would decide, Gemma knew.

"I appreciate what you have done," Gemma answered.

When Psyche and her sister had left them at Louisa's home and departed, Miss Pomshack was eager to gossip.

"What an honor to meet Lady Sealey, and such a gracious lady she is! You really must not repine, my dear Miss Smith. With such a patron ready to offer you credence, not to mention the goodwill of Lady Gabriel, even if Lord Gabriel himself does not formally acknowledge you—and it is understandable if he does not wish to, no slight intended toward you, but it is his mother's reputation at stake here, after all—you will not be totally ignored. It is a great pity that the sins of the fathers shall be visited upon the children, but the Good Book says—"

"Yes," Gemma interrupted. "Thank you, I am familiar with the quotation, and it is always good to reflect upon Holy Writ. But just now, my head is aching." And she was not in a mind to endure platitudes, no matter how well meant, she thought ruefully.

"You poor child," the other woman said. "Would you like me to make up one of my special tisanes?"

"That would be most kind of you," Gemma told her, reflecting that she could always pour the noxious mixture into the slop jar. "If you would have Lily bring it up to my bedroom, I will drink it there and take a short rest."

"Of course, just what you need after such an eventful day," Miss Pomshack agreed.

Feeling a little guilty, but only a little, Gemma went up to her room and did indeed lie down upon her bed. As kindhearted as Lady Sealey had been, Gemma still felt overcome with trepidation. In the end, she always returned to the same question. Who was she, who was Gemma Smith, really? It seemed now there would never be a definite answer. . . .

To make up for her slight subterfuge, she forced herself to drink Miss Pomshack's herbal concoction when the maid brought it up, then she tried to shut her eyes. She was short of sleep from several turbulent nights. And she thought of the countess's suggestion that those who cared for her would not mind what her origins might be. Would Arnold agree?

Then she thought of Captain Fallon, still in the west of England occupied with the search for his sister. She admired him so much for his unswerving loyalty to his sibling. She could have been Clarissa, could have shared

Clarissa's peril. Gemma so wanted the young woman to be found, to be safe, and to be reunited with her family.

Family. It always came back to that. This time she did weep, a little, from overwrought nerves and the old sadness. But then she rose and washed her face and resolved that she must be calm and resolute—she would not give up. With that thought in mind, she dressed for dinner and resolved to present a serene face to Miss Pomshack.

The other lady was happy to take credit, through her tisane, for Gemma's improved state of mind, and they shared a quiet dinner together. Gemma thought a bit uneasily of Louisa. She hoped her friend would send word, soon, if she did not plan to return to London. Gemma would like to know that all was well. But Louisa was of age, and Gemma did not think that Lieutenant McGregor would abuse her. In fact, thinking briefly of just what the two newlyweds might be doing this evening brought a slight blush to her cheek. To change the highly improper direction of her thoughts, Gemma inquired of Miss Pomshack about the book the lady had been reading.

She was then forced to listen politely to a discussion of weighty theologic topics, which was more than enough to take anyone's mind off the possibility of riotous lovemaking.

*The next day, they had another unexpected visitor.*

"Mrs. Andrew Forsythe," Smelters announced from the doorway.

Gemma looked up in surprise. Miss Pomshack put away her book, and they both stood to receive their visitor, who was a fashionably clad matron with brown hair and merry brown eyes, who was shorter and more rounded than her friend Psyche.

"I thought I should pay a call and get acquainted before the ball tomorrow night, so that we will all be at ease," she explained.

"I am delighted to meet you. Your invitations were so

generous," Gemma said. "I know I can speak for my friend. Louisa is out of town, but she will be so sorry to have missed you." Gemma realized she had a new worry. Would Louisa return in time for the ball? And if she did, could she bear to face the possibly censorious Ton with rumors of the veiled lady at the brothel perhaps already circulating?

A rumble of wheels outside the opened window made her turn her head, and Miss Pomshack hurried over to look. "Oh, how fortunate. I believe Miss Crookshank—that is, Mrs. McGregor—has returned."

Mrs. Forsythe raised her brows, but Gemma hesitated, not sure she could even begin to explain. Fortunately, she heard the bustle of the new arrivals, and within a short time, Louisa herself appeared in the doorway.

"Colin has gone back to the hotel to collect his things—" she began, untying the ribbons of her hat, then halted. "Oh, hello."

"Mrs. Forsythe has kindly paid us a call," Gemma hurried to explain. "Mrs. Forsythe, this is my friend Louisa—"

Then she hesitated.

Louisa dipped a curtsy and came forward. "Mrs. Forsythe, it was exceedingly kind of you to invite us. I have been anticipating the ball with great delight. But I fear I must tell you—" She paused and seemed to gather her courage. "I am not sure if I should presume upon your benevolence when my appearance at your home may cause talk. I have just recently—I have ended my engagement to Sir Lucas Englewood and formed a new attachment. Although it may seem sudden, I was married two days ago in Brighton. My husband is Lieutenant Colin McGregor."

Gemma held her breath, and Louisa seemed to brace herself.

But instead of looking shocked or affronted, Mrs. Forsythe gave a peal of laughter. "You mean there might be a touch of scandal about your sudden marriage? How delightful, just the thing to make my party the talk of the Ton.

My dear, you must come! And I wish to hear all the particulars. I love a good romantic tale."

Louisa looked surprised for a moment, then she sat down on a chair across from them. "You are very good, Mrs. Forsythe."

"Oh, call me Sally," the lady told them. "And now, tell me all."

Louisa glanced at Gemma, and Gemma bit back a smile, glad that this time it would be Louisa who had to pick careful steps among the true and the not-so-true details about her quick marriage, deciding what to share and what not to reveal.

So they were still going to the ball? Louisa was being very brave, risking the frowns of Society. And Gemma . . . like Cinderella, Gemma would go dogged by fear, waiting for the clock to strike midnight and her assumption of gentlewoman's status to melt away like the fairy-tale heroine's magical gown. She still felt unsure, an impostor, vulnerable to exposure and ridicule.

Almost, almost she would have wished that they could decline the invitation. But if Sally Forsythe was being so generous, and if Louisa was ready to face the Ton, how could Gemma say no? She had to back up her friend.

Mrs. Forsythe had taken her leave by the time Lieutenant McGregor returned from the hotel with his clothing and other personal items. But he was entirely in favor of going ahead with their plans.

"Of course you should go," he agreed. "Look your enemy in the eye, and force him to blink first. No McGregor ever turned tail and ran from a confrontation!"

Louisa smiled at the reminder that she was now a McGregor, too, and the pair exchanged a quick kiss.

Gemma thought that Louisa seemed to glow with happiness. Louisa had always possessed a merry spirit, but Gemma had never seen her friend look this joyful before. Watching the newlyweds, Gemma felt a slight sense of wistfulness. If only . . .

She shook away her own doldrums and went upstairs to change for dinner. But while she slipped into her same old dinner dress, and then when she stared absently in the looking glass while Lily brushed out her dark hair and arranged it becomingly, she still thought about Louisa and the lieutenant's obvious devotion to each other. It must be lovely to be so sure of your heart. Thank goodness Louisa had not married Sir Lucas, even though it had seemed the more appropriate marriage.

And if, after dinner, Louisa seemed ready to retire to bed very early, Gemma was determined not to think about the reasons for her hostess's declared weariness and somewhat unconvincing yawns. Gemma said good night to the newlyweds and pretended not to see the look the two exchanged as they climbed the stairs hand in hand. Yet it left her feeling, somehow, very lonely. She certainly could not recall Mr. Cuthbertson ever gazing at her in just that way. . . .

Gemma was about to ascend to her own chamber when she heard a knock at the door. Who on earth, at this hour? She paused, waiting for the footman to appear.

"Captain Fallon, miss," he announced. "Shall I tell him that the household has retired for the night?"

"No!" she said quickly. "I'm sure he has good reason for a late call, and anyhow, it's only nine o'clock. Show him into the drawing room, if you please."

Ignoring his disapproving expression, Gemma went back into the room and sank onto the settee, trying to compose her expression. Oh, was it possible the captain had at last located his sister?

But when he appeared in the doorway, his bleak expression revealed—before he uttered a word—that his quest had been unsuccessful.

"I apologize for calling at this late hour," he said.

She hurried to him and, without thinking, held out her hands. She had seldom seen him look so discouraged. "There was no sign of her?"

He held both her hands between his and shook his head.

"Oh, Matthew—I mean Captain Fallon—I'm so sorry."

He didn't seem to notice her slip. "I am so full of fear for her, fear that I will fail her. When I returned to the hotel, I couldn't bear to sit alone in my rooms, and there was a note from McGregor, with a rather strange tale, which I have barely deciphered. Then, too, I thought you would be waiting to hear about my trip." She explained quickly about the trip to the brothel, their fear of scandal, and Louisa and Colin's elopement.

He frowned. "I will check out this place again, just in case. You should not have taken such a risk, but thank you. And again, forgive me for coming so late. I just wanted to see—"

He paused, and for a moment, something besides his frustration and constant anxiety glinted in his dark eyes.

Still hurting for him, Gemma said quickly, "Of course. I was anxious—we are anxious—for the latest news. I only wish it had been more happy."

She became aware that he still gripped her hands, and that they were standing very close. She was acutely aware of his male presence, the virile strength that he projected without any conscious effort . . . and of how her body responded to it. Why had Arnold never made her feel this way?

She should step back, put a respectable distance between them. Captain Fallon had every excuse for not thinking rationally, but she should be more circumspect. She should, Gemma thought, but she didn't move.

"I wanted to see you," he finished at last, and now he seemed to be looking at her, not at the unhappy fears that haunted his thoughts, looking at Gemma, seeing Gemma.

Gemma felt her heart beat faster. It was only that she reminded him of his sister, she told herself. No doubt because of their similarities in circumstance.

Yet when he bent even closer to her, his expression was not in the least brotherly. "Gemma, Miss Smith—"

"Yes?" she whispered. For a heartbeat their faces were only inches apart, then—she felt as if the whole world had stopped its spinning, and time itself seemed to slow—he bent to kiss her lips.

She gave herself to the embrace, and he pulled her closer. His mouth was hungry. She kissed him back just as eagerly, her whole body tingling with awareness, with need, with pure delight. . . .

When at last he pulled back, the room seemed to whirl about her for an instant, and she had to draw a deep, shaky breath. For another long minute he simply held her, gazing at her as if he had never seen her before.

Finally, when he spoke, it was only to softly speak her name. "Oh, Gemma." He released her with apparent reluctance. "Duty is a harsh taskmaster. I learned it at sea, and even now—"

"Yes?" Her mouth was dry. Did emotion leap inside his dark eyes?

But he seemed to conquer his feelings, and now he dropped his arms. "That was—that was—"

"Wonderful!" she finished for him, and to hell with being ladylike.

He smiled, and she was glad to see his expression lighten. "More than wonderful," he agreed. "Enough to shake any man's resolve. But it is late, and I should not have come at all. It was just, I had to see you. Somehow, you always give me new hope. And someday . . ."

This time she bit her lip, afraid of what she might blurt out.

But his voice trailed off, and only his hungry gray eyes betrayed him. "I must go."

Yet, he lingered another silent minute, gazing at her as if she were the lantern that lit his darkness. And when he bowed and strode rapidly away, as if to make up for his hesitation, she watched him go, her heart still beating very fast.

One thing was certain, Gemma thought. She could not marry Arnold Cuthbertson when another man made her feel so alive. She would write Arnold a note tomorrow and break the news as easily as she could.

❧

*The next morning, Gemma was not the only one writing* notes. Louisa spent several hours writing a long letter to her uncle and aunt in Bath. "Really, I'm quite glad I don't have to explain the hasty marriage in person," she confessed to Gemma. "By the time we go to visit, they will have had some space in which to come to terms with the whole situation!" Then she penned another letter to be sent to the aunt who was abroad.

After a light luncheon, they went upstairs to bathe and began leisurely preparations for the ball. Only then did Louisa remember to send down the dress she had had altered for Gemma to wear.

Lily laid it out on the bed. "Isn't it pretty, miss? Such a fine silk, and the trim really sets it off."

Gemma stared at the ball gown. It was blue, a delicate pale blue. Louisa had obviously forgotten her aversion to the color.

And now there was no time to prepare anything else, even if she had been willing to risk offending her friend, who had been so generous to pass on such a lovely and expensive dress.

She would have to wear it.

"Yes, indeed," Gemma muttered, and the maid beamed. Taking a deep breath, Gemma allowed Lily to help her on with the gown. After Lily did up the small hooks on the back of the blue bodice, its curved neckline trimmed with lace and seed pearls, and arranged the blue overskirt with its flounce, Gemma turned to stare at her reflection.

The gown looked elegant. Her blue eyes, made even more brilliant by the clear tones of the dress, seemed more vivid. Her dark hair had been arranged high on her head, with only a few curls left loose by her temple to soften the effect, and her face looked fashionably pale.

Louisa had lent her a short circlet of pearls, which Lily fastened about her neck. The necklace was just right for a young unmarried lady and went perfectly with the dress, and there were matching ear drops.

She looked quite grand. Amazed, Gemma stared at herself. She did not look like a former inhabitant of a foundling home, a girl without a name, a woman with no family to claim her. She stood up a little straighter.

Louisa had given her more than a dress. She had declared her unqualified friendship, and that was a beginning, surely, perhaps the first of more bonds that would connect Gemma to people whom she loved.

It had been so lonely, not knowing who she was or where she belonged. But perhaps, perhaps, she would be alone no longer.

Gemma ran her palms lightly over the fine smooth silk. This dress fit as if it had been made for her from the start, and the color, clean and clear, was nothing like the faded blue-gray of the foundling home garments. She should push aside those old memories, wash them away just as she had helped scrub out the filthy home itself. Since Psyche had taken charge of the orphanage, its appearance was changing rapidly, as was the condition of the girls who lived there. No one would go hungry again, or labor in cold hallways, or be subject to the harsh discipline of an uncaring matron.

Perhaps it was high time Gemma wore blue again and exorcized the memories of the worst year of her life, putting those ghosts to rest forever.

When Louisa came to knock on the door and look inside, she said, "Oh, Gemma, you look ravishing! I knew that dress would become you."

"Thank you." Gemma turned to observe her friend, a fairy vision in pale pink and gold. Louisa's new dresser had done her fair hair into an intricate arrangement of curls and silk flowers. "You look beautiful yourself. And thank you for the dress. It is so generous of you."

"It's nothing." Louisa waved away the expression of gratitude, but she looked pleased. "Do you think we are ready to brave the lions of the Ton? My stomach feels as if it is full of hissing geese."

Gemma laughed at the image. "We shall be a menagerie, then," she agreed. "My stomach feels about as calm as a pond full of leaping carp."

Louisa giggled. "Oh, there is another surprise for you. A package came for you a little while ago."

"For me?"

Lily was sent to fetch it, and when she brought back the box, Gemma tugged at the string that held it shut. She couldn't imagine what it might be, unless Louisa had been even more generous. . . .

When the lid was lifted, Gemma sighed in appreciation. Inside was a lacy white shawl, just the thing to wrap about one's shoulders for a formal evening.

"How lovely," Louisa said, looking over her shoulder to see what the box contained. "Who is it from?"

There was a note. Gemma unfolded the paper and glanced first at the signature. "Captain Fallon," she said in surprise.

Louisa, however, showed no astonishment. "He has very nice taste, for a man," she said, and to Gemma's relief, made no more comment upon the unexpected gift. "I have to put on my ear drops," she told Gemma. "I will see you downstairs. Colin says we are fearfully behind the time, and there is a limit to even fashionable lateness. He sounds like a husband already!" She giggled.

After Louisa departed, Gemma said, "You may go, Lily. Thank you for your help."

The maid curtsied. "You look that beautiful, miss. I hope you all have a wonderful time. Perhaps by the end of the Season, you'll be a new bride, too."

"I doubt that," Gemma murmured. As soon as the servant had shut the door behind her, Gemma opened the note again to read the few lines scribbled there.

*A small token to make your evening more pleasant. Just remember, you are as worthy as any lady or gentleman there.*

Gemma smiled, and for a moment, she held the note close to her heart. But now she had to descend the steps, be greeted pleasantly by Lieutenant McGregor, looking very fine in his dress uniform, and be handed up into the carriage. Miss Pomshack waved her handkerchief cheerfully as they departed.

Louisa chatted all the way to Mrs. Forsythe's house, but her voice was a little high, and Gemma knew that her friend was nervous, too. What reaction would Louisa and her new husband receive from the Ton? Would they be ostracized, slighted, gossiped about?

Gemma had no social presence to lend weight to her friends, but she would certainly never desert Louisa. They would sink or swim together, she thought, swallowing hard.

When their carriage swung in line to wait for their turn at the door, she saw that the ball was an even bigger event than she had guessed. The street was crowded with carriages and grooms milling about, and flambeaux burned outside the doors of the handsome dwelling. From tall windows, soft golden light flowed out into the street, and sounds of laughter and music and the chatter of many voices could be heard.

When they had at last reached the entrance, Louisa's groom opened the door and handed them down. Inside, the Forsythe home looked just as fine, but Gemma hardly noticed the fashionable furnishings. Everything, from the brocade chairs and polished side tables at the edge of the hall to glittering crystal chandeliers overhead, was a blur. She could feel her heart pounding almost as hard as it had the night of the dreadful visit to the bawdy house, and she wondered if their guilty secret could be read, branded upon their foreheads as criminals were sometimes marked.

They would know the reaction of the Ton only when they were announced to the other party goers, and then it would be too late to retreat. She and Louisa and Colin would have to face them down, censorious or not, just as she had once advised Louisa. How simple it had seemed

then, and how little this social debut into the center of Society compared to surviving the taunting of jealous school
girls.

Or perhaps not. Either way, they were committed.

Louisa looked pale, but the lieutenant offered her his
arm, and gallantly gave his other arm to Gemma. They
made their way up the staircase toward the sounds of gai-
ety. A few gentlemen and a matron or two stared at them
from the landing, but Gemma kept her expression calm.
No need for anyone else to know what armies seemed to be
marching through her midsection.

Music was playing somewhere behind the high-pitched
babble, a cacophony of ladies' shrill tones occasionally
deepened by lower-pitched male voices. The footman at
the door had to almost shout as he intoned the names of
new arrivals.

Louisa paused, and she looked for a moment as if panic
had overcome her. "What if they don't—what if they
say—"

"Courage, my love," her husband murmured. Gemma
threw her friend a look of encouragement.

Then Colin bent his head toward the servant's ear. In an
instant the footman repeated, his voice loud, "Lieutenant
and Mrs. Colin McGregor."

Gemma dropped his arm so that the married couple could
walk in side by side. From just outside the doorway, she
could see heads turn, and a hush fall over the crowded room.
Where was Mrs. Forsythe? Sally would welcome them,
Gemma was sure, but their hostess seemed to have stepped
away from the doorway. Oh, they should not have been so
late in arriving!

Shoulders back, Louisa raised her chin and stepped into
the room. Her hand rested lightly on her husband's arm.
Lieutenant McGregor looked fiercely proud of his wife,
and even from the side, Gemma could see that the glance
he threw toward the party-goers was rimmed with menace.
If anyone dared to insult Louisa, he would make that mis-
creant pay dearly.

And, my, but they made a very handsome pair, Gemma told herself—fair-haired Louisa in pink, with gold and diamonds flashing in her ears and about her throat, Colin with his wicked smile and military bearing, so dashing in his uniform. Still, Gemma's throat tightened with tension.

She could detect whispers running about the edge of the room, but it was hard to judge the expressions on the faces that turned toward the door. What were the other guests thinking?

And now the newlyweds were inside the big room, and it was Gemma's turn to run the gauntlet of curious stares. She gathered her courage and muttered, "Miss Gemma Smith," to the footman.

As she stepped into the doorway, she heard someone else behind her speak to the servant. It was taking all her courage just to face the staring eyes in front of her, and, her heart hammering in her ears, she did not make out the words. It would have been bad manners to look back, and anyhow, she didn't dare. She felt just as frightened as Louisa, and if she turned, she might lose her resolve and flee in terror from the ballroom.

So she braced herself and tried to smile pleasantly, instead of looking like some doomed French aristocrat ascending the steps of the guillotine. But when the footman spoke again, his tone seemed to peal across the suddenly hushed room. She paused, and her blood might have turned to ice.

"Lady Gemma Sinclair," the footman said.

## Seventeen

*Gemma couldn't move. Everyone was staring. She felt* for an instant as if she might be dreaming.

"Lord and Lady Gabriel Sinclair," the footman intoned.

Someone stepped up beside her and offered his arm. Somehow, she was able to tuck her hand into it and be guided farther into the big room before she made a total spectacle of herself by tarrying too long in the doorway. A few feet inside the ballroom, they paused.

Gasping, Gemma drew a deep breath, feeling as if she had been submerged in an icy pond and was just now coming up for air. She looked around and discovered who supported her—it was Lord Gabriel, his expression composed. On his other side Psyche appeared incredibly elegant, her gown a slim gold-hued column, a delicate diamond tiara ornamenting her pale hair.

Still stunned, Gemma struggled to recover her voice and her wits, but before she could speak, a wave of people surged up to them.

"My lord, what surprise is this?" an older man inquired.

"A very pleasant one," Gabriel answered, flashing an easy smile. "I am pleased to introduce my sister, Gemma."

"But—but where have you been hiding a sister, for goodness' sake?" a stout matron demanded.

"Do not tell me this is another humbug!" someone else added, turning to stare at Gemma. "More impostoring?"

To Gemma's intense relief, Psyche smiled sweetly and stepped a little forward. Although Gemma had not yet found her tongue, Psyche sounded unruffled as she admonished, "Now, my dear Mrs. Blount, what a way to welcome our new arrival."

Meanwhile, Gabriel murmured, "Shall we risk a waltz?"

Seeing his intent, Gemma nodded. She was not sure she could make her feet move, much less follow the rhythm the musicians played from the back of the room, but at least while whirling on the dance floor, they might snatch a few moments of private conversation and escape the horde which threatened to engulf them.

Making a path through the crowd with apparent ease, he led her to the floor. With one hand at her waist and the other gripping her hand, Gabriel guided her through the steps. To her mild surprise—how many more miracles could occur tonight?—she found she could follow his skillful lead without stumbling over her own feet. And at last she could say quietly into his ear, "What brought about your decision, my lord?"

"You must call me Gabriel," he corrected. "It was the handwriting, partly. Psyche told me about the strong similarity. And the curious fact of the eye broach. And then, Circe made several sketches of you, did you know?"

Gemma blinked. The girl had been so quiet, sitting in Louisa's drawing room with her pad and pencil, that Gemma had not realized what she was drawing.

"It seems we have the same shaped eyes, and brows, and ears," he said, his tone light as if he discussed matters of little import, in case anyone else circling on the floor overheard a few words.

Gemma withdrew her hand from his arm for an instant and, without thinking, touched her own ear with its borrowed pearl ornament. Yes, she could see the same shape to his lobe, the same neat alignment against the head, although again, the resemblance had not occurred to her before.

He continued, "But when she showed me the sketches, and we compared them to ones she has done of me, it was impossible to deny the likeness. In addition, when I took out the miniature of my mother, it seemed to me that you resembled her as she might have looked when she was younger and happier. And my brother told me once—"

Pausing as another couple almost careened into them, he swung her out of harm's way. A few feet across the room, Gemma saw that Louisa and Colin were dancing, too. Her forehead creased in concern, Louisa glanced toward her. But Gemma was intent upon her partner, and she waited impatiently for him to continue.

"About me? About a baby sent away?"

Gabriel shook his head. "No, only that he suspected I was not the marquess's son. My father had said the same, but I thought it was only his insane jealousy of my mother. I did not believe it even when John said it. And as for you, how could she have hidden the fact that she was increasing? But perhaps she did not—hide it from her husband, that is. I paid a not-very-fruitful visit to your solicitor this morning, but he still will not talk—damn the man! But all in all, I think it may be true. My father, that is, the late marquess, made my childhood hell, and he only suspected I was not his child. When I was grown, he cast me out." He grimaced, then quickly smoothed his expression.

"If, when you were born, he had been even more suspicious of your birthright, our mother may have feared for your very life. It is the only reason I can think of, can believe—knowing her loving nature—that she would have sent you away."

Gemma blinked hard. She would not, could not, weep in front of all these staring eyes. She could feel the other guests watching their every step, studying their expressions.

They might just as well have been upon a stage, enacting a drama for the Ton's amusement. For the sake of their audience, she struggled to keep a smile on her face. When she could trust her voice, she said, her tone still husky, "Thank you. You have given me a name."

He shook his head. "I should rather beg your forgiveness. I have spent time in exile, too, Gemma, longing for a home and a family. All I can say in my defense is that I did not know you were in need, or had been lost, set adrift like an infant Moses in his bulrush basket, with no one to name your heritage or bring you back to your own people. We will do what we can to remedy that."

"Your brother, the current marquess, what will he say?" Gemma still could not credit that this was really happening.

An emotion crossed his face that she could not identify. "John and I have had our differences, but I believe he will back me in this. He would not wish to inflict more hardship upon you, and I know, and he will know, what our mother would have desired us to do."

They circled the polished floor for another minute, and Gemma realized that the tune was dying away. Soon, the curious would flock about them once again.

"What will we say?" she whispered. "How on earth can it be explained?"

"That you were sent away for your health and are now recovered and being welcomed back by your family," he said. "Details are not needed."

No one would intimidate such a man, she realized, and Lady Gabriel, Psyche, also had more than enough mettle to resist any attempts to elicit familial gossip. So Gemma simply had to be as resolute.

A fact she would remember, later. Just now, all she could hear, echoing inside her mind, were the words, *family . . . welcomed . . . family.*

"I have dreamed of this all my life," she murmured.

The last notes of the waltz faded. Lord Gabriel— Gabriel, her brother—lifted her hand to his lips and kissed

her fingers lightly, fondly, as a brother would, not a sweetheart.

"It's long overdue, then," he told her. "But welcome
home, Gemma Sinclair."

*Louisa watched her friend closely, trying to see past the*
somewhat set smile. "She looks happy," she muttered to
Colin. "I think. Doesn't she?"

Her new husband pulled her a little closer into his arms
as they swayed to the music. "It will be well, Louisa. Do
not look anxious—it will not help her case."

Louisa nodded, lifting the corners of her lips whether
she wished to or not. True, on one hand, she was in the
midst of a glittering social scene such as she had long as-
pired to join. On the other, she knew full well the social
jury was still out, and neither the fickle mood of the Ton,
nor their own fates, had yet been determined.

One minute at a time, Louisa told herself. She had her
husband beside her. With his love and support, she could
withstand any storm. So they danced, gliding to the rise
and fall of the melody, and when the music died, she
looked up at him and saw the glimmer of love, of desire,
that always lingered in his eyes when he looked her way.
Louisa smiled, with no effort at all.

But then she saw Gemma and Lord Gabriel making
their way off the dance floor. She and Colin lingered until
the other couple approached, and Gemma paused long
enough to reach out and squeeze Louisa's hand.

Gemma's fingers were cold, as if she were in shock, but
this time Louisa could see that her friend smiled easily, and
her expression was almost giddy.

It was all right, then. When Louisa had heard the name
Gemma Sinclair—*Lady Gemma Sinclair*—announced by
the footman, she had almost squealed in surprise. Only
Colin's warning touch on her arm had stilled her expression of awed delight.

Now Gemma released her hand and turned to make introductions. "Lord Gabriel, these are my friends Lieutenant and Mrs. Colin McGregor. Louisa, whom I believe you have met, has been very dear to me and very kind."

"Then I am in your debt. Louisa, so good to see you again." Lord Gabriel made a graceful bow, and they returned the greeting. "McGregor, my wife and I will look forward to knowing you better."

Lord Gabriel and Gemma moved on to respond to some of the other guests trying to waylay them. Watching them go, Colin chuckled beneath his breath. "To think I bothered to create an on-dit for the Ton's rumormongers, in order to overshadow any other possible scandal! Gemma has done that much more effectively. I should not have worried."

"But if you had not come up with that ridiculous plot, we would not have eloped." Louisa flashed him a smile. "I would change nothing."

He pressed her hand, and the wicked glint in his hazel eyes made her blush. She hurried to say, keeping her voice low, "What happiness for Gemma, to be acknowledged at last. I suppose now—"

But she paused, and for a moment a band seemed to constrict her heart. A familiar matronly form, elegant in puce, swept up to them.

"Lady Jersey." Colin bowed. "How lovely to see you. Have you met my wife, Louisa McGregor?"

"So I hear! What is this, my dear lieutenant?" the countess demanded, her tone arch. "First you desert me for weeks on end, and then I hear you are suddenly married. Did you at last find a fortune big enough to entice you into matrimony?"

Louisa glanced at Colin, who merely raised his brows. She had no idea what to reply, so she held her tongue.

The unpredictable countess shook her head, and the ostrich plumes that adorned her headdress trembled. "No, I observed you two on the floor just now. I do believe your heart has been captured at last, despite all your talk of mercenary matches. Good for you, my girl. May I dare to take him away for one tune? There is no one else who dances quite as well as he, and I shall miss his partnering exceedingly!"

Louisa felt a childish impulse to hold tight to her husband's hand. This was the woman whom Colin had flirted with and squired about London. Instead, she released him and bestowed a calm smile on them both. "Of course."

She watched Colin escort Lady Jersey toward the dance floor, chatting easily, bestowing his charming smile on the older woman. But then he glanced back toward Louisa, and the look in his eyes changed, grew intimate. Even from a distance she could easily see that when he smiled at her, it was so much more, and his glance held a different warmth, a depth of feeling that no one else evoked from him. He would always display the easy charm that drew people, women especially, to him, but Louisa had more.

The constriction around her heart loosened, and Louisa put aside her last fear about her impulsive marriage.

She sighed. And then two more figures approached, and she felt a moment of alarm. It was the two young ladies from the theater who had snubbed her so unmercifully, and whom she and Gemma had ignored at the park.

Whose turn was it now to be slain with a cold look, she wondered, trying not to giggle, not sure whether to be frightened or amused.

But this time, both ladies smiled upon her with undisguised eagerness. "You are to be congratulated, dear Mrs. McGregor," Miss Hargrave said, her thin lips curving into a wide smile. "A married lady and the Season hardly begun. What fun."

"And you are acquainted with Lady Gemma Sinclair? You must introduce us," Miss Simpson added. "Everyone is abuzz. No one knew Lord Gabriel, such a dashing, handsome man, had a sister! You must tell us all you know about their secrets."

"I know very little, I fear," Louisa said, her voice calm. "And I'd love to chat, but I fear I see a friend I must speak to. Excuse me."

And with almost no guilt at all at her atrocious behavior, Louisa swept away without a backward glance. It was quite true. She had, in fact, glimpsed a young lady whose face was familiar, sitting at the edge of the big room among the older ladies and looking bereft.

The young woman looked up in surprise as Louisa approached. "Miss Marriman? I believe we were introduced last year, when I was visiting my aunt in London."

Miss Marriman, a shy-looking brunette, flushed in apparent pleasure. "Of course I remember. You are as lovely as ever, Miss—I mean—Mrs. McGregor. How nice to see you again. My felicitations upon your marriage."

Louisa sat down beside her and chatted. Presently, Gemma came up to them, evading a couple of determined-looking matrons who seemed to wish to cut her off, and was introduced.

"How are you?" she said to the young lady, and to Louisa she added, with a different intonation, "How are *you?*"

Louisa followed her glance toward the dance floor, where Lady Jersey circled in Colin's loose embrace. "Perfectly at ease," she said, and meant it.

Gemma smiled, and the three of them talked until the tune ended and Colin escorted the countess back to their side.

Louisa performed introductions once more and hinted to her husband that he might wish to escort Miss Marriman through the next round dance. The young lady turned bright red in delight.

Colin agreed with his usual charm, although he said over his shoulder as he led his partner away, "Mind you, the next one is for the two of us, wife o' mine, so do not promise it to anyone else."

Left alone with the countess, Louisa tried to think of a polite remark. The woman still made her nervous. But Lady Jersey could fill a silence with no effort at all. In fact, Louisa remembered her aunt commenting that Silence was the lady's nickname, a title awarded her by certain irreverent wits, although never spoken in her presence, of course.

Just now, she looked from Louisa to Gemma, regarding them with shrewd eyes. "So you are intimates, are you? At least someone has known where you have been hiding. Lord Gabriel has had his secrets before, but this is beyond anything! My dear Lady Gemma, you must divulge more about your amazing absence from Society. I'm sure there is more here than your brother is telling us."

"Nothing of interest," Gemma said firmly, though she tempered her remark with a smile.

"Nonetheless, I shall expect some juicy tidbits, though not here, perhaps. The ball is a sad crush, is it not? Although Sally Forsythe does give the best parties, she has invited too many people, as usual, even for a house this size," the countess declared. "I know, I shall speak to one of the other patronesses and send you around vouchers for Almack's, shall I? Lord Gabriel's sister could not be excluded, and besides, we can have a nice quiet chat there."

Louisa stiffened. But to her surprise, Gemma smiled brightly and tucked her arm through Louisa's. "How very kind of you. Louisa and I should love that, Lady Jersey."

Lady Jersey glanced back at Louisa. "Of course, my dear lieutenant's wife must have vouchers as well. With so many tales of romance and mystery to unravel, I think we shall have a lively Season at Almack's this year."

Louisa managed to stutter her thanks, and the three of them chatted briefly. When the matron marched away, Louisa drew a deep breath. After the countess was safely out of earshot, she said, "Gemma! You are a marvel."

Gemma laughed a little under her breath. "You have no idea how much my presence is suddenly in demand. It is ridiculous. As Lady Sealey would say—oh, she is here tonight and spoke to me very kindly, although in this mob, you may not have seen her as yet, and I also found our hostess, who says you and I and Colin and Lord and Lady Gabriel are to sit at her table at supper—Lady Sealey would say that I am the same person I have been all along."

Louisa laughed, and they chatted as the musicians played a sprightly tune. Louisa felt her feet wanting to tap, and she could hardly wait for her turn to dance. She felt gay, suddenly, as her long-held tension faded. What a wonderful ball this was! Could it all truly work out so well?

Then she hesitated, as another familiar face appeared at the edge of the crowd. It was Lucas, and he gazed at her, his expression difficult to read.

"Oh, dear," she said.

Gemma had seen him, too; she glanced back at her. "Do I stay or go?"

"I suppose I should talk to him," Louisa said. "Alone, please."

Gemma slipped away, and Lucas approached her. "I heard the footman announce your married state. Quite a shock, Louisa—you might have sent me a note! I didn't really think you were serious about ending our engagement."

She met his gaze. He looked affronted and very much on his dignity, but she saw no sign of a broken heart. And as for herself, Louisa realized that the happiness she had found in her marriage had dissipated the anger and disappointment she had felt over her former fiancé's betrayal. "Lucas, I was perfectly serious. Most women do care what their fiancés and husbands do, whether with ladies or—otherwise, you know."

"Smythy says that all men—"

She interrupted him gently. "As an old friend—we have known each other since we were both in short skirts—I would advise you to seek out a more worthy source of information than Mr. Harris-Smythe."

Lucas frowned for a moment, then his expression relaxed a little. "I would have made you a perfectly amiable husband, Louisa."

"I don't dispute that," she told him. "But really, I think our feelings had faded into friendship some time ago, don't you?"

He shrugged. "Perhaps so. I thought—I thought that was how it always went, a few weeks of excitement, and then, well . . . It's more complicated than I thought, perhaps. I don't think I shall marry."

*Not until you find a woman with whom the excitement doesn't fade*, she thought, *a woman you actually want to be loyal to*, but perhaps it was too soon to tell him that.

"But we are still friends?" he suggested.

"Of course," Louisa said. She gave him her hand, and he bowed over it.

"You have my felicitations," he told her. "Not the fellow I would have thought you'd prefer, but I wish you the best, anyhow."

"Thank you," she said and bit back the impulse to offer a defense of her husband, who needed none. Lucas still nursed his wounded dignity, she thought, and even though he had brought it on himself, she could afford to be magnanimous.

Lucas walked away just before Colin returned to reclaim his bride. He threw a dark look toward the younger man.

"Is he distressing you? Should I say something? Wring his silly neck?"

"No," she answered. "He is part of my childhood, part of my past."

"You don't regret his going?"

The question sounded serious, and she looked at him in surprise. "Of course not," Louisa said. "You are my future, my love."

Colin pressed her hand, and as she smiled up at him, escorted her to the dance floor.

*Gemma had run into entanglements of her own.* After chatting briefly with two determined matrons wanting to gossip, she escaped them only to see the square form of Arnold Cuthbertson appear before her.

"Mr. Cuthbertson," Gemma said, her voice weak. "You did manage to solicit an invitation, then. Did you not receive my note?"

"Didn't have time to read it. I had an appointment this

afternoon with a wool merchant," he explained. "But it would have been remiss of me not to attend your first ball. Mrs. Forsythe was most kind when I apprised her of our prior relationship. I would not step forward earlier, of course, until you had your chance to be presented to Society. And I must say, your brother came through swimmingly for you. *Lady* Gemma. Good lord, my mother will never credit it!"

Gemma felt a strange stirring inside her. She regarded him with a cool glance. "And if the Ton had not accepted me? What if my brother had not acknowledged me as his kin? Would the plain, orphaned Miss Smith still not have been worth your while? Would you have walked away and ignored me?" His attitude had made a kind of cynical, worldly wise sense, once, when she'd believed so little in herself. Now, his attitude seemed cold-hearted.

"Now, Gemma," the squire's son said in his usual ponderous manner. "You're overwrought, not your fault, a female thing, I know. You recall my parents' concerns. My father may not have a title, but his lineage goes back for generations. I must think about my family's reputation, too, as well as my own."

"Of course," she said, knowing that her tone was still icy.

But he didn't seem to notice. "Knew you'd be sensible. Always was a sensible girl, one of the things I liked about you."

"Really."

"But now that it's all square about your parentage, we can puff it off, you know. Announce our betrothal in the papers, I mean. And you can likely buy your bride clothes before we return to Yorkshire in a week or two. I expect your brother will come through with a handsome dowry for you, eh? Any idea how much? At the least, a few hundred pounds, no doubt. I can buy another pair of prize rams, and that pasture on the north side of Father's holdings I've had my eye on for some time."

She stared at him. "Arnold, that is, Mr. Cuthbertson, as

tempting as the idea of prize rams may be, you must remember that you have never proposed to me! And I have
certainly not accepted you."

"Perhaps not in so many words, but it was understood,
don't you know?" he protested. "I only waited to find out
about your name and your family ties."

"To determine if I was good enough for you," Gemma
suggested.

"Well, I wouldn't say—"

"I wouldn't say that you could possibly be good enough
for this lady," someone interjected.

She knew the voice, and the coldness inside her melted.
She looked up to see the tall form of Matthew Fallon,
looking amazingly urbane in a black evening coat and
buff-colored pantaloons, his evening shoes gleaming, his
neckcloth in perfect form. Beside him, poor Mr. Cuthbertson looked as shaggy and countrified as one of his Yorkshire rams.

Arnold Cuthbertson gazed at this newcomer with patent
astonishment. "I say, you must have mistaken me, or the
lady, for someone else. We have an understanding, don't
you know?"

"No, Mr. Cuthbertson, we do not," Gemma told him,
her voice firm. She felt as if a weight had fallen from her
shoulders. "I fear you have assumed too much. You must
give my regards to your sister when you return home. I
shall always value her friendship, and I will write her again
soon. But you and I have no announcement to make."

"I say, really, all this—this attention—has all gone to
your head," he sputtered. "When you have calmed down—"

"That is no way to speak to Miss Smith," Fallon interrupted. The captain's gray eyes glinted, and the line of his
mouth was grim. "And unless you wish to be taught better
manners, I would advise amending your tone."

The squire's son flushed, and his mouth dropped open
for a moment. Then he drew himself up, gave them both a
stiff and offended bow, and stalked away.

Gemma thought she must be smiling much too broadly.

"Captain Fallon, I wasn't sure you would attend the ball, with so much on your mind. And the shawl is lovely, thank you so much."

He smiled at her. "I'm told Miss Crookshank—Mrs. McGregor, I should say—went to great trouble to procure my invitation. And anyhow—"

He paused, and she waited, her heart beating.

"Anyhow, amid all the strangers here, I wanted to be sure you had someone nearby who cared for you," he said, his tone very low. "And by the by, who was that lout who seemed determined to insult you?"

She tried not to laugh; it was unfair. "I will explain later. But I must tell you that I am not Miss Smith any longer."

She told him quickly about Lord Gabriel's acknowledgment, and how suddenly her background had altered.

"I am glad for you," Captain Fallon told her.

But he gazed at her just the way he always had, Gemma thought, with the same mixture of strength and restraint and just-leashed passion, not at all like Mr. Cuthbertson's awestruck relish at his luck in nabbing a potentially wealthy, suddenly socially acceptable bride.

"I believe there is one dance yet before we go into supper," she amazed herself by suggesting.

"May I have the honor?" He met her gaze, and Gemma knew she saw her true self reflected in the depths of his steel gray eyes.

Had she promised this dance earlier to any of the young men who had thronged around her, now that she had a name, a class? She couldn't remember, and she didn't care. She held out her hand, and he took it, and with more strokes of magic, the musicians were playing another waltz. It might be considered a bit fast for a young lady to waltz at her first ball, but Gemma didn't care about that, either. To have Matthew take her hand, pull her so close, to see the pulse beating in his temple and the way his fair hair almost shone beneath the light of the glimmering chandeliers, and to glide across the floor under his sure guidance—she had never been so happy in her life. Her heart thudded in her ears, and the music was sweeter than any she had heard before. She found it a little hard to breath. And the captain, was he breathing quickly, too? She thought of their kiss last night. It was too bad they could not do it again, but too many people circled around them. So she was left to wish that the dance stretch endlessly on.

She wanted to stay inside his arms; she wanted the music to never end. Cinderella had vanquished her curse, the magic was real, and Gemma longed to dance until the darkness outside the tall windows lightened to dawn. But although the violins trilled and the flutes lilted, the notes faded too soon. They were forced to step apart, make their bow and curtsy, and she had to release his hand.

She found she could wish for more, after all.

There were people around her, wanting to chat, to claim her attention, but Gemma ignored them. She smiled up at the captain, noticing no one else until Louisa came to fetch her.

Louisa exclaimed, "Captain Fallon, you are here! I am so glad. You must come and dine with us. I know our hostess would wish you to join our table."

Gemma threw her friend a look of gratitude. They went in to supper, she with her hand still on the captain's arm, feeling the firm muscle beneath his evening jacket, her breath still coming a little too fast.

And food was the least of what she hungered for.

*The supper was excellent, although later Gemma could* not remember what she had eaten. Sally Forsythe chattered on and made them all laugh, while her quiet, stolid husband did his part as host, making sure their plates were continually replenished, and their glasses filled high with champagne.

Gemma found she hardly needed the sparkling wine. She was heady with sheer exhilaration. She had found a family, and her brother seemed determined to be all that any sister could ask for. With Captain Fallon on one side, and Gabriel on the other, she felt as if she might overflow with gratitude.

Gemma told Gabriel about Captain Fallon's search for his missing sister.

"I went first to Clapgate, a village in Hertfordshire," the captain explained.

Across the table, Louisa dropped her fork. It clanged as it hit the china plate, and she blushed. "Excuse me," she murmured.

Grinning, Colin picked it up for her. Still pink, Louisa refused to meet her husband's mischievous gaze.

"And then to the west and—and other places—but without finding any trace of her," Matthew went on.

Gabriel listened to the tale and offered advice about the search.

As the men talked in low tones, Psyche remarked to Gemma, "We shall have to plan a genuine coming-out ball for you, Gemma. If you give us the time, at least."

Not following her sister-in-law's thought, Gemma blinked before she realized that Psyche had cast a wry glance at Captain Fallon. If she did not marry before a ball could be organized, Psyche meant.

Were her feelings so obvious? Gemma blushed and hoped that Matthew had not heard the remark. In fact, a servant had leaned over to speak to him, and the captain was nodding and then speaking to Mr. Forsythe.

As soon as the meal was completed, Matthew drew Gemma aside. "I hope we may have another dance presently," he suggested. "But the agents I hired to watch the ports and the ships leaving England have sent me more passenger lists from Dover. Our host has kindly offered me the use of his study so I can go over them at once. I would not distract from the party, but tomorrow will be five days since the solicitor's threat, and I feel the weight of the passing hours heavily upon me."

Gemma nodded. "Of course," she said. "I understand."

So Captain Fallon withdrew. Gemma returned with the others to the ballroom and found herself with more than enough young men eager to claim her hand for a dance.

But although she went through the motions, smiling politely and enjoying the music and the brightly lit room filled with elegant people, without Matthew Fallon the ball had lost its sparkle.

Louisa and Colin seemed to be enjoying themselves, and Gemma found time to talk with Psyche, and with Gabriel, who danced with her again. And her heart was filled with happiness, except—except for her awareness of the shadow in Matthew's eyes and the knowledge that somewhere, another lost sister still waited to be found.

After several dances, Gemma told herself that even poring over lists of names and ship's ports of call, surely, the captain might use some refreshment. So when one of the footmen passed by with a silver tray, she accepted a glass of wine and went to locate the study. She could have sent a servant with the wine, of course, but she wanted to steal a few minutes with Matthew.

Another footman directed her to the right door, and she knocked lightly, then turned the knob. Inside she found Matthew Fallon sitting behind a large desk. He had already unsealed three packets, she saw, and lists of names covered the polished wood top. The look of despair on his face cut her to the heart.

She brought him the glass. "I thought perhaps you might enjoy some wine."

"Thank you," he said. He took a sip and tried to smile, but although his lips lifted, his expression was more of a grimace.

"You've found nothing?" she asked, wanting to weep for him.

He shook his head. "I have one more ship's list to read. And there are more lists coming from Plymouth. I don't know how to judge what I am looking for, except I told my agents to look particularly for a young lady of about eighteen, no matter what name is given. There are two here about the right age, but the description does not seem to match that of my sister."

He rubbed his hand across his face. "Mind you, since I have not seen her in years, I could be wrong about that, too. I am going to fail her, Gemma, and if what that villain said is true and I miss the last chance to find her, I will never forgive myself."

Despite the bleakness of his tone, her heart leaped at the ease with which he used her name. She stepped closer to look over his shoulders as he unsealed the last packet of papers.

He drew a deep breath and scanned the columns: lists of merchants and bankers, families traveling on holiday, young men going abroad for education or adventure. Gemma glanced over the names, too, wondering about all these people coming and going, and how on earth they would ever detect one missing girl among so many.

Matthew finished the first sheet and tossed it to the desk, then picked up the next. And suddenly, he froze.

"What?" Gemma demanded. "You saw something? A girl of Clarissa's description?"

"No, but—I know that name. What—" He grabbed the first sheet and ran his finger down the list. "There! P. Nebbleston, of Clapgate."

"Clapgate?" Gemma stared down at the list. "Is a young woman listed in his party?"

Matthew inspected the list as if he might, by sheer force of will, force the desired words to appear. "No, he is traveling with his son, a lad of ten, that is all. But—but I have a feeling that there is something here I must investigate. It is a remarkable coincidence that he should turn up leaving England, after Temming's threat."

He read quickly through the rest of the ship's passengers, without finding more, but Gemma saw that he had made up his mind.

"I must leave at once. I can barely get to Dover in time for this ship's departure even if I ride hard through much of the night. I regret I cannot stay for the end of your ball, Miss—Lady Gemma."

She shook her head. "It doesn't matter. This is more important."

"It may well be a wild goose chase," he told her, "but still—"

"You must follow your instinct," she told him, happy to see some hope return to his gray eyes.

"I will not even take time to go back to the hotel to change," he told her. "I will look a sight tomorrow morning in my evening dress, but compared to Clarissa's fate, it doesn't matter. However, I don't think I can ride in these damned dancing shoes. I wonder if I might borrow some boots from our host? Do you know where Mr. Forsythe has gone amid this mob?"

"I saw them before I left the ballroom. I'll guide you," she agreed quickly. She led him back to the large room where, fortunately, the Forsythes were just coming off the dance floor.

However, one glance at Mr. Forsythe's short, wide foot showed how impossible it would be to fit Captain Fallon's longer one into one of the older man's boots.

Gabriel stood nearby, however, and his feet looked much more of a size. And the Sinclair residence was only a few blocks away, unlike the captain's hotel. "I will send a servant for boots at once," Gabriel told them when the situation had been explained, "and the rest of my riding kit, though it may not fit perfectly. Also, I will have my best mount prepared for you. You'll make better time on horseback than in a carriage."

While Matthew expressed his thanks, Gemma listened, and an idea dawned inside her. For a moment, she thought of all the potential drawbacks, but somehow, she knew this instinct was true. So while the men talked, she took their hostess aside. "Sally," she said. "You mentioned over supper that you sometimes ride in the park. Do you possibly have a riding outfit I could borrow?"

Sally's eyes widened at the strange request, then she nodded. "You're a bit taller and a bit slimmer than I, but if we belt it tightly, it would do. But it will be terribly improper, you know."

"I know," Gemma agreed. "But I must."

Sally smiled. "I will send a servant out to tell the groom to saddle my mount. He's a sedate gelding, but he has bottom. He will keep up with the captain, especially with such a light load as you on his back. I fear I would not last ten miles, but if you are a good rider, it might be done. Now come along."

They slipped away and up the stairs to Sally's dressing room, where, with the help of Sally's maid, Gemma changed quickly into the riding outfit. As irony would have it, it was a navy blue, trimmed with red piping. A hat with a light veil was the final touch, and Gemma tied its strings firmly beneath her chin and pushed the veil back. "Tell Louisa where I've gone," she told Sally. "She will understand. And don't tell Gabriel just yet, if you can help it. He might try to act like a very proper brother and forbid me to go!"

Sally giggled and showed her a back staircase, which let Gemma slip out of the house without meeting any of the other guests.

In the stable she was in time to find Matthew, now clad in his borrowed riding boots and riding breeches, and mounting a tall black horse. And a groom was bringing up another steed, Gemma was glad to see, a reddish-brown animal with a lady's saddle on its back.

Matthew looked at her change of clothes and shook his head. "No, impossible, even if time were not so short."

"Captain Fallon, I am coming with you." Gemma motioned to the groom to help her up and prayed that this horse—how could it seem so tall?—was as placid as Sally had promised.

He stared as she was thrown up and hooked her knee around the pummel. "Such a course is unthinkable. You would have to have a chaperone—what about your friend?"

"Louisa doesn't ride," Gemma told him as she settled into the saddle.

"Lady Gabriel?"

Gemma shook her head. She had considered that, herself, but she was afraid her formidable new sister-in-law would simply forbid her to go. "You said yourself, there's no time. And there's too much at stake to worry about what is proper," she told him. "Matthew, if you find your sister, you may need a woman there—she may need a woman's aid. She is a woman herself by now, you know, not a child any longer. And we don't know how or in what condition—well, I just think I should be there."

"But you are risking your reputation—your good name, just when you have been established in Society," he pointed out. "This is not a little thing, Gemma, to ride off alone with a man. Your brother might very well call me out!"

"He will understand," Gemma said, and was somehow sure it was true. She still felt touched by the magic of the evening, invincible in some inexplicable way. "It is for your sister."

Gabriel would not cast off the sibling he had just acknowledged, or at least, she believed it to be so. As for the rest of Society—she had never had their approval before, and, unlike Louisa, social success had been the least of her concerns. It was a family, an identity, she had longed for, not just a social presence. And as much as she valued—cherished—her brother's presence in her life, her family-to-be, her future, lay even more with Matthew. She knew it, though she was not totally sure if he had realized it yet.

She picked up the reins, and the captain watched her with a critical eye. "Do you know how to ride?"

"I had lessons at school," she told him, her tone dignified. And indeed she had. She remembered both of them distinctly, sedate walks through a local park, half a dozen girls in line on plodding steeds. Fixing her knee around the horn, Gemma prayed she would not fall off this beast. She felt a hundred leagues away from the ground. Matthew was correct, of course. On the face of it, this was insane. But this journey was for Matthew, for his happiness, for his sister, so her choice was not merely a capricious whim.

And if Matthew could have his hunches, so could she, and she felt in every ounce of her being that it was imperative that she be at his side when he reached the port.

He hesitated only for a moment. Turning to the groom, Matthew said, "Do you have another horse ready?"

"Yes, sir, Mr. Forsythe's mount. I saddled them both, just in case, not sure why they was sending down for her horse at this hour."

"Good, you will accompany us in case this lady needs an escort home," Matthew commanded, for all the world as if he still stood on the deck of his ship.

In case she couldn't keep up, he meant. Gemma vowed to herself that she would ride this animal to hell and back, if need be, and she would not slow them down.

"Come, we cannot lose a moment more of the moonlight," he told them. He turned his borrowed steed, which stamped and snorted and then settled beneath the captain's skilled hand, and trotted out toward the street.

Gemma nudged her own mount with her foot and was relieved that the animal followed the first horse without further urging and did not show up its rider's ignorance before they had even left the stable yard. The groom, who looked as if he thought them both mad, followed her without a word.

# Eighteen

They trotted through the streets of London, which still bustled with carts and carriages and hackneys, though the avenues were not as crowded as during daylight hours. Too soon, they left the lighted avenues of the west end behind, and the lanes became narrower and darker. And then they put the city itself behind them and rode across the heath, with only dappled moonlight showing them the way.

Sometimes the moon emerged with a clear silver light, and the captain urged his mount into a canter. Gemma had no choice except to urge her horse to increase its speed, too, and hang on for dear life, glad that she rode a few paces behind Matthew and he could not see her face, where fear might have been too easily revealed. Fortunately, her steed seemed to be a natural follower, and it did whatever the captain's horse did, trotted through darker patches, walked when the footing was uncertain, speeding up again when the conditions of the road and the illumination of the pale moonlight allowed.

It was a curious sensation to have a living beast beneath her, and at first it was quite pleasant to feel the powerful animal move smoothly, to feel the warmth of its coat and to pat its coarse hair. But the position in which a lady had to ride felt so unnatural, perhaps because Gemma had had little practice, that after a time, she thought her legs had gone quite numb, and she feared that she might fall off from sheer lack of sensation. Her knee cramped, then her thighs and her back, and she shifted her position a little from time to time, trying not to lose her balance.

If she fell off, she would put the captain in a terrible position, torn between the race to find his sister and the need to tend an irrational female who had insisted, against all reason, on coming along.

Was he angry at her? It was impossible to talk as they trotted or cantered, and he looked so intent that even when the horses picked their way through a patch of muddy ground, she hesitated to catch his attention.

The groom rode just behind them, and he was silent, too, of course, so all that could be heard was the steady pounding of horses' hooves. Several times she noted the hoots of an owl, and once a nightingale sang, invisible in the darkness, its presence made clear only by lyrical notes that seemed to express an aching sadness.

Gemma stopped worrying about herself, or even about Captain Fallon's mood. It was Clarissa whom they had to think of, and Gemma was still sure that she was meant to come along to help in Clarissa's rescue. Whether it was an irrational whim, arising from her strong identification with the other girl's plight, or not, she had chosen her role and she would see it through.

By the time the moon was setting and the darkness became too dense, the horses were beginning to tire, as well. They had pushed their steeds and themselves hard, but Matthew's impatience and sense of urgency could not be debated. Indeed, Gemma felt he was most likely correct in his assumption of a desperate need for haste.

The darker hours caught them in the countryside, with

no convenient inn nearby to shelter them for a few hours. Gemma remembered her journey back from Brighton, when finding lodging had seemed simple. But then she had had a coachman who knew his way. This was a different road, unfamiliar to all of them.

"I have traveled this way, but not in several years," Matthew spoke finally out of the darkness. She could just make out the darker shape of him on his great black horse. "I thought we might be coming up to a village, but it's too dark now to continue."

He pulled his horse up, and the tired beast tossed its head and snorted. "Do you know this road?" Matthew called to the groom.

"No, sir," the man answered. "I'm London bred, sir. And I do think my 'orse is going lame, sir. May have thrown a shoe."

Matthew swore softly beneath his breath, and Gemma pretended not to hear.

The captain said, "I heard water gurgling. By the sound of it, there is a rill just beyond the road. We will water the horses and rest for a few hours till dawn."

He dismounted—Gemma could hear his feet hit the hard-packed dirt—and came to help her down. A good thing, or she would have fallen. When he lifted her off the saddle, she found her legs numb, and they did not seem to want to bear her weight.

He supported her while Gemma trembled inside his arms. Her legs felt as rubbery as overcooked rhubarb, and her feet prickled with returning sensation. He steered her to a stout oak beside the edge of the road, with a low limb upon which she could lean.

"I'm all right," Gemma lied.

She could not make out his face, but his tone sounded skeptical. "Rest here. I will take the horses down to the water."

She heard the horses pass by her, the rustling of grass and bushes until they reached the stream, then there was splashing as the horses drank.

Her own mouth was dry as dust. When some of the sensation had returned to her feet and legs, she was able to stand and follow the sounds, stumbling a little over the sloping ground.

"Stay upstream of the horses so that the water is cleaner," Matthew told her. She obeyed, kneeling to splash her dusty face with the cool water and then lift it in her cupped palms to drink. It felt good against her parched throat, and she swallowed as much as she could.

The captain had taken the horses away and tied them to trees beside the road. She tried to stand and almost fell; her legs were still weak. Glad that no one could see her frailty, she straightened and made her way back up the sloping ground.

Matthew was waiting. He held out his hand—she could barely make out his form, but she felt his fingers catch her arm.

"Here," he said. He wrapped his coat around her and led her to a sheltered area where the ground was flat. "Lie down and try to sleep. I will be only a few feet away if you need me."

She let him help her down, and, with the coat beneath her, she lay back against the hard-packed dirt. She listened to slight rustling noises as Matthew arranged himself in the grass. A little farther away, she could hear whistling sounds from the groom, who was already snoring.

Grass cushioned her a little, but the ground was firm, and despite her weariness Gemma felt sure that she could not sleep. So she closed her eyes, resigned to waiting out the few hours until daylight returned. A frog peeped somewhere nearby, and there was the flutter of wings as an unseen owl, disturbed by their presence, winged its way through the blackness. Some kind of insect hummed, and she hoped dimly that nothing came out of the grass and walked across her, when she could not see. . . .

So she was surprised to open her eyes and detect the first flush of light rimming the horizon. The blackness had turned to gray, she could hear faint noises as the horses munched on grass, and a bird chirped.

Matthew was up, frowning at the sky. Of course—Clarissa, the ship leaving Dover. They had to go on.

She sat up and tried to get to her feet, but protesting muscles made her gasp. Her body, unaccustomed to hours of riding, had stiffened, and her legs and back felt knotted with soreness.

Matthew came over and gave her a hand up. Trying not to moan, Gemma made it to her feet.

"Are you stiff?" the captain asked, his tone sympathetic.

"A bit, yes," she told him, trying to disguise her pain.

He went to wake the groom. Gemma hobbled away to find a private spot among the trees to empty her bladder, and then went down to the water to rinse her face and hands and to drink. She pushed her hair back into place and returned to retrieve her hat and tie the ribbons beneath her chin. By now the birds sang a riotous chorus.

The men were inspecting the horses. Matthew looked up at her and shook his head. "The third horse is lame. The groom will have to lead it to the next village and wait there. You are not used to this kind of hard travel, Lady Gemma. It would be best if you remained with him."

Gemma lifted her chin. "I have come this far. A little soreness will not stop me now. I still believe you may need me before this journey is done."

She saw a reluctant respect in his eyes. "As you will."

This time, he helped her into the saddle, and she bit her lip not to gasp at the pain in her legs and bottom as she arranged herself and picked up the reins.

After the captain gave the groom money and more instructions, they left him on foot to lead the lame horse. As light flushed the sky and birds sang in increasingly agitated chorus, they took once more to the road.

In the better light, the captain was determined to make good time. Gemma blinked away tears of pain, but she would not admit to her weakness. She clung to the reins and concentrated on staying in the saddle, urging her mount to keep up with the pace he set.

They passed through several villages before they finally saw the coast ahead of them, and at last the streets of Dover came into view.

This time, Matthew remembered his way and led them straight to the port itself, the wharves busy as ships and boats of all sizes completed last-minute chores and made ready to catch the tide.

He knew the name of the ship he sought, and they rode up to the edge of the piers before dismounting.

"This is it, the *Merry Partridge*," he said, nodding to the small ship that swayed on the shifting waters. "Wait here while I locate the captain and find out if Mr. Nebbleston has gone on board."

She nodded. Her horse tossed its head, looking as tired as she felt. Gemma used her vantage point from her mount to look about the dock. Men rolled barrels and toted large boxes. Hot pie vendors called their wares, and young boys ran hither and yon on unknown and important errands. A family group approached the gangplank, and Gemma's gaze sharpened. But the only female was a motherly figure who shepherded several lads before her. No one the right age to be Matthew's sister could be detected.

Sighing, Gemma continued to watch.

Presently, Matthew returned. "Nebbleston has not yet presented himself, and the boat will sail within the half hour. I will check with the harbor master." His tone was harried, and he seemed unable to be still.

He had to be searching, trying, Gemma thought with a pang of sympathy. She watched as he strode away, and then she returned to her survey of the dock.

A young woman appeared with a man in brown, and Gemma stared hard, wondering if Matthew's sister could be that plump. But then the woman turned, and Gemma saw that she was much older than Clarissa would be.

Would their frantic ride be for nothing?

Then a carriage pulled up, and a tall scrawny gentleman

got out and called for assistance. "Make haste. I must make the ship before it weighs anchor," he called to some sailors nearby, tossing them coins.

The men hurried to untie his luggage and take the trunks aboard. "Matthew, where are you?" Gemma murmured. She watched as, aided by the groom, a boy climbed awkwardly out of the carriage. Was there a young lady with them?

No, only a maidservant, her arms full of parcels, who seemed hardly older than the boy. Her heart in her throat, Gemma waited, but no one else appeared from the inside of the carriage.

Perhaps this was not the right person.

But just then one of the sailors asked, "Who should I tell the captain is going aboard, sir?"

And the man snapped, "Nebbleston, and make haste. Harold, hurry up, boy, the ship is about to depart."

Oh, it was him! She had to let Matthew know. Gemma unhooked her leg and slid awkwardly down from the horse. Her abused muscles throbbed, and her legs again felt rubbery and uncertain. She had to lean against her mount, who seemed too tired to mind, until she could be sure that her limbs would support her weight.

Nebbleston had strode up the gangplank, and the boy shuffled along behind him. A sailor and the little maid followed. The girl was dressed in drab clothes, and her dress was ill-fitting. As Gemma watched, she noted the silhouette as the servant half-turned for a moment to grab at one of the bundles that slipped out of her hands. As she bent to retrieve it, Gemma observed the girl's shape, and the slight curve of breasts beneath the enshrouding gown. Despite her short stature, the girl was older than she first appeared.

"Matthew!" Gemma called. She saw him now, coming out of one of the port offices, but he was too far away. She waved frantically to him, and he broke into a run. The Nebbleston party had reached the deck of the small vessel, and sailors were moving to take away the gangplank.

Releasing her horse, Gemma took unsteady steps, running, hobbling, and hurried up before it could be removed.

"Wait!" she told the nearest seaman.

"We got to release the ropes, miss," the man said. "The tide is turning."

Shaking her head, Gemma stepped onto the plank. He could not move it without dislodging her and throwing her into the dirty harbor water below. She lifted her head to look up at the ship—Nebbleston was out of sight, and the rest of the party were also heading inside. With some glimmer of desperate instinct, she shouted, "Clarissa!"

And the little maid turned her head.

# Nineteen

Gemma stood stubbornly on the gangplank until Matthew reached her, took her hand, and pulled her up with him the rest of the way onto the ship. He called to the port official who had followed him more slowly and now gaped up at them both from the dock, "Take care of my horses! I will see you are rewarded when I return."

Then the grumbling seamen pulled the boards away, and other sailors unloosed the ropes that had secured the ship to the dock. Almost at once, the deck shifted beneath them, and the small vessel was moving out to sea. No mere personal crisis would keep it from sailing with the tide.

Gemma didn't care. She stared at the young woman in the shabby outfit, who stared back at them in bewilderment.

"What's your name?" she asked, her own voice breathless with anxiety.

The girl bit her lip. "They call me Mary," she muttered.

Matthew bent his tall frame to see her face more clearly. "But what was your name, once?" he asked, his tone very gentle.

The girl hesitated. She had hazel eyes, and her hair, what Gemma could see of it beneath the cap, was as fair as Matthew's, but with glints of reddish-gold. Her face was oval and lacked his firm jaw, but the deep forehead was the same.

Was this his sister? Did Matthew recognize her?

He looked very pale. "What was your name?" he repeated. "Before they took you away from the foundling home? Or even before the home itself?"

"How'd you know about that?" the girl demanded, frowning. "Did Matron send you to bring me back? 'Cause I ain't going. This ain't the best master to work for, but it beats the home, any day."

Gemma swallowed against the lump in her throat. "The matron has left the home," she told the girl. "And no one will be unkind to you again. But what is your name?"

Her expression wary, the girl hesitated, glancing from Gemma to Matthew. "My mother called me Clarissa. But she died long ago, and I had no place to go."

Gemma glanced at Matthew, but he seemed to have lost his tongue—his face was as white as the sails flapping above them in the breeze.

"Did you have a brother, perhaps?" Gemma prompted, keeping her voice gentle. The girl looked as skittish as a hare startled by the distant baying of hounds, ready to flee at any increased suspicion of danger.

"I had, once, but he went to sea. He died, Matron said," the girl replied, gulping. "She gave me a black armband to wear."

Matthew shuddered. "I am not dead, Clarissa. They lied to you and to me. I did not know you had been sent to the foundling home. It is a long story, but I have been searching for you for months. Do you not know me?"

She stared up at him. Her skin was naturally fair, although her face could use a good washing, and there was a yellowish bruise on her chin. "Matthew? Is it you? You're not a ghost?"

He reached and took the bundles out of her arms, dropping them on the deck. Then he could close her fingers inside his, holding her hand as if he never wished to let it go. "It is me, whole and returned to you. And thank God, I have found you at last."

She hesitated, still, then drew a deep tremulous breath and threw herself into his arms. Tears flowed down her face, although she made no noise of weeping.

Matthew held her, tilting his face to kiss the top of her head. Gemma blinked away tears of sympathy.

"Mary, come along. Harold needs you," a new voice interjected. "Why are you dawdling, girl? Do you need another cuff?"

Clarissa trembled, wiping her wet cheeks and looking ready to obey, but Matthew held her within one arm.

"If you have laid hands on my sister, you will regret it," Matthew shot back, his expression savage.

"What's this?" Nebbleston demanded. "Unhand my servant. What does she have to do with you? You have no cause, sir, to interfere with my business."

"This lady is my sister and a gentlewoman by birth. I am anxious to hear how you came to claim her as a maid-servant?"

His expression faltering, the man stared at them. "It's not true. She's making up lies again."

"Really? Did she make claims before, assertions that you ignored, perhaps?" Matthew's voice hardened, and his eyes glinted like burnished steel.

Hesitating, Nebbleston swallowed visibly, his adam's apple bobbing in his long scrawny neck. "I—that is, I don't—"

"How did she come to be in your employ?" Gemma put in.

"I paid—I got her from a foundling home. The matron was seeking positions for her orphans. I did the girl a kindness!"

"You bought her, you mean, like an indentured servant, from someone who would not ask questions. I shall have more words with you about this matter and your role in it later, sir," Matthew vowed.

Nebbleston winced. "But my son wants his tea! He has a clubfoot—the boy needs cosseting! I promised his mother—"

"You will have to take care of your son yourself," Matthew told him. "My sister will stay with me. The boy is no longer her concern."

Her expression amazed, Clarissa gazed from one to the other.

Nebbleston drew himself up. "I was good to the girl. She should be thankful to have had an honest job!"

"Not bloody likely!" Clarissa muttered, turning a defiant face up to her former employer.

Matthew ignored his sister's bad language and kept one arm around her in support as Nebbleston stamped back inside the cabin. Gemma bit back a giggle. Clarissa might need some lessons in deportment before she remembered how to behave like a lady. But at least her spirit did not seem to have been broken.

The deck shifted as the ship rolled with a wave. Gemma looked back at shore. The port was rapidly falling behind them. They were aboard for the voyage, now, without any chance of turning back. She glanced at Matthew, who seemed to be thinking much the same.

"I will see about obtaining cabins for us," he told them. "I hope this wretched boat is not full; it's hardly bigger than a fishing dory. Clarissa, stay with Lady Gemma. She will look out for you until I return."

The girl seemed reluctant to let go of her brother, but in a moment, she relinquished her grip.

Gemma reached to take her hand. "You are safe, now, I promise."

"You won't disappear again?" Clarissa asked, looking from Gemma to Matthew.

His expression twisted. "On my sacred oath," he told her.

So Clarissa did not object when he headed inside, but she clung hard to Gemma's hand. They stood side by side and watched the seagulls hover above the deck, filling the air with their raucous calls. "Have you been to sea before?" Gemma asked the younger girl.

Clarissa shook her head. "Mr. Nebbleston said we had to go to France. He's found a cheap cottage there. I think he's running from his debtors and needs to hide out for a time. He's a terrible gambler, his valet tol' me, before the man walked out for lack of pay."

Gemma remembered the solicitor's warning and repressed a shiver. They had almost been too late.

"I didn't want to go," Clarissa added. "I thought maybe I would drown like my brother did. I used to have nightmares about him, watching him sink into a black sea, and not even a gravestone left to remember him. Except he's not dead, after all. I feel like mayhap I'm dreaming, and when I wake, someone will be yelling for his breakfast, or for fires to be laid and slop jars emptied."

Gemma tightened her grip on the girl's shoulders. "I understand," she said. "But it will seem real to you, presently. Your brother has resigned his commission, and he will not leave you again."

Clarissa gazed out at the shifting waves and the sunlight, which glinted on the whitecaps of the heaving channel waters. "I 'ope not. You sure this bloody ship won't sink?"

Gemma sighed. It would take time, she thought, for Clarissa's change in circumstance to seem real to her, for her sense of security to return—and for her vocabulary to improve! "I promise, it will not sink. When we reach Calais, we will wait for the ship to ready itself for the return voyage, and for the next tide, and then we will bring you back to England."

The girl nodded.

When Matthew returned, he looked grimly satisfied. "As I feared, the ship's cabins were all taken."

"Oh dear," Gemma said. "Do we get to sit on the deck for the rest of the day? How many hours does it take to get to France?"

He shook his head. "Not to worry. I have paid a merchant

handsomely to give up his berth to us so you two will be more comfortable. I will be fine in the main cabin. And I have taken two cabins for the return voyage."

"So, all will be well," Gemma agreed, smiling down at Clarissa. "My dear, are you hungry? Would you like a cup of tea?"

The younger girl nodded. "I'm always hungry," she said simply. She had a petite figure, barely coming up to her brother's shoulder, and she was very thin. Gemma wondered if his mother had been slight of build, too, or if the poor meals at the foundling home had slowed his sister's growth.

Matthew frowned for a moment, then when Clarissa looked hesitant, smiled at her instead. "Then come along. We will see about tea and something to go with it."

"We won't see Mr. Nebbleston, will we?" his sister asked, glancing at the door that led into the ship. "He'll yell and he might wallop me."

"It doesn't matter if we see him," Matthew promised her. "I will be with you. No one is going to hurt you, ever again."

So Clarissa took his hand and followed him inside.

*Now that Clarissa was safe, the trip across the Channel* seemed more like a pleasure jaunt. It was Gemma's first time afloat, too, and she could enjoy the novelty of the boat's deck rising and falling beneath her feet, the touch of the moist salt air against her face, and the wide and scenic vistas.

They marveled at the snowy chalk cliffs that dropped behind them as England faded into the distance. And if Matthew watched his sister as if she might vanish in a whiff of smoke before his eyes, and if Clarissa jumped at every sound, Gemma told herself again that it would take time for both, each wounded by the girl's abduction, to recover. She herself was still smarting from the hurried horseback ride to the coast, but her pains were nothing compared to Clarissa's emotional scars.

They spent part of the day outside, watching the gulls flit over the waves and dip occasionally into the water to snatch a fish. Gemma found it more comfortable to stand than to sit, and Clarissa waved at passing fishing boats and larger ships wending their way through the Channel. The air was mild, and the breeze smelled of brine and fish. Later, they went inside and enjoyed an ample dinner. When the ship docked at Calais and made ready for its return voyage, they were able to move to the larger cabin, with a small sitting room and a bedroom on either side, one for the ladies and one for Matthew.

Gemma helped Clarissa get ready for bed. A steward brought them warm water and soap, so that the ladies could wash up, although they had no nightgowns to change into. Clarissa went to bed in her threadbare shift, and Gemma sat beside her for a time after Clarissa climbed into the bunk.

"He's not angry at me, is he?" Clarissa asked, yawning. She had eaten a large dinner, and after her bath, Gemma had asked for warm milk to help the girl sleep. It had been a tumultuous and emotional day.

"Matthew? Of course not, why should he be angry at you?" Gemma asked.

"I—I don't know. Just because. I tried to write to him, you know, but I had no money to post a letter with, and I think Matron threw my notes away."

Gemma felt a jolt of anger, but she kept her tone serene. "He's your brother and he loves you," she assured the other girl. "He was greatly troubled by your disappearance, but he does not blame you. If anyone, he blames himself. But truly, it was no one's fault except the solicitor, Temming, and he is already in prison."

"Is he?" Clarissa brightened. "He took me to the foundling home, you know, after Mama died. I never liked the blighter!"

Gemma bit her lip so that she would not laugh. No, she

thought Clarissa would recover. She sat with her until Clarissa drifted into sleep, then Gemma went out of the room, closing the door quietly behind her.

Matthew sat alone in the sitting room, and his brooding expression made her heart contract. She hurried across to him.

"She's sleeping soundly. She seems well, Matthew. Although I must tell you, she has bruises all over her arms and legs."

His face darkening, Matthew looked up. "Nebbleston? I will have him horsewhipped! If I had not thought it would further distress Clarissa, I would have done it today."

Gemma sighed. "I think many of them are from the boy. Clarissa says he has a terrible temper and was very difficult to deal with, pinching or kicking her if he didn't get every whim instantly fulfilled. His clubfoot makes him somewhat clumsy, but it's more that he has been shamelessly indulged. His father could not keep governesses or even nursery maids. That's one reason he may have bought Clarissa's services. She could not quit; she had nowhere to go back to."

Matthew groaned, and she reached out to him to touch his shoulder. "I don't mean to distress you further."

"No, better to have the truth out. Do you think she will be able to heal?"

"Of course," Gemma told him. "It will take time, but I am sure her spirit is still whole. With your love and patience—"

"She will have that," he promised.

"She will mend, in her body and her mind," Gemma assured him. "She can be happy again." Just as she herself would be, Gemma thought, and a few words from a sermon heard long ago drifted into her mind. *The lost children had been found; there would be no more weeping in the wilderness.*

"Gemma, you are a marvel. And to think I tried to persuade you not to come. How can I thank you?" Matthew took her hand and gripped it tightly. "Without your sharp eyes, I could very well have missed finding Clarissa, despite my rush to the port."

She smiled at him. "I did very little, and I thank God for the happy outcome." His fingers felt warm against her own, and she made no move to break the contact.

"I will do all I can to prevent gossip," he told her. "I do not wish you to suffer for this journey."

She shrugged. "The groom was with us through most of the ride down. And now your sister will share the journey back." After wrestling with life or death issues, she could not be concerned with a few unchaperoned hours. Anyhow—

A knock at the door interrupted her thought, and to her disappointment, the captain dropped her hand.

"Come in."

A servant opened the door and brought in a large tray with a teapot and other dishes.

"I thought you might like some tea before bed," Matthew told her, motioning her to a chair.

The steward put down the tray and departed. Gemma sat down carefully, trying not to wince, and watched as the captain poured two cups of tea. She added sugar and cream and sipped her tea, pausing to watch as he poured hot water from another pot into an empty cup. To her mystification, he took a small vial from his pocket and placed it in the water.

"What is that?" she asked.

"It's oil of bitter almond," he told her. "I bought it from a merchant's sample case."

"Why?"

He smiled, and suddenly his gray eyes sparkled. "My dear, you have been limping all day. I suspect that Clarissa is not the only person here with bruises."

Gemma blushed. "It was a long ride," she muttered.

"And for someone not accustomed to hours in the saddle, an ordeal. You must be aching all over."

"Ah, in some spots more than others," she admitted.

"I have a friend, a fellow seaman who has sailed several

times to the Orient," Matthew told her. "He informed me of a trick that ladies in the Far East use to soothe aching muscles. It seems the least I can do."

Still not sure of his meaning, Gemma nodded. She sipped her tea and waited. Then, after she rose carefully and went to check once more on Clarissa, finding the girl deeply asleep, she came back to the main cabin and saw him bending over the tea tray. The captain took the vial out of the warm water and uncorked it. She smelled a pleasant nutty scent.

"You will have to lie down upon your berth," he told her. "You will need to rub the oil into your, ah, afflicted areas."

"I don't wish to risk disturbing Clarissa."

"Then use my cabin," he said. "I have no need to retire just yet."

She followed him into his room and leaned against the berth as he pulled off her borrowed riding boots, then he said, "If you put the oil on your palms and—"

"Matthew," she said, "I don't think I can reach the sore spots."

"Ah." He considered. "We really should have your lady's maid perform the task, but unless we wait until we return to London—"

"No," she said, aware of her body's soreness and the stiffness with which she moved. It seemed to be growing worse. Every step hurt her. And when she rose or sat— She drew a deep breath. "I don't suppose that you could do it?"

His expression was hard to read. "It would be extremely improper for a man to do to a lady."

"Yes, but it hurts," she told him, giving up the last pretense. "I've already broken almost every law in the social canon, why stop now?"

He seemed to struggle with himself, then said a little abruptly, "Lie facedown upon the mattress."

Gemma did as she was told, and looking over her shoulder, saw that he still hesitated. "I will have to lift your skirts and rub the oil into your legs. Perhaps this is indeed too far for us to stray past the bounds of propriety."

"If it will ease the pain, I don't care," she told him. "Pretend you are my physician. This cannot be more unpleasant for you or me than bloodletting."

He lifted his brows. "I should hope not!"

Gemma lifted her skirts herself, and then lay with her head to the side so that she could see him from the corner of her vision. She watched as he rubbed the oil onto his hands.

Then, very gently, he touched her right foot. Gemma jumped, then lay still. He ran his hand over her foot, stroking the top of it, careful not to tickle, flexing the toes, then allowing his strong fingers to slip up to the ankle, massaging it, too, and then her calf. He touched the sore muscles, kneading out the knots and soothing her aches, his oiled fingers caressing her with a touch as smooth as warm butter.

Gemma shivered. It was an amazingly sensual sensation, his strong hands moving across her skin, and the feel of the warm oil only enhanced his touch. She smelled the nutty scent over the slightly briny smell that invaded even the inside of the cabin, just as did the faint sound of waves hitting the side of the ship. But all her thoughts were here, with Matthew so close, his hands upon her limbs.

"Higher," she urged.

He pushed her heavy riding skirt up farther and groaned. "Oh, Gemma."

Sighing, she nodded. When she had bathed earlier, she'd seen the enormous purple bruises that marked her thighs, the result of her hours on horseback. She could not see her buttocks, but she suspected the bruises there were even darker. It was no wonder she was hurting.

Matthew poured more oil onto his hands and then rubbed lightly along the outside of her thigh.

It hurt, for a moment, then the gentleness of his touch soothed the deep ache inside her legs. He stroked and eased his way along her thigh, first one, then the other, and the knotted muscles began to unkink. Gemma sighed in pleasure.

He rubbed again, ran his strong hands up and down her leg, smoothing and pushing against the muscles, caressing the skin, gentle over the bruises, his fingers always in motion. She felt her body respond to his touch, and more than her ankles and calves were tingling.

This was indeed a wonderful combination, she told herself. Warm oil and Matthew's strong hands . . . She did not think a maid's ministrations would begin to compare to it.

But he had stopped. Looking over her shoulder, Gemma saw that Matthew had straightened and backed away from the bed.

"What is it?" she asked. "Don't stop. Are your arms tired?"

He turned away from her and seemed to stare out the porthole into the darkness, where the sea crashed against the boat.

"My dear—" His voice seemed husky. "I fear I cannot be as impersonal in this as I should, as a physician might."

Gemma wanted to urge him back, but she bit her lip. "I'm sorry. If you find this unpleasant—"

He laughed, but his laughter, too, seemed hoarse. "No, no, that is the last word I would use. But although my self-control has been tested before, every man has his limits. And you are so—you are—"

Still she waited, and when he turned back to face her, she saw a glint of perspiration on his forehead, even though the cabin was not overly warm.

"Gemma, you have been so courageous, so selfless in your attempts to help me find my sister. And even if that were not true, I have discovered I have such feelings for you—"

Gemma felt joy leap inside her. Of course, now she understood. She was not the only one of them affected by his touch on her body.

"I could not consider myself and my own feelings, not until I knew my sister was safe. Even now, I know it will take time for her to recover. But if you can have patience, if you are willing to wait, then at the earliest possible moment

I will court you properly, grant you every attention, and shout my honorable intentions from the rooftops of London, if need be. I adore you, Gemma Sm—that is, Lady Gemma Sinclair."

Gemma bit her lip. He watched her, his expression anxious. "Can you wait, my dearest heart?"

"No," she told him.

His face darkened in disappointment and chagrin. "My dear—I cannot deny that you deserve more, but, my sister, I must—"

Gemma gave up trying to keep a straight face; she smiled at him. "Matthew, I know your sister will require time to heal. Of course I would not rush her. But I am not waiting any longer. There is no need for an extended courtship. I don't want bouquets of flowers or theater visits or fancy balls. I wish to be at your side, dearest, and I will help you with your sister. I'm sure I can be of assistance to you both. I know more about what she has been through than most gentlewomen would. But I am not going to wait any longer." She gritted her teeth and rolled over to sit up, holding out her arms.

He leaned closer, and she put her arms about his neck. "Matthew, can't ship captains perform marriages? Can we be married tonight?"

He lowered his face and kissed her, a long, deep, hard kiss that sent a thrill of response all the way to her toes. But when he lifted his face, he shook his head. "They can, in deep waters, but I rather doubt that the English Channel would qualify."

"Then as soon as we get back to London," she suggested.

"After all this, your brother may insist on just such an action," Matthew told her, his tone grim for an instant. "But I don't wish you to be rushed into—"

"Matthew, I am not a pampered society lady who needs a drawn-out courtship," she told him again. "I know now who I am and what I want—and I am proposing, drat you. Will you not marry me now, or at least as soon as possible?"

"You cannot propose. I have already told you of my intentions," he argued, his brows lifting and his eyes lightening, as they sometimes did with inner laughter. "I'll not have you telling our children one day, or grandchildren, that I was such a sluggard that you had to urge me to the altar!"

"I am not your midshipman, Matthew," she said, tossing her head.

He glanced down at her tucked-up skirts and exposed legs. "You do not look anything like my midshipman, dearest."

"Just remember that when you start giving orders," she directed. "However, if we cannot have the ceremony immediately, we can start the honeymoon tonight, at least. And first of all, you will finish my massage. I'm still aching." And now from more than her abused muscles, but it seemed unladylike to say that aloud.

Perhaps he knew.

Matthew kissed her again. "Very well," he said. "Then we shall do this right."

He unbuttoned the back of her bodice and helped her out of the riding outfit, removing the bodice and heavy skirt and the rest. When presently she wore only her thin linen shift, Gemma lay back down, face to one side, her chest against the bed.

Matthew leaned over and kissed the back of her neck, then her cheek, then found her lips. Gemma kissed him back, relishing the firm touch of his lips, even enjoying the slightly scratchy feel of his unshaven cheeks. He had had no razor with which to shave today, and much of his face was now covered by a blond stubble, which rasped against her skin when he nuzzled her neck.

"Oh," she said, but it was such an exciting touch that she hardly minded the slight discomfort.

"Did I hurt you?"

"No, but remember the massage, if you please."

Chuckling, he poured more oil into his palms. He sat beside her and again rubbed her feet, circling her ankles, going lightly up her calves and now onto her thighs.

Gemma tried not to shiver. It was a delicious feeling, his hands warm against her skin. Her soreness began to fade as he traced the muscles and tendons up toward her buttocks, rubbing gently, then hard and then softly, until the soreness eased beneath the silky touch of his fingers, and a different kind of ache arose, deep inside her. The light touch of oil that ran up and down her legs seemed to be trails of heat, pulsing against her skin, calling up an even deeper warmth from inside the center of her being.

Now he pushed the shift farther up and put his palms upon the cheeks of her buttocks. Gemma bit back a gasp. He held her rounded cheeks, kneading the soft curves, rubbing the sore spots, the bruises that discolored her body here, too, and again, the ache seemed less, but the delicious shivers that his hands induced ran up and through her, leaving her breathing quickly.

She tried to turn, but he pushed her gently back. "We're not done," he told her. "Patience, madam."

She was not a "madam" yet, but she soon would be, Gemma thought happily. She had not expected to trade her new surname in so quickly, but she would always have the Sinclair in her heart, even when she became a Fallon.

But she couldn't think of that now, couldn't think of anything except Matthew's touch as he ran his hands up along her hips, curving around her bottom, stroking her thighs until heat seemed to follow every motion, and this time, it was not the warmth of the oil she felt, but an inner fire that only his touch could stoke.

Now he pulled the linen shift up and over her head and tossed it aside. And his sleek oiled hands touched her back, tracing the line of her spine, easing the soreness in the small of her back from the jolting ride. Again, his hands left a trace of fire behind. When he reached her shoulders, she sighed, feeling the ease of his touch, feeling light enough so that she might almost float out of his arms. And at the same time, she knew how much she wanted his hands on the rest of her body.

For just an instant she hesitated, never having shown

herself naked to any man, but this was Matthew, whom she loved and trusted and would soon claim as husband. So she rolled over, and when she saw his face gazing down at her, his expression almost awed, she managed a smile.

"You are so beautiful," he told her. "Gemma, my love."

He touched her neck, ran his hand down her chest, and she quivered. His hand was so warm and so strong as it cupped her breast, and the sensations he invoked were so intense. . . . He stroked her skin, and Gemma felt the delight of it seep through her, as if the joy pierced flesh and bone. Her breast seemed to strain against his hand, wanting more, and when he bent to place his lips on the nipple, she gasped from surprise and joy.

"You taste like bitter almonds," he said when he lifted his head for a moment.

She laughed, but when he dropped his head again, she forgot everything in the swirling sensation of joy that seemed to pull her deeper and deeper into this intoxicating new passion. Now the other breast needed his touch, too, and he stroked it gently, then kissed it, touched his tongue to the nipple and took it inside his mouth, suckling, kissing, gentling it, and she moved beneath him, filled with a restless need that she could not have explained.

"Oh, my love," she whispered.

His hand dropped lower, caressing her belly, his touch still leaving fire in its wake. Now he stroked the sharp angles of her hip bones and then slid past, lower again. And still his hand lingered, sliding into the crevice between her legs and touching the parts of her that had developed a deep ache of their own, one that had nothing to do with the long ride.

Gemma stiffened for a moment, from surprise, from the unexpectedness of the sensations his touch evoked. He waited for her to draw a deep breath, then he touched her again, his fingers slipping inside her, where she was liquid with need. Gemma shivered as he touched and stroked and probed gently. His fingers sent shivers of joy running deep inside her, through her, and as she moved beneath his hand, she wanted still more.

He paused now long enough to pull off his own clothes and borrowed boots and then lay beside her, putting his hand once more on her belly. He stroked her again and lowered himself over her, but when his weight touched her, Gemma stiffened, biting her lip at the pain her abused back and buttocks exacted.

Matthew shook his head and moved away.

"Don't go," she protested, hoping that her present indisposition would not end his lovemaking too soon.

He leaned over to kiss her, the touch of his lips warm and salty, tasting—as he had said—slightly of almonds. "By no means," he agreed. "But I think we shall have to be creative." He lay beside her, circled her with his arms, and before she realized it, turned her deftly atop him.

She blinked in shock as she felt him beneath her, felt the warm firmness of his naked body. She shivered with the newness of it and the wonder, but before she could voice her surprise, he pulled her closer, kissed her neck, his touch whisper-soft, then her breasts, making her quiver once more with delight and impatience.

"If you sit up a little, slide just a little," he murmured, showing her, his hands lightly guiding her hips, how to position herself over him, and then, what an amazing thing, Gemma thought, that they could fit together so neatly. She moved just enough, and he slid slowly, carefully inside her.

Gemma's eyes widened in surprise. He felt firm and hard, and he filled her completely. But it felt good, more than good, and then he moved inside her, arched his body against hers, and Gemma's thoughts burst like bubbles above a soapy bath, and all conscious thought faded.

He pushed himself deeper inside her, and the pleasure grew. The ripples of feeling spread through her body, running over her skin like fire and ice until she thought that she must cry out from the sheer joy of it. She pressed her lips together to hold back the sounds, but small cries slipped out, and still he moved, thrusting again and again, rising and falling in a rhythm as natural as that of the waves that hit the outside of the ship, up and down, in and out, and she thought that she might explode from pure sensation. She discovered that she could move with him, meet him, aid him, and intensify their exquisite joining. She felt as if she were rising, like a bit of flotsam on a wave, then falling into the slough, then rising again on its crest, tossed up once more by this elemental cycle, moving and swirling and sliding deep into the whirlpool of the passion they created together.

Then just as she seemed to be falling deeper and deeper into the bluest depths of the sea, he thrust again, and she was rising to the height of passion itself, calling out his name . . . and joy exploded inside her, and she was replete, filled with the ecstasy of complete release.

He turned so that she could lie on her side, weak with the aftermath of passion, and lay her head against his chest while Matthew held her in the circle of his arms. For a time, they lay quietly until Gemma's breathing at last slowed to normal, and she could feel his heart falling back into its usual rhythm. He pressed a kiss against her shoulder.

"I love you, Matthew," she whispered. Just now, her sore muscles seemed a distant thing, and everything inside her glowed with a quiet joy.

"I love you, Gemma, my dearest heart," he answered, kissing her again as if he could hardly believe she lay inside his arms. "I found you when life seemed darkest, and you helped bring the sunshine back. I will never let you go."

She smiled, pulling his hand close enough to kiss his fingers. "That promise, I will hold you to," she assured him. "Just be sure to bring along the oil of almond."

Laughing, he hugged her even closer.

# Epilogue

$T$he wedding was small but very elegant. Both Louisa and her new sister-in-law did a great deal of conferring with Gemma about the church and the wedding dress that the couturier whipped up in record time. As for Gemma, the days passed in a haze of joy. Matthew had found a house he thought she might like, and when she was not enduring yet another fitting for the wedding gown or for the extensive trousseau that her brother insisted on paying for, she was picking out dining room chairs or choosing colors for the drawing room or the bed chambers, and she made sure that Clarissa was included in all the new plans, as well.

And when the time came for Gabriel to walk her down the aisle, Gemma wondered yet again if she must be dreaming. She glanced up at him. He had given her a terrible scolding—"such a mad venture!"—after they had returned to London, a brother's prerogative, he said, and then had hugged her fiercely. Just now, Gabriel looked very serious, but he caught her eye and gave her a quick smile.

Gemma smiled back. Only a few months ago she had felt so alone. And now—she glanced about them—in the pews were people she cared about, even though many of them had only recently come into her life. But Lady Sealey, Sally Forsythe with her husband beside her, even Miss Pomshack, teary-eyed with pleasure, all beamed at her with genuine delight. And closer to the front stood her family— such a lovely word!

Psyche waited in the front pew for her husband to join her, and Louisa and Clarissa stood in their places as matron and maid of honor. Colin and a mariner friend of Matthew's stood on the other side, and in front of the altar and the waiting vicar, Matthew himself smiled at her, his gray eyes alight with happiness. Gemma felt her heart soar.

Now Gabriel pressed her hand one last time, then gave way to her future husband and took his seat. Gemma stood beside Matthew, and the lump in her throat was almost too large to permit her to speak her vows.

But Matthew's luminous gray eyes met hers, and her throat cleared. "I take this man . . ." she said.

Afterward, the Sinclairs hosted a wedding breakfast, and everyone was very merry. Gemma felt the magic again, just as she had on the night of the ball when she'd found her place in the world, found herself, and claimed her future husband. . . .

Watching the newlyweds eating cake and sipping champagne, laughing and talking, Psyche sighed in pleasure and clasped her husband's arm.

"So you see, after all your blustering, it's quite all right. And the wedding was beautiful."

He shook his head. "A good thing, too, that they had already decided to wed, after going off with my sister like that—"

Psyche made a face at her husband. "Hush. Gemma has her own mind, and you know perfectly well whose idea it was."

Gabriel tried to frown at her for a moment longer, then

gave it up and stole a quick kiss. When she scolded him, he grinned. "It is a wedding celebration—we are allowed a little levity, ourselves. And I'm sure you're right. When did we poor menfolk ever stand a chance of defying the ladies we love?"

"Never," she told him, her tone complacent as she turned back to watch their guests. "I'm glad we chose that shade of pale green for Clarissa. It's most becoming. Now if she will just learn to mind her language—what—what is it?"

Gabriel hesitated, but he knew well enough it was impossible to mask his thoughts from Psyche's blue-eyed gaze. "Only that after the wedding, I have a mission to undertake."

She waited.

"It doesn't seem to have occurred to Gemma yet, she was so set upon determining the identity of her mother, but—"

"But?"

"But somewhere out there—if the late marquess was not our father, Gemma's and mine—is the man who sired us, the man who wrote the letters that John burned, the man whose eye may be painted on the broach my mother kept hidden away but close to her heart."

Psyche looked grave. "It was many years ago. He may be dead, my darling."

"True, he may be. But he may not. And either way, someone must know who he is. And I mean to find out."

She did not argue, only reached to touch his face with her hand. Gabriel put his fingers over hers and held her close, his talisman, his deepest love.

At the other side of the room, her cheeks flushed, Gemma was laughing at Colin McGregor's jest. Beside them, Matthew grinned, too. She looked totally happy. Gabriel would not dream of offering her a new concern to fret about. But she would think of it, too, sooner rather than later, and he suspected her resolve would equal his own.

Did they not have the right to know their father's name?

Psyche took his arm. "Come and mingle with our guests, my love. Later, we will discuss this."

He nodded and reached to take up a glass of champagne from one of the silver trays. "Yes, we must toast the bride."

Gemma looked up and flashed them a smile as, arm in arm, they crossed the room to stand beside her.

Continue reading for a preview of

## *Truly a Wife*

The fourth novel in Rebecca Hagan Lee's
Free Fellows League series

Coming soon from Berkley Sensation!

"*Good evening, Miranda. Fancy meeting you here.*"
Sussex gave the Marchioness of St. Germaine an
awkward little bow.

"This isn't funny, Daniel." She glared at him. "Your
mother was very surprised and none too pleased to see me.
She made it quite clear that my name was not on the guest
list."

"Not on *her* guest list," Sussex corrected.

"Your mother's guest list is the only one that matters,"
Miranda snapped at him.

"Not to me," he countered. "And I invited you."

"Then you should have had the decency to inform your
mother because hers is the guest list they use at the front
door."

He winced.

Miranda frowned. "You do this to me every year,

Daniel, and you know she doesn't like me crashing her party."

It was true. His mother had never liked or approved of Miranda. There was, the duchess always said, something unseemly about a girl Miranda's age inheriting her late father's title and becoming a peeress in her own right. Something unseemly about a young woman who considered herself the equal to male peers. Daniel suspected his mother might be more jealous than disapproving, for the duchess had been born an honorable miss and had gained her lofty title by marrying a duke while Miranda had rightfully inherited hers. So, Daniel invited Miranda to the gala every year knowing his mother had deliberately omitted her name from the guest list.

It began on a whim as a way to right his mother's injustice, but Daniel had continued to invite Miranda year after year because he enjoyed her company. He had wanted to see her again, to hear her voice and resume the verbal sparring they'd enjoyed during their brief courtship—a courtship that had come to a rather abrupt end.

He had been a few months shy of his majority and certain his dream of becoming a member of the Free Fellows League was within his grasp when he met her. Miranda had just inherited her title and Daniel's mother had made her disapproval well known. Although he'd liked Miranda immensely and found her physically and mentally stimulating, he hadn't wanted anything more than a light flirtation, and Daniel had been very much afraid that he was in danger of falling in love with Miranda St. Germaine. So he'd stopped calling upon her and he and Miranda had gone from being would-be lovers to complete adversaries almost overnight.

And their adversarial relationship had continued. Every year he invited her to his mother's society gala and every year, Miranda responded to his invitation. And Daniel was convinced it wasn't just to avoid the humiliation of having everyone else in the ton know that hers was the only prominent name that didn't appear on the duchess's guest list.

She enjoyed their verbal sparring every bit as much as he did.

"Yet, you came," he mused.

"I must be as daft to accept as you are to invite me," Miranda admitted. "Because I thought, this time, Her Grace was going to have footmen escort me back to my carriage."

"If she had, it would have marked the end of her gala evening and her role as hostess here at Sussex House."

Miranda glanced up at him. A thin line of perspiration beaded his upper lip and the look in his eyes was hard and implacable. "Daniel, you don't mean that."

Daniel met her gaze. "Oh, but I do. After all, it is my house."

"Your mother has had it longer," Miranda reminded him. "And she is the duchess."

"Dowager duchess," he corrected.

"A duchess all the same." Miranda sighed. "You know I don't like coming here uninvited."

"You didn't."

"How many other guests did you invite?"

"None," he answered truthfully. "Only you."

"Why am I the only recipient of the Duke of Sussex's largesse?"

Daniel smiled at her. "Because I didn't want to suffer alone."

She opened her mouth to speak, but he stopped her with his next words. "Let's not argue anymore, Miranda."

"We always argue," she told him.

"Not tonight."

"What shall we do instead?"

"I'm here," he said, reaching for her hand. "You're here. And the orchestra's here. Why not do me the honor of a dance?" He nudged her onto the edge of the dance floor.

Miranda blinked up at him, not certain she'd heard him correctly. "You're asking me to dance?"

"It would seem so." Lifting the dance card and tiny pencil dangling from her wrist, he penciled in his name for the current dance and all the others that followed, blithely crossing out the names already listed and adding his own. "And it seems I've done so in the nick of time before your card was full."

"You want to dance to this?" She frowned. The orchestra was playing a quadrille and in all the years she had known him, Miranda had never seen Daniel Sussex partner anyone to the music of a quadrille.

"You know better than that." He gave her his most devastating smile. "I despise quadrilles." Turning in the direction of the orchestra, Daniel held up three fingers, then four, designating the three-quarter time of the waltz.

"Daniel, you can't!" Miranda protested as soon as she realized his intention. "You know your mother doesn't allow waltzing at her galas."

"She'll allow it at this one." Daniel ignored Miranda's protest and signaled for the waltz once again. The orchestra leader glanced at the dowager duchess before giving Daniel an emphatic shake of his head.

Miranda turned to Daniel with a smug I-told-you-so look on her face.

But the Duke of Sussex was undaunted. He lifted his right hand, indicated the signet ring bearing the ducal crest and signaled, once again, for a waltz in three-quarter time. "There, now." Daniel smiled at Miranda as the orchestra leader acquiesced. "See, Miranda, with the right incentives, one can accomplish the impossible."

"As soon as she hears the music, your mother is sure to put a stop to it," Miranda warned.

"Then it's our only chance."

"Chance for what?"

"To escape in each other's arms."

The thought of being held in his arms while they circled the room at a romantically breathtaking pace filled Miranda with pleasure until she caught a whiff of his breath. "Daniel, you're foxed!"

"I am," he confirmed.

"But why?"

"Because I've been drinking."

"Yes, you have." Miranda struggled to keep from smiling, but lost the battle. "My guess is whisky. Quite a bit of it."

"Quite." Daniel nodded, swaying on his feet once again, leaning on her more heavily.

Miranda put out a hand to steady him and felt dampness against his waistcoat. He groaned in obvious pain. "Daniel?"

Daniel glanced down. "Bloody hell," he cursed beneath his breath. "Mistress Beekins won't be pleased."

Miranda's ears pricked up at the sound of an unfamiliar female name. "Who is Mistress Beekins?"

"The lady who sewed me up," Daniel replied, matter-of-factly.

"Sewed you up?" Miranda parroted.

Daniel nodded. "In nice, neat stitches." He frowned. "But it appears to be for naught because I seem to be bleeding again." He fought to keep his feet, leaning heavily on Miranda for balance. "There's the end of the quadrille. Come, Miranda, I want to waltz with you. Now."

"Daniel, you're in no condition to waltz." Miranda looked closely and saw that he was flushed with fever. "You ought to be in bed."

Daniel stared down at her. "I'm doing my damnedest to get there."

"I'm serious," Miranda replied, her tone of voice laced with concern and a certain amount of disapproval.

"So am I." He spoke through clenched teeth. "I'm willing to go to bed—just as soon as you waltz me out of here and into the carriage I hope to God you left waiting."

"But your bed is upstairs."

"Up sixty-eight stairs I can't negotiate," he admitted. "And even if I could get to my bed without anyone noticing, how long do you think it would be before *she* discovered the reason for my absence?"

"She's your mother," Miranda reminded him. "She should know you're injured."

"No." He spoke from behind clenched teeth. "No one

can know." He leaned forward, pressing his forehead against the top of Miranda's head. "Except you."

"Why me?"

"Because I trust you," he told her. "And . . ."

Miranda's heart swelled with pride. "And?"

"You're the only woman tall enough and strong enough to manage."

Miranda's romantic dreams died a sharp, quick death. "Thank you for informing me of that, Your Grace." Miranda's reply was sharper than she intended, but she was struggling to keep her hurt and the tears that stung her eyes from showing. "No doubt I needed to be reminded that I'm always the biggest girl anywhere," she muttered.

"Miranda . . ." he began.

"No."

He knew she couldn't refuse him. "Please, Miranda, waltz me out of here. I can't walk out of here on my own and I bloody well can't quadrille out. Waltzing is the only way. We'll head for the terrace."

"The terrace?"

"If I hold on to you, I know I can make it. . . ."

"You're an ass, Your Grace. . . ."

"I know," he answered as the orchestra began the waltz.

"You're lucky I don't leave you bleeding all over your mother's marble floors," she told him, as he took her in his arms and guided her into the first steps of the dance.

Daniel inhaled deeply, gathering his remaining strength. "I know."

Miranda felt the trembling in his arms and carried as much of his weight as she could. "Good heavens, Daniel, you weigh a ton."

He grunted in reply and did his best not to lean so heavily on her. But he was fighting a losing battle and they were both keenly aware of it.

Miranda knew the effort it took for him to waltz so effortlessly and she did the only thing she could think to do to keep him upright and moving. "If you stumble and fall or step on my feet, I swear to God, I'll leave you where you lie and let Her Grace deal with you."

Squeezing his eyes shut against a wave of dizziness, he faltered.

Miranda felt the slight breeze from the open terrace doors and realized victory was within reach. She moved closer, taking on more of his weight as she whispered, "Hold me closer."

"Too . . . close . . . already . . ." He ground out each word. "Your rep—"

"Hang my reputation! You're bleeding through your waist-coat and onto my new ball gown. So, don't give up on me now, Daniel. Because when this is over and you're recovered, you're going to accompany me to my dressmaker's and buy me the most exquisite ball gown anyone has ever seen. . . ."

Daniel barely spared a glance for her pale green dress. "Help me and I'll buy you a ball gown fit for a queen," he promised.

"You'll have to do better than that," she warned. "This ball gown *was* fit for a queen." Miranda looked Daniel in the eye and realized that his face was grayish white, and his upper lip was dotted with perspiration. Fearing he might pitch face forward onto the hard marble floor at any second, Miranda wedged her knee between his and nudged him through the terrace door. "The queen and I share a dressmaker."

The night air helped cool his feverish brow and Daniel murmured a brief prayer of thanks as he lowered his gaze and found himself staring at the cleavage Miranda had pressed against his chest. The view was spectacular and Daniel was relieved to discover that, despite the fog of pain surrounding him, he could still appreciate the sight of the truly magnificent bosom pressing into him. "I've no doubt your seamstress is thrilled to have your patronage for I doubt that dressing the queen compares to dressing you." Or undressing you, he silently added.

"Flattery isn't going to get you out of this, Daniel," Miranda advised. "You think I'll take pity on you and allow you simply to pay the bill because you were foxed and injured when you made the bargain. But no matter what you say or do, when you're recovered, you're going to accompany me to my dressmaker's and buy me the ball gown of my choosing."

Daniel squeezed his eyes shut, trying to block out the sight of Miranda's cleavage as much as the burning pain in his side. "So long as you live up to your end of the bargain and help me out of here." He would live up to his end of the bargain and accompany her to the most expensive dressmaker on earth so long as she got him away from Sussex House before he fell flat on his face. Daniel opened his eyes and blinked several times before he managed to focus on her lovely face—*both* her lovely faces.

"Hold on," she ordered, dropping her hand from his shoulder to his waist, and wrapping her arm around him.

Daniel tried to muffle his groan of pain and failed.

"I'm sorry," she whispered as she tightened her grip, feeling dampness at the back of his jacket as she half pushed, half carried him across the terrace.

He stumbled twice and nearly sent them tumbling down the steps that led from the terrace to the garden, but Miranda managed to keep them upright as they made their way along the gravel path through the garden to the street. For once, she was grateful for the fact that she towered over most of her acquaintances. But she was trembling from exhaustion and perspiring through her silk ball gown despite the heavy mist and the cool breeze that blew her skirts against her legs. "I take it back," she complained. "You don't weight a ton, Daniel. You weigh a ton and a half."

"It's a good thing you're no featherweight yourself," he murmured.

"Insult me again and you'll be buying me jewels to match my new gown."

"I didn't insult you," he said.

"What do you call it when you tell a lady she's bigger and heavier than average?" she demanded.

"A compliment." Daniel sucked in a breath. "The fact that you're no featherweight is one of the things I like best about you. You give the appearance of being solid and reliable and trustworthy."

"Instead of beautiful and mysterious and romantic," Miranda murmured.

"The world is full of beautiful, mysterious, and romantic women," he said. "Solid, reliable, and trustworthy women are rare."

"Take it from me, Your Grace," she informed him. "That is *not* a compliment."

"It should be," he muttered, aware that Miranda was the only thing keeping him upright. She thought she'd already born the brunt of his weight, but until a few moments ago, Daniel had supported more of his weight than Miranda realized. That was no longer the case and Miranda gave an unladylike grunt as Daniel's strength abruptly deserted him and the pressure on her shoulders increased tenfold. "How much farther?" he asked.

"About ten feet," she answered.

Daniel braced himself for another wave of pain and nausea. "I think I can make it."

"That makes one of us," Miranda replied, bluntly. "Because I'm not certain *I* can. Especially across the lawn in full view of the late arrivals." She pushed him down onto a stone bench and sat down beside him.

Daniel groaned once again. Damn, but he'd forgotten about late arrivals! "You must," he ordered. "I can make it with your help. I can't make it alone."

Miranda took a deep breath—as deep as her laced half-corset would allow—and forced herself to her feet, then turned and faced him. "Then wait here," she instructed, "while I go back inside for help."

Daniel's face must have mirrored his alarm, for Miranda gave an exasperated sigh. "I understand the need for discretion, Your Grace, but we need help and Alyssa told me she and Griff were coming tonight. If I can't find Alyssa and Griff, I'll look for Lord Grantham or Shepherdston or your cousin, Barclay. They're sure to be here." She named the men with whom she knew Daniel associated, the men she knew he trusted, and the men she knew the dowager duchess wouldn't exclude from the guest list. "Rest a bit," she urged. "I'll be back as soon as I can."

Shaking his head slightly, Daniel reached inside his jacket and removed a pewter flask.

Miranda looked askance at the pewter flask. The plain pewter vessel was at odds with Daniel's otherwise elegant attire, as was the fact that he carried a flask at all. She'd never known him to carry one before—even on cold mornings in the country where riding and tramping the moors for grouse and pheasant were the local pastimes. And if he carried a flask, Miranda somehow expected that the Duke of Sussex would carry a silver one.

"What is it?" he demanded, uncapping the flask and taking a long drink from it.

Miranda spoke her thoughts. "In all the years I've known you, I've never seen you carry a flask."

"In all the years you've known me, you've never seen me shot and bleeding like a stuck pig despite Mistress Beekins's best efforts. Besides"—he drawled, frowning at the flask—"it's almost empty."

"Shot?" Miranda's voice rose an octave. "You complained of tearing some stitches," she accused. "You didn't say anything about being shot."

"If I hadn't been shot, I wouldn't *have* any stitches to tear." He took a long swallow from the flask and returned it to his inner pocket amazed that he had the dexterity to do so. He'd always prided himself on being able to hold his liquor, but he'd consumed an inordinate amount of whisky during the past twelve hours. He'd needed it in order to sleep through as much of the journey to London as possible, but Daniel had still been awakened by the pain during the trip inland and asked for whisky often enough to know

Micah had refilled the flask several times. And Daniel remembered Micah refilling it once more before Micah had left him at the side entrance to Sussex House and gone to deliver the leather pouches to the Marquess of Shepherdston's London residence.

Daniel was so foxed, he'd passed the stage of sloppy drunkenness and was able, once again, to feel pain and to realize that the wound in his side wasn't going to be the only part of him aching on the morrow. His head would feel the size of a melon and be accompanied by a full company of drummers.

He focused his gaze on Miranda. There were still two of her, but he was able to see both of them clearly. "What did you think happened?"

"I don't know what I thought," she admitted. "That you'd been in an accident of some sort. That you'd cracked a rib, or cut yourself climbing a trellis up to the mysterious Mistress Beekins's bedroom . . ." She stared at him. "I never dreamed you'd been shot."

"Cracked ribs don't bleed, Miranda. And although a cut generally bleeds, a cut from a climb up a trellis to gain entry to a woman's bedchamber wouldn't bleed like that." Daniel nodded toward the blotch of crimson marring her bodice and trailing down onto her skirts.

"Good heavens!" Miranda glanced down at her dress. The bloodstain on her ball gown had spread. It had grown from a stain the size of a coin and blossomed into a stain the size of a man's hand. Staring down at her bodice, Miranda realized there were, in fact, two stains on her dress. The original one and a nearly perfect impression of Daniel's bloodied handprint on the curve of her waist and hip. They had known he was bleeding through his waistcoat, but she was certain that neither she nor Daniel had realized he was bleeding so profusely.

"Surprised you, didn't it?" He looked at his waistcoat. The blood wasn't visible on the black brocade, but the garment was wet with it. "Surprised me, too."

"You need help." She let out the breath she hadn't realized she'd been holding. "Someone experienced. Someone who knows what they're doing . . ."

"You can't go back in there to get it," he said, glancing toward Sussex House. "Not looking like that. Not without attracting attention."

"But, Daniel, you need—"

"The ball went through the front and out the back, and Mistress Beekins cleaned and stitched the wound," he said. "I'll be fine with some rest."

"Not if you bleed to death first."

Daniel winced. "I won't. Not as long as I rest. But rest is the one thing I won't get if anyone in there suspects I'm injured. All I'll get is questions I can't answer and a stream of curious callers I'd rather avoid." He reached out and took her hand. "You've got a good head on your shoulders and you spent an entire summer helping Alyssa Abernathy devise all sorts of healing concoctions. I know you learned something, and despite our past differences, Miranda, I trust you to keep this *our* secret."

"Daniel, I can't," she faltered. "I can't keep a secret that might endanger your life. I won't use the front entrance. I'll go around back to the service entrance and ask to speak with your mother. . . . I'll tell her it concerns you. . . ."

"You'll be wasting your breath." Daniel sighed. "My mother won't believe anything you have to say."

"She can't deny the blood on my dress," Miranda argued.

"Of course, she can." Daniel attempted a lopsided smile. "Her son is a duke and everyone knows that a duke's blood is royal blue."

"Daniel, this isn't a joke."

"No, it isn't," he agreed. "It's a matter of life or death. *My* life or death and believe me, my dear Lady St. Germaine, my life won't be worth a penny if word of my injury gets around. And it *will* get around if you return to the house like that. Someone is bound to notice and ask questions I cannot afford to have asked, much less answer."

Miranda knew he was right. She couldn't return to the party with bloodstains on her gown and she had nothing with which to cover them. She hadn't worn a wrap and her evening cloak was no doubt lying on a bed upstairs along with a hundred other evening cloaks deposited there by the footmen and maids collecting them at the door as the duchess's guests arrived. Without her cloak, there was no way Miranda could hide the damage that had been done to her dress, and the only other option was to dispense with her gown and go back inside Sussex House in her undergarments.

As a peeress in her own right, Miranda had always been a bit more independent and daring than was considered proper for an unmarried lady. She had garnered her share of gossip since she'd made her curtsy and had earned a reputation as the ton's perpetual bridesmaid. She was unconventional in many ways, but Miranda was a lady to her core and dispensing with her ball gown wasn't an option she could seriously consider and unfortunately, a bloodstain the size of the one on her dress was nearly impossible to disguise.

Nor could she dismiss Daniel's concerns. He knew the situation better than she, and Miranda would never forgive herself if what Daniel said was true and some eagle-eyed member of the ton raised a hue and cry and demanded to know what happened. If someone recalled the fact that the Marchioness St. Germaine's exquisite ball gown hadn't been stained until *after* she'd accepted the Duke of Sussex's invitation to dance the waltz—an unprecedented occurrence at his mother's annual gala.

Miranda gritted her teeth in frustration. If only she'd realized how foxed he was before he'd asked her to dance, before he'd ordered the orchestra to play the waltz, she might have persuaded him to make his exit in a less noticeable manner, but she'd foolishly succumbed to the temptation of being held in Daniel's arms once again, and now, they were both going to suffer for it. But once they were safely away and Daniel was settled into bed with someone to look after him, Miranda was going to demand an explanation.

She looked at Daniel. "You're right," she stated, matter-of-factly, extending her hand to him in order to pull him to his feet. "Unfortunately, we've no choice but to make a run for it. So, let's be about it, Your Grace, before you're too weak to support your weight or before you expire on the spot."

# NICOLE BYRD

## Widow in Scarlet
0-425-19209-1

When Lucy Contrain discovers that aristocrat Nicholas Ramsey believes her dead husband stole a legendary jewel, she insists on joining his search.
Little does she know they will be drawn into deadly danger—and into a passion that neither can resist.

Also Available:
## Beauty in Black
0-425-19683-6

Praise for the romances of Nicole Byrd:

"Madcap fun with a touch of romantic intrigue...satisfying to the last word."
—Cathy Maxwell

"Irresistible...deliciously witty, delightfully clever." —*Booklist*

Available wherever books are sold or at
www.penguin.com

# NICOLE BYRD

## LADY IN WAITING
### 0-515-13292-6

A talented artist, Circe Hill has no interest
in the affairs of the heart—
until the man she secretly loves pretends to court her to
silence his matchmaking mother.

## DEAR IMPOSTOR
### 0-515-13112-1

She's Psyche Hill, a lady in want of a fabulous
inheritance. There's only one way to secure it: by
marriage. There's only one problem.
She's not at all in love.
He's Gabriel Sinclair, a handsome gamester on the run
and in need of a place to hide. Psyche can offer him a
safe haven. There's only one problem.
He's falling in love far too fast.

"The real thing—a story filled with passion,
adventure, and the heart-stirring emotion that
is the essence of romance."
—Susan Wiggs